C000272987

THE ELF TANGENT

LINDSAY BUROKER

Copyright © 2022 by Lindsay Buroker

All rights reserved.

No part of this book may be reproduced in any form or by any electronic or
mechanical means, including information storage and retrieval systems, without
written permission from the author, except for the use of brief quotations in a book
review.

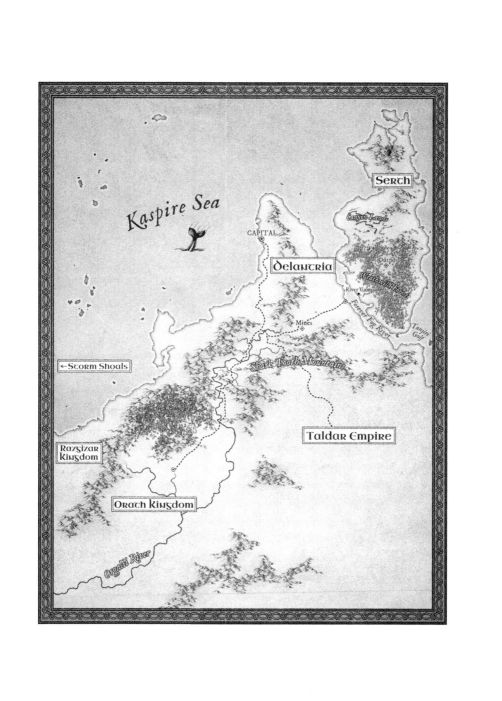

ACKNOWLEDGMENTS

Thank you to my editor, Shelley Holloway, and my beta readers, Cindy Wilkinson and Sarah Engelke. A shout out to Vivienne Leheny for narrating the audiobooks, Alec McKinley for the map, and Deranged Doctor Design for the cover.

1

"*Mathematical Models on the Creation of Economic Prosperity Through Capital Creation*—are you *kidding* me, Your Highness?"

From the top of a rickety library ladder with squeaky wheels, Princess Aldari ne Yereth frowned down at her bodyguard. "My father sent you along to protect me from the riffraff, not spy on the books I'm borrowing."

"It's not spying if the book is so thick that the letters on the spine are legible from the circulation desk. You said you were picking up some light reading for the trip. That's not *light*. Or is your plan to throw it at enemies if your wedding caravan is attacked by highwaymen?"

"That's a possibility." When Aldari pulled the fat tome from the shelf, the wobbly ladder lurched at the additional weight. Maybe the book *could* be used as a weapon. "I could also use it to thump a lippy bodyguard on the head."

"Hilarious, Your Highness." Theli propped her fists on her hips and twisted her mouth into a pucker more suitable for a disapproving nanny than a faithful bodyguard. Thanks to the mace hanging from her belt, her severe black trousers and tunic, and the tight braid she always chose for her thick black hair, she didn't need the pucker to appear stern. "You'll slay me with your attempts at wit."

Since they'd grown up together, Aldari wasn't intimidated by the sternness. "They're not attempts; they're successes. I can tell from the quiver of your body that you're struggling to restrain mirth." Aldari waved at Theli, though she was as steady as a rock, not so much as an eyelash quivering. "It's understandable. Princesses are known for their wit. I'm sure it's in all of the ballads you sing when you think nobody's listening."

"Princesses are known for their *beauty*, not their wit," Theli said, ignoring the comment on her songwriting and singing hobby. "Occasionally charm, grace, and good manners. Wit is never mentioned."

"*Grace*? Are you sure?" The ladder wobbled again as Aldari took an awkward step down with the heavy book under her arm.

"It's possible minstrels rarely get to interact with real princesses."

"Then it's your good fortune that you get to study one up close." Aldari winked at her.

"Uh huh." Theli pointed to the book before reaching out a hand to steady her. "If you read aloud from that on our trip, I'm going to flee the caravan and leave you to the highwaymen."

Judging by the wistful expression Theli sent toward a stained-glass window letting in wan northern light, she would be tempted to flee the caravan regardless of the conversation topic.

Aldari, whose stomach knotted with dread every time she thought of her rapidly approaching wedding, understood the temptation perfectly. She made herself smile and pointed to another title. "Perhaps that one will be more to your taste."

"*Principles of Economic Survival in the Ancient Nation-State of Argodor?* Doesn't this library have any murder mysteries about heroic bodyguards solving crimes while protecting the royal family?"

"Those are popular. They all get checked out as soon as they come in." The ladder squeaked as Aldari pushed off a bookcase to roll closer to the second tome. After plucking it off the shelf, she gave both books to Theli, afraid to climb down from the decrepit ladder without both hands free.

Theli accepted the books with a frown. "This reminds me of something. Last month, after you were late for that dinner with the dignitaries from the Orath Kingdom because you were caught up in your reading, didn't the king forbid you from visiting libraries?"

"Of course not. Father values knowledge and education."

He just didn't value his youngest daughter studying economics and writing papers full of ideas for fixing the financial woes of their tiny impoverished kingdom. As the minstrels in Theli's ballads promised, princesses weren't supposed to be academics; they were supposed to look pretty, speak little, and attract princes from powerful neighboring nations.

Aldari didn't think she'd been doing any of those things particularly well, but the marriage proposal from the Orath prince had come, regardless, promising an alliance in exchange for Aldari's hand in marriage. And Father had accepted. With the aggressive Taldar Empire leering down from the Shark Tooth Mountains, what choice did he have?

"So..." Theli eyed the books dubiously. "I'm *not* aiding you with a forbidden activity?"

"Of course not." Aldari's second smile was even more forced. Being reminded that she was going against her father's wishes made her uneasy.

What if he one day found out that she was publishing under a secret pen name? What if her future husband did? Would she be monitored more closely when she moved to Orath? So closely that she wouldn't be able to study and write?

Aldari gripped the ladder tightly as the nerves tangling in her belly threatened to blossom into full-fledged panic.

"Uh huh," Theli said. "I wondered why you dragged me across town to this decrepit library on Tavern Row, where the homeless drunks like to sleep under the tables."

"There are untapped resources here. And perhaps instead of lecturing me on my wayward ways, you could take those books up to the clerk and check them out for me."

"I'm busy keeping the riffraff away. Like that surly elf with blood stains on his armor. He looks like he came straight from battling water serpents on the Forever Fog River."

Aldari spun so quickly the ladder lurched and she almost fell off. Though Theli didn't take her gaze from the doorway, she reached out and steadied it for her.

"Damn," Aldari whispered. An elf *had* walked into the library. "I think that *is* blood."

The tall elf gazed across the pitted travertine floor toward them, his forest-green eyes intent. He appeared to be in his early twenties and was handsome, with angular cheekbones, a straight nose, and elegantly pointed ears, but his battle-stained black clothing and black leather armor gave him a grim visage. Dirt smudged his jaw, a bruise darkened one cheek, and long scars marred the side of his neck—some predator must have nearly taken his life with that attack. Uncombed, his long blond hair fell around his shoulder guards, it too stained with grime and blood. A sword was sheathed at his hip, and a bow and quiver of arrows jutted over his shoulder.

"I know blood when I see it," Theli whispered, her hand resting on the hilt of her mace. "I've been trained since birth to be your bodyguard."

"I thought you started training when you were ten because you were jealous of all the time your father spent with your brothers."

"I was *nine*."

Aldari might have rebutted, but a second elf walked in, this one older and more battle-worn, with a scar slashing across one cheek. He had *two* swords belted at his hips, and his blond hair was cut short, making his dyspeptic expression prominent. The bloody gouges in his armor might have accounted for his dark mood. He pointed at Aldari, curled his lip in disgust, and said something to the younger elf in their own language.

"Do you and your *knowledge and education* know what they're saying?" Theli asked without taking her gaze from them.

The clerk behind the desk disappeared through a door and closed it, the *thunk* of the lock ringing across the silent library.

"I'm familiar with their number system and how they set up their equations," Aldari offered.

"I'm sure *math* is what they're discussing." Theli glanced toward the door in the back of the library. "We should slip out and report their presence to the City Guard."

"Elves are permitted to be in Delantria." A true statement, though Aldari had only seen a couple of them in her entire twenty-two years of life. Now and then, elven mercenaries who'd grown tired of the Ever War their people had been fighting on their continent for centuries traveled south and found work in human lands, but that was rare. From what she'd heard, such people were shunned by their own kind and called cowards for leaving. "As long as they don't cause trouble."

The younger elf started toward them while the older folded his arms over his chest and glowered at the back of his head.

"Those two are *oozing* trouble," Theli grumbled.

Not certain whether to disagree or not, Aldari climbed down from her perch. Since she didn't want to take her gaze from the approaching elf, her foot slipped off a rung, and she almost pitched off the ladder for the second time in as many minutes.

Once more, Theli reached out and steadied her.

"Thanks." Being ungraceful in front of her bodyguard hadn't bothered Aldari, but with strange witnesses watching, she blushed in embarrassment.

"Good afternoon," the elf said in a pleasant if precise and accented baritone. He stopped in front of them, bowed deeply to Aldari, then offered a broad smile that was almost startling for its contrast to his grim attire—and the blood stains. "I am *Vethsel* Hawk of the Moon Sword mercenaries. Ah, your people would call me Captain Hawk. And that's *Veth—Lieutenant—*Setvik." He tipped his thumb back toward his scowling comrade. Interesting that the older man was the lower ranking of the two. "Am I correct that you are Princess Aldari?" he added.

Theli shot her a warning look as the nerves returned to Aldari's belly. Should she lie?

Despite the elf's warm smile, these two looked like robbers or kidnappers. Theli was a capable bodyguard, but even if Aldari jumped in to help, she doubted they could fend off two hardened elven warriors. According to legend, their people were the best fighters in the world, the males and females both honed by generations of constant battle.

"You're mistaken," Theli said when Aldari hesitated. "This is my sister Amma."

Aldari stifled a wince. Thanks to the raven hair and dark brown eyes that Theli had inherited from her islander mother, she looked nothing like the freckled, blue-eyed, and strawberry-blonde-haired Aldari.

"Adopted sister," Theli amended, perhaps having similar thoughts.

"Yes," Aldari said, then, not being a natural liar, felt the need to embellish. "I'm the librarian."

That earned her another warning look from Theli. After all the years they'd spent together, Theli well knew that lying wasn't one of Aldari's strengths. It was a small miracle that Aldari had kept anyone except her tutor from finding out about her pen name.

"Interesting. You look familiar." The elf—Hawk—gripped his chin and tilted his head as he considered her thoughtfully. "I'm certain I've seen your portrait before."

"Have you? In our little kingdom, I *am* a rather famous librarian. Perhaps you've seen my picture in academic journals on athenaeum studies." Aldari eyed his armor, wondering if he'd picked up an academic journal in his life. And also wondering if that brown tuft stuck to his sword scabbard was a chunk of human hair or animal fur. She swallowed uneasily.

"Ah, yes. That *must* be where I've seen your face before. We try to get all of the latest human journals and periodicals delivered to the battlefield. Especially on such scintillating subjects as athenaeums."

Behind him, his fellow officer rolled his eyes.

"Perhaps you can help me find a book, madam librarian? Amma, was it?" Hawk offered his broad smile again, the gesture charming even through the bruises and grime.

That didn't reassure Aldari, not in the least. It was possible he was the charming cutthroat sent in to negotiate with the underground buyers of the things—and *people*—they stole.

"Certainly," she made herself say, though a part of her was tempted to make an excuse and hurry out the back door. But what if he gave up his pretense and tried to stop them? She didn't want Theli to be injured, or worse, because she flung herself at the elves to buy time for Aldari to escape. "Are you interested in economics?"

"I'd like a book on whaling. Your seafaring people are known for their fishing and whaling, aren't they?"

Yes, since the empire had taken over their ore-rich mountains and pushed the Delantrian border out onto the peninsula, whale oil was the only commodity they had the means to collect and trade.

"They are," was all Aldari said, not wanting to highlight her kingdom's deficiencies.

"As a librarian—a *famous* librarian—I trust you know where everything is in here?" Hawk's smile turned challenging, and Aldari realized he didn't believe her story.

"My sister usually shelves the books—" Aldari tilted her head toward Theli, "—but I can certainly guide you to an appropriate title."

"Your sister carries a large mace—for a librarian."

"To appropriately punish miscreants who dog-ear the pages or overly crease the spines." Aldari walked slowly, her gaze darting from bookcase to bookcase as she searched for the appropriate row. In the castle library, she could have found anything with ease, but as Theli had pointed out, this wasn't where she typically checked out books. But the kingdom, however impoverished, was well-organized when it came to education and had a kingdom-wide cataloging system for organizing books. She found the section on hunting and fishing roughly where she expected it. "Are your people thinking of getting into whaling?"

"Perhaps if the material is suitably stimulating. My comrade *loves* hobbies that involve driving pointy sticks into things." Hawk smirked back at his lieutenant, who remained by the door, glowering at what he seemed to believe was a waste of time.

"Judging by your martial accoutrements, I would guess you both do." Aldari eyed the feathered shafts of arrows visible in his quiver.

Though Hawk's smile lingered, the hint of a grimmer emotion flashed in his green eyes. "It has been the elven pastime of these past centuries."

Aldari pulled a book off the shelf. *A History of Whaling Techniques and the Origins of the Two-Flue Harpoon.* "Here you go."

"Excellent. I'm certain this will be riveting reading."

"My sister is incapable of selecting riveting reading," Theli muttered without glancing over. She must have decided the lieutenant was the more dangerous of the two elves, for her focus was on him.

Aldari was less certain. Hawk might have a handsome face and charming smile, but he wouldn't have risen so quickly in the ranks if he hadn't been competent. Very competent.

The elves had a monarchy, the same as Delantria, but from what she'd read, their military ranks were granted to those with the talent to prove themselves, not out of nepotism or a relation to the throne. Admittedly, she didn't know if that applied to the rogues who left their homeland to start their own mercenary companies, but something about Hawk made her suspect he was highly capable. And dangerous.

"I'm certain you're wrong," Hawk told Theli, "and I shall look forward to delving into this fine piece during my next journey."

He bowed again to Aldari and walked toward the doorway.

Aldari thought about pointing out that those who weren't subjects of the kingdom were supposed to fill out a form and leave a deposit when they checked out books, but she didn't want to do anything to keep those two from leaving. Why they'd been looking for her, she couldn't guess, but she doubted it was for a good reason.

2

"Are you sure you don't want to take my place?" Aldari asked her sister—her *real* sister—as they walked through the castle courtyard toward the train of carriages waiting to whisk Aldari off to Orath for her wedding. A wedding to a man she'd never met, in a kingdom she'd never visited. How could it fail to be a delight?

Shydena, her elder by two years and prone to sarcasm, gave her a surprisingly sympathetic look. The kind usually reserved for geriatric relatives wasting away from a fatal illness. The sympathy made Aldari feel uneasy rather than heartened, and she wondered if Shydena had heard more about Prince Xerik than she had.

"Don't take this the wrong way," Shydena said, "but I'm still surprised he chose you over me. You're gangly, bookish, and don't know the first thing about pleasuring a man. You'll probably show up in his bedroom on your wedding night with ink on your fingers."

"How would *ink* affect anything?"

"I'm certain a prince doesn't want his favorite protrusion stained black."

Aldari rubbed her face. "I know how to wash my hands. And I'm not planning on touching any of his protrusions."

"If that's true, you're going to be a disappointing wife." Shydena arched her eyebrows. "Trust me, touching is required. Surely, with all the books you've read, you have *some* awareness of the basic mechanics of sex."

"Most of our library's books that cover the topic of procreation discuss it in terms of animals." Aldari still remembered being mortified when she'd read about the mating practices of dolphins and sharks. She'd been twelve at the time. Since then, she'd stayed out of that aisle in the library.

Shydena shook her head. "Just ask him what he likes, and do it. And hope he doesn't have any perversions that are too odious."

Whether her expression was startled or horrified, Aldari didn't know, but Shydena slanted that sympathetic look toward her again. "I can't say I'd be eager to visit Orath, especially permanently, but I think Prince Xerik picked the wrong sister."

"*Neither* of us is supposed to know anything about sex, you know. You'll recall Father's frequent and vociferous opinions on the matter."

"That we remain virgins until our weddings because we live in ridiculous backward times when some men believe that's a more desirable trait in a woman? Please. Whatever prince I marry will be *ecstatic* to find out that I'm experienced in bedroom matters. I'd be disappointed if *he* wasn't experienced." Shydena wrinkled her nose. "I know arranged marriages are usually far from romantic, but I hope I don't get stuck with a thirteen-year-old who can't even find the right hole."

Aldari almost dropped the bag of books she was carrying, and the pencil she'd tucked behind her ear fell out. Maybe she should have been accustomed to her sister's ribald streak, but when Mother had been alive, she'd always insisted that little princesses weren't supposed to speak of or even think about sex, and Aldari's own distraction with other topics had left her a touch naive on such matters.

"If you mean Xerik's little brother Xarloran, I believe he's fourteen now." Aldari bent to pick up her pencil and almost lost one of the pouches of candies that she'd tucked into her dress pocket for the trip. Beltzi, the castle chef, had made them for her, as he'd been doing since she'd been a toddler. He'd wept as he'd hugged her goodbye. All day, she'd been trying not to think about how it might be years—if ever—before she was permitted to return home for a visit, but the tears and hugs from the staff had made that difficult. "Besides, we should only need to wed one Orathian prince to secure an alliance for our kingdom."

Aldari looked wistfully toward the sea just visible through the castle gate, the portcullis up and waiting for the wedding caravan to depart. The armed soldiers who would accompany it through the dangerous Skytrail Pass in the Shark Tooth Mountains were stationed around the carriage and wagons, some on foot, some on horseback.

Fortunately, Theli was among the blue-uniformed men, though her head was bent as she conferred with one of the soldiers, and she frowned with worry at something. Aldari was glad her bodyguard and friend of so many years was being sent with her, but she also felt guilty that Theli had to leave her parents and siblings, perhaps forever.

Though Aldari hadn't yet left, a wave of homesickness washed over her as she imagined spending the rest of her life in landlocked Orath with a man who'd chosen her over her sister because of her virginity rather than romantic feelings or common interests. From what she'd heard, Prince Xerik favored hunting and horse racing to reading or academic pursuits. All she could hope was that the alliance was worth it, that Xerik's father would do as he'd promised in exchange for Aldari marrying his son: send weapons, black powder, and a legion of troops to deter the Taldar Empire from encroaching farther into Delantrian lands.

"Let's hope," Shydena said as they stopped in front of the carriage where Aldari's belongings had been packed. "My preferences run toward mature handsome studs who can stroke a lover like a master violinist in a concert in the Great Hall."

One of the guards stepped around the corner of the carriage, a startlingly familiar man in black leather instead of the blue military uniform of Delantria. A startlingly familiar *elf*.

This time, Aldari *did* drop her bag. What were elven mercenaries doing here within the castle walls?

"Good morning, Librarian Amma." Captain Hawk addressed her with a bow, plucking up her bag and holding it out to her. He'd washed up, cleaning the dirt off his face and the blood off his armor, and he'd run a comb through his long blond hair. "Is this patron of the musical arts another of your sisters?" He extended his hand toward Shydena.

"Uh," Aldari uttered.

"Librarian Amma?" Shydena propped a fist on her hip and assumed the haughty tone she usually only adopted when she wanted to chastise a servant or guard for failing to use proper decorum in the presence of royalty. "This is Princess Aldari, and *I* am Princess Shydena. Who are *you,* and what are you doing in the castle? With *weapons* no less." She looked pointedly at his sword and bow.

"I'm *Vethsel* Hawk. You may call me Captain."

"I may call for the castle guard to escort you out of the courtyard. What are you *doing* in here?"

"He might be here to see Father." Aldari put a hand on her sister's arm, hoping she would tone down the haughtiness. Though Aldari felt safer from would-be thieves and kidnappers in the castle than in the library on the far side of the city, she hadn't forgotten her first impression of Hawk, that he was as dangerous as the tales about elves promised.

When his lieutenant stepped into view, she jumped. Only then did she realize that there were no fewer than twenty blond elves in black leather armor among the military men.

"Princess Aldari?" Hawk raised his eyebrows in feigned shock. "That's not the name she gave me when we met yesterday. As for the rest, I'm inspecting the caravan carriages for soundness. If we end up in a battle, I'd like to know that the first arrow fired won't pierce the walls and perforate a passenger. As an experienced mercenary and occasional guard of important persons, I can tell you how poorly they react to perforation."

"You're coming along?" The significance of the elves mingling with the military men came to Aldari, though her mind stuttered with confusion. Why would her father have hired *mercenaries* to protect her on the journey to Orath?

Yes, Delantria was poor, but it wasn't as if they didn't have men of their own. Reliable men who were natives of the kingdom, not sell-swords with no allegiance to Delantria or humans in general.

"We have been retained to escort you to Orath, yes," Hawk told her. "As my first duty, I'd like to inform you that you've already picked up a stowaway."

"What are you talking about?" Shydena frowned at Aldari— did she also find this addition of mercenaries alarming?

Hawk held up a finger, then crouched and pointed under a carriage. His lieutenant was watching their exchange with as dark an expression as he'd worn the day before, his hands resting on the leather-wrapped hilts of his twin longswords. He looked like the villain in one of Theli's murder mysteries, not a dependable caravan guard.

"Father's coming." Shydena stepped back, nodding for Aldari to come with her. "We'll ask him about this."

Hawk arched his eyebrows. "You don't want to do anything about this stowaway?"

Though she was inclined to go with Shydena and speak to Father, curiosity prompted Aldari to crouch and peer under the carriage. To her surprise, her ten-year-old brother clung to the framework underneath, his arms wrapped around one axle and his feet propped against the other.

"Hello, Rothi," Aldari said.

He shifted his grip so he could hold a finger to his lips. "Sssh. I'm going with you."

"To protect me on the journey?"

"To see the world! I want to have adventures. Like Grandpa!"

"The view from under the carriage won't be spectacular, and you'll have trouble hanging on to the axles once they start rotating."

"I was going to come out once we camped for the night. Once we're far enough away, the caravan won't be able to turn back. You can't be late for your wedding. Father said so. We're depending on those troops. You'll *have* to take me the whole way, and I'll get to see the monster-filled mountains and Orath too. Then the whole world."

"Father and your tutor would be disappointed if you didn't show up for your afternoon lessons," Aldari pointed out. "You are the heir to the throne, after all."

Rothi wrinkled up his nose as if he'd bitten into raw liver. "I wanna be like Grandpa. He travels and writes to us about all kinds of adventures. I don't want to sit on a throne all day. Father's job is *so* boring."

Making a disgusted noise, the mercenary lieutenant crouched down beside Hawk and dragged Rothi out from under the carriage. Rothi yelped and kicked and swung at him, but the elf held him out at arm's length, as if he weighed no more than a cat.

"What's going on here?" came Father's rumbling bass voice.

He strode up, looking as powerful and regal as ever, even if his robes were frayed and shabby compared to the attire the Orathian dignitaries had worn. Gray shot through his trimmed brown beard, and his blue eyes were piercing as he surveyed the elves. He didn't appear surprised to see them—did that mean they *were* supposed to be there? He didn't even seem that surprised to see Rothi dangling from the lieutenant's grip, though his frown did convey disappointment in his son.

Hawk tapped his lieutenant's arm and pointed to the ground.

The older elf—what was his name again? Setvik—set his captive down but not without a glance of supreme irritation toward his captain. Irritation and... was that hatred? Or maybe resentment because Hawk had been promoted over him? Or had Hawk taken charge of the company because he'd bested Setvik in a fight?

Aldari knew little about elven ways or mercenary companies and could only guess at the reason for that animosity, but it unnerved her. Might not someone with such distaste for his captain betray him? Or walk away from the company in a crucial moment?

"Stowaway, Your Majesty." Hawk bowed toward Father.

"Go inside, Rothlar," Father said. "You have lessons."

"I wanted to see the world," Rothi whispered, though he studied Father's shoes instead of meeting his eyes.

"When you're older, you'll be able to."

Rothi shook his head bleakly.

Aldari, who couldn't remember a time when Father had taken a vacation, much less traveled to another country, perfectly understood her little brother's feeling of being trapped by his fate. But what could they do? This was the life they'd been born into. It came with comforts that few in the kingdom enjoyed, so they shouldn't complain, but it was hard at times not to feel bitter about having their lives chosen for them.

"Say goodbye to your sister, and go find your tutor," Father said.

Rothi hugged Aldari, what he intended to be a brief hug, but Aldari wrapped her arms around him and struggled to let go as that feeling of homesickness returned. Rothi endured the embrace for more seconds than he might usually have, but then he squirmed and protested.

"*Aldi...* I can't *breathe.*"

"Sorry." She made herself release him. "Be good while I'm gone. Don't forget to practice your multiplication tables. What's seven times eight?"

Rothi rolled his eyes so hard it was a wonder they didn't dislodge from the sockets and fall to the flagstones.

"Fifty-six. What's a hundred and seven times nine-hundred and eight?" He squinted at her, his voice full of challenge.

"97,156," she said dryly. "Do you know if I'm right?"

"No," he admitted.

Aldari slid her pencil out from behind her ear and pulled a small notebook out of her pocket.

"Why are you taking *math* stuff with you?" Rothi asked.

"Math is important." Aldari pushed the implements into his hand. "If I'm wrong, and you can prove it, I'll give you an elf ear." She drew out one of her pouches of sweets before it occurred to her that the common candy name might be offensive to the mercenaries. Warily, she looked over and found the captain and lieutenant watching her intently.

"What if you're *right*, and I prove it?" Rothi started writing the digits on an empty notebook page.

"I'll still give you a, uhm, piece of candy."

The surly lieutenant asked Hawk something in their tongue and pointed to his ear.

Hawk, who didn't look offended in the least, replied with a shrug and a single word.

That only angered Setvik, who rattled off several increasingly heated sentences as he pointed at Aldari and the pouch. She didn't understand a word but had no trouble telling that he *was* offended, either by the candy name or something else she'd done.

"Is there a problem?" her father asked in a tone that suggested there had better not be.

His soldiers, trained to pay attention to their monarch's cues, turned to focus on him and watch the elves. They didn't reach for their weapons, and the nervous glances they shot each other implied they didn't want to fight the mercenaries, but they would if they had to. Aldari had little doubt.

"No problem, Your Majesty." Hawk held up a hand to his lieutenant, and Setvik fell silent. "We're prepared for the journey and are honored to serve you and your daughter in this small way."

"Let's hope it's a small way," Father rumbled with a sigh, "and that the journey is uneventful. But be alert in the pass." He nodded toward the senior military officer as well as Hawk. "Since the Taldar Empire has designs on our kingdom, it's possible they don't want to see this wedding—this *alliance*—go forward."

For the first time, Aldari—who'd been more worried about life with her future husband and, since her sister had spoken, what he might expect in the bedroom—realized that the Taldarians might try to keep her from arriving.

"Taldar's soldiers are no match for Moon Sword mercenaries," Setvik said, his words more heavily accented than Hawk's. "If they *dare* attack the caravan with our people present, we will handle them."

"Good." Father nodded at the elves. "Thank you."

He drew Aldari aside and hugged her. "I will miss you, my daughter, but I'm certain you'll arrive safely. Our soldiers are capable, but I hired the elves to make sure of that. With their reputation, I'm hoping you won't be bothered in the least. Even if you are, they can protect you."

"Thank you, Father." Aldari thought of her sister's comment about possible perversions and wondered if she could pay the mercenary captain to accompany her into her husband's bedchamber on the first night. That probably wasn't the best way to start off a marriage.

"You will write," Father said. "Often."

"Of course. You know of my fondness for words."

"I do." He smiled, glancing at the pencil that she'd given to Rothi, but his expression soon grew grave. "I know you've been aware since your earliest days that it would be your duty to marry for the sake of the kingdom, but I regret that I can't give you a choice in your husband." He lowered his voice. "I sometimes feel like a hypocrite in that, since I married your mother for love, not because of political machinations."

"She used to tell us the story."

"Yes." Father swallowed, a hint of moisture filming his eyes. Even after ten years, speaking of Mother caused him sadness.

Aldari wondered if she would ever feel such an attachment to Prince Xerik. Maybe he wouldn't be so bad, and she would grow to care about him.

"But had I listened to *my* father and done as he wished, selecting a wife from one of the more prosperous kingdoms... perhaps we would not be in such straits now." He gripped her shoulders and gazed earnestly into her eyes. "We need this alliance if we're to have any chance of fending off the empire, of retaining our sovereignty. Our freedom."

"I know, Father. I understand." And she did. It was just... hard. "Maybe you could read a few papers by Professor Lyn Dorit while I'm away. She has a lot of interesting ideas about improving the wealth of the kingdom and its subjects."

It was the first time she'd mentioned her pen name to her father—she well remembered how he'd scoffed at the *ridiculously fanciful* economic theories she'd shared with him when she'd been younger, and she'd been afraid to bring up the subject with him since.

He scoffed. "By giving land to the commoners and allowing people to start businesses tax-free?"

Well, at least he'd heard of Dorit's ideas.

"By allowing commoners to *buy* land and earn the money to do so by starting farms, industries, and businesses where they have the potential to reap rewards and are thus incentivized for their efforts," she said. "We need to encourage the development of industry. With fewer and fewer whales in our seas these days, we can't rely on whale-oil exports forever. Have you read Professor Dorit's paper showing calculations for our future prosperity if that resource continues to dwindle?"

"Dorit is a naive academic with no experience governing a nation."

Admittedly true, but Aldari didn't think she was wrong. Besides, what was the harm in making a few changes and seeing if they worked? It wasn't as if things could get much worse.

"The morning is advancing, and you need to leave on your journey." Father released her. "Be safe, my daughter."

"Aldari." Rothi waved the notepad. "Your math was right. Look."

She managed a smile as she took the implements back from him. "I'm glad to hear it."

"Elf ear, please." Rothi held out his hand.

"Just call it candy," she whispered, glancing at the elves again as she gave him a piece.

Fortunately, Setvik had moved around to the other side of the caravan and was speaking to some of his men. Hawk was still watching them though. For several seconds, his eyes locked on to the notepad and the math Rothi had worked out, then he lifted his gaze to hers and smiled. Something akin to triumph flashed in his eyes, as if he'd found what he sought, but the expression disappeared, leaving only the pleasant smile behind.

He opened the carriage door and offered his hand. "Are you ready to go, Your Highness?"

No. Aldari looked bleakly around the castle and out toward the sea again, desperately wanting to stay, to run back and hide in her room. But her father was watching, and she had no choice but to nod and step forward.

She could have climbed into the carriage without help—she wasn't *that* much of a klutz—but a princess was supposed to accept a gentleman's offer of assistance, or so her nanny had always informed her, so she rested her hand on Hawk's calloused palm. Whether a mercenary counted as a gentleman or not, she didn't know, but he politely guided her into the carriage and closed the door behind her.

Aldari glanced back in time to catch that flash of triumph in his eyes again, and uncertainty crept into her belly. Had her father made a mistake in hiring the elven mercenaries?

3

THE MORNING HOURS PASSED UNEVENTFULLY, THE SOLDIERS RIDING horses and the elven mercenaries striding along on foot in front of and behind the caravan as it traveled south along the King's Road, the ancient stone passageway following the sea for the first twenty miles. Aldari rode inside, alternately reading and speaking with Theli. Her bodyguard had brought along one of her murder mysteries, but the book lay unopened in her lap as she gazed out at the sea, the sun sparkling on the waves. Was she feeling the same homesickness that already plagued Aldari?

Theli kept mouthing something. Song lyrics? Or curses for her fate? Earlier, she'd been absently murmuring a shanty about sailors lost at sea, never to see their loved ones again.

"I can send you back, if you like," Aldari said quietly.

Theli stirred, startled. "Your Highness?"

"I mean, not right away, but if I get there, and the royal family has their own bodyguards... maybe I wouldn't need you anymore." Aldari's throat tightened at the thought of losing Theli and being all alone in a strange land with a husband and a family she didn't know, but it wasn't fair to ask Theli to give up everything back in the capital just because she had to. This was Aldari's duty. Theli was a free woman, paid by the crown but not *owned* by the crown.

"You think their scruffy bodyguards could replace *me*?" Theli thumped a hand on her chest in indignation.

"Never." Aldari smiled. "But if you decide you would prefer to go home, I won't stop you."

"I'm not leaving you there without protection. I—" Theli glanced out the window and frowned.

Aldari followed her gaze and saw Captain Hawk striding along beside their carriage, his long legs having no trouble keeping pace with the horses pulling it. It wasn't the first time Aldari had noticed him out there. She hoped it was a good sign, that it meant he wanted to keep an eye on her and make sure nothing happened, but she couldn't help but wonder if those pointed elven ears heard better than human ears, and their voices were audible to him.

"He's awfully interested in you," Theli said.

"My great beauty, no doubt." Aldari waved a self-deprecating hand down the length of her pale blue dress.

Theli frowned at her. "Your beauty is fine. You're not as *voluptuous* as your sister, but you're pretty. Especially when you focus on who you're talking to instead of vacantly thinking about some book."

"You don't *vacantly* think about books. You assiduously and academically ponder them."

"Not the way I do it." Theli waved at her murder mystery.

"That's possibly true."

Captain Hawk jogged out of view, heading up to talk to one of the elves.

"Maybe I should go out there and have a chat with the mercenaries," Aldari said.

"A *chat* with mercenaries? Why don't you just jab your pencil in my heart? You know they kill people for a living, right? We have no idea whose blood that was on their armor when they first arrived in town."

"Father hired them. I'm sure he researched them before he did so and believes they're trustworthy." Aldari would have believed that more herself if she hadn't caught those calculating glances from Hawk. No, not calculating, exactly. Triumphant—that was the word that had come to mind. "But just in case, they might be more predisposed to risk their lives for us if they like us."

"How are you going to inspire that feeling in them?"

"By being personable and offering them candy." Aldari patted her pocket and reached for the door handle.

"Don't you have anything else you can share? They may find *elf ears* offensive. Do you think their people name candies after *our* body parts?"

"All the stories I've heard suggest the elves are too busy fighting for their lives to have time for confectionery-making hobbies." Aldari wasn't sure she could even imagine the battle-worn elves eating candy. Well, maybe Hawk. He knew how to smile. "If only I could trust it," she muttered.

Theli raised her eyebrows.

"Never mind." Aldari poked into one of her bags. "I have the latest *Puzzles Quarterly* that I could share with them." She withdrew and waved the cherished periodical that her grandfather had first ordered for her on her fifth birthday, when she'd solved a little puzzle he'd brought back from the Yi Kingdom. "Do you think they like hedge hoppers? Or word scrambles?"

"We've been on the road for four hours. Haven't you solved everything in there yet?"

"Well, I haven't done the mazes. Those hardly count as puzzles." Aldari usually saved those for Rothi. Sadly, she wouldn't be able to share them with him this time.

Theli shook her head. "If you're not back in ten minutes, I'm coming out after you. Mistress Haproh would be horrified by the idea of you *chatting* with mercenaries without a chaperone. Or at all."

"That's because it was her duty to guard our virtue when Shydena and I were growing up. Fortunately, we're mature adults now and don't need chaperones."

"Uh huh, and that's why your father asked me to make sure none of the soldiers ogled you inappropriately—and vice versa." Theli rested a hand on her mace, as if she was already rethinking her willingness to grant Aldari ten minutes.

"He did *not*."

Theli raised frank eyebrows.

"Did he really?" Aldari asked.

"He was more worried about *them* than you, I gather, but yes. We're on a days-long journey and surrounded by nothing but men. I'm not here only to guard you from bandits."

Aldari sighed. "You're welcome to come with me to chat and make sure nothing untoward happens."

Theli waved for her to go. "I'm more concerned about untowardness that might happen at night when we're camped."

Aldari tucked her puzzle periodical back into her bag, suspecting military men would find candy more appealing, then eased the door open. After deciding they were moving slowly enough for her to jump down without falling and embarrassing herself, she hopped out. When she landed, a hand reached out to steady her. Captain Hawk.

"You're sticking close," Aldari observed, hoping he wouldn't prove overprotective and try to stuff her back into the carriage.

She snorted to herself, not sure why she'd used the word *try*. Her half-hearted self-defense and swordsmanship lessons with Weapons Master Jerfor meant she wasn't completely helpless, and could doubtless escape a drunken sailor in an alley, but the elves were neither seamen nor inebriated.

"Are you charmed by my attentive nearness?" Hawk asked. "Or appalled by my stifling aegis?"

"Aegis? You have an impressive vocabulary for a non-native speaker."

Admittedly, it was a good vocabulary for a native speaker as well. Not many of the soldiers around the castle threw around words like *aegis*.

"As the leader of a world-traveling mercenary company, I need to be able to communicate with employers of all sorts."

A gruff call in Elven came from behind. Lieutenant Setvik. He walked at the rear of the caravan between two alert elves scanning the shoreline and the roadside cranberry bogs and blueberry farms. Berries were among the few crops that didn't mind the short northern summers and the salty sea air.

Father's horseback soldiers were gossiping with each other, less attentive here in their homeland. Aldari trusted they would be more alert as they drew nearer the mountains.

"Also gruff colleagues. My pardon, Your Highness." Hawk gave her an abbreviated bow before trotting back to join his lieutenant.

The idea of chatting with any of the other elves daunted Aldari, and she didn't know if any more of them spoke Hyric—the language of the Seven Kingdoms—but she spotted Lieutenant Sabor, the officer in charge of her father's troops, at the head of the caravan and jogged to catch up with him. As with the other soldiers, he was riding on horseback. Aldari wondered if the elves opted to walk on foot for some military reason, such as to harden their bodies with greater exercise, or if horses simply weren't used in their homeland.

"Your Highness," Lieutenant Sabor blurted in surprise when she caught up with him. "What are you doing on foot?" He glanced back at her carriage, as if expecting to find it on fire, for what other reason could have prompted her to get out? "Can I get you a horse?"

"That's not necessary, Lieutenant. I just wanted to ask you something." Aldari glanced back to make sure none of the elves were close and wondered again about how keen their hearing was.

"Yes, of course." For a moment, Sabor looked like he might order one of his men to dismount and provide her with a horse, but he settled for sliding off and walking beside her. "If it's about the elves, I've heard of them. At first, I was a little affronted that your father believed we *needed* such assistance. Pardon, Your Highness, as I mean no disrespect to king or crown, but my men are very capable. But there have been numerous incidents in the pass this summer, and... you've heard about the villages we lost in the foothills, I trust." His forehead creased as he considered her. "Does your father keep you abreast of politics? I know your brother is the heir, but..."

"I'm aware of how threatened our people are and how precarious our independence is right now, yes." Aldari managed not to sound affronted herself—it wasn't as if the lieutenant knew her well enough to know if she followed kingdom events closely or not.

"The Moon Swords are supposed to be very good. They helped defend the Razgizar Kingdom against the buccaneers harassing their shores last year. Defeated them utterly, if the stories can be believed, even though their numbers were far fewer. The elves are amazing warriors."

"I'm glad to hear it."

Hoofbeats on the road ahead drew their attention. A blue-uniformed rider was pounding toward them at a gallop, concern in his eyes. They were between villages with only a few houses visible between the bogs and farms. The wide road behind the soldier was empty.

"That's Corporal Gomoth, our scout." Sabor swung back onto his horse and rode out to meet his man.

If Aldari had been on horseback, she would have gone after

him. As it was, she was half-tempted to hurry up to the meeting, but the feeling of being watched came over her. When she glanced back and found Hawk jogging toward her, she wasn't surprised. He didn't make a sound, neither weapons nor armor jangling as he glided over the stone highway on light feet.

She was about to say she'd decided his constant attention was more stifling than charming, but he merely nodded at her on his way past and ran up to join the troops. That made her feel foolish for her assumptions but not so foolish that she didn't jog ahead to catch up with the group. She was glad she'd opted for practical travel boots instead of the sandals her sister had said looked good with her dress.

"There are bodies ahead," the scout was saying when Aldari caught up. "Men and women with their throats torn out in and around a farmhouse. It looks like vorgs were responsible, but the vorgs are dead too. There are dozens of their furry bodies, the animals taken down by blades and bows."

Aldari stared at him and then toward the farmland ahead. She'd heard of the furred, fanged, and horned vorgs, and there were two stuffed vorg heads mounted over one of the fireplaces in the castle, but she'd never seen a living one. The big predators resided in the mountains where they hunted wolves, bears, and elk. Or at least, that was where they were *supposed* to reside.

"There could be more vorgs in the area, hiding in the bushes. It's not safe to continue until we've checked it out and—" The scout noticed Aldari and gawked at her in surprise.

"Go ahead, Corporal Gomoth," Aldari urged, wanting him to continue. Who had killed the vorgs? And why had the creatures been here to start with?

Gomoth looked uncertainly at Sabor.

"Your Highness," Sabor said. "Perhaps you could wait in your carriage. Once I've learned everything, I can give you a full report."

"If I hear your scout's report for myself, you don't need to give me a separate accounting." An accounting that would doubtless be edited to be less gruesome and thus more appropriate for the ears of a princess.

"It may be dangerous, Your Highness," Sabor said. "I'd like you to stay in the carriage until we've dealt with the creatures and made sure the road is suitable for a lady to pass along."

What were they going to do? Drag all the dead bodies out of view and wash away the blood before they let her come?

"We don't always get what we like, Lieutenant. Continue the report, please." Aldari waved toward the scout.

"That's not necessary," Hawk said. "I can tell you what happened."

The soldiers turned toward him.

"We killed the vorgs yesterday." Hawk pointed to himself and his mercenaries. "We came this way to report for our duty at the castle. It was early in the morning, and the vorgs were attacking the people coming out of their house to work. There were a *lot* of them, and we were too late to save everyone. The humans who survived ran off to neighboring properties instead of speaking with us."

"Why didn't you report this when you arrived at the castle?" Sabor asked.

"We weren't allowed into the castle until it was time to join the caravan this morning." Hawk twitched a shoulder and glanced at Aldari. Had they been wandering around *sightseeing* and killing time when they'd stumbled into the library and found her? Since they'd walked up to greet her by name, that was unlikely. "This is not our land, and we don't know what's common or rare. I assumed the people who got away would handle the necessary reporting." Hawk lifted his chin. "Also, there are no vorgs left alive. We handled the problem fully."

Sabor looked more flabbergasted than appreciative as he peered around the countryside. "We should have had warning. If we'd known vorgs had come down from the mountains— *Why have they come down from the mountains?*" Sabor waved at Aldari. Implying what? That her father wouldn't have set her caravan out if he'd known there would be threats?

"Nothing would have changed," Aldari said firmly. "I have to reach Orath by the end of the week to meet my future husband and his family before the wedding next week. I understand the Orathians set the date before Father even accepted the proposal. They have a big festival coming up, and Prince Xerik planned to marry *someone*."

Maybe she shouldn't have said all that—or hinted that she wasn't that pleased about her fate—for Hawk looked at her oddly. Were arranged marriages not common in his land? If so, she envied him that, the option to choose whomever he pleased.

"It would have been nice to know there was an additional threat," Sabor muttered.

Not wanting the elves to think her people unappreciative, Aldari faced Hawk. "On behalf of Delantria, I thank you and your mercenaries for coming to the assistance of these farmers and for risking yourselves to attack the vorgs."

"You are welcome."

"Lieutenant Sabor." Aldari pointed to a spot a ways off the road. "May I have a word with you in private?"

"Of course."

After glancing at Hawk—and his pointed ears—Aldari led Sabor farther away than she might have otherwise. "Please send your scout ahead again," she said softly, "and confirm that all the vorgs are dead and that there aren't any... discrepancies in Captain Hawk's story."

Sabor arched his eyebrows. "You don't think he's telling the truth?"

"He probably is, but let's verify it, all right?" Aldari found it strange that the elves hadn't mentioned the vorgs to anyone when they'd arrived, especially since people had been killed, but it was also possible that dealing with packs of predators was so commonplace to them that they didn't think much of such events.

"Yes, Your Highness."

"Also send one of your men back to the capital to report this. Father will want to know about it, and he'll likely send out troops to make sure there aren't more infestations of deadly predators in the mainlands."

"We may need all of our men for the journey ahead," Sabor said.

"I'm sure we can spare one, especially since we have the elves. If their company is as deadly as you say, and if they killed dozens of vorgs..." She spread her palm toward the sky.

Sabor's expression was mulish, but he didn't argue further. Aldari was glad for that. This was her first trip into the countryside without the rest of her family or an older chaperone along, and she hadn't been positive the men would defer to her.

"I'll tell my soldier to ride quickly and return as soon as possible," Sabor said.

"Perfect." Aldari smiled at him, hoping he didn't find her too difficult. Her sister likely would have remained in the carriage and let the men handle everything, but Aldari preferred to know what was going on and have input. "Thank you."

"But do us a favor, please, Your Highness. As we continue on, stay in the carriage." Sabor glanced toward the road ahead. "With the curtains drawn. You shouldn't be exposed to death and gore. It'll give you nightmares."

"I'll ride in the carriage."

Aldari didn't make any promises about the curtains. Though she had no desire to see *death and gore*, she also couldn't imagine shutting herself off to its existence, to the knowledge that her people had been killed. What if the Taldarians had driven the vorgs out of the mountains, either by accident, through their mining operations, or on purpose, to further weaken Delantria in preparation for a full-out invasion?

That possibility was what would give her nightmares and ensure she would, whether she wished it or not, hurry to reach Orath and walk down the aisle with Prince Xerik.

4

THE NEXT MORNING, THE CARAVAN WOUND ITS WAY INTO THE mountains, what had once been part of the King's Road but now had numerous signs marking it as the Taldar Highway. Bumpy and full of potholes, it hadn't seen any improvements since the empire had taken control of the mountains. At least they hadn't closed it to travelers and posted sentries to keep citizens from other nations from using it.

Towering evergreens rose to either side of the highway, their branches sometimes stretching out over the road and blocking out the sun, and Aldari almost missed a sign that promised a cross-roads ahead. In one direction, over the mountains to the south-east, lay the heart of the Taldar Empire. Toward the southwest, the way they would go, lay the Orath Kingdom. She started in surprise at a third destination that was mentioned, the Forever Fog River and the elven continent of Serth.

At any point, they could have cut across the Delantrian Penin-sula and headed east and reached that wide river, but no roads in the kingdom went toward it. The dangers of the river and the elven lands beyond were well known. Aldari was surprised there was a road here and wondered if the mercenaries had come that way.

"I saw a cougar watching us from a cliff," Theli said, her nose pressed to the window as she gazed out, "but no vorgs, drajkar, packs of dire wolves, or anything else likely to attack the caravan."

"We're probably safe until nightfall."

Unfortunately, they would have to camp in the shadow of the great peaks. No matter how fast they traveled, the caravan wouldn't make it through the mountains in a single day.

"That might be what those farmers thought," Theli said grimly.

Her grave expression made Aldari wonder if she'd caught a glimpse of some of the bodies. The *human* bodies. They hadn't closed the curtains as they rode past the farm, and some of the soldiers had been pulling vorg corpses away from the road. The people who lived in the area had been in the process of burning them in a pyre, but Aldari had spotted a number of the dead two-legged furred and horned creatures. Larger and more powerful than grizzly bears, they were known to run in packs, but she'd been shocked by the sheer number that had descended on the farm. Once again, she wondered if someone could have manipulated them into attacking.

Old tales of witches and wizards and magic came to mind, though Aldari had never seen proof that humans had any aptitude for the ancient arcane arts. Even the elves, who'd supposedly made all of the magical weapons and relics that existed in the world, had lost the knack for it. Though magic existed in strange and sometimes deadly places around the natural world, its cultivation was a lost and forgotten art from a past age. If the vorgs had been coerced, it had likely been with arrows or perhaps explosives. The Taldarians were reputedly refining handheld black-powder weapons to rival the power of cannons on warships.

"Tell me a tale of death and woe," Theli sang softly, "and into the shadows I'll not go."

Not recognizing the lyrics, Aldari was about to ask if she'd composed them when the thunder of hoofbeats reached her ears. Frowning, she closed the book she'd been halfheartedly reading and scooted closer to the window.

A fist pounded on the door, startling her, and she jumped to her feet and cracked her head on the ceiling. Theli surged into a crouch, her mace in hand.

"Hostiles ahead," a uniformed soldier on horseback yelled. "Stay inside!"

He galloped out of view, and other mounted soldiers, as well as several of the elves on foot, rushed past in the same direction. Captain Hawk appeared, peering in at them, and he hesitated for a moment, matching pace with the carriage. Did he think he needed to stay behind to guard Aldari?

"Go ahead," she called. "I've got Theli. And a book the size of a coffee table."

Theli shot her an exasperated look. "Get your *dagger* out, Your Highness. Just in case."

In the confines of the carriage, the last thing Aldari wanted was to tumble when they hit a pothole and inadvertently cut Theli, but she did pull out the weapon. Ahead of the caravan, the distant clang of steel striking steel sounded, and her hands shook with the realization that they truly were being attacked. And not by vorgs—vorgs didn't carry swords—but by men. Men from the empire? Men who wanted to rob them? Or men who'd been sent to stop her wedding and the alliance with Orath?

The carriage lurched and sped up, almost pitching Aldari back into her seat. Horses squealed, and the coachman cursed, trying to calm them down. From inside, Aldari couldn't see the man, but she had no trouble envisioning him struggling to keep the scared animals under control.

A boom rang out amid more clashing of steel. One of the

black-powder weapons she'd been thinking about? If so, their attackers were almost certainly from the empire.

"We should have sailed," Theli said.

"Orath is landlocked." Aldari sank to the carriage floor to steady herself as it wobbled and clunked into potholes. They were going even faster now.

"They've got a river."

"With the mouth in the desert in another kingdom. Besides, by the time we sailed around the horn and through the Storm Shoals, it would have taken weeks instead of days, and there are plenty of pirates in those waters."

"Why don't you just stab me through the heart with your logic and kill me here?"

"Have I mentioned how delightful it is that you're always implicating me in your hypothetical deaths?"

"It's to make you feel guilty enough to ensure good behavior." Theli braced her free hand against the doorjamb and peered out the window as the carriage rocked. "Since bodyguards aren't allowed to spank princesses."

"Ha ha."

Something snapped, and the carriage jolted so hard that it pitched them both into the back wall. One of the wheels had broken.

The coachman's frantic voice sounded, ordering the horses to stop, but the team kept tugging the wobbling carriage along, even as it rocked ferociously, hurling Aldari and Theli from side to side. Aldari swore and tried to sheath the dagger she'd drawn, afraid she would cut herself or Theli as they flew about. Pain battered her from all sides as her shoulder, head, and hip clunked against the walls and floor.

"We need to get out of here," she yelled, crawling toward the door.

If Hawk was still out there, maybe he could protect them if

they leaped out.

Theli grabbed her arm. "We'll be easy targets out there. Don't assume they want you alive."

No, Aldari wouldn't. If all the empire wanted was to stop the wedding, killing her would achieve that just fine.

"We could be pummeled to death in *here*."

No sooner had her words come out than another snap sounded, this one thunderous in the confined space. The carriage pitched sideways and tumbled off the road. As they rolled down an incline, Aldari couldn't keep from shrieking as the floor became the ceiling, then the floor, and then the ceiling again. She flew through the air and crashed into Theli before hitting a bench. They tumbled together into a wall, with Theli landing on her.

Glass shattered as a branch thrust through the window in the door. An instant later, the carriage slammed into a tree and halted so abruptly that Aldari hit her head and bit her tongue. Blood tainted her mouth as she gasped in pain.

Theli squirmed off her and tumbled to the floor. No, the ceiling. The floor was above them now, with the sides of a wall smashed inward. The scent of pine needles filled the air, the branch thrusting through the window taking up half the interior.

Hoofbeats raced past on the road that was now uphill from them. The clangs of swords clashing were much closer now.

Though her entire body hurt, Aldari squeezed past the branch, hoping to see out through the broken window. Which side was winning? Were Lieutenant Sabor and the elves still alive?

Something warm trickled down her forehead. Blood.

"Stay here," Theli rasped.

With the branch thrust through the window, Aldari couldn't have opened the door to get out if she'd wished to. "I just want to see outside."

"I just want to die," Theli groaned, her hand to her ribs.

There were medical supplies under the coachman's seat, but

getting to them would be a challenge. Aldari couldn't tell if the man—or the horses, for that matter—was still out there.

They'd landed such that Aldari could see up the slope back to the road, and Hawk and Setvik were visible, crouched back to back as they fought six men who'd surrounded them. Two blue-uniformed soldiers lay nearby, their weapons fallen from their hands, their eyes open but glazed as they stared upward. Lieutenant Sabor was one of them, and Aldari feared he was dead.

Big shaggy men with beards, wild hair, and chain mail vests swung huge two-handed swords and heavy axes meant not to log trees but to cleave off heads. Taldarian mountain men. They roared as they attacked, their dark eyes blazing with battle lust.

With the elves surrounded, Aldari didn't see how they could win, but they were as fast and deadly as the stories promised. Their feet, hands, and blades moved so quickly that Aldari struggled to follow the battle, except through the reactions of those they struck. One of the six men stumbled back, dropping his sword. Another followed, leaving an opening in the knot of enemies surrounding the two elves.

Aldari thought Hawk and Setvik might come out on top, but one of those black-powder weapons fired from up the road. A projectile clipped Setvik's shoulder, knocking him back.

Two men sprang for him, weapons raised as they tried to take advantage. Somehow, Hawk blocked them both even as he kicked a third man and parried a sword meant for his head.

Aldari shook her head in amazement at his speed but worried it wouldn't be enough. Someone had to stop the shooter, or he would be able to pick off the elves.

She fumbled for the door handle, but it was warped and only half accessible. Aldari struggled to turn it, then shoved at the door with her shoulder, swatting aside pine needles in her face. Maybe she could lever her dagger into the gap and that would help.

"Aldari," Theli warned. "Don't—"

Metal screeched as a shadow fell across the broken window, and someone ripped the door from its hinges. A hulking bear of a man snarled as he stepped into view. His eyes lit when he spotted Aldari, and he hefted his battle-axe over his head.

Aldari reacted instinctively. Her dagger was still up, and she thrust it toward his belly, toward a gap in the chainmail. As soon as the weapon drove into his flesh, she let go and flung herself backward.

His axe came down, smashing into the branch and the broken frame of the carriage. It missed her by scant inches. Theli grabbed her shoulder, pulling her farther inside.

The man bellowed, a mixture of pain and rage. He yanked the dagger free—it had only sunk in a couple of inches—and threw it to the ground before thrusting his axe into the carriage. The branch impeded him, but he jabbed and swung, trying to force his way to them.

As Aldari sucked in her belly and pressed her back to the warped wall of the carriage, Theli lunged forward with her mace. She avoided the swinging blade and smashed her weapon onto the man's wrist. He bellowed again, jerking back, but unfortunately, he didn't drop his weapon. Knowing he would keep trying to kill them, Aldari grabbed her heavy book to use as a shield—or maybe a club.

Abruptly, the man's roar halted and he stiffened, arching his back. Only when his axe dropped from his limp fingers did Aldari realize what had happened. The brute pitched sideways, revealing Hawk standing behind him, a sword and dagger in his hands.

Blood dripped from a cut in his temple, and his wild blond hair was matted with crimson stains. He looked like an avenging scythe lord out of ancient mythology, ready to cart them off to the River of Death, but he'd saved their lives. Outside, the sounds of battle had faded, the mountain air growing still, not even a bird calling.

Aldari slumped back, the book falling from her lap. They'd lived.

But how many others had died? She thought of Sabor's vacant eyes and swallowed, her mouth dry and her throat tight. Tears threatened, but she blinked them away. She had to hold it together.

"Thank you, Captain Hawk," she managed to say as he lowered his weapons, his gaze scouring Aldari and lingering on the wound that was dripping blood into her eyes. She wiped away the moisture. "Are you able to give me a report?"

"We were attacked by approximately forty wild mountain bandits, or so they appeared," Hawk said. "Several shouted orders at each other and used rank, so it's possible they were dressed to pass as a motley band but were in fact military men. They were well trained and fought as a unit."

"Men sent by the empire."

"Or someone else who objects to your trip. Or its ultimate goal?" Hawk raised his eyebrows.

"The wedding is to cement an alliance between my kingdom and Orath. My father has been promised that once I'm married to Prince Xerik, Orath will send troops to help keep Delantria independent. We've surmised that those who want our kingdom for themselves would prefer we remain unable to defend ourselves against the empire's superior numbers." She couldn't keep the bitterness out of her voice.

Setvik walked up, gripping his shoulder where he'd been shot as blood trickled through his fingers. He also sounded bitter, or maybe disgusted, when he spoke to Hawk in their language.

Hawk pointed at the mountain road that had turned into a battlefield, with bodies strewn up and down its length, and said something curt in return. Setvik argued. Hawk grew even more curt. Setvik glowered at him without moving. Hawk asked a soft question as they glared at each other, neither breaking eye contact.

Aldari wished she understood their language.

Setvik finally looked away and shouted an order to their mercenaries.

"I'm not sure if any of your soldiers who remained in the area survived," Hawk told Aldari, the calmness returning to his voice and face.

Did that mean that some of her father's troops had fled? Aldari frowned at the idea of them abandoning their duty.

"My people are checking now," Hawk added, "but several of them were also injured."

"I'm sorry." Aldari looked over her shoulder to Theli, feeling even more fortunate that they'd survived. "I'm not sure I can speak for my future husband, but I know my father will reward your people for staying with us."

Hawk smiled sadly. "I'm afraid he won't."

"Why?"

Setvik folded his arms over his chest.

"Because that is the way to Orath Kingdom." Hawk pointed to the rightmost road branching off from the crossroads ahead. It was as the sign had announced, with two roads forming a V, each continuing deeper into the mountains but toward different passes and different destinations. What looked like little more than an overgrown animal path meandered off to the left, following the mountains instead of crossing over them.

"Yes..." Aldari couldn't keep the puzzlement from her voice. "I read the sign, and I've seen maps."

Hawk shifted his finger to point at the animal trail. "And that is the way we're taking you."

"I don't understand."

Did he not think it would be safe for them to continue toward the pass? Was there an alternate way through the mountains, one where they'd be less likely to encounter imperial soldiers?

Setvik smiled coldly. "We're kidnapping you, Princess."

5

ALDARI RODE ON HORSEBACK, A LEATHER THONG BINDING HER WRISTS together. Her legs weren't tied to the stirrups, and her mouth wasn't gagged, but there would have been little point in yelling. Who out here—besides vorgs, wolves, and possibly imperial men who wanted her dead—would hear her? All she could do was watch the ferns and pines pass by, her brain absently picking out patterns in the foliage.

Behind her, Theli was in a similar state, astraddle another horse. Both of their mounts had belonged to soldiers, soldiers who'd been alive that morning and were now dead. They'd died saving Aldari's life, but at the moment, she struggled to find gratitude. All along, she'd been wary of the elves, something about them seeming off to her, but she hadn't trusted her instincts. She hadn't told her father to send them away, that she didn't want to go with them.

Would he have listened? Or would he have dismissed her instincts as quickly as he dismissed the work she published under her pen name?

She sniffed surreptitiously and blinked away tears—she did

not want to cry in front of these people, especially that smug bastard, Setvik. He was behind her on foot, leading Theli's horse. Hawk also walked and led hers, though he hadn't spoken more than five words to her since his lieutenant's odious announcement.

Most of the rest of the elves were riding now. They'd rounded up the horses they'd recovered after the battle. It wasn't as if the soldiers had needed them, and if the horses had been left to fend for themselves in the mountains, they likely would have been killed by predators. Even so, it was hard for Aldari not to think of it as theft, and she wondered if the elves had colluded with or even arranged for the imperial attack as a distraction, so they could get what they'd wanted.

What would have happened if the Taldarian men hadn't attacked? Would the elves have waited until nightfall, slit the throats of the sleeping soldiers, and stolen Aldari all the same?

She glanced back, wishing she dared confer with Theli, but the trail was too narrow for them to ride side by side, even if the elves would have allowed it. Theli, her cheek purpled from a rising bruise, lifted her chin attentively, as if awaiting some command. Did she want Aldari to suggest an escape attempt?

Unfortunately, the elves had taken their weapons. Even if, by some crazy stroke of luck, they could escape their fearsome captors, they would be as helpless in the mountains as the horses would have been.

Still, Aldari nodded and mouthed, "Later."

She had no idea where the elves were taking them or why they wanted her, but as soon as she and Theli got an opportunity, she *would* order an escape attempt.

Setvik, who didn't seem to miss anything, caught the exchange and snorted. Hawk glanced up at Aldari.

She looked away, glowering off into the woods. Her first thought was to say nothing to him, but maybe that was foolish.

She ought to learn whatever he was willing to share on the off chance that it would help them formulate an escape plan.

"Why did you kidnap us, Captain?" Aldari asked, forcing herself to be respectful and use his rank. Maybe if she was courteous with him, he would be less likely to treat them poorly later. "If you intend to ransom me to Prince Xerik, I doubt my value to him is equal to the injuries your men took." Or the deaths of those poor soldiers. "We haven't even met yet."

Maybe she shouldn't have said that. Would it have been better to have Hawk believe she was tremendously valuable? If he couldn't get whatever coin he sought, he might cut her throat.

"We have no interest in the Orath Kingdom or its prince, Your Highness," Hawk said. "My duty is to my people."

"And your people need me?" she asked skeptically.

"They do."

Setvik spoke sharply, some warning to Hawk. An order for him not to share their secrets? Which one of them was truly in charge?

Hawk snapped back over his shoulder at Setvik. He glowered at the trail ahead for a moment before taking a breath, smoothing his face, and looking up at Aldari.

"I regret that our act is inconveniencing you and your maid. If it's possible, we'll return you unharmed, so that you may continue with your wedding plans."

"*Maid*?" Theli blurted a protest. "Do I look like the kind of woman who helps a princess take a bath and pick out her clothes?" She waved her bound hands as much as she could to encompass her black trousers and tunic, the clothes chosen because they allowed athletic movement, not because of a fashion choice.

Aldari wished *she* wore trousers and a tunic rather than a dress that was as much grime as fabric now. "She's my bodyguard. If she were my maid, she wouldn't have been clubbing enemies with a mace."

"Two days ago, she was a librarian," Hawk said mildly.

"A lie I wish you'd believed." Aldari shook her head.

"We did our research before coming."

"Research about what I look like? Why? I hardly believe the elves have some prince of their own that they want me to marry for an alliance."

Hawk, who'd been nothing but graceful up until that point, stumbled. He shot her a glance she couldn't read, but he recovered quickly, his face smoothing, though a hint of amusement—or maybe irony?—brightened his green eyes.

"No, Your Highness," he said. "The elves do not seek an alliance through marriage with a human princess."

His tone was polite, but Setvik's wasn't when he muttered, "As if our people would seek an alliance with a puny kingdom of fishers and farmers who can't even fight off a few vorgs."

Thinking of those who'd died at that farmstead, Aldari couldn't keep from blanching and feeling insulted on the behalf of the fallen.

"Or spread the legs of some human wench, wishing her to bear a feeble half-breed child," Setvik added.

"*Wench*?" Theli roared.

Aldari clamped down on her tongue, barely holding back an angry retort of her own. Maybe she should have let it out, but if Hawk spoke the truth, and he intended to let her and Theli go eventually, she didn't want to irritate the elves so much that they changed their minds.

"Enough, Setvik," Hawk said over his shoulder, anger taking the light from his eyes. "You will not insult our guests or be crude around them."

Setvik, grip tightening on the reins he held, shot an icy glare forward, not at Hawk but at Aldari. It was as full of murderous anger as she'd seen in the eyes of the imperial axeman, and she barely kept from shrinking away.

Her decision not to irritate the elves seemed wise. Though she tended to believe Hawk would do as he'd said, and let them go when he'd finished… whatever he planned for them, she was a lot less certain about Setvik. He seemed to be fantasizing about driving a dagger between her shoulder blades. What she'd done to offend him, she couldn't guess, but she didn't want to give him a reason to fulfill his fantasy.

Setvik spoke softly in his own tongue, the words for Hawk. Hawk flicked his fingers in dismissal and faced forward. Was he aware of Setvik glowering at the back of his head? Or the rest of the mercenaries stealing glances toward them?

Not wanting to give them a reason to argue further, especially when she had the feeling her fate would be much more question-able if something happened to Hawk, Aldari tamped down her curiosity and didn't ask any more questions.

All she could hope was that when they camped for the night, she and Theli would be able to slip away. Somehow. If the elves succeeded in taking them across the Forever Fog River and into their strange and ominous land, rumored to be full of creatures far deadlier than vorgs, Aldari doubted escape would be possible.

6

AT TWILIGHT'S APPROACH, THE ELVES CREATED A CAMPSITE alongside the trail near a stream that meandered down the slope. Aldari's butt was sore from the long day's ride, and her entire body had stiffened painfully, bruises rising in all the places that she'd struck as the carriage had tumbled from the road. She stifled a gasp as she dismounted, not wanting her captors—especially Setvik—to have the satisfaction of witnessing her distress. At least neither she nor Theli, as far as Aldari knew, had broken any bones.

She wouldn't have minded walking around and returning the blood flow to her body, but Hawk directed her and Theli to a log. While his men cared for and fed the horses, he pulled leathery green bars and water out of his pack for them.

"If I untie your hands so you can eat more easily," Hawk said, "will you give me your word that you won't try to escape?"

"No." Aldari wondered if he would have believed her if she'd said *yes*. Maybe she should have, as it was her duty to do whatever she could to get away.

He snorted softly. "Very well then."

He handed them each one of the dubious green bars, then waved for them to sit on the log. Gingerly, Aldari lowered herself onto the moss-covered bark and sniffed at what was apparently food. Macerated and compacted plant material with darker bits dotted in, it had a strong earthy scent.

"What is it?" she asked.

"A moss bar."

"*Moss*? I didn't know moss was edible." Aldari stared at the leathery rectangle.

Theli, who was still standing, jerked her bar out to arm's length, as if it had bitten her. A nearby horse nickered, nostrils twitching as it turned its head toward the meal. If Theli wasn't that hungry, her bar might end up in its mouth.

After the long day, Aldari couldn't imagine refusing food, however dubious. Her stomach growled uncertainly.

"Much of it is," Hawk said. "Most isn't very nutritionally dense, but we have a few species that we cultivate that are high in protein and keep well when preserved. The bars are good for travel. We add cranberries to give them a more palatable flavor."

"Remind me to get the recipe from you before I leave," Aldari said. "I'm sure cranberry-moss bars would be popular at the Solstice Day Festivities."

Hawk arched his blond brows. "I sense you're mocking my food."

"You're astute for a kidnapper."

"Because the moss keeps me sharp. What do *your* people eat regularly?"

"Fish and potatoes. We're far enough north that our growing seasons are fairly short. Potatoes are among the few crops that are reliable and store well over the winter." She realized that most of his continent was even farther north than Delantria. No wonder they ate moss.

"Potatoes?" Hawk asked. "Aren't those poisonous?"

"Only when they're raw. And it would be rare for one to kill you. Usually you just get some, uhm, digestive distress."

"The *moss* doesn't have that effect." He sounded smug.

Setvik walked past, glancing at them and saying something dismissive in his language. Probably that human culinary practices were barbaric.

A few other elves sank down with groans, men who'd been injured during the fighting. After the battle, Hawk must have been worried about more enemies in the area, because he hadn't stopped to let his people treat their wounds. Now, however, a silver-haired elf with a brown leather bag that might have been a medical kit moved among the mercenaries, asking questions and probing injuries.

If he was a doctor, he was impressively capable with a sword. Aldari had glimpsed him fighting.

"Does either of you need medical attention?" Hawk glanced at the top of Aldari's head, where she'd hit it and bled. "I can call over Medic Mevleth."

There was a painful knot up there—she had painful knots *everywhere*—but Aldari shook her head, not wanting one of her captors probing her all over.

"I'd take a painkiller," Theli muttered, sinking down clumsily onto the log. Having their hands bound made even simple acts difficult. "Or five. Do you have any waywar root?"

"We have something similar." Hawk spoke to the medic.

Mevleth grunted and tossed over two packets of something, then knelt before a young elf who was grimacing as he peeled out of his armor. Hawk caught the packets and handed one to Theli and one to Aldari, though she hadn't asked for anything.

"If you're in dire straits, he has some magical healing potions," Hawk said, "but he must think you're unlikely to die and that something to dull the pain will be sufficient."

"Lucky us," Aldari said.

"Lucky *us*." Hawk smiled and placed a hand on his chest. He hadn't yet said what he wanted a human princess for.

Theli unwrapped her packet, revealing a gray powder redolent of crushed rocks. "Appealing."

"They're aged and dried aslavar berries from our homeland." Hawk sat on the log next to Aldari. "The powder is potent. Take only half, and see if that's enough. If you're still in pain, you can consume the second dose, but you might fall asleep afterward."

Aldari eyed him, wishing he would go away. With their captors so close all day, she hadn't been able to conspire with Theli. She didn't quite know what they would conspire about, as she hadn't been able to formulate a plan beyond *wait for them to fall asleep, grab horses, and run.*

She had been considering the horses and which ones appeared strongest and most athletic. Since she and Theli were lighter than the elves, it was possible the horses they selected might be able to outrun theirs, but the idea of charging blindly down a mountain path in the dark daunted her. She also doubted all the elves would allow themselves to sleep at once.

Aldari dabbed her tongue to the powder, puckered at the rancid, ashy taste, and couldn't keep from coughing. Crushed rock would have been less abhorrent. She thought about drowning out the taste with the moss bar, but that was probably as loathsome. Instead, she grabbed the canteen from Theli and swigged water as tears ran down her cheeks.

Several of the elves laughed, their voices oddly musical for hardened killers.

"Our medicine is rarely delicious, I fear," Hawk said.

"You said this came from *berries*?" Aldari rasped. "Isn't the purpose of berries to get birds to eat them and spread the seeds to help the species survive? I'm shocked that whatever bush these came from hasn't been extinct for eons."

"Ah, I believe the medicine may be from the seeds *within* the berries."

Aldari made herself touch her tongue to the packet again, forcing herself to take the suggested half dose.

Theli eyed hers in the darkening gloom. "Maybe I can deal with my pain."

"It's not that bad." Aldari coughed and took another swig.

"Yes, the cheerful glow to your face makes me eager to tongue it up."

"In addition to lessening pain," Hawk said, "it's supposed to boost your body's natural ability to heal itself."

Aldari handed the canteen to Theli. "Enjoy."

While Hawk chewed on a moss bar and Aldari unsuccessfully willed him to go away, the mercenaries worked around them. Setvik also worked, setting up tripwires and other defenses Aldari could only guess at in the dim light. She tried to make note of where they were placed, since they could as easily impede an escape as an invasion, but what she found herself noticing was that the mercenaries looked to Setvik, asking him questions and nodding obediently at his orders. None of them asked anything of Hawk.

"Are you really in charge here?" Aldari nibbled from the corner of her bar. It was as dreadful as she'd feared, only slightly less bitter than the medicinal powder. Maybe she would pick out the cranberries.

"Of course. Veth Setvik is my second-in-command, and I delegate duties to him while I lounge on logs with pretty ladies." Hawk waved his ration bar in the air. "Privileges of command. Is it not so in the human lands?"

Though he smiled, ignoring a dark look that Setvik gave him, Hawk watched her intently. Wondering if she believed him? Despite his quick smiles, his eyes were always intent. He had a way of holding her gaze that made her feel that she had his undivided attention, that she was important to him. But why?

"I guess." Aldari thought of Lieutenant Sabor and the other soldiers who'd died, and shivered. "Did you collude with the Taldar Empire and arrange for their men to attack our caravan, so you could more easily steal us away?"

"We did not," Hawk said without hesitation. "We were aware that they had men in the mountains who might be a threat, because we came this way as we traveled to your kingdom, but we did not interact with them."

"But you planned all along to kidnap us."

"To kidnap you, yes." Hawk glanced at Theli but pointed at Aldari. "We planned to subdue and tie up the human soldiers during the night. It is unfortunate that there were deaths."

He seemed sincere, but Aldari didn't trust her ability to read a near stranger. A near *elf* stranger, at that. Though they smiled and glared similarly to humans, it was possible some of their facial expressions were different. It was also possible Hawk was a practiced liar.

"And why do you want me?" she asked. "You rudely neglected to answer that question the last time I asked it."

"My apologies, Your Highness. Mercenaries aren't known for their manners." Hawk bent toward her in a sitting bow.

As long seconds passed, Aldari realized he didn't intend to answer her question this time, either. She made an exasperated noise and was tempted to throw the moss bar at him.

"Once we've reached Serth, I'll be at liberty to speak more freely," Hawk offered.

Aldari had no plans to stick around that long, but she sensed that interrogating him further wouldn't get her anywhere. What she truly wanted was to plot and scheme with Theli. In private.

"To keep your mercenaries from resenting your lounging-with-ladies privileges," Aldari said, "maybe you could build us a fire. It's getting chilly."

She had a feeling Hawk was sticking close to make sure they didn't escape—or weren't the target of imperial bowmen lurking in the forest—not because he made a habit of relaxing while others worked.

"We can't risk a fire. It would act as a beacon that could help others find us."

"You think there are others out here who'll be looking for us in the middle of the night?" As she finished the question, a wolf howled nearby. Something that might have been a vorg or another large predator roared farther up the hillside. "A fire might keep the animals away."

"We can handle the animals."

"*We* can't." Aldari held up her bound hands.

"I will protect you."

"Because you need me for something."

"Yes."

"But you won't tell me what."

Hawk glanced at Setvik, who never seemed to be far away. "We're taking you to elves who will explain everything. My understanding is limited. I'm a warrior, not a scholar."

"And you need a scholar?" Aldari glanced at Theli, but she only shrugged and raised her eyebrows. "What makes you think I qualify, Hawk?"

She remembered the math problem she'd shared with her brother and how intently Hawk had watched their exchange. But being able to do multiplication in her head didn't make her a scholar. It was something lots of people could do, including her tutor. She *had* studied mathematics and economics for years, but how would an elf from another kingdom have known that? Her own family didn't know her pen name, so this couldn't have anything to do with the papers she'd published. Besides, what would the elves care about the economics of human kingdoms?

"You seem smart," Hawk said, smiling again.

He was only flattering her to avoid answering her question, so she shouldn't have been anything but irritated, but he had a roguish charm, and *irritation* wasn't the feeling that arose within her when he smiled and gazed into her eyes.

She scowled and looked away, refusing to experience any kind of *attraction* to her captor. Her captor who might have, despite what he claimed, colluded with the imperial men so he could more easily kidnap her. If he had, the deaths of Lieutenant Sabor and the other soldiers were his fault. Even if he hadn't, he was stealing her away from her journey and her wedding, a wedding that would seal an alliance her people desperately needed.

Theli gagged, coughed, and drank from the canteen only to sputter and dump half the water on her tunic.

"You either disagree that I'm smart," Aldari said, "or you tried the powder."

"It's dreadful. Better to pass out and die on the mountainside."

"You get used to it," Hawk said, then called to the medic for a packet of his own. Maybe his body was stiffening up after the battle and the long walk. When the medic tossed him a packet, Hawk dumped all of it in his mouth, despite having warned them to start with a half dose. He must have had a rough day of fighting and kidnapping.

"Don't let that make you drowsy," Setvik told him. "If their people are vaguely competent, we'll have company tonight."

"Doubtful," Hawk said.

"You let that man get away." Setvik slapped the scabbard of one of his swords and switched to his language for the rest.

"We came for the princess," Hawk said, opting to continue in the human tongue, "not to kill their people. We don't need any more enemies."

Aldari frowned and sat up straighter. Who'd gotten away? One of her father's soldiers? If he escaped the mountains and reached the garrison in the mainland, was it possible the troops there could send a rescue party? One that would catch up in time? Before they reached the Forever Fog River?

"The rest were dead," Setvik said, following Hawk's lead to speak in the human tongue and letting them understand. "If that soldier fell to a knife, nobody would have known who was responsible."

The admission that Setvik would have killed a soldier in cold blood sent a chill through Aldari, but it didn't surprise her, not in the least. He glared at her, and she had to fight the urge to scoot closer to Hawk. He was her kidnapper, not her savior. She needed to escape him as much as she did the others.

"We're not here to kill anyone, unless in self-defense, as it was today. Or to protect her." Hawk tilted his head toward Aldari. "I know you're a bloodthirsty brute who abandoned his people years ago, but you agreed to this mission."

Rage flared in Setvik's eyes, and his fists wrapped around the hilts of his twin swords, his knuckles white against the skin. "I did not *abandon* our people. I came to the human lands to work."

"You're a capable soldier, and we needed you to defend the outpost and drive back the enemy."

Setvik switched back to their language to reply, his hands still tight on his weapons.

Hawk remained sitting on the log, calmly eating his moss bar.

"Is it wise to goad him?" Aldari whispered, again worrying that she and Theli would be in trouble—*more* trouble—if Hawk died and Setvik ended up in charge of their mission.

"Not in the least." Hawk took a casual bite from his bar. Despite that casualness, he kept his gaze on Setvik. "He's an extremely capable warrior."

"I've had a lot of practice fighting," Setvik said.

"The better to come home and help our people?"

"As I promised the king I would. I gave my word, but don't push me, Hawk." Setvik released his weapons, though his jaw was clenched, and loosening his hands required a visible effort. "If her people catch up with us and attack tonight, we'll have to kill them. And it'll be your fault because you intentionally let one get away."

"They won't catch us. It was half a day back to their border and closest garrison. We'll get up early and reach the river by noon. They won't follow us across."

"You'd better hope you're right." Setvik stalked into the woods, disappearing into the gloom.

Thanks to the encroaching darkness, Aldari could barely see the mercenaries anymore. She hadn't been lying about the night air cooling. It snowed in the mountains even in the summer, and she hugged her arms in close, wishing for a blanket. But the elves were traveling light, and she doubted they had such luxuries.

Since they'd been in a hurry to leave the attack site, they hadn't allowed her to bring any of her belongings along—not even her books. They couldn't appreciate academics *that* much.

"You two fought well today," Hawk surprised Aldari by saying. "When I heard that axeman rip the door off its hinges, I didn't think I would get to the carriage in time. Imagine my surprise when I reached him, and he already had a dagger hole in his gut."

"It was just reflex," Aldari muttered, hardly feeling she should take credit for that wild stab. "I got lucky."

"*I* didn't," Theli said. "When I whacked him with my mace, it was calculated."

Aldari elbowed her. "That's why she's the bodyguard, and I'm the princess."

"We brought your weapons along." Hawk pointed over his shoulder; he'd tied Theli's mace and Aldari's dagger to his pack. "When we reach our land, I'll remove your bindings and return them."

"Are you certain we won't be able to use them to escape?" Aldari asked.

"I'll explain our land to you when we reach it, but I'm positive you won't want to wander alone there."

"Are you also positive," Theli asked, "that if you give us our weapons, we won't crack you on the head when you're not looking?"

"I'm positive the princess won't." Hawk's voice turned dry. "I'm less certain about you."

"Good," Theli said.

He chuckled and stood, but he paused to touch Aldari's shoulder. She started to draw away but stopped when he spoke, his voice full of earnestness.

"I know you don't care about us or our people, Your Highness —you have no reason to—but we *do* need you. If the scientist I was working with is right, you may be able to help us do something we've been trying and failing to do for centuries."

He lowered his hand and disappeared into the darkness in the same direction that Setvik had gone.

"What do you think that means?" Theli whispered.

Aldari sighed. "That they're going to do their damnedest to keep us from escaping."

7

A BOOM FLOATED THROUGH THE MOUNTAINS, AND ALDARI YANKED her attention back to the trail ahead. All morning, she'd been peering back, hoping to catch a kingdom rescue party about to thunder in to save them. Unfortunately, the elves were maintaining a quick pace, and Hawk had seemed confident when he'd said they would reach the river before the man who'd escaped had time to report and form a rescue party.

During the night, Aldari had woken often—sleeping with her hands bound and on the lumpy ground hadn't been conducive to quality rest—and each time, Hawk had been nearby. Further, she'd spotted elves standing guard in the shadows. No opportunities for escape had presented themselves.

She kept mulling over ideas about how she could *create* opportunities, but thus far, nothing had been practical. All her mind wanted to do was guess how many miles they'd come and calculate how far they were from the river.

A second boom followed the first, and her horse's ears flicked. Its gait remained steady, but she doubted it liked the noise. *She* didn't.

"Was that a cannon?" Theli asked from her mount. Once again, she rode behind Aldari, an elf holding the reins to her horse.

Surprisingly, Hawk still led Aldari's horse himself. Despite his talk about privileges of command, this was one duty he hadn't delegated to anyone else. Some of the elves, including the medic who'd given them another packet of that awful pain medicine that morning, were taking turns riding, but Setvik and Hawk remained on foot.

"Explosives," Hawk said. "A mine has been carved out not far from this trail."

Setvik muttered something dark in his own tongue. For once, Hawk's response sounded like one of agreement. They both looked up a scree-covered slope in the direction of the booms and shook their heads.

"An imperial mine?" Aldari asked.

"Yes."

She looked back, meeting Theli's eyes. If there were imperial soldiers guarding the miners, soldiers who had heard that their people's attack on the caravan hadn't gone well, and if they spotted Aldari, they might try to capture her.

"We passed by it during the night when we came before," Hawk said. "It is an eyesore and probably the reason animals are leaving the area."

Aldari thought of the farm the vorgs had attacked—perhaps they hadn't been intentionally driven from the mountains but had simply been fleeing the noise. Of course, just because that may have been inadvertent didn't mean the Taldar Empire wasn't to blame.

A few minutes later, an angry roar emanated through the forest. The booms were off to the side and over a ridge they were walking below, but that roar came from the trail ahead. It prompted the elves to converse, several looking to Setvik.

Hawk issued an order, and the mercenaries fell silent. Aldari guessed it had been the equivalent of *keep going but be ready.*

The trail took them through a field of boulders and more scree, then twisted to follow a slope upward. Soon, their group walked along the top of the ridge. The elves remained alert, looking in both directions as their hands rested on their weapons. Several had taken their bows off their backs and rode or walked with arrows nocked.

"What is *that*?" Theli lifted her bound hands to point at a deep miles-long scar that had been dug—or blown—into the mountainside. A river ran near it, and mills had been set up to pulverize rock. Men, tiny from the group's vantage point on top of the ridge, labored at pulling out ore.

Thus far, none of them had noticed the elven party, but Aldari couldn't help but feel vulnerable out in the open. She hoped the trail descended out of their view soon.

"That is the mine," Hawk said. "The humans destroy the mountain to tear iron and precious metals from the rock."

When Delantria had controlled this part of the mountains, they had also mined, but her people hadn't done anything to such a large scale. They'd dug tunnels rather than blowing open massive pits.

"They must need the ore to make weapons," Aldari said quietly. "For the invasion they're preparing."

Hawk looked up at her.

"The Taldar Empire wants Delantria—what's left that they haven't already taken—so they can have a port on the Kaspire Sea. We need powerful allies to stave them off, and my wedding is our people's best hope. If we don't get help from Orath, our entire kingdom could fall in the next year." Aldari doubted Hawk would change his mission because of her plight, but she couldn't help but hope that he would realize that a great deal was at stake and that it was selfish of him to kidnap her.

"The Orath Kingdom will not assist you if there is not a wedding?" Hawk asked.

"No." Aldari didn't go into all the negotiating and bargaining her father had been attempting these past years, not only with Orath but with the Yi Kingdom and some of the larger island nations as well. Unfortunately, few people cared if Delantria retained its independence. To other nations, it did not matter who ruled the peninsula, and Father hadn't been willing to offer whale oil for free—the one thing the kingdom had that others wanted. Her people could ill afford to give away their one major export. They could only afford to give away daughters.

"They do not sound like good allies," Hawk said.

"They would become so once the two royal families were bound by matrimony."

"You think so?" Hawk sounded skeptical. "If they would not help your people without that contingency, are you so certain they will help once they have you?"

"Yes," Aldari said firmly, though it had crossed her mind before to notice how little help they'd offered in the time between the betrothal and the wedding. Even so, she didn't appreciate this foreigner who knew nothing of their people insinuating that there was something wrong with the arrangement. "We have few options. It's not as if *your* people have ever crossed the Forever Fog River and offered to help."

"*Your* people did not help *us* when we asked for assistance," Setvik said, though he didn't look back, merely kept eyeing his surroundings with his bow half drawn. "Why would we come to your aid now?"

"When did you come to our kingdom and ask for help?" Aldari would have remembered elven visitors.

"Many times centuries ago," Hawk said as they descended from the ridge, entering the forest once more.

Another boom rang out from the mine. Another roar came from ahead—closer now.

"*Centuries* ago?" Aldari kept her voice to a whisper, not wanting to draw the attention of whatever was ahead of them. It sounded irked.

"Yes."

Was Hawk truly judging her kingdom for things that had happened generations before her father and everyone else had been born? Not that her people had the resources to help the elves with their problems today, even if they'd asked more recently. Perhaps it had been the same in the past.

"None of the human kingdoms were willing to risk sending troops to our land to help us with our problem. Eventually, we stopped asking. That is why we are now forced to take." Hawk spread his hand toward her.

"Well, it's not right for you to do so. Not when—"

A roar rang out, this time from the trees only a few dozen yards away. The elves spun in that direction, several raising bows and firing into the woods.

Aldari glimpsed brown furry creatures on two legs. They had bear-like heads, lupine snouts, and antlers. Vorgs. At least four of them.

The creatures used the trees for cover, and most of the arrows pierced trunks instead of fur and flesh. More roars came from the trail ahead.

Aldari's horse shifted, nickering nervously, its eyes wide as it looked toward the vorgs. Though Hawk drew his sword, he didn't release the reins. As his mercenaries fired, he cooed at the horse and tried to keep it calm.

Behind Aldari, Theli's mount reared up. She cursed and grabbed at the saddle horn as the elf with the reins struggled to keep it under control.

Setvik stood ahead of the group, firing calmly into the woods, and he caught one of the vorgs as it ran from one tree to another. The arrow lodged in the side of its neck, and it screeched in pain, but it still managed to lunge behind cover.

The big creatures were hard to kill. And more of them were coming, gathering forces in the woods before making an attack.

"I want to take the fight to them," Setvik told Hawk. "Before they gather more."

"Some of our men must stay with the princess," Hawk said.

"*You* stay."

"Leave two others."

A grunt came from the other side of the trail, and a huge boulder flew toward the bowmen. They scattered before it struck down, gouging the earth and flinging up dirt. It had to weigh hundreds of pounds. Had one of the creatures hurled it?

Two elves turned and fired in that direction as more vorgs appeared on the trail ahead. They were surrounding the group. Aldari glanced behind them. As of yet, the trail was clear in that direction.

As several bowmen drew swords and ran into the woods toward the vorgs, it occurred to her that this might be the opportunity to escape that she'd wanted. The Taldarian miners had been busy and might not notice fleeing captives. If she and Theli could keep their horses—and keep them under *control*—they might be able to outrun the elves, especially if more of Hawk's men were injured.

"Duck!" Hawk sprang into the air.

Aldari flattened herself to her horse's neck as he swept his blade up, connecting with a long stick hurtling through the air toward her. A *spear*.

She gaped as his blade sliced through it, both ends clattering to the ground. The spear had been flying straight at her head and would have killed her. She hadn't even realized the animalistic vorgs were capable of using tools—of crafting weapons.

Grunts and screeches of pain sounded as the elves reached and engaged with their furred enemies. The mercenaries were as fast and agile as they'd been in other battles, but there were so many vorgs that Aldari wondered if it would be enough.

Her horse reared up, as frightened by the battle as Theli's mount. With her heart pounding in her chest, Aldari tried to wrap her arms around its neck to help her stay mounted, but with her wrists bound, all she could do was grip the saddle horn and lean forward. She squeezed her legs tight to keep from falling off.

Hawk tugged on the reins to convince the horse to drop to all fours again, crooning at it as he watched the forest to either side for more spears.

"Let us go." Aldari lifted her bound hands. "Please. I can't defend myself or even hold on properly."

She wanted to slide off, but even that was problematic with her wrists tied. The trail was narrow, boulders and trees to either side.

Hawk looked up at her. "Will you promise not to try to escape?"

"*Yes,*" Theli called with exasperation.

"No." Aldari still couldn't bring herself to lie. "But if you give us weapons and our hands, maybe we can help—or at least be less of a burden."

Movement caught her eye—another spear sailing toward them. This time, it flew past overhead, too far above to threaten her, but she couldn't help but give it a pointed look.

Hawk hesitated, looked in all directions again, then drew a knife and cut her bonds. "Very well. May the Hunter guide you."

Aldari didn't know what that meant, but she nodded as Hawk untied Theli's mace and her dagger from his pack. After handing her the blade, he gave her the reins to her horse.

"Thanks." Aldari gripped the weapon, though she couldn't imagine getting in a knife fight with one of the powerful vorgs.

The elf restraining Theli's horse questioned Hawk when he

ran back to cut Theli's bonds and hand her the mace, but a boulder flew toward Aldari, and Hawk didn't answer. He sprinted back toward her horse to pull it out of the way, but Aldari nudged it with her heels, and it lunged forward on its own.

The boulder tumbled through the air behind her and cracked against a tree. Two vorgs followed it, running toward Aldari and Theli with their claws raised, their furred appendages similar to human arms and hands.

Hawk charged out to meet the hulking creatures. The elf with Theli took a step, as if to run to help, but he seemed to realize that would leave Aldari and Theli unguarded.

"Go help him!" Theli barked to him. "Your boss will get pulverized by himself."

The elf started to shake his head, either because he'd been ordered not to leave them or he was certain Hawk could handle two vorgs, but two more great furry creatures ran out of the trees to join the first pair. They roared and raised spears, pointing them at Hawk.

The other elf cursed, gave an order in his language—*stay here*, no doubt—and ran to help his captain.

"Now's our chance," Theli whispered, the words barely audible over the roars of the vorgs and the shouts of the elves.

She was right. With fighting on both sides, and even more vorgs up ahead, their captors were as distracted as they would ever be.

Still, as Aldari lifted the reins, intending to tug her horse around and back the way they'd come, Setvik scowled over at her. Hawk, even though he'd sprung into battle with the first two vorgs, also glanced back. As busy as they were, they hadn't forgotten about their prisoners.

Aldari nodded at Theli but raised a finger. If they waited another couple of moments, the elves might stop checking on them so frequently. Hawk might believe Theli had spoken truthfully and didn't plan to flee.

Watching them fight, Aldari willed Hawk and Setvik to be so absorbed that they couldn't pay attention to their captives. The vorgs were over eight feet tall and tremendously powerful. *Aldari* wouldn't have glanced away from them.

One shoved aside a tree, tearing its roots from the ground, then hefted the trunk and threw it at the elves. But Hawk and the other mercenary only jumped aside, easily avoiding the unwieldy projectile. Immediately, they sprang back in, blades cutting into furred flesh. As they fought, leaping and dodging blows that would have crushed elven bones if they'd landed, Hawk glanced back often. Checking on Aldari and Theli.

Though that exasperated Aldari, she couldn't help but admire Hawk's skill as he fought. The elves were *all* incredibly gifted, leaping and twisting in the air to avoid blows, performing feats of athleticism that humans couldn't have managed. She admired it, but it scared her as well, especially when the realization hammered into her that if a rescue party *did* catch up to them, it would be outmatched. Unless she got lucky, and the vorgs, through sheer numbers, injured and killed most of the elves.

She couldn't bring herself to wish Hawk would die, even if he'd orchestrated all of this, but she wouldn't shed any tears if his lieutenant was killed.

"*Aldari,*" Theli barked and pointed at the trail ahead.

Aldari wrenched her gaze from the fight, cursing herself for being mesmerized by the elves' skills—by their *captors'* skills. Four of the vorgs that had been milling on the trail had committed to the battle. They roared and charged toward Aldari and Theli.

"Go," Aldari whispered, glancing at Hawk. For the moment, he was distracted by his battle; he wasn't checking on them. "Now!"

She worried their mounts would rear up again and fight their guidance, but the horses' desires were perfectly in line with theirs. At the first nudge, they wheeled around.

They charged back along the trail toward the ridge, in the only direction there weren't any vorgs. And they ran at top speed. If not for Theli's horse ahead of it, Aldari's might have sprinted even faster.

She bent low, hanging on for her life as her horse raced along the rocky trail far faster than she would have asked it to. But maybe it was for the best. As wind blew against her face, the sounds of battle receding, Aldari believed they might get away.

As the horses raced toward the ridge, she thought about the miners and wondered if there was any possibility that she and Theli could hide among those men. But they were enemies as surely as the elves were—perhaps they were even *greater* enemies. Whatever the elves needed Aldari for, they wanted her alive. The empire was another story.

Ahead of them, a vorg sprang up from behind a boulder and landed on the trail. It roared and waved a spear.

Both horses halted too quickly for their riders to compensate. Aldari shifted and tried frantically to hang on, but her mount reared up, and she tumbled free. All she could think about was trying not to break every bone as she landed—and keeping a grip on her dagger.

Her shoulder struck first, pain blasting her as she rolled down the slope. A cry came from Theli as she also landed hard. She came down closer to the vorg than Aldari, and it focused on her as the horses sprinted off the trail and down the slope.

Rocks shifted and scree clattered as the big vorg ran toward Theli. Aldari scrambled to her feet, but the air had been knocked out of Theli, and she appeared stunned. As the vorg thundered toward her, it hefted its spear to throw.

"Get up!" Aldari yelled and hurled her dagger, praying it would strike its target.

The blade glanced off the vorg's arm, barely gouging it. Fortunately, it was enough to distract the creature from throwing its spear. In that second, Theli recovered enough to roll out of the way. She'd managed to keep hold of her weapon. Mace raised, Theli yelled and ran toward the vorg.

Weaponless now that she'd thrown her dagger, Aldari grabbed two rocks.

The vorg saw Theli coming and swung its spear at her head. As powerful as the creatures were, they weren't that fast, and she successfully ducked under the attack. She lunged in and hammered her mace into the vorg's groin.

It roared and dropped its spear so it could try to grab her. As Theli darted away, Aldari threw one of her rocks. This time, her aim was off, and the projectile flew past its head. Though Theli was fast, a meaty fist clipped her and sent her stumbling.

Aldari threw her second rock. It struck the vorg in the back of the head, but the creature barely noticed. She needed a more deadly weapon.

She circled the fight, trying to spot her dagger among the rocks. Theli ducked low under another swipe and came in once more. Her second attack angled toward the vorg's knee and cracked as loudly as if she'd smacked the metal weapon into a boulder. The creature howled, but the pain didn't keep it from lunging at Theli.

Though she tried to dart out of range, its legs and arms were so long that it caught her. It hefted her from the ground and shook her.

Theli yelled as she kicked, connecting with its jaw. She also smashed her mace into its wrist, but whatever pain the vorg felt, it didn't deter it. Only the knee strike had truly hurt it.

Metal glinted among the rocks. Aldari's dagger.

She ran and snatched it up, then whirled, looking for a vulnerable spot. As the vorg shook Theli, looking like it might hurl her in the same way its allies had hurled boulders, Aldari ran in behind it. She had no idea where its vital organs were, but she lunged in and drove the dagger into its lower back with all her strength. The creature ought to feel *that*.

It roared and flung Theli to the rocks before spinning to face Aldari. Its spin tore the dagger from her grip, and she cursed, backing away as fast as she could. But she couldn't outrun it, and she didn't have another weapon.

As it lunged for her, something sped in from the side. An arrow.

It lodged in the vorg's eye, sinking in deep, green feathers quivering. Even that deadly blow didn't immediately fell the creature. It threw its head back and roared, raising both fists.

Horse hooves clattered on the scree-covered slope, and Aldari turned as Hawk bent low on the mount he'd acquired, his bow already replaced by his sword. Without slowing, he grabbed her arm and pulled her up.

"Theli!" Aldari shouted, afraid Hawk would race off and leave her bodyguard.

Hawk draped Aldari across his lap and kept riding. He'd passed the raging vorg but soon circled back, heels nudging the horse to pick up speed. The vorg, now blind in one eye, the arrow sticking out of its skull, recovered its spear and turned its attention to Theli.

She crouched, her mace ready, as the vorg threw the weapon. From her awkward position, Aldari couldn't see what happened, but having an eye knocked out must have affected the vorg's aim, for the spear didn't hit Theli. She ran into view, her mace raised.

But on horseback, Hawk reached their enemy first. He rose up in his saddle, one hand keeping Aldari from falling off, and swung a mighty blow with his sword. It sank into the vorg's neck, cutting through muscle and into flesh to strike an artery.

Unlike Aldari, *he* managed not to lodge his blade in too deep and lose it. He turned the horse to come in for another attack, but the vorg tottered and collapsed on the rocky slope, blood spewing from its neck.

Theli stepped forward and tugged Aldari's dagger out of its back. As Hawk slowed his horse, Aldari realized the sounds of battle in the forest behind them had fallen silent. She slumped and met Theli's grave eyes, afraid they'd lost their only chance to escape. And after the failed attempt, their captors would be more alert than ever.

8

AS THE PARTY DESCENDED FROM THE MOUNTAINS, THEY ENTERED A dense fog. Aldari eyed the trees to either side of the trail, noting how poor the visibility was growing, how close another pack of vorgs might creep before anyone noticed them.

At the moment, however, she felt safe. She was no longer draped across Hawk's lap—thankfully, as it had been humiliating when he'd ridden back to his mercenaries with her in that position—but sat in front of him on the horse. His arm was wrapped around her, ensuring she wouldn't go anywhere.

She should have found it overly familiar and annoying, but after the encounter with the vorgs, she admitted it was comforting. In the last two days, she'd almost been killed not once but twice. Both times, Hawk had saved her. Even though the rational part of her mind kept pointing out that she'd only been in trouble from vorgs because he and his people had kidnapped her, that didn't keep the scared and emotional part of her from being glad that he and his sword would be between her and any further threats.

Another of the elves rode behind them in a similar position with Theli. He'd been injured during the battle, so that was why he'd been given a mount, but his sword was out, and he appeared as ready as Hawk to protect his captive.

Judging by the glower on her face whenever Aldari glanced back, Theli didn't appreciate the protection as much as Aldari did. *She* had been faring better in that fight with the vorg. Aldari's strengths of writing papers and solving math problems weren't particularly useful in battle.

"We'll reach the river soon," Hawk said, his mouth not far from her ear.

Aldari had never shared a horse with a man and found herself very aware of him. The forced closeness made it hard to miss the hard muscles of his arms, the warmth of his skin through his clothing, and the way their bodies shifted against each other with the movement of the horse. She would not allow herself to feel attraction to her kidnapper, but she kept catching herself wanting to lean back into him, to enjoy the experience. What would she do, she wondered, if his grip were a little less professional, and his hand drifted higher?

Swat it away, she assured herself with a firm nod. And tell him she would rather walk than be manhandled by her kidnapper.

But there was nothing unprofessional about his grip. He was a polite and courteous kidnapper. Whose breath tickled her ear as it whispered across her skin, sending a weird little tingle through her.

"Do you have a boat waiting?" Aldari asked, forcing her mind to more practical matters. "Or do we have to swim?"

"Swimming the Forever Fog River would be unwise."

"Are there really monsters in it?" She'd heard numerous stories of deadly river serpents that sometimes attacked fishing boats, slipping in close in the deep mist that always covered the waterway, destroying the craft and devouring the crew. But there were also pirates that hid out in those waters, striking at trade ships that were leaving the ports on the western side of the peninsula, then slinking back into the fog to escape reprisal.

"It borders the eastern side of your peninsula, and you don't know?" Hawk asked.

"Our ships don't travel up it, and most of our cities are along the western coast."

Because of all the stories of the river, and because nobody wanted to live that close to the elven continent, the land supposedly infested with monsters reputed to suck the blood of the living and prey on old women and children. They had no mercy, no humanity. Even the magic that was said to permeate the continent was cruel, luring travelers into quicksand and sinkholes or to the maws of deadly predators.

Aldari turned her head to look at Hawk, wondering how much from the tales was true. Supposedly, even the elves who left their homeland rarely spoke of it.

His earlier words that his people had once sought help from humans had surprised her. The elves always came across as aloof, as believing themselves superior to humans. She wouldn't have envisioned them ever asking for help, but she'd had so few interactions with their kind that she didn't know what was true and what was myth. Hawk didn't seem aloof.

"There are large river serpents capable of destroying ships, yes. There are also magical currents and whirlpools that are equally dangerous for one who doesn't know the waters well." Hawk sighed. "The river is as cursed as our land."

Sadness lurked in his green eyes, and Aldari had the urge to say she was sorry, but she reminded herself that he was an enemy. He wasn't a friend that she should try to comfort.

"It wasn't always that way, I'm told," Hawk said, "but the fog has been there for centuries. Nobody who lives today remembers a time when it wasn't. Except perhaps some of the Twisted. Unless they're killed by blades, they live forever. If you can call what they do living. The curse keeps them from passing into the next realm and finding peace." He shook his head, the sadness turning to utter bleakness.

The urge to comfort him returned, to lift a hand and touch his cheek, as if that might take away his pain.

Aldari clenched her jaw and faced forward, irritated with herself for her feelings. She needed to focus on escaping, nothing more. Yes, the mountains were dangerous, but she had a duty to her kingdom. Besides, she and Theli wouldn't have to be out there alone for long. All they had to do was hide out until the inevitable search parties came looking for them.

"Do not try to escape while we are on the river," Hawk said softly, as if he could read her thoughts.

A shiver went through her as she wondered if maybe he could. The stories said the elves had lost their magic, but long ago they'd had tremendous power, fielding wizards who could singlehand-edly turn the tide of a battle. Was it possible the ancestors of those old magic users still had a few inklings of power?

"I did not tell you those things to scare you," Hawk continued when she didn't reply. "The river is genuinely dangerous. If you tried to swim, you could be killed. The serpents can survive on fish, but they are known to crave the flesh of animals—and humans and elves. Even though they can't walk on land, they have long necks, and I've seen someone kneeling on the shore, filling a canteen, be plucked up and stolen out into the water, pulled under and killed, before I could reach him to help. In the end, only his canteen floating on the surface remained."

The story sent more chills through her, but she refused to show her fear or fully trust that he was telling the truth. "So, I should escape *before* we reach the river."

Hawk snorted softly. "Probably. But have you no fear of the vorgs? I believe the mining has riled them up and made them more aggressive than usual. Many times in the past, Setvik has passed through these mountains, and he said he's never seen so many band together to attack before."

"I'm not unafraid of them—" Aldari wouldn't be brave but foolish to claim otherwise, "—but I have a duty, Captain. As I already informed you."

"You will risk your life to marry this prince who would not help your people until he got his prize?"

Aldari gritted her teeth, annoyed to be called a *prize*, even if she couldn't deny it was true. "I will risk my life to secure an alliance that my people desperately need, yes."

Hawk didn't respond right away. She wished she could make him see that what he was doing was wrong and endangered her entire kingdom.

"Do not risk your life," he finally said. "As I told you, I will protect you, and once our mission is done, I'll return you to your people. If we're successful..." His tone grew achingly full of longing, and his arm tightened around her, as if he feared he would lose her and thus lose everything. "If we're successful, I'll escort you to your prince's castle myself, and woe to any animal, human, or elf who attempts to stand in our way."

The words were spoken so earnestly and with such force that she couldn't keep from looking at him again.

"I promise," he said with equal fervor, his eyes full of determination.

Her belly shivered with an unfamiliar feeling of nervousness —or maybe anticipation?—as she met his gaze. The urges she'd been pushing aside returned, not only prompting her to comfort him but to help him with his problem. Especially if humans had refused to help his kind before. Was that true? She had no way to know, but she found herself wanting to believe his words. She'd seen him fight twice now, risking his life to keep her safe, and he'd refused to let his mercenaries go after the soldier who'd gotten away, to kill someone who didn't deserve that fate. He'd kidnapped her, but he didn't *seem* like a loathsome bandit, some thug who wanted only to ransom her and get paid. He seemed a noble man —elf—driven by desperation.

"What do you need that you think I can help you with?" she asked for the third time.

The first two times, he hadn't told her, but he opened his mouth, and she thought he might tell her now.

Until his lieutenant jogged up, distracting him.

Setvik squinted at them, at the closeness of their faces, at Hawk's arm wrapped tightly around her. "You think bedding her will convince her to help us?"

"What?" Hawk's eyebrows flew up, and he jerked his arm away from Aldari. "Of course not."

"Good. Because we have enough trouble without *distractions*. And she is—" Setvik curled his lip at Aldari, "—*human*."

"Clearly an inferior species," Hawk said dryly.

"*Yes*. You do not need—" Setvik switched to their language for the rest, which didn't keep it from sounding derogatory.

With Setvik walking so close to their horse, Aldari could have kicked him. Or at least tried. From what she'd seen, Setvik was as capable a fighter as Hawk and would likely have dodged the blow.

Hawk sighed and flicked his fingers. "Run ahead, Setvik, and have the boatmen prepare to launch. The sooner we can return home and finish our task, the better."

Setvik glared at Aldari before turning and trotting off down the trail. He said something to the elf in the lead as he passed, probably instructions to admonish Hawk if he started smooching with a human. Not that *smooching* had been about to happen. Other than the fact that they were sharing a horse—against her wishes—Aldari couldn't imagine what Setvik had seen to believe that a possibility.

"As you've doubtless determined," Hawk said, resting his hand on his thigh instead of wrapping his arm around her again, "Setvik is the diplomatic one in our group, here to ensure that you develop a fondness for elves and are eager to assist us."

Aldari wondered if she should mention her fantasy of kicking him. "What *is* his role in your company? He seems to dislike you and gives you a lot of lip. Don't commanders frown upon such behavior from their subordinates?"

"He's an excellent warrior and an experienced veteran."

"Who gives you a lot of lip."

"Yes. Shall I have him flogged? Is that how it's done in human armies?"

"I've not endured military life, so I'm not sure. I think a human commander would give him extra duties, like scrubbing floors and peeling potatoes."

"Interesting. I would be vastly amused by watching Setvik scrub floors. There aren't an abundance of floors in the forest, however." Hawk peered through the trees to either side of the trail. "Perhaps he could sweep with a pine bough and round up all those untidy cones littering the ground."

Aldari caught herself smiling before remembering that she shouldn't. She had a feeling *Hawk* was the diplomat in the company. Maybe that was why he was in charge. Though she couldn't imagine that rulers who hired mercenaries cared if their fighters were charismatic or not.

She was about to steer the conversation back to the question she'd asked before—why did the elves need her?—when the trail disappeared, ending at a field of rocks, and the thuds of horse hooves turned to clacks. No, not a *field of rocks*. A riverbank of stones.

Butterflies flew erratically through Aldari's stomach. They'd arrived at the Forever Fog River.

9

THE FERRY CREAKED AS IT FLOATED SLOWLY ACROSS THE RIVER, rocking left and right with the currents. So much armor covered the hull that it sat low in the water, and harpoon launchers were mounted along the railing in between upturned dinghies—lifeboats. Aldari had almost run into one of them when they'd boarded. The fog was so dense that they couldn't see more than ten feet ahead—or across to the opposite side of the ferry.

Aldari stood at the railing with Theli, Hawk's elves speaking quietly with the four elven boatmen who had been waiting for them at the shore. They'd left the horses behind to be found by the rescue parties, people who would arrive too late to help.

As they'd left, Aldari had cast longing looks back at the forest, hoping vainly that her father's soldiers would charge out of the trees to get them, but no one had come. She and Theli had been ushered into dinghies and rowed out to the ferry, a paddleboat that hissed periodically, a steam-engine powering the big wheel in the back.

Whether the craft belonged to the elves or they'd stolen it, Aldari didn't know. A malaise settled over her as they traveled farther and farther from shore, the fog perhaps swallowing them for all of eternity, and she didn't bother asking.

Theli seemed equally affected by the gloom. The ballad she'd chosen to hum was in a haunting minor key that made Aldari think of funerals and graveyards.

When no elves were nearby, Theli paused to whisper, "You're still thinking about ways to escape, right?"

Aldari looked over her shoulder. Hawk was watching them, but he was also speaking with and receiving what sounded like a report from one of the boatmen, so she and Theli might have a private moment. But not very private. As soon as they'd boarded, Setvik had started a patrol with one of the other elves. With their hands on their weapons, they circled the deck. Ostensibly, they were watching the water for threats, but Setvik gave Aldari and Theli long assessing looks each time he passed.

"I'm thinking about them," Aldari whispered, "but if half of what we've heard about this river is true—and Hawk said it *is* full of serpents—we dare not jump overboard and swim for shore. I'm not even sure where shore *is* at this point." Aldari had no idea how the boat captain was navigating in the fog. By the current, she supposed, but she didn't think even that was reliable. People said the river rose up from a spring at the center point, with half of the water flowing northwest, toward the Kaspire Sea and half to the southeast, toward the Tanjiri Gulf.

"*Hawk* said?" Theli raised her eyebrows. "You're taking his words for truth?"

"Not necessarily, but our people believe the same thing. It's not like he gave me contradictory information."

"Is that what you were talking about when you were gazing raptly at him on your shared horse?"

Aldari stifled a groan. Had *everyone* seen them looking at each other and thought some weird romance was going on? *Why?* The only reason their faces had been close together was because they'd been riding on the same mount.

"I wasn't gazing raptly at him or anything else. I was listening to him talk."

"While he cuddled you in his arms?"

"I believe that was called restraining me so I wouldn't escape. Your elf was doing the same thing to you."

"And groping and rubbing against me whenever the bastard got the opportunity," Theli growled.

Aldari scowled. "Are you serious?"

As soon as the words came out, she regretted questioning her bodyguard. Theli had a sarcastic streak and could exaggerate at times, but Aldari doubted she would about something like that.

"Of course I'm serious," Theli said. "He was excited to have a woman in his arms. They probably don't come to him voluntarily."

"I'll tell Hawk." Aldari pushed away from the railing.

Theli grabbed her arm. "It's not important. Besides, what do you think *he's* going to do?"

"He's in charge of them. He can punish his soldier or at least make sure it doesn't happen again."

If Hawk wanted their help, he would. Aldari extracted her arm from Theli's grip, set her jaw with determination, and strode toward the elves.

"I don't know if you noticed, but he *kidnapped* us, Your Highness," Theli whispered, following her. "Anyone who does that is a *villain*. Don't you read any fiction in between all those economics books? Villains are vile and evil and *villainous*."

"Yes, I could have guessed that even without picking up a murder mystery."

"Are you sure? The way you chat with our kidnapper suggests your grasp on the subject of villains is weak."

When Hawk and the others looked at them, Theli fell silent, though her glower remained firmly in place.

"The mercenary who was riding with Theli—with my body-guard—touched her inappropriately," Aldari said.

Theli groaned, possibly due to mortification, possibly due to Aldari's word choice.

Hawk's brow creased—with confusion? Thus far, he'd understood everything she'd said. She found it hard to believe he didn't grasp her meaning now, but his expression was questioning when he looked at Theli. She hoped it wasn't because he felt his troops could do whatever they wanted with their prisoners. That would be hard to believe. He'd told his lieutenant not to be crude in front of them.

"He grabbed my boob," Theli explained. "Twice."

Maybe the plainer words were best, for the puzzlement vanished from Hawk's face. "I understand." He peered into the fog —anyone on the other side of the ferry wasn't visible or was an indistinct blur at best. "*Vun* Pheleran," he called, then switched to his tongue for the rest.

The young elf who'd been guarding Theli jogged over. With short tousled blond hair and buck teeth, he looked like he was about eighteen, but he didn't appear innocent. Maybe it was the black leather armor and weapons, but none of the mercenaries had that mien about them.

As soon as Hawk began speaking sternly at him, the elf—Pheleran—lifted his hands in what looked like feigned innocence. Hawk asked a clipped question. Pheleran started to shake his head, but Hawk narrowed his eyes, and Pheleran hesitated. Finally, he pointed at Theli and offered some kind of protest. Maybe he felt prisoners didn't have to be respected.

Hawk said something slowly and steadily, his enunciation precise. Pheleran wilted under his gaze and bowed his head, muttering what had to be the equivalent of, "Yes, Captain." Hawk raised his voice and repeated the words for the rest of his troops— and perhaps the boatmen too.

Hawk considered Aldari for a moment, and she thought he would ask a question, but he waved over one of the boatmen and asked him something. The elf's brows rose, and he nodded, then led Pheleran into the structure at the back of the ferry that housed the steam engine.

"I apologize to you for my soldier's behavior," Hawk told Theli. "It is my fault that they didn't understand clearly that you are *guests*, not prisoners, but the behavior was unacceptable, regardless."

Setvik, who'd been doing his circuit during the talk, approached now, a frown on his face.

"Can we truly be considered guests when we were kidnapped?" Theli muttered to Aldari.

"If it prompts them to treat us better, I'll take that label," Aldari said.

The boatman and Pheleran reappeared, the latter carrying a bucket and mop. He glanced at Hawk, who nodded at him, and started washing the deck.

It took Aldari a moment to remember their conversation about punishing men by forcing them to clean, and she smiled faintly. The soldier might have deserved a harsher punishment—he would have received such if he'd been a soldier in her father's army—but she was relieved Hawk had believed Theli and hadn't brushed off the accusation. She had little doubt that Setvik would have.

The lieutenant watched Pheleran mopping for a moment, and his scowl darkened. He glanced at Aldari and Theli and asked Hawk a question. Hawk's answer was short and delivered calmly, but Setvik's scowl went from dark to pitch black.

"You are punishing my troops because of *them*?" Setvik pointed at Theli. "We have risked our lives to protect them."

"I corrected *our* troops' poor behavior. *Vun* Pheleran will not suffer from that punishment."

"Are you sure he's guilty?"

"He denied it at first, then admitted it. He thought it was acceptable behavior because she's a *human*." Hawk's calm was evaporating as he returned his lieutenant's glower.

Aldari didn't know why they'd switched to her language, but their anger wasn't any more comforting because she could understand it. She didn't regret speaking up on Theli's behalf, but she hadn't wanted to stoke the fire that always simmered between these two.

"I don't know why he would want to touch a *human* female," Setvik said, "but you surely can't consider it a crime."

"If he'd touched an elven princess, the price would have been his life," Hawk said coolly.

"That is *not* an elven princess, and she's not even the one he touched. He groped the maid."

"*Bodyguard*," Theli said, but they ignored her.

"She should be honored that he was interested enough to do so." Setvik curled a lip as he glanced dismissively at her. "I can't imagine it."

"She's *not* honored," Hawk said.

"Why do you care? They are not allies to our people. They care *nothing* for our people. As they've proven many, many times." Setvik shifted his gaze toward Aldari, as if she'd committed a crime or attacked him personally. "There is a reason we had to kidnap them. And we don't even know if there was any point or if she's the right one."

"She's the right one," Hawk said firmly.

"How can you be sure?"

"The king's... advisor did her research." Hawk looked at Aldari. "What is the square root of 5,041?"

"Seventy-one." Aldari shrugged, knowing that one without having to do any calculations.

"What does *that* prove?" Setvik asked.

"That she's smarter than you." Hawk smiled tightly.

Setvik spat on the deck and strode off.

Aldari only gazed at Hawk with puzzlement. What math-related problem could the elves have that they couldn't solve and thought she could?

"*Vun* Pheleran," Hawk called, crooking a finger.

The young soldier hurried over with his mop. Hawk pointed at the spittle and said something in Elven.

The soldier bobbed his head and mopped the area assiduously. Hawk patted him on the shoulder.

With his focus on the soldier, Hawk didn't notice that Setvik had stopped and was watching—seething—as his mercenary was forced to do menial labor. Aldari, afraid for Hawk, almost directed his attention to his lieutenant, but Setvik spun and stalked off into the fog.

She rubbed her face. She hadn't intended to start a fight or foster more animosity between them, not when her and Theli's continued existence might rely on Hawk. The other elves weren't as belligerent toward them as Setvik was, but she'd seen the way the mercenaries leaped to obey his orders. If Hawk wasn't around and Setvik ordered them to kill Aldari and Theli, she believed they would do it. Of course, Setvik was a highly capable warrior and could do it himself. He might enjoy it.

Aldari shivered from more than the chilly fog.

"May I speak with you?" Hawk asked her quietly.

"Yes." Aldari was glad for the excuse to move away from the rest of his mercenaries.

She and Theli trailed him to the railing. A fish—or something larger—jumped out in the water, but the fog hid the details as it splashed back in. The fog hid everything. It had been noon and sunny when they'd approached the river, but out here, it was perpetual twilight.

"May I speak with you *privately*?" Hawk glanced at Theli.

Theli scowled. "I'm not a maid or a nanny, but that doesn't mean I won't stick close to Princess Aldari and protect her virtue."

"Her what?" Hawk asked, and Aldari realized her culture's terms for skirting blunt language related to sex were what he wasn't familiar with.

"Nothing," Aldari said before Theli could elaborate—what did she think would happen out in the open on a ferry? Or at all? Aldari knew her duty and wasn't the type to fling herself at men, even if a future husband *hadn't* been waiting for her. "But you can trust my bodyguard, Captain. There's no need to shoo her away."

"She knows all of your secrets?" Hawk raised his eyebrows.

Aldari started to nod, but she caught herself as a realization slammed into her. He might not only know that she had a penchant for mathematics; he might know her pen name. Her pen name that nobody except her tutor had discovered.

How could elves from a kingdom that never interacted with hers have found out? And why would they *care*? They were embroiled in a perpetual war and few of their people ever left their continent. She failed to see how economics could solve their problems any more than math could.

"Will you give us a moment, Theli?" Aldari asked.

Theli rocked back. "You keep secrets from me?"

"Isn't that allowed? I'm sure you don't tell me everything going on in your life."

"Yeah, but you share *everything* with me. Even your dreadful reading tastes. Actually, *mostly* your dreadful reading tastes." Theli scratched her jaw. "I guess that's usually what you blather on about, not what you write in your diary."

"Princesses don't blather. They speak eloquently on subjects that are important to them."

"Last month, while we were supposed to be enjoying a concert, you lectured me on harmony analysis for an *hour*."

"*Harmonic* analysis, and I'm not sure if that was a rebuttal or you were making my point."

Theli squinted at her. "Oh, you're sure."

Hawk cleared his throat. "Pardon my rudeness, but I'd prefer to have this discussion before we land." Dry amusement lurked in his tone, so he probably wasn't that impatient.

"Fine, fine." Theli lifted her hands and backed away.

The eerie fog swallowed her before she'd gone more than ten feet.

Aldari joined Hawk at the railing, the water directly below barely visible. Long seconds passed as he gazed out into the fog. He seemed to be gathering his thoughts—or debating how much he could tell her? Earlier, when he'd started to answer her question about what the elves wanted with her, his lieutenant had stopped him.

What secrets was he about to divulge? An uneasy feeling came over her, a sense that whatever he said, it might change her mind about her kidnappers and make her want to help them. But she couldn't. Not when her people's future depended on her getting to her wedding in time.

10

A DISTANT BELL CLANGED, THE SOUND MUTED BY THE FOG. WAS IT guiding the ferry to the far shore? Or did it represent another ship out on the shrouded river?

"We're nearing the halfway point," Hawk said. "There's a magical bell that clangs eternally, a beacon to guide the rare boats that risk these waters."

"Ah." A sound between a roar and a shriek came from their left. It was off in the distance, but that didn't keep the hair on Aldari's arms from rising. "And that?"

"A serpent."

"It sounds cranky."

"Hungry."

"I hope humans and elves give it heartburn, and it's irritated because something more delicious isn't paddling across the river."

"Judging by past actions, their kind find elves sumptuous. I don't know how they feel about humans."

"You know, some men lie to women about dangers, wanting them to feel safe through obliviousness."

"Would you prefer I lie to you?" Hawk asked.

"I guess not. Though you haven't been terribly forthright with me thus far."

"I know." Hawk propped one elbow on the railing and faced her. "You're not what I expected from a princess."

"You're not what I expected from a kidnapper. Your surly lieutenant is. He oozes villainy."

"I'll be sure to let him know."

"Maybe you shouldn't antagonize him. Every time he looks at you, his eyes say he wants to plunge a dagger between your shoulder blades."

"He won't attack me, but if he did, it would be from the front, and he would meet my eyes as he plunged the dagger into my heart."

"You're a gloomy people, aren't you?"

"Our world has made us so." Hawk tilted his head as he seemed to search her face for something. "I'm not sure why I expected you to be haughty and without a sense of humor. Princess Hysithea is—*was* friendly and witty. We all mourned when she was taken last year."

"Taken? By some illness?" Aldari thought of her mother, gone these past ten years. "Or in childbirth?"

"By the Twisted. She thought it was worth the risk to unleash her magic to heal the scarred land around the outpost—our last remaining city and refuge. They sensed it and came for her and took her. We weren't strong enough to stop them." Hawk touched the long scars on the side of his neck.

"And she's dead now?" Briefly, Aldari worried the elves had kidnapped her out of some notion of her replacing the princess they'd lost, but that was silly. The elves seemed to consider humans an inferior species, and Hawk was more interested in her math skills than her royal blood.

"I don't know." Hawk gazed sadly out at the water again, the ringing of the bell growing louder. "Sometimes, the Twisted kill people, but sometimes, they take them, especially those with strong magic. When they do that, they make them their own, turning them into crazed enemies that attack their own kind. *Us.* We're forced to kill them to protect our people. We know we're attacking those who were once our kin, but we have no choice. If we didn't fight, they would destroy us all, and nothing would remain of our people, our heritage, our... hesitant hope for a better future."

"How do they turn people? You spoke of magic? I thought... Our stories say that elves no longer have magic, but you say your princess did?"

"We're all born with it and are inherently magical, with varying degrees of power. But we must sublimate it, for magic draws the Twisted in droves. Even though we fight them and occasionally strike them down, once they're turned, they're immortal. There are Twisted in our forests who were elves when the twins lived, when Zalazar originally cursed our land eight hundred years ago." Hawk pushed up his sleeve to reveal a leather bracer with a dark gray metal oval embedded in the top. The bracer covered half of his forearm.

Aldari had glimpsed it before and assumed it was protection from his bowstring, especially since he wore it on only one arm. The other mercenaries had similar pieces.

"This sublimates the magical power within me." Hawk touched the metal oval. "All of our people wear jewelry with a *ryshar.* It is the only way to ensure the Twisted can't bind our magic to theirs, lure us out of the protection of our cities, and make us their own."

"I'm sorry. It sounds awful. Why did that elf—Zalazar, you said?—curse your people? And how could one person have done so much damage? Or was he a god?" Aldari was aware that the elves had multiple gods, but she didn't know how many or if they believed such beings had once walked among them.

"The twins were not gods, though Zalazar might have believed he was." Hawk snorted and pushed his sleeve back over the bracer. "As I said, elves are inherently magical and born with power that they once learned how to use in school, just as they learned writing and arithmetic. But every generation or two, someone is born with *immense* power, far beyond the norm. It often corrupts such souls or leads them to believe they are so great that they should take the place of our kings and queens and have power over all. That is what happened with the twins.

"Zedaron wasn't that bad. He was so absorbed with his academic pursuits and building inventions that it wouldn't have occurred to him to use his power to subjugate others, but Zalazar wanted to replace their king, and he wanted all to worship him. He especially wanted the king's daughter Cedensra, whose singing voice was as beautiful as her face, and who drew the devotion of many, many young suitors. When the king let her choose another and marry him, Zalazar was furious. That's when he put the curse on our land, turning all of those around him into the Twisted and ensuring they wanted to go out and spread their magical disease. He said he would turn them back if the king gave him his daughter, but the king refused. He sent all of his best warriors and wizards to fight Zalazar. This only enraged Zalazar, and he turned them into more of the Twisted, and he sent them to march on and destroy our cities. Even worse, he used his power to cause a volcano in the canyon lands to erupt—that was the home of our capital back then, a beautiful crystal city built between the cliffs. It was the home of the king and held our great libraries and stores of culture and wisdom. Only through the sacrifice of many did the king and his children escape before the lava flows poured through the canyons and buried the city.

"Horrified by what had befallen their people and their city, Cedensra offered to leave her husband and give herself to Zalazar. The king didn't want her to do it, but she sneaked away. Unfortunately, she died on the way to give herself to Zalazar, killed by his own creations. When he found out, he was so distressed over her loss that he killed himself, leaving our land cursed these past eight centuries. All this time, we have been at war with the Twisted. Ironically, if we were able to let our power develop, and could spend time learning the ancient arts, someone of great magical ability might have been born in that time, someone capable of ending the curse, but the risk is too great. As Princess Hysithea demonstrated." Hawk paused and blinked a few times, taking a deep breath before continuing. "It takes a lifetime to learn how to use one's power, and the Twisted, when they sense magic, come right away."

"I'm sorry," Aldari said again, wishing she could offer something more useful. "Are the Twisted confined to your continent? Couldn't some of your people leave to study magic elsewhere and then return to help your homeland?"

Hawk gazed sadly at her. "They are not confined. Because humans do not have magic, the Twisted are not drawn to your lands, but if our people left without a *ryshar*—" he held up his bracer, "—some of the Twisted would be drawn by them and go after them. And even though it is magic that pulls them, they will kill everything in their path. They are awful. Zalazar made them so to terrify the king into giving him his daughter."

Aldari sagged against the railing, horrified by the story, by the thought of these Twisted coming into her kingdom and wantonly killing her people. Even though she didn't yet know what they looked like, she was already certain they were worse than the vorgs.

"It is our problem," Hawk said, "and our people long ago vowed to do our best to keep the taint in our lands, to not let it spill out and destroy the world, so none of our kind leave without a *ryshar*. A few have gone rogue in the past and tried, and our people were sent to hunt them down." He waved in the direction of his mercenaries. "It is allowed for elves who cannot stand the battle anymore to leave, but not with their powers."

That chilled her almost as much as the rest of the story, the idea of the elves hunting down their own kind for the greater good of the world. Aldari peered into Hawk's eyes, trying to tell if everything he was telling her was the truth. Her instincts told her it was, but how much could she trust someone who'd kidnapped her?

"What do you think *I* can do about any of this?" she asked.

"The other twin, Zedaron, who'd been busy with his studies and experiments and oblivious to Zalazar's atrocities, saw toward the end what was happening. He had a great mansion and laboratory in the capital, protected by all manner of magical booby traps, so he was insulated from the Twisted, but when the lava flows came and started destroying his own city, he finally realized the extent of the threat. Before Cedensra's death and Zalazar's suicide, Zedaron confronted his brother and tried to get him to stop, but as powerful as he was, he was an academic and a tinkerer and hadn't trained to use his magic in battle. Zalazar defeated him but did not kill him, saying that because their mother would have wished it, he spared his brother. Zedaron retreated to his laboratory to nurse his wounds and study. If he couldn't defeat his brother with raw power, he thought he could build something to fix what he'd done, to change back the Twisted and end the curse on our land.

"He sent a message to the king and said he was doing exactly that. Unfortunately, that was the last message the king received. Months passed, and it's believed that Zalazar found out what his twin was up to and killed him. All we know is that when Cedensra was killed and Zalazar passed, the Twisted remained, and Zedaron was never seen again. The king sent warriors to Zedaron's mansion to check on him, or at least find what he'd been making and had, they hoped, finished, but they found that the damage to the capital was too great and even Zedaron's laboratory was gone, as buried by the lava flows as everything else."

When Hawk paused, Aldari almost said again that she was sorry. And she was. Her people had problems, but they were beginning to sound simple in comparison to what the elves had endured over the centuries.

"As I said, the capital was made from crystal, the walls and towers shaped by magic," Hawk continued. "Many believed that parts of it were intact under the hardened lava, and over the centuries, numerous expeditions ventured to the area to hunt for the lost city, to try to excavate their way to Zedaron's mansion in the hope that he *had* succeeded in making a device that could change the Twisted back and end the curse. It was always danger-ous, for the number of the Twisted has always been great in that area, but a few months ago, a team succeeded in unearthing part of the old city." Hawk rubbed the side of his neck, fingers lingering on his scars. "They found what they believed was Zedaron's home, but you'll remember that I said it was protected by booby traps? It still is. Nothing so simple as tripwires. There are puzzles, puzzles based on mathematics, including a large one embedded into the cliff by what we think is the front door. We believe that if someone could solve that puzzle, that person would be granted entry."

"Oh," Aldari mouthed, as she finally understood why the elves wanted her. She *was* good at puzzles, with a knack for solving them more quickly than others. But how could the elves have found out? Her economic theories, all backed by mathematics, were out there under the pen name, so it was believable that an academic elf might have stumbled across them, but it wasn't as if she published books of puzzles she'd solved. That was just a hobby. "How did you know I have a knack for puzzles? And what makes you think I'd be better at solving a puzzle created by an elf than your own people?"

"A few months ago, the king's advisor came across the papers written by Professor Lyn Dorit," Hawk said. Her pen name. "In one of those papers, the author used an analogy that referenced an old elven puzzle that has long challenged our youth. It was created by Zedaron."

"Oh," Aldari repeated, numbness spreading through her as she remembered the complicated dodecahedron puzzle her grandfather had brought back from his travels and given her. It had been part of what had become his quest to stump her. The puzzle had taken her all summer to solve and then the better part of a year to come up with a series of rules and formulas to truly master it.

"She was surprised to see it referenced and even *more* surprised when the author spoke of a formula for solving it. Our people weren't *aware* that there was a formula. The king's advisor said it's a children's toy that's been around a long time, and people occasionally tinker with it enough to solve it, but nobody had thought to figure out the steps so that it might be solved quickly and easily. She believed that the author of that paper might be able to solve the puzzle that is currently denying our people access to Zedaron's laboratory."

"And you think the author is me."

"It took our advisor some time to ferret out that information, but yes." Hawk arched an eyebrow, a hint of humor touching his face for the first time since he'd started his tale. "She was vastly bemused that the author was so young. *I* pointed out that young people are not simpletons and occasionally have good ideas."

If only her father believed that. Oh, he didn't think her a simpleton, but he was convinced her radical ideas had no merit.

"How old are you?" She'd heard stories that elven magic somehow allowed them to live longer lives, but now she wondered if that referred to the curse and the Twisted. Or if it was only true of elves who were allowed to access their magic. She glanced at his bracer.

"Twenty-three," Hawk said.

When he smiled and joked, he looked it, but when he was

grave and somber, he seemed so much older. Because he carried an ancient pain with him, she supposed.

"I wasn't supposed to tell you any of this. I'm just the, uh, delivery boy." Hawk waved ruefully at her. "The king's advisor planned to explain things to you, but perhaps this is for the best. The king wouldn't have approved of this mission, of kidnapping a princess from another kingdom and possibly starting a war. Also…"

Aldari raised her eyebrows.

"As I said, you're not what I expected. What any of us expected. Maybe it's naive on my part, but I thought if I explained this to you, you might agree to come along and help voluntarily. I… like to consider myself honorable, and this kidnapping scheme has disturbed me from the beginning, but we feared it was the only way. As Setvik so diplomatically pointed out, in the past, our people have asked your kingdom—humans in *many* kingdoms near our borders—for help, and none of your kind has ever granted it. We came to believe that humans, at least humans in that era, resented our kind, because we had magic and power that they didn't. And maybe back then, we were haughty about it. I can't truly know what happened in the past." The haunted expression returned to his eyes. "There are some of our people who feel that we deserved what we got. Regardless, we felt that kidnapping was the only sure way. But I ask you now if you'll come voluntarily."

"I…" Aldari groped for a response. If her wedding hadn't been on the horizon, and if her people hadn't needed the Orath alliance, she might have said yes. Even though the journey and the chance of surviving it sounded terrifying. But now? "My people need me to marry Prince Xerik," she said quietly.

"I see."

"It's my duty to try to escape and return in time for the wedding."

Hawk's face had grown closed, and disappointment darkened his eyes, but he said, "I understand." He opened his mouth, as if he might say more, but he frowned and looked out at the river instead. "Someone else is out here."

Aldari listened but heard only the faint lapping of water against the hull and the clanging of the bell, softer now as they'd moved past it.

"The serpent?" she asked.

"No. Voices. Another boat." Hawk held a finger to his lips. "Find your bodyguard, go inside, and stay with her. I'll alert the others."

"You think they're enemies?" Aldari whispered as he started away.

Hawk paused and looked back. "There are few valid reasons for risking the Forever Fog River."

With her kidnapping on her mind, Aldari could only agree.

—————

11

"BOAT HO!" SOMEONE CALLED FROM THE FOG.

The words hadn't come from the ferry, and they were in the language of the Seven Kingdoms, not Elven, but it wasn't the Delantrian dialect. Aldari immediately thought of pirates. Who else, besides kidnapping elves on a mission, would be lurking in the fog on this cursed waterway?

"This could be an opportunity to escape," Theli said.

Aldari and Theli stood inside an open area in front of the steam engine and boiler, peering out a window at the deck as machinery hissed and clanked behind them. Along the walls, several bins held coal, shovels thrusting out of them, and a huge firebox in the back emanated heat.

The warmth rolling off the machinery had felt good when Aldari first walked in, but now she barely noticed it. Hawk's words —*all* of them—circulated in her mind as she tried to tell what was happening outside. Thanks to the ongoing fog, they could barely see their own crew, much less the other ship.

"Our last opportunity to escape didn't go well." Aldari rubbed her sore hip, remembering being thrown from the horse and their terrifying battle with the vorg, a vorg that might have killed her if Hawk hadn't ridden up in time. "But I agree," she added, aware of Theli's frown, "that we need to be ready in case an opportunity arises."

As sympathetic as she was to the elves' plight, Aldari had been honest with Hawk. As her father's daughter, it was her duty to put her people's needs first. Even if the idea of going off on an adventure with Hawk sounded more appealing than walking down the aisle with a stranger.

It *shouldn't* have. She'd never been like her ten-year-old brother, who longed to follow in their grandfather's footsteps. If she could have rejected *both* options and stayed home with her books and studies, she would have preferred that.

"Who's out there?" came another call from the fog.

Hawk answered from the bow, giving his name and company in his language. Did he think that whoever it was would be more likely to leave them alone if they realized they were dealing with elven warriors? Anyone who'd seen their people in battle shouldn't want to pick a fight with them.

"Shit," someone else in the fog said, perhaps having that very thought.

"Are you the elves who kidnapped the princess of Delantria?" the first speaker asked.

Theli gripped Aldari's shoulder. "The word got out! They know about you. These could be our saviors."

"I don't know about that. They're speaking in a foreign dialect. Sounds like people from Yi or maybe islanders. If they're interested in us, it's probably because they're thinking they can ransom me to Prince Xerik."

Once again, Hawk answered in Elven, a hint of confusion in his voice, as if he didn't understand. Right.

"Who *cares*?" Theli whispered. "That'll still get us to Orath. Maybe even before we'd be late for the wedding."

"I hadn't planned to meet my future husband for the first time while being tied up and toted over a pirate's shoulder. Or having him need to open his coffers to pay a ransom fee." Aldari shook her head bleakly. Was she even positive Xerik's father would agree to do so? If the pirates wanted a ludicrous amount, he might not. And her own father could ill afford to pay a ransom.

"I'd think *anything* would be better than our current situation. Besides, some loutish pirates might be easier to escape from than these elves. You and your pride could still walk freely into Orath."

"That does appeal."

"Good." Theli squeezed her shoulder.

"...don't want to deal with elves," a whisper floated across the water.

"Don't worry. We've got the..."

A clunk sounded, and the deck shuddered. The entire boat did. Had they hit something?

Theli pointed to the left. Beyond the railing, the dark outline of a ship was just visible, a ship much larger than their ferry. It looked like an ocean-going sailing vessel, not some barge for crossing the river. And were those cannons mounted near the railing?

"Princess Aldara, are you aboard?" one of the ship's crew called.

"Aldar*a*?" Aldari whispered.

If the accents hadn't convinced her that these were foreigners, their not knowing her name would have. People in the kingdom knew their monarch and his family.

Theli cracked open the door—Hawk hadn't locked it when he'd escorted them inside. "She's here! We need help!"

Aldari lunged and grabbed her arm, pulling her back. "What are you *doing*?"

Theli yanked her arm free. "What *you* should be doing."

The door banged open, almost smacking Theli in the face. If Aldari hadn't pulled her back it would have.

Curses came from the elves on the deck as Setvik strode in, fury twisting his face. He grabbed Theli.

Terrified for her bodyguard, Aldari sprang and tried to put herself between them. As far as she knew, Theli had no value to the elves.

"I'm sorry," Aldari whispered, lifting a hand. "I'll keep her quiet."

Setvik shoved her away and yanked something from his belt. A knife?

As Aldari caught herself on a coal bin, knocking a shovel to the deck, Theli snarled and tried to punch Setvik. But his hand blurred upward, and he caught her fist as if it had been the slow, puny strike of a toddler. Aldari had seen Theli spar enough to know it hadn't been.

She ran back in, aware of mercenaries barking orders and weapons being drawn on the deck.

Setvik pulled out gags and bonds, not a knife. Aldari hesitated. She didn't want to be tied up, but it was better than watching Theli be killed.

"I *told* him to keep you bound," Setvik snarled, blocking two more punches from Theli without a hitch in his words, then spinning her around and jamming her against the wall. He forced her to her knees and leaned against her back with crushing force.

Afraid he would break her ribs as he bound her, Aldari rushed in and grabbed his shoulder.

"We won't resist you, but do *not* hurt my bodyguard," she said in her most imperious tone—and her loudest tone. Though she didn't know if her fate would be any better among the pirates—it might be worse—Aldari felt compelled to go along with Theli's plan and hope the pirates could steal them from the elves and would take them to Orath.

Without releasing Theli, Setvik grabbed her hand and shoved it away. "Do not touch me, *human*. And know that you've just condemned more of your people to die."

"Those aren't my people."

"They are human, and if they try to board our ferry, we *will* kill them." Setvik's snarling visage promised that he wouldn't mind doing so; he might even relish it. He pushed Aldari farther away, released her, then went back to tying Theli.

Theli struggled, bucking and trying to escape the lock he had on her. Against a lesser foe, she would have been successful, but she couldn't push away the powerful elf. She cried out as he wrenched her harder, punishment for resisting, and wrapped a leather thong around her wrists.

Aldari took a step toward the door, hoping Hawk would be more reasonable, but she almost kicked the shovel she'd knocked free. She grabbed it. Setvik's back was to her. She might be able to strike him before he finished tying Theli. But fear gripped her. She could envision him glimpsing the attack, halting it, and punishing Theli because he couldn't hurt Aldari.

"Get *off* me, you bastard," Theli snarled. "You're going to break my—" She arched her back and cried out again.

Her pain dashed away Aldari's indecision. She sprang and swung the shovel at Setvik's head as hard as she could.

He must have heard her, for he started to turn but not quickly enough. The shovel cracked into the side of his head.

Cursing, Setvik sprang toward Aldari. She swung again, but he caught the haft in midair.

Theli squirmed, attempting to free herself to help Aldari, but he'd already tied her wrists. Aldari tried to twist the shovel out of Setvik's grip, but he yanked it away from her with such power that it wrenched her shoulder.

The notes of a flute floated through the fog from the direction of the other ship. Who was playing a musical instrument *now*?

Aldari scrambled back, looking around for something else to use against Setvik. Surprisingly, he didn't follow her. He crouched with the shovel in the air and looked toward the window. The notes played again.

He swore. "They've got a *heyselka.*"

"A what?"

"An ancient elven flute that commands animals—and serpents." Setvik threw the shovel down with enough force to dent the head and rushed outside.

The same roar-shriek that Aldari had heard earlier pierced the fog. It was much closer now. Laughter came from the deck of the other ship.

"Send a team down," someone barked. "Get the princess."

The clash of swords rang out on the deck, and a cannon fired, so close that the boom was deafening. The ferry rocked, throwing Aldari into a wall. She pushed off, grabbed the shovel that Setvik had left behind, and ran to Theli. She put the tool down and knelt behind her, digging into her bonds.

"I have no idea what we're going to do," Aldari whispered, "but let me untie this."

"Gladly." Theli looked over her shoulder. "Did you hit that bastard with something?"

"A shovel." Aldari pointed to the dented tool she was kneeling on to ensure it wouldn't skid across the deck. Since Hawk had taken their weapons again, it was the closest thing to a weapon she had, and she didn't intend to lose it.

"*Good.*" Theli's voice was savage. "I hate that one."

"I know." Aldari could hear Hawk giving orders in his language as the fight raged. Setvik was out there too, his words sounding more like curses than orders, though they might have been both. "I think he hates us too."

"Let me tell you how sorrowful that makes me. I wish you'd knocked him out. Or *killed* him."

"His head was harder than the shovel." Aldari scowled as she struggled with the knots and wished she had her dagger.

"In murder mysteries, hitting a villain in the head always knocks him out. Distressing that it doesn't really work like that."

The roar-shriek erupted from the water beside their ferry. Aldari finally loosened the knots, and Theli pulled her arms free.

She cursed and rotated her shoulder. "He almost tore it out of the joint. I pity his lovers."

"Let's hope he doesn't have any." Aldari helped Theli to her feet.

Theli winced but shook out her arms. "I can still swim."

Something struck the hull of the ferry, shoving them sideways and almost sending Aldari tumbling into another wall. Outside, the fighting on the deck paused. Hawk shouted an order, and footsteps pounded across the deck.

Another strike—a hit from a serpent's head?—jostled the ferry, and Aldari remembered the armor on the hull. If it weren't there, the serpent, if that was truly what was out there, might have been taking bites out of the side.

"I don't think swimming is a good idea right now." Aldari wrapped both hands around the shovel haft.

"We can't stay here, especially after you clubbed Setvik. He'll want revenge later." Theli touched her shoulder and winced again.

"We've got them," someone on the other ship yelled. "Keep firing."

Another cannon boomed, and the wall exploded inward. As a cannonball plunged past scant feet away, Theli pushed Aldari to the deck, using her body to shield her.

The serpent struck from the other side of the ferry, metal wrenching terribly. This time, it *had* managed to bite into the hull.

"Are you all right?" Theli lifted her head.

"Yes. Thanks." Aldari stared at the hole in the wall—it was ten times the size the cannonball had been. The other ship was visible outside of it.

"That's our way out," Theli said over the *thunk* of a harpoon launcher firing. "We'll only have to swim a few feet. They'll pull us up before the serpent can get us."

A roar-shriek hammered their eardrums. From the thumps and its cries, Aldari believed the serpent was on the opposite side of the ferry from the ship, but she hesitated, certain it could swim fast, and even more certain it would be drawn by the scent of people in the water.

Out on deck, weapons clashed again as another harpoon was fired.

"They're distracted." Theli rose and pulled Aldari to her feet. "Come on, Your Highness. This is the losing boat. If we don't get off now, we might never."

Aldari might have argued in favor of the elves coming out on top, even though their enemies had cannons and a serpent, but Theli didn't stick around to discuss it. She ran to the hole in the wall, jumped up into it, and balanced on the jagged wood. She peered up and waved at someone.

"Get a rope," Theli called softly to whoever she saw, the words barely audible over the cacophony of battle.

The door to the engine room flew open, and Hawk stood there, his sword and dagger in his hands, the blades dripping blood.

"Thank your god," he blurted when he spotted Aldari. "Stay there and..." He trailed off when he noticed Theli, still poised in the hole—poised to leap off the ferry.

He took a step into the engine room, but the wall near him exploded inward. Wood flew, and the viper-like maw of a giant serpent plunged toward him.

Aldari shrieked.

The monster startled Hawk as much as it did her. He sprang away from its fanged maw but not quickly enough to avoid it completely. It smacked into him, sending him flying toward Aldari, his head striking the deck hard. For an instant, that stunned him, and he didn't move. The serpent roar-shrieked, its head darting inward on its long sinewy neck.

Aldari sprang over Hawk and swung her shovel at it. Focused on him, the serpent didn't see her attack coming—or maybe it was indifferent to her puny weapon. She cracked it in the face. It hissed and jerked its head up, yellow reptilian eyes locking on to her.

Hawk's eyes focused, and he recovered enough to plunge his dagger into the bottom of its jaw. The serpent screeched and whipped its head up so hard, it struck the ceiling.

Aldari might have clubbed it again with the shovel, but Theli cried out her name and grabbed her from behind, pulling her away from the fight.

As Hawk leaped to his feet, sword raised, an enemy cannon fired once more. A cannonball blew through the window, passing close enough to Hawk to whip his hair about, and struck the boiler. An explosion ripped through the engine room and blew Aldari into Theli. It knocked Hawk into a wall so hard that he lodged in the wood, but at least it battered the serpent too.

As Aldari tumbled to the deck with Theli, she hoped the explosion would kill the serpent, but it merely shook its head and pulled back out through the hole it had made. Half of the ceiling collapsed on Hawk as he tried to pull himself out of the broken wall.

"Look out!" Aldari yelled too late to be helpful.

Outside, a harpoon launcher fired. At the pirates, or was the serpent still attacking?

"Aldari," Theli whispered—it was almost a groan.

The fight had gone out of her voice, but she managed to point toward the hole the first cannonball had made. A rope was visible dangling down the hull of the other ship. A rope waiting for them.

Aldari shook her head and wobbled toward Hawk, wanting to help him out of the wreckage, to make sure he hadn't been killed. But the serpent's head blasted through one of the remaining walls. Aldari halted, hardly able to believe it still lived. A harpoon stuck out of its scales, and Hawk's dagger jutted from its lower jaw.

The serpent roared, plunged downward, and pulled Hawk out of the rubble. His sword was still in his hand, but he dangled limply from its mouth. Impaled on its fangs?

With the shovel still in hand, Aldari lunged toward him, but Theli caught her.

"It's too late," she said.

And it was. The serpent pulled its head back out through the wall, taking Hawk with it. Outside, harpoons fired. Maybe the elves would succeed in killing the serpent, but Aldari didn't see how Hawk could survive. And if he was gone, Setvik would be in charge of the mercenaries.

When Theli tugged her toward the hole, Aldari didn't resist. Shovel still in hand, she turned and followed her bodyguard. They sprang for the rope and the escape that Aldari hoped didn't turn into a greater nightmare than what they'd already endured.

12

A<small>S SHE CLIMBED THE ROPE UP TO THE DECK OF THE SAILING SHIP</small>, Aldari kept glancing back, hoping to catch a glimpse of Hawk—hoping that he was somehow still alive. But the fog was too thick. She could only see the closest side of the ferry, the roof and walls of the engine room torn to pieces thanks to the serpent, the cannons, and the exploding boiler. The entire mercenary company would likely end up dead, their vessel sunk.

They were still fighting, splashes and the shrieks of the serpent clear through the fog, but they seemed to be focused on the monster instead of the ship. That left their human enemies free to continue to pummel the ferry with cannon fire.

Aldari shook her head. Even though she should have been glad to be free of her kidnappers, she hadn't wanted Hawk killed. Not for trying to help his people.

As Aldari neared the top, the shovel making the climb awkward, someone pulled her over the railing. Once she joined Theli on the deck, several burly men with greasy hair and beards surrounded them. Aldari couldn't help but wonder if they'd truly put themselves in a better position.

"We've got them," one man called, smacking Theli on the backside. "Push off and leave the crazy elves to deal with the serpent."

Theli spun on him, her fists raised. Unfortunately, her mace was back on the elven ferry, strapped to Hawk's pack.

Fingers tightening around the haft of the shovel, Aldari glared at the group of men surrounding them. A rumble went through the ship, suggesting that more than wind powered it, and they floated away from the elves.

A shaggy man in a wool cap came forward and looked Aldari and Theli up and down, his gaze lingering on their breasts. "I'm the captain here. Janjo. You the princess?" He pointed at Aldari.

"Yes. Aldari."

"And are you grateful to us for saving you from those heathens?" He smirked, eyeing their chests again.

"Not that grateful," Theli said.

Aldari flexed her fingers on the shovel, contemplating smacking him and leaping overboard. As awful as Setvik was, he hadn't shown any sexual interest in them. If anything, he'd been disgusted by the idea of mating with a human.

"No?" Janjo grinned, his teeth yellow and pitted. "You will be."

Aldari lifted her chin. "As you may have heard, I was kidnapped on the way to my wedding to Prince Xerik of Orath." She hoped that invoking the royal family of a powerful kingdom would make the captain think twice about abusing them. "If you treat us well and take us directly to Orath, I'll see to it that you are rewarded."

As she'd told Theli, Aldari would prefer to walk into her future husband's castle of her own volition, but she had to make sure the wedding took place. She couldn't be choosy about how it happened. All she could hope was that Xerik's father would indeed pay these men and wouldn't make a liar out of her.

"A reward?" Janjo smirked and stepped closer, lifting a hand to her cheek. "We're pirates, princess. We get ransoms, not rewards, and *we* set the price."

Theli stepped in as Aldari stepped back, not wanting the man's hands on her. But Aldari paused. She didn't want him to paw over Theli either.

"Whatever you want to call it," Theli said, "you better not touch her. The prince is expecting a *virgin* bride."

Aldari winced as embarrassment heated her cheeks. She understood why Theli was pointing that out, but she also didn't want her sexual status announced to a ship full of strangers.

"I'll bet he is," one said, grabbing Aldari's shoulder from behind. "We *all* like virgins."

Aldari tried to pull away, but she'd backed away from the captain and right into the rest of the group.

"Who are you?" Janjo asked Theli. "Her maid?"

"Her bodyguard," Theli said coolly.

"Hah, figured. You've got a lot of muscles for a maid. Not bad looking though. You can *both* join me in my cabin tonight."

"*Captain*," someone whined. "You're not going to share? We haven't had any women since Port Tungar."

"This was my idea, and that makes it *my* reward." Janjo tried to step past Theli to reach for Aldari, but Theli grabbed his wrist.

Before he could pull away, she stepped in, twisted, and jammed her hip into his stomach. She crouched, thrust, and threw him over his shoulder. He landed hard on the deck, and a few men laughed.

"Feisty," one said.

The captain sprang up with a snarl, his fists in the air. Theli raised hers and glowered at him. Aldari tried to step forward, wanting to stand with Theli and fight back to back with her if need be, but the man who'd grabbed her tightened his grip.

She whirled, swinging the shovel. He ducked and rammed into her, knocking her into another pirate. Catching her from behind, he wrapped both arms around her waist and hefted her into the air. Furious, Aldari shouted and managed to whack him in the back with the shovel, but another man tore it out of her grip.

The thuds of punches landing came from behind her, but Aldari couldn't see Theli and didn't know if it was a fair fight. As more and more men surged around them, she doubted it.

Helpless as her captor slung her over his shoulder, Aldari tried to knee and elbow him, but even when she connected, it didn't bother the brutish pirate.

A dying squeal floated over the water, and the fighting paused.

"Sounds like they got the best of the serpent," someone said.

"It doesn't matter. It did its job. Their boat's a wreck, and they aren't catching us."

"I say we help the captain enjoy his prize right here."

Janjo laughed, not objecting, and clothing ripped. Theli's clothing?

Tears sprang to Aldari's eyes as the enormity of their mistake came to her. "You won't receive any ransom if you molest us," she yelled. "Me *or* my bodyguard."

"Intruder!" someone cried. "Coming over the rail—"

Several men swore. The one holding Aldari dropped her.

Though startled, she rolled away as soon as she hit the deck. She was ready to jump overboard and take her chances with the serpent, but through the knot of men rushing the railing, she spotted familiar short blond hair. Setvik. And he wasn't alone. Another elf had climbed aboard with him. It was two against ten or more, but maybe the elves liked those odds. She hoped they did.

Theli lay crumpled on the deck, groaning, her tunic torn off her shoulder and her lip bleeding. Aldari crawled toward her, pausing only to grab her shovel. The men had left it behind, attacking the elves with swords.

As steel clanged, Aldari wrapped an arm around Theli's waist. "Can you get up? We need to..."

She didn't even know what. Run? Help? She looked toward the battle, and her breath caught. Setvik was fighting with his back to the railing, a whirlwind as he slashed and stabbed against multiple opponents, and at his side...

"He's still alive," Aldari breathed, hope rising in her chest.

As much blood streamed from Hawk as water, and his torso armor was mutilated with bite marks, but he fought alongside Setvik, his face twisted with rage as he attacked the pirates. The two elves were terrifying, pirates falling to their deadly blades, battle fury in their eyes, but in that moment, Aldari didn't think she'd seen a more wondrous sight. Setvik and Hawk were outnumbered and should have been outmatched, but pirates crumpled at their feet, blood washing the deck.

Some of the humans realized they were losing and tried to run, but if they turned away, the elves took advantage. A couple of pirates leaped over the railing and escaped that way, but a fresh roar-shriek came from the other side of the ship. There were more serpents in the river, drawn by the scent of blood and eager for a meal.

Soon, the elves stood alone, their chests heaving, blood streaming from their weapons. Hawk met Aldari's eyes, and some of the rage left his face. He strode toward her with determination, though he limped. The water and his dark clothing made it hard to tell how much he was bleeding, but the serpent's fangs had punctured his armor all over—and him as well.

Aldari dropped the shovel and ran forward, not wanting him to have to walk farther than necessary.

"I'm sorry," she blurted, flinging her arms around him.

For a moment, he stood stunned, his sword and dagger drooping to his side. Maybe he'd expected her to run, that he would have to chase her down and force her off the ship.

"I'm sorry," she repeated, regretting that she'd made things more difficult for him and relieved he'd somehow survived. She kissed the side of his neck, then buried her face in his shoulder.

Hawk shifted his weapons to one hand so he could return her hug. He said something in his language, something that sounded achingly weary, but he patted her on the back, so she didn't think it was a curse or that he was calling her an idiot for fleeing. Even though he would have been correct if he had.

"She hit me in the head with a shovel," Setvik said, "and she *hugs* you?"

He was leaning against the railing for support as he peered around the pirate ship, watching for further threats. A few men remained, watching them through portholes or from behind corners, but Janjo lay dead on the deck, and nobody else came forward to challenge the elves.

"I didn't think you wanted hugs from humans," Hawk said.

"I didn't want them to club me with shovels either."

"Maybe you should be more personable then."

Setvik spat on the deck.

"Bodyguard Theli," Hawk said, "are you all right? Able to walk?"

Aldari drew back, guilt swamping her as she realized she'd abandoned Theli. And she felt foolish for having kissed Hawk—she'd just been overcome with relief that he'd survived.

"Yes." Theli had been kneeling, but she grimaced and pushed herself to her feet. "I would have beaten that ugly pirate captain if the others hadn't jumped on." Her torn tunic hung off her shoulder and she pushed it up to cover herself.

"I have no doubt." Hawk inclined his head toward her.

Theli squinted at him, as if she suspected him of teasing her, but the comment seemed sincere.

"Come." Hawk stepped back, though he kept a hand on Aldari's arm. "The blood will draw more serpents. We need to hurry and get to shore before they all converge." He shook his head grimly. "They prefer live prey to dead."

"I suppose they wouldn't be lured away by some of your moss bars thrown in the water," Aldari said.

"*Nobody* would be lured away by those."

She snorted. "I knew you couldn't really believe they tasted good."

Hawk smiled weakly, leading her and Theli to the railing. "When we reach our outpost, I'll make sure a feast is prepared to celebrate your arrival."

"A feast made from moss?"

"No, many kinds of meat. Elves are good hunters." Hawk eyed her. "There may be moss side dishes, but it's better when its warm and mixed with dressing."

"I'll attempt to look forward to it."

Aldari caught Theli frowning over at her. Maybe she shouldn't have admitted that she was willing to go along with the elves to their outpost and enjoy their feast.

Was she? She'd been bantering with Hawk because she was relieved he was alive, not because she wanted to go with him. She couldn't want that. Her duty called her to Orath. If she got another opportunity to escape, she would be obligated to take it. But she wouldn't fling herself into the arms of more pirates. If Theli suggested something like that again, Aldari would have to put her foot down. After all, *she* was in charge.

13

THE DINGHY SKIMMED THROUGH THE FOG, SETVIK AND HAWK ON separate benches, rowing toward an invisible shoreline. The ferry had been destroyed, but most of the mercenaries and boatmen had gotten off in similar dinghies. Hawk had been terse as he'd explained that to Aldari and Theli, his eyes especially grim at the word *most*.

He bled as he rowed, his face tight with pain. The two elves were both in need of medical attention, but Hawk had shaken his head when Aldari offered her and Theli's service, saying they needed to get to the other side as quickly as possible, while the serpents were distracted by the dead in the water. If the armored ferry hadn't been able to stop a serpent, the wooden dinghy would be flotsam within seconds.

The idea that some of the crew were back there serving as meals for monsters chilled Aldari as much as the fog. She scooted closer to Theli on the bench they shared, hoping for warmth. No breeze blew on the eerie river, nothing that would stir the fog, but the chill northern air sucked the heat from one's body. She wouldn't have minded taking a turn at rowing, if only to warm up, but neither she nor Theli could match the powerful strokes of the elves.

"We have a permanent camp on the shoreline," Hawk said. "It has food and medical supplies and is relatively safe. We'll spend the night there."

Hawk glanced toward the sky, though they couldn't see the sun any more here than they had elsewhere on the river. It seemed to be getting darker, but Aldari couldn't tell if that was because evening approached or the fog had grown thicker. She could barely see Setvik rowing silently behind Hawk.

"*Relatively* safe because it's not in the water, and the serpents don't come up on shore?" Aldari asked.

"That, and the Twisted shouldn't attack us while we're there. There are *phyzera*—magical orbs that create a protective barrier around the camp."

Setvik said something grumpy in his own language.

"I doubt she's going to tell her people all of our secrets," Hawk replied.

That earned an even grumpier response.

Hawk sighed and let his chin droop to his chest, choosing to focus on his rowing. Sweat beaded on his forehead.

"Do you have any medical supplies with you?" Aldari asked, though she'd already noticed he didn't have his pack. It and her and Theli's weapons might be on the bottom of the river. "I could try to treat your wounds. Or Theli could. She has more experience in that area. You're, uhm, bleeding on the bench."

"And the oars and into that puddle there." Hawk nodded toward his boots. "I know. Sadly, I didn't think to grab my pack before being swept up by the serpent."

"How did you get away from it? When last I saw you..." Aldari swallowed, remembering how certain she'd been that he would die.

"My pride wishes me to inform you that I was merely playing

dead while luring the serpent to complacency so that I could strike," Hawk said.

This time, Setvik's comment sounded sarcastic.

"I was marshaling my strength to deliver a valiant strike with my sword, which I *did* do," Hawk said. "It helped that Setvik threw a knife and hit it in the eye first."

"I *lost* that knife too," Setvik said. "Next time, before you kill the serpent with my knife lodged in its eye, pull my blade out for me."

"You couldn't pull your own blade out?" Hawk asked over his shoulder.

"*I* wasn't the one dangling from its maw like a piece of meat. The serpent sank before I could swim out to retrieve it."

Hawk sighed at Aldari. "It's difficult being a mercenary commander."

"I've heard that," Setvik grumbled.

Aldari smiled, glad for their grousing at each other. It wasn't exactly oozing brotherly love, but if they were feisty enough to argue, maybe she didn't need to worry about them keeling over at the oars.

Theli hadn't reacted to the conversation and was staring numbly at her feet.

"Are you all right?" Aldari whispered, worried Theli had been traumatized by the pirates and their manhandling. Or maybe the entire kidnapping adventure. Still, Theli was so tough and resilient that it seemed like it would take more than either of those to deeply disturb her. "Are you composing song lyrics about our adventure?" Aldari added, hoping to lighten her mood.

"I'm just tired," Theli mumbled, not glancing at Aldari as she absently held the torn flap of her tunic closed. They would have to find something else for her to wear, or at least a needle and thread. Did mercenaries carry such domestic things?

"Are you mad at me?" Aldari asked even more softly, though

there was little point in whispering in the small boat. The elves would doubtless hear.

"No." Theli glanced at her. "Also, that's not permitted."

"Being mad? Or being mad at *me*?"

"Bodyguards aren't permitted to be irked with their clients, especially their royal clients."

"No matter how foolish the things are that those clients do?"

"No matter." Theli eyed the elves and lowered her voice. "I'm annoyed with my choice, not yours. I've been so focused on escaping and trying to get you back to safety and your wedding that I haven't accepted that the dangers out there could be greater than the dangers here with them."

"It's a difficult situation."

"Yes."

"I'm glad you're not irked with me," Aldari said. "I thought you might have been perturbed when I hugged Hawk, even though that was a perfectly reasonable thing to do, given the circumstances."

"Given the circumstances, I might have hugged him if you hadn't, but there wasn't room."

"You could have hugged his lieutenant."

Setvik was rowing in sync with Hawk and ignoring their conversation, so it was only in Aldari's mind that he flinched, aghast at the thought of a human woman touching him. Even Hawk didn't seem to be paying much attention to them. Maybe because of his pain, rowing was the only thing he could focus on.

"I would rather have hugged the serpent," Theli said.

"It *was* cuddlier."

"Not true," Hawk grunted, proving he *was* paying attention.

He paused rowing long enough to lift his tunic and the bottom of his torso armor, inasmuch as the stiff leather would allow it. Thanks to its recent maceration in the maw of a serpent, it was more pliable than typical, and Aldari got a glimpse of deep puncture wounds still leaking blood. The skin around them was water-logged and inflamed. If he didn't have an infection by the next day, she would be shocked.

She hoped his camp *did* have medical supplies—very *good* medical supplies. That nasty gray powder the medic had shared couldn't possibly be sufficient to deal with injuries like that.

Aldari forced a smile, not wanting her horrified expression to worry Hawk—it was possible he didn't yet realize how bad the wounds were. "Did you not feel cuddled as its fangs were sinking in?" she asked lightly.

"I did not. On the other hand, Setvik and I may have a some-what contentious relationship, but he's not bitten me yet."

Aldari doubted it would feel any better if Setvik plunged a dagger into Hawk's chest, but she didn't bring that up. A current caught the dinghy, and it lurched as they started floating sideways —rapidly.

With a curse, Hawk hurried to lower his tunic and armor and return both hands to the oars. The dinghy rocked hard in the current, then floated past a huge rock jutting out of the river.

It was the first obstacle Aldari had seen in the deep, formerly placid water, and they barely avoided wrecking the dinghy upon it.

Setvik barked orders, as if *he* were in charge, and the two elves rowed vigorously to get the bow pointed downstream. Did they actually want to *go* in that direction? They were supposed to be crossing the river, not following it out to sea.

As the dinghy rocked in the current, more rocks jutting out of the water to either side of them, Aldari gripped Theli's hand. She didn't know if it was for comfort or in the hope that they would be less likely to be thrown overboard if they were attached to each other. With her other hand, she gripped the side of the dinghy.

Surprisingly, once the bow was pointed downstream, the elves stopped rowing.

"You're not giving up because there's no hope of us escaping being swept out to sea, right?" Aldari asked.

"Elves never give up." Hawk held her gaze. "The fact that our people have survived centuries of attackers at our door and having our brothers and sisters stolen and turned into the Twisted should attest to that."

The intensity of his gaze was unsettling, and it gave her the sense that he would do anything for his people—anything to stop their torment. The fact that he'd kidnapped her, when he didn't seem like someone who would usually lower himself to such criminal activity, spoke to that.

"Not to mention being cuddled by river serpents," Aldari said, preferring levity to intensity.

Hawk managed a quick smile. "Indeed."

The hint of something roasting reached Aldari's nose. Meat? Were they nearing the camp the elves had spoken of?

Her stomach whined pitifully, reminding her that she'd eaten nothing except a couple of those awful moss bars since she'd been kidnapped.

"There's something glowing purple up ahead." Aldari pointed.

No sooner had the words come out than the current shifted. The rowboat wobbled again as it turned toward what Aldari hoped was the bank. The thickness of the fog kept her from seeing anything but three glowing spheres ahead. Their height suggested they were hanging well above the water. Or above land?

As the current carried the boat in that direction, the outline of dark, shadowy trees grew visible. The spheres hung among their branches.

The dinghy hit a rock or some other underwater obstacle, and Aldari almost pitched off her bench. Hawk released an oar long enough to lean forward and steady her.

Once the current spat them into a calm cove, the dinghy settled. After a few more powerful strokes, the elves pulled in the oars. As their momentum carried them forward, the outlines of tents grew visible, as did the orange of a couple of campfires and numerous torches.

The dinghy glided until it scraped the beach beneath them. Hawk and Setvik climbed out and pulled it ashore. Several other dinghies rested on the pebbly beach—Aldari recognized them from the ferry—as well as a couple of canoes. Perhaps someone stayed year around and maintained the camp for travelers.

Once the elves stepped back, Aldari and Theli climbed gingerly out. With her entire body aching, Aldari longed for medical supplies not only for Hawk but for herself. Somewhat miraculously, she hadn't broken any bones, but she could feel fresh lumps and bruises rising all over, and her hip and knee pulsed with pain when she put weight on her legs. Her shoulder and back also ached, and she longed for the steam baths in the castle back home, and for one of the maids to tend her wounds and bring her a healing herbal tea.

"Welcome to the elven kingdom of Serth." Hawk spread a hand toward the camp and towering evergreens stretching inland, then bowed to them. Twilight darkened the shoreline, and the trees reminded Aldari of the creepy forests of fairy tales, places where wolves and vorgs and worse lurked, waiting to devour children who wandered too far from their homes. "I regret that it's not the place the legends promise us it once was," Hawk added, "and that I can take you only to the outpost where the king lives and rules, and not one of the great cities of eld, but perhaps you'll be able to help us return our land to what it once was."

Hawk smiled at Aldari, a smile full of appreciation and hope.

In another situation, she might have found that smile handsome and appealing, but all she could think about was that he might expect far too much of her. How would he feel if she *couldn't* get him into the ancient laboratory of a crazy dead elf wizard? Or, even if she could, what if they opened the door and found nothing there to help?

14

ALDARI GRIMACED AS SHE ENDURED THE POKING AND PRODDING OF the mercenary medic, whose touch was not gentle in the least. She'd hoped a friendlier doctor would be waiting for them—or at least one who didn't also ram swords into people for a living—but the camp, though stocked with supplies and guarded by the glowing purple orbs, had been empty of anyone other than the mercenaries who'd arrived first. They'd started the fires and had meat cooking.

Now, with night darkening the forest outside, Aldari and Theli shivered in little more than their undergarments. At least they had a modicum of privacy. They were inside a large tent with numerous cots, only two of which were occupied by elves, both of whom had their eyes closed. A couple of weak lanterns burning on crates left the interior largely in shadow.

Theli had objected to the idea of either of them removing clothing, and she hadn't wanted any man—elven medical expert or not—touching Aldari. Only when he'd held up bandages, jars of astringent-smelling ointment, and a potion in a glass bottle had she stopped objecting. Or maybe it had been the pained grunt

Aldari had made as she sat on a cot that had convinced Theli she needed treatment. They *both* did.

That didn't keep Theli from glowering at the other patients or scowling toward the tent flap whenever voices sounded outside. Not that anyone except the medic had been looking at them. The tent's other occupants hadn't stirred since Aldari and Theli had come in.

"I didn't see any horses as we entered the camp." Theli dug into a crate of medical supplies near their cots. "Do you think we'll be walking on foot to this elven outpost?"

"Unless a magical chariot shows up to whisk us along the elven highways."

"Do elves *have* highways?" Theli pulled out suturing thread and a needle.

"I don't know." Aldari hissed as the medic applied ointment to scrapes and bruises on her side. His touch continued to be brusque rather than gentle, and the stuff managed to burn and chill at the same time.

Maybe the medic hadn't gotten the word that Aldari was supposed to be a treasured guest rather than a loathed prisoner. Admittedly, only Hawk had treasured her thus far. Maybe the other elves didn't believe Aldari could do anything. Or maybe they hadn't been filled in on his mission.

"I don't know if they have magical chariots either," Aldari said. "It's possible the legends we've heard about their people aren't entirely accurate."

"Why do they think you can help them with their problem?" Theli threaded the needle and attempted to sew the torn flap on her tunic. "What did Hawk tell you when he pulled you aside on the ferry?"

"They need someone who's good at puzzles, and they'd read some of my work, so they believe that could be me." Aldari kept her answer vague. She hadn't spoken about her pen name to Theli before, in part because she'd doubted Theli would care, and in part because she'd gotten used to keeping it a secret, out of the fear that her father would find out and forbid it.

"I didn't know your keen ability to thwart word scrambles was known in other kingdoms."

"Some people enjoy keeping tabs on the royals in other kingdoms."

Theli glanced at the medic, then squinted at Aldari. If the elf spoke their language, he hadn't given any indication of it yet.

"What aren't you telling me?" Theli asked her.

Aldari sighed, not wanting to lie to her bodyguard of years or keep her unnecessarily in the dark. "I publish economics essays under a pen name. An example I included in one led the elves to believe I'm an expert puzzle-solver. If we get out of this, don't tell my father about the papers, please." Aldari supposed it wouldn't matter if he knew once she was married and living in another kingdom, but after keeping the secret all these years, the idea of everyone finding out made her uneasy. Maybe part of it was that Father didn't respect her pen name's theories. *Her* theories.

"I won't. Besides, he doesn't invite me into the throne room for tea that often. Are those secret papers the reason you check out all of those tediously boring books from the library instead of scintillating murder-mystery novels?"

"They are. One must do research. Mystery novels rarely have much to say about the economic state of the kingdom and neighboring nations."

"Thank the One God."

Theli finished her sewing job but only sneered at her grimy, wet tunic. Aldari wished they could get changes of clothing, but since they were still out in the wilds, that seemed unlikely.

Hawk's voice came from outside the tent. It sounded like he was giving orders.

Aldari tapped the medic on the shoulder and pointed toward

the tent flap. "Captain Hawk has some garish puncture wounds that could get infected. Did you see him get snatched up by the river serpent?" She had no idea what the medic had been doing during the battle. "It crushed him in its maw, and then he fought pirates, and then he rowed us all the way here. You should make him come in here and get treatment."

The medic squinted at her. What was his name? Mevleth. That was it.

Assuming he didn't understand her, Aldari started to pantomime her message, but he waved away her gestures and spoke. "He is you captor, no? Why you care he get healed?"

"We like him more than Setvik, though your lieutenant probably needs healing too." Aldari pointed at the flap again. "Seriously. Hawk is much worse off than we are. You should drag him in here, toss him on a cot, and rub him all over with your nasty ointment."

Mevleth snorted, but he called to Hawk in their language, giving what sounded like orders, a lecture, and a reprimand all in one or two sentences.

The tent flap lifted, and Hawk limped in, a hand pressed to his abdomen.

Theli leaned over, picked up a blanket, and wrapped it around Aldari's bare shoulders.

"What are you doing?" Aldari asked.

Mevleth had paused to address Hawk, but he was still in the middle of treating her.

"Covering up your modesty," Theli said.

"My modesty, which nobody here is interested in anyway, is suitably hidden beneath my undergarments."

"You've got more skin on display than a dancer in one of the men's bars on the seedy side of town."

"My skin is so covered in these purple and blue bruises that a prison escapee who hadn't seen a woman in twenty years wouldn't be interested."

"Nonetheless." Theli adjusted the blanket to drape more fully over Aldari.

The medic ignored their antics as he pointed Hawk to another cot and continued to lecture him. After a moment, he pointed at Aldari, saying something that prompted Hawk to raise his eyebrows. She was positive it had nothing to do with her *modesty*.

Hawk smiled faintly, said something, and waved for Mevleth to finish with Aldari and Theli before tending to him. That earned him a scowl and an order to undress.

The tent flap stirred, and Setvik walked in, leaning on a stick. The smell of a nearby campfire wafted in with him. He ignored Aldari and Theli, said something to Hawk, and both elves started undressing.

Mevleth lifted the bottle he'd shown Aldari earlier. Inside, a bright green liquid sloshed. It was so bright that it almost glowed.

"Where do you think *that* goes?" Theli touched a bruise on her shoulder, freshly applied ointment giving it an oily sheen.

"Maybe we drink it." Aldari nodded as Mevleth uncorked the bottle.

"It's *green*."

"So are the moss bars."

"You say that as if it's an argument *for* consuming it, not a vehement protest against. At this point, I'm hungry enough to eat a shoe, but..." Theli trailed off as she looked not at the medic as he swirled his potion in the bottle but toward Setvik and Hawk.

Unconcerned about their own modesty, they'd stripped to their underwear and were settling onto cots. Their wounds were even more garish than Aldari had realized, and she wanted to shove the medic immediately over to take care of them.

Since Theli didn't seem to care much what happened to the

elves, Aldari didn't know what was holding her attention, but she was eyeing them with new speculation. Because of their physiques? They were both extremely fit, with lean bodies and powerful musculatures that were now fully on display, but given how much Theli detested Setvik, it was hard for Aldari to imagine her wanting to ogle his naked body. And Hawk was so wounded that Aldari struggled to think about anything beyond how badly he needed attention.

Though as she gazed over at him, her mind produced the thought that *she* wouldn't mind being the one to rub ointment over him. The gruff and brusque Mevleth shouldn't be the one to do it. A man—an elf so badly injured should be treated by someone with a *gentle* touch. Someone who cared. Someone who'd never run her hands over the muscled arm or chest of a man and couldn't help but find the idea intriguing.

Aldari blinked and looked away. It was all right to care—if the story he'd shared of his people was true, Hawk deserved to be cared for—but she couldn't fantasize about *touching*. Her wedding might have been delayed, but she still intended to find a way to Orath to marry Xerik. It was her duty.

"Drink," Mevleth said.

How long had he been holding the bottle of green liquid before her eyes? Judging by his exasperated expression, more than a few seconds.

Aldari accepted it, waving to indicate she would share it with Theli, and Mevleth took his medical kit over to Setvik and Hawk, kneeling first beside Hawk's cot.

Setvik said something cranky, and Hawk gestured for the medic to attend him first. But Mevleth shook his head, pointed to Hawk's awful puncture wounds, and did some more lecturing. Even though Aldari couldn't understand any of it, she fancied it was a long diatribe on how foolish it was to stick one's body into a river serpent's mouth.

"He didn't have any choice," she said, startling herself by interrupting, but she didn't want to see Hawk berated. He'd done what he had to do to protect the ferry—and them.

"It's all right," Hawk told her. "It's his way. If he's not railing at his patients for being foolish, he's not happy."

Setvik growled, surged to his feet, and grabbed the medical kit out of the doctor's hand. Instead of waiting for help, he dug inside and found some of the packets of the gray pulverized berries and helped himself, tearing one open and licking the contents.

Theli stared at Setvik's chest, new wounds crisscrossing over old scars. He was older than Hawk and looked to have seen a lot more battles, but he was still all sinewy muscle and power. The elves clearly trained hard.

"Leave some for the rest of us," Hawk said dryly.

Setvik tossed him a packet, then flopped down on the cot. Mevleth grunted something and pointed to the green liquid.

"I guess we better drink so he can enjoy it too." Aldari had only seen one bottle of the stuff.

"*Enjoy.* Right." Theli pulled her gaze from Setvik to glare at it.

"I assume it'll taste medicinal." Aldari lifted the bottle to her nose to sniff the liquid. It smelled like moldy socks basted in vinegar.

"I assume it'll taste like piss," Theli said.

"Oh, it's worse than that." Hawk winked over at them as Mevleth pulled out what looked like antiseptic to clean his wounds. "But it's magical and will help more than the dried berries. Even though our people no longer dare draw upon their innate power, there are substances that grow around Serth that are inherently magical. We harvest the ones that are edible and make medicinal compounds like that one."

Heartened by his words that it would help, Aldari held her nose and quaffed the medicine. It tasted even more dreadful than it smelled and burned all the way down her throat. She coughed, tears coming to her eyes, and the blanket that Theli had so diligently wrapped around her shoulders fell on the ground. Aldari was lucky *she* didn't fall on the ground.

"Smooth, isn't it?" Hawk asked.

"*So* smooth," she rasped, offering the bottle to Theli.

Hawk looked like he might say more but glanced down at her chest, and his gaze lingered as his forehead creased. Sadness, or maybe regret, stole the humor from his eyes. Aldari was fairly certain he was looking at her bruises rather than her breasts, but Theli noticed his gaze and lurched to her feet to recover the blanket. She wrapped it firmly around Aldari, then glared over at Hawk as she sat back down, not on her own cot but right beside Aldari. Even though she didn't have her mace, she appeared ready to thump Hawk with a blunt object.

"Are you *sure* she's not your maid?" His smile returned, though the regret hadn't left his eyes.

"All I would have to do," Aldari said, "is ask her to wash my clothing or scrub my butt in the bath to get confirmation on that."

Hawk arched his eyebrows. "Humans don't scrub their own butts in the bath?"

"Most do, but royalty naturally has special needs. Is it not so with elves?" Aldari hoped he could tell she was joking. She had heard of royal families who had servants to do *everything* for them, and who were quick to flog those servants for the slightest transgression, but nobody back home was like that. Given how tight money was in the kingdom, it wasn't as if even her father could afford to hire legions of servants.

"I don't believe so," Hawk said. "Setvik, you don't think the king has servants to scrub his butt, do you?"

Setvik lay on his back with an arm flung over his eyes, waiting for the medic's attention. "You'd be far more likely to know the answer to that than I. It's not like I've visited the king's home."

"I do spend more time in Serth and visit the outpost often, but

I only rarely wander into the king's bathroom to investigate his bathing practices."

Setvik switched to his tongue to say something that might have been *shut up.*

Mevleth pointed to the bottle of medicine, spoke a few sharp words, and waved toward Hawk. *Hurry up.* Right.

"I'll pass," Theli said. "I'm not that injured."

Aldari wanted to urge her to try some, but the taste was dreadful enough that she couldn't recommend it, especially since she didn't yet know how much it would help. After bracing her tastebuds, she took another sip, then handed it to Mevleth to give to Hawk.

As Mevleth pulled out suture and bandages, Hawk drank deeply from the bottle. He offered it to Setvik, but his lieutenant only flicked his fingers and remained on his cot. Hawk took another long swig, sighed, lay back, and closed his eyes while the medic attended his wounds.

A distant keening sound drifted into the camp. It came from the forest rather than the river and sounded much different from the serpent's roar. Aldari couldn't tell if it belonged to a person or an animal, but she suspected the latter. Whatever it was, it made goosebumps rise along her arms, and she pulled the blanket tighter around her for reasons that had nothing to do with modesty. The elves didn't stir or even glance at each other.

"Don't get too relaxed around him," Theli whispered. She still sat close, sharing Aldari's cot.

"Who? Hawk?"

"Yes, Hawk." Theli glared over at him.

Like Setvik, he'd flung an arm over his eyes. The medic was suturing the deepest of his wounds.

"He likes the way you banter with him a little too much," Theli said.

"My banter is delightful. All who encounter me enjoy it."

Theli turned the glare on Aldari. "You *know* what I mean. He was eyeing your assets, which you were not keeping properly covered."

"Because we're receiving medical attention, and I'm positive you're wrong. He was concerned about my bruises." And maybe felt guilty about them, Aldari added silently. That was how she'd interpreted his look. Like her, Hawk had a duty, and he would do what it took to fulfill it, but that didn't mean he didn't regret that she'd been hurt.

"Don't be naive," Theli whispered. "He could be as dangerous to your future marriage as those pirates. If not more so, because I think you *like* his attention."

"There hasn't *been* any attention. I'm scraped up and bruised and bedraggled. You're the one who's naive if you think anyone except some desperate pirates who get excited by hurting people would be interested in our bodies right now."

"I hope you're right. I don't have to remind you that your marriage is contingent on the prince getting a *virgin* princess."

"No, you don't, but you mention it at least once a day, regardless. Drop the subject, all right? And go sit on your own cot. I'm tired, and I want to sleep."

Theli held her gaze. "I just don't want you to do anything you'll regret."

"I won't."

"Good. Because I don't think writing economics papers pays very well. You'd be out of luck if your father disowned you for cavorting with elves."

Another eerie keen came from the forest. Was it closer this time?

Aldari shuddered. "I'm positive nobody here has cavorting in mind."

"Good," Theli repeated and returned to her cot.

Somewhat hypocritically, she looked over at the shirtless

Setvik before lying down. Aldari hoped it was because she was contemplating his weaknesses, and how to best him in a battle, not cavorting of her own.

The flap stirred, and the young mercenary she'd last seen swabbing the deck stepped in with two trenchers of roasted meat and pale-yellow root vegetables. Aldari's stomach whined.

Setvik sprang up and grabbed one of the trenchers for himself and maybe Hawk. The way he used his teeth to tear meat off a bone didn't suggest he had sharing in mind.

The mercenary started to bring the second trencher to Hawk, but without taking his arm from over his eyes, Hawk waved for the elf to deliver it to Aldari and Theli.

Aldari had no idea what kind of meat it was, but by that point, she would have eaten anything that wasn't green. As soon as the mercenary dropped it off, she waved Theli over, and they sat together with the trencher between them.

Not caring that they didn't have silverware or napkins, Aldari grabbed a slice and bit into it. Juices ran down her chin, and she grabbed a root vegetable. It turned out to be similar to a parsnip, and she chomped it down.

Only after she'd taken the edge off her hunger did it occur to Aldari that she and Theli were eating like cavemen. If she'd done this at home, the visiting dignitaries and members of her father's court would have gaped in disgust. Feeling self-conscious, she looked at Hawk.

With Mevleth still stitching his wounds, Hawk hadn't stirred, but he was looking over at her. Less with disgust and more with a faint smile.

She lifted a meaty bone, offering to bring it to him. After the day's fighting and all that rowing he'd done, he had to be as hungry as she.

He shook his head, instead saying something to Setvik. His lieutenant snarled—he'd descended further into caveman-ness than Aldari—and tossed a slice of meat over. It would have splatted onto Hawk's chest, but he caught it. Juices struck the medic in the face.

"So savage, Setvik," Hawk said in mild reproof. "No wonder the king doesn't invite you into his home."

He might have meant it as a joke, but Setvik glared icily at him. The meat that had been comfortably settling into Aldari's stomach turned into a stone, and she again wondered if Setvik would betray his captain during this mission.

As if he could hear her thoughts, Setvik looked over at them. With meat juice dripping onto his bare chest, the word *caveman* floated through Aldari's mind again. Cave-elf. He tore more meat off the bone, then turned his back on all of them.

Another eerie keen came from the forest.

15

When Aldari slept, she dreamed. Not of home or her wedding or her family, as she might have expected, but of Hawk and Setvik.

In the perpetual fog of the forest, they argued heatedly, then sprang together in a battle, fighting each other with as much fervor and deadly skill as they'd used against the pirates. They were evenly matched, neither able to gain the upper hand until Setvik spotted Aldari and threw a dagger at her. It plunged into her side, and horror stamped Hawk's face. When he lowered his sword and took a step toward her, Setvik took advantage. He grabbed Hawk's shoulder and plunged another dagger into his chest. Into his *heart*. Hawk died immediately, and Setvik strode toward Aldari with hatred in his eyes, and she knew he would finish her off.

A touch woke Aldari from the dream. She lurched upright with a gasp, her heart pounding. Mouth dry, she struggled to swallow and push away the vestiges of the nightmare.

Hawk knelt beside her cot, a low-burning lantern the only source of light in the tent. After the meal and the exhausting day, Aldari had slept deeply, despite the scary keens coming from the forest, and she had no idea if it was dawn or the middle of the night. The medic was gone, as was Setvik. Hawk had dressed, so she couldn't see the extent of his bruises and bandages. One of the other elven patients was awake, chewing on leftovers from the trenchers of meat.

"We'll be leaving after the sun comes up," Hawk said quietly. "May I speak with you privately for a few minutes?" He glanced at Theli, though she was still asleep on her cot.

"You know you're my kidnapper, right?" Aldari whispered, rubbing gunk from her eyes. "It's not as if I could object if you tossed me over your shoulder and toted me into the forest."

"I believe you would object *vociferously* to that and that your bodyguard would leap on my back and thunk me with her mace." Hawk smiled. "But I would not wish to treat you with such a lack of respect, regardless." He extended his hand toward the exit.

Aldari nodded and found her dress, wishing it was clean. She'd draped it over a crate the night before, but thanks to the damp climate, it wasn't fully dry. By the time she joined Hawk outside, she was shivering. At least her body didn't ache as badly as she'd feared it would after the previous day's battering. Maybe the magical elven potion had worked.

Since the camp was on the edge of the river, they hadn't yet escaped the fog, and the fires had burned low, so she couldn't see much beyond Hawk's shadowy form. In his dark clothes and armor, even he blended into the night.

"This way," he said quietly, touching her arm, then heading toward the trees. His movements were slow and stiff, a sign that his injuries had been far greater than hers and even magic potions couldn't cure him overnight. "The scouts are awake, and I would prefer to speak without being overheard."

"Do elves have better hearing than humans?" Aldari asked as she trailed after him.

"Do you ask that because our ears are larger?"

"No." She thought of the elf-ear candy and wondered if he was offended by her assumption. "They seem well-proportioned. But I've heard stories that your people have keen senses. After seeing you fight, you do seem, uhm, keen."

"I'm glad you find me so." He smiled over his shoulder at her. "We do have good hearing."

It wasn't a flirtatious smile, but for some reason, Theli's words from the night before came to mind. She didn't *think* Hawk had any sexual interest in her, but Theli, like everyone else in Aldari's life, was more experienced in such matters. Was it possible Aldari was wrong?

No. She shook her head. As she'd pointed out, she was a bedraggled and bruised mess right now. No man, from elven kidnapper to her future husband, would be moved to ardor by the sight of her.

A twinge of nerves came to her as she envisioned Prince Xerik drawing back in disgust when she walked into his castle, battered from an escape attempt, her clothes in shreds, her hair a mess. She assumed he'd seen portraits of her, but they'd never met before. What if that first impression drove him to cancel the wedding?

"This is far enough." Hawk stopped near one of the dangling purple orbs that beamed light into the camp and the surrounding woods. "We don't want to leave the protection of the *phyzera* before we have to." He tilted his head toward the sphere.

By its light, she could see his face, the strong lines set with determination, thoughts of his duty never seeming far from his mind. Aldari relaxed. Whatever Hawk wanted, she was sure Theli was wrong. Sex with a prisoner wasn't what he had in mind.

But what he *did* have in mind didn't come up immediately. After he turned to face her, he paused, as if he was searching for the words he wanted.

"Are you sure your lieutenant won't betray you?" Aldari asked, her nightmare still at the forefront of her mind.

"Reasonably sure." Hawk tilted his head. "Are you worried for me?"

Was she? Maybe a little, yes. But should she admit that to him?

"I'm not entirely *not* worried for you," she said, twisted words that prompted an eyebrow raise from him, "but I'm especially worried about what would happen to us if something happened to you. Something such as him plunging a dagger into your heart and killing you instantly."

"Ah. If that happened, Setvik ought to complete the mission and take you to the king's advisor."

Aldari frowned. *Ought* wasn't the same as *absolutely would*, and Hawk hadn't rejected the possibility that Setvik might use a dagger on him. "So... you trust him?"

Hawk hesitated. "He promised his loyalty, insofar as completing this mission, to the king's advisor, and she is someone of importance in the king's court."

"He promised his loyalty to her, not to you? His commander?"

An insect buzzed around the sphere, drawn by its light. Hawk eyed it for a moment before answering.

"I have also sworn an oath to her," Hawk said. "Even if Setvik and I have no love for each other, it will bind us together in this."

"If you brought me out here to comfort me, you're not succeeding." Aldari thought about sharing her dream, but it wasn't as if she was prone to prophetic visions in her sleep.

"That's not why I brought you out here, but I lament your discomfort. Among other things." He smiled sadly at her. "Back on the ferry, when the serpent smashed me to the deck and you ran forward with that shovel, I appreciate that you cracked *it* in the head instead of me. My first thought was that you saw your opportunity to end your kidnapper's life." He spread a hand over his chest.

"That didn't cross my mind. I'm sorry that little shovel didn't do more to keep the serpent from picking you up and mauling you."

"It only injured me." Hawk lifted his chin. "I mauled *it*."

"My apologies. I was unwisely following Theli off your ferry and didn't see the final blows." Aldari lowered her voice. "I didn't think there was any way you would live, and we didn't want to stick around if Setvik was in charge."

"He is a grump."

His *grumpiness* wasn't her primary concern.

"Thank you for coming after us. Those pirates were dreadful. Never has someone so quickly proved how loathsome they are to me."

"Pirates aren't known for their charisma."

"Or intelligence. You're supposed to treat prisoners you want to ransom well."

"Indeed. I have something for you." Hawk tugged on his belt and stuck his hand in his trousers.

Aldari almost fell over. "I don't want *that*."

"Are you sure?" Hawk pulled out a silver baton an inch and a half thick and a foot long with a single large symbol engraved in the bottom. "I believe you'll find it intriguing."

Aldari pressed a hand against a tree for support and squinted at him. "Theli would assure me that a princess shouldn't be intrigued by anything a man pulls out of his pants."

"I offer this to the puzzle-solving part of you, not the princess part." Hawk held it across his palms, shifting closer to the sphere, so she could see it better.

Though made from silver, it reminded her of a branch or maybe finger bones with symmetrical knots or knuckles segmenting it. The purple light played across a dozen different sections, showing numerous tiny symbols engraved in the surface in addition to the one in the bottom. Some she recognized as elven numbers. Were the others letters? She wasn't familiar with their alphabet.

"It's a historically significant artifact," Hawk said, "so I can't outright *give* it to you, but I'd like you to have it for the duration of our mission. You might want to study it. It's possible you can even figure out what it does."

"You don't know?"

"It spins," he offered, turning a few of the sections. "The king's advisor gave it to me to lend to you. It supposedly belonged to Zedaron. He went to the various elven cities, giving lectures, and he left this in what was once one of the remote outposts but is now the largest population center we have left. It's possible it does nothing, that it's merely a baton to rap inattentive students with, but it's magical, and these are all numbers and letters and math symbols in our language, so the advisor believes it has some purpose. She thinks it might even hold the key to evading the booby traps Zedaron placed around his laboratory, or, at the least, provide a hint into his mind and how he thought. Perhaps, by understanding Zedaron, the puzzles he created would be easier to figure out."

"Oh." Aldari took the baton from him, much more intrigued now, whether it had come out of his trousers or not.

Hawk fished in a pocket and drew out a folded paper. "I translated all of the numbers, letters, and symbols that I know for you."

"Thank you. That will be extremely helpful." Aldari smiled broadly at him, ridiculously pleased. The numbers she'd recognized, but the other symbols had been gobbledygook to her.

Her smile seemed to startle Hawk, but he recovered and pressed the paper into her hand. His touch was warm, his fingers brushing hers, and a little shiver went through her. The memory of him shirtless on that cot came to mind, and her cheeks heated. She didn't know why. She didn't feel embarrassed.

"I'm glad." Hawk clasped his hands behind his back. "I hope

it'll mean more to you than it has to those of our people who have studied it."

"How many have studied it?" Aldari eyed the baton, wondering if she could discover something that the king's advisor hadn't been able to. Presumably, an advisor was an experienced and well-educated person. Still, Hawk had implied that his people had lost a lot when they lost their cities, and in the following centuries when they'd been forced to focus on battle. Maybe that included some of their more advanced mathematics.

"Oh, just the advisor and a handful of elves in the king's court, I believe. It was in a trunk, forgotten for a long time. It was only with the rediscovering of the Crystal City that someone remembered it existed."

"All right. I'll try to study it along the way."

"Good." Hawk nodded to her, started to turn back toward the camp, but paused. "There was one other thing I wanted to assure you of." He met her gaze, the purple light glinting in his eyes.

"Yes?"

"I know what your bodyguard said last night, but neither I nor anyone in my party will make a sexual advance on you. You or her. If anyone *does*, tell me immediately. I regret that we had to take these extreme measures to steal you from your people and delay your destiny, but we are not—*I* am not—" his chin came up again, "—a pirate."

That should have been a relief. Why, then, did she feel a twinge of disappointment?

"I didn't think you were," Aldari said, "but thank you."

Hawk bowed to her, then extended a hand toward the camp, inviting her to go first.

A shriek sounded not fifteen feet away, and Aldari couldn't keep from crying out in alarm. She whirled toward the noise and raised the baton.

Hawk lunged in and caught her wrist. "Don't throw it."

"I wasn't going to," she said, though she had been thinking about using it as a *club*.

The dangling orb glowed brighter, purple light flashing outward. It shone across a humanoid creature crouching in the shadows, blue skin stretched taut over a skeletal chin and cheek-bones. Blunt yellowed teeth leered from its open mouth, and its white hair was a tangled mess with twigs sticking out in all directions. Claws protruded from curled fingers, its hands poised, as if to rake them. The creature screeched like a falcon as it pinned them with yellow eyes.

No, it pinned *her*. Those horrible flat yellow eyes bored straight into her soul as hatred and hunger emanated from the creature. A creepy premonition flashed through her, that it wanted to leap on her, claw her to the ground, and tear her to pieces and feast on her flesh.

But the purple light brightened, shining in its eyes and keeping it from advancing. It slashed at the air, snapping its jaws, even as it arched its back, thrusting its chest forward as pain seemed to grip it. It wore torn fabric, the remains of clothing—of a dress—and startlingly human breasts pressed against it. Or... *elven* breasts?

The light flared brighter. The creature shrieked again, then whirled and ran off into the fog. Several long seconds passed before the light softened, the orb returning to its normal glow.

"What was it?" Aldari whispered.

"One of the Twisted." Hawk released her wrist, leaving her shaking.

"They're terrifying."

Hawk had drawn a dagger with his other hand and hesitated before returning it to its sheath. "I could have gone after her. Perhaps I *should* have. She'll tell the others, and they may trouble us on the road back. We can't take the *phyzera* with us. This camp must be protected for other elves out there who may return home."

"Why didn't you?" Aldari had little doubt that the creature had wanted to kill them. Had it been her imagination that it had focused on her in particular? "Are they hard to kill?"

"Yes, and if they cut you, the wounds fester like nothing else. Many have died from them. Others have been turned, those whose magic is strong and can't entirely be cut off by the *ryshar* we use to sublimate our power. But that isn't why I hesitated to go after her." Hawk sighed. "I told you they used to be elves, right?"

"You did." Aldari struggled to imagine it.

"It's hard not to hope, especially now, that some way might be found to turn them back. Even if you don't believe that's possible, it's difficult when you know you're killing what were once your kin. They're hard to identify once they've been Twisted, but if you've ever lost someone, you can't help but wonder..." His eyes were haunted as he gazed in the direction the creature had gone.

"Have you lost anyone close to you?" Aldari asked softly.

"Yes."

"I'm sorry." She hesitated, then stepped closer and hugged him. What comfort her touch might be, she didn't know, but if he'd lost a parent or sibling, she could only imagine how horrible that had been for him. What if he'd been married—married because of love and not something arranged—and had lost his wife? Whether Hawk had volunteered to come kidnap her or he'd been chosen by the king's advisor, she could understand now why he'd agreed to do it.

Her hug seemed to surprise him, but after a moment, he accepted it and rested his chin on her head.

"You're an unusual prisoner," he murmured.

"Well, you gave me a gift, so you're probably an unusual captor too."

"I have little doubt." He chuckled and stroked the back of her head.

The gentle touch sent a tingle through her, and she had the urge to lean against him. When she'd hugged him the day before, after he'd saved her from the pirates, it had been quick and impulsive, and she'd been too relieved to think about it, but now, she noticed the warmth of his body, the hard muscles of his arms, and though he once again wore his leather armor, she remembered the contours of his chest from the night before. She'd kissed him on the neck on the pirate ship, but she barely recalled it, and she wished she'd let her lips linger, inhaling his scent, tasting his skin.

He stepped back, and she released him and scooted away, relieved she hadn't acted on that bizarre impulse. What was she thinking?

A disgusted comment came from the side, and she skittered even farther back. Setvik stood there, close enough to have seen them clearly through the fog.

Hawk must have heard his approach, for he didn't seem surprised. Whatever his lieutenant had said, Hawk merely shrugged and waved in the direction the Twisted had been.

Setvik sneered, pointed at Hawk's crotch, said something curt, and stalked back toward the camp.

"He says the mercenaries are ready to go," Hawk said.

"Are you sure? It sounded... cruder."

"There were embellishments. He also said your bodyguard is looking for you." Hawk bowed to her. "I apologize if I caused her to grow concerned. Protect the artifact, please, and let me know if you learn anything from it."

"I will."

As he led the way back to the camp, her gaze fell to his backside before she pulled it away, chastising herself. This week was already complicated enough. The last thing she needed was to make things worse by falling in love—or lust—with her captor.

16

THE COBBLESTONE ROAD WOUND THROUGH THE DARK FOREST, THE wagon creaking and groaning with each step of the animals pulling it. Not horses but reindeer. *Large* reindeer.

When Aldari had returned to the camp after talking to Hawk, two mercenaries had ridden up, leading more than a dozen of the antlered animals. A team of six had been assembled to pull the wagon that Aldari and Theli rode in with the two injured elves from the tent. The remaining reindeer had been divvied up among the less injured mercenaries, and they were riding bareback on the shaggy creatures. That included Hawk, whom Aldari considered *more* injured, but he must have been too proud to recline in a wagon when others were walking or riding.

On a reindeer as big as a horse, he rode beside them, glancing into the wagon often to check on Aldari, Theli, and the injured elves. Despite his proximity, he hadn't been chatty or offered many of his usual smiles. Maybe he was thinking of the Twisted they'd seen and wondering if it had been someone he'd once known.

"First rule of being a princess," Theli said as the wagon

bumped along, jarring their teeth. "Don't go anywhere without your bodyguard."

"Actually, that's rule thirty-seven," Aldari murmured, absently studying the way the cobblestones had been laid. The pattern was different from those favored in Delantria, but judging by the weathering of the stones, the road was ancient and had held up well over time. "There are many, *many* mandates on etiquette, including how to greet royalty visiting from distant lands, which fork to use first at a meal, and how far to stick your pinky out when you sip from a teacup or wine glass."

"Those rules don't matter out here. I'm superseding them all with the bodyguard one."

"Probably a good idea."

"Damn right, it is."

One of the wagon wheels hit a hole left by a missing cobblestone, and they lurched into each other. Their conveyance had been designed for carrying crates and barrels, not people, as evinced by the lack of benches, cushions, or places of any kind to plant one's backside. Still, it saved them from having to walk, and after all the bruises she'd accumulated, Aldari appreciated that.

The road appeared to be centuries if not millennia old, with thorny vines and branches that hadn't been cut back recently stretching toward them. The fog of the river had faded, but a mist clung around the trees, and the sun hid behind a haze that seemed like it might be perennial.

"I might get out and walk," Theli muttered, pushing herself back up and leaning against the side of the wagon. "It would be gentler on my body." She rubbed her shoulder, a reminder that she'd also taken a beating during the various attacks.

"I might stay where I am and keep figuring this out." Aldari held up the baton and the notes she was scribbling, an attempt to decipher everything on it, using the translations Hawk had given her. Not every symbol on the baton was on his paper, but she believed from what surrounded them that they were less common mathematical symbols. The average mercenary probably didn't solve sines, cosines, and tangents that often.

The only symbol that she couldn't guess what it might be was the one engraved in the bottom, four leaves entwined. Maybe it had been the maker's sign.

"What is that thing, anyway?" Theli asked.

At first, she hadn't commented on it, perhaps assuming Aldari had found it in the wagon. After all, *she'd* found a notebook and a pen when scrounging in a box bolted to the floor. There were also a few of those awful moss bars and some tools in there, but only the notebook had interested Theli. She'd started penning lines in between peering into the forest and checking for threats.

"A gift from Hawk." Aldari smiled.

Theli scowled.

"Technically, he's lending it to me to study. It's a bit of an enigma. Their people don't know what it is, but he says it's magical. Look, see all these interlocking cylinders? They rotate and click into place when the various symbols are lined up in these notches. The symbols are mostly numbers, but there are also letters, which I believe to represent variables, and this is an equals sign here near the top. And down here, that's a plus sign. I'm guessing the other options on that row are subtraction, multiplication, and... I wonder what this is? Maybe a command to raise a number to a higher power?"

"Our captor gave you a puzzle?" Theli asked.

"Yes."

Theli groaned. "How did he know the *one thing* he could give you to make you fall in love with him?"

"That's not going to happen," Aldari hurried to say and glanced at Hawk, well aware that he was close enough to hear them.

Fortunately, his focus remained forward. That didn't mean he hadn't heard, of course.

"And I'm sure that's not what he's trying to do," Aldari added. "If he was, he would have given me flowers. Or jewelry or candies."

"Sure. *That's* what interests you. You don't even wear jewelry. You're a very odd princess."

"Well, you're a very odd bodyguard." Aldari pointed to the notebook in her hands. "I bet you're passing the time by writing song lyrics."

"What else am I supposed to do? Our captors weren't kind enough to let us bring along our reading material. Or—" Theli sniffed her armpit and wrinkled her nose, "—changes of clothing or laundry soap."

"A change of clothing would be nice," Aldari admitted wistfully. She did not sniff her own armpit.

"I'm writing about the lieutenant." Theli lowered her arm and scribbled another stanza, the words *stranger* and *danger* standing out at the ends of the lines.

"Oh? Love sonnets?"

"No, I'm making him the villain in a ballad about prisoners who free themselves from their savage captors. He's going to get mange, fleas, and genital warts, and then die a horrible death."

That prompted Hawk to snort and look over while Aldari wondered what Theli would find to rhyme with *warts*.

"Your choice to make him the villain is surprising," Aldari said, "given that you were admiring his chest last night."

"I most certainly was not."

"You looked longer than necessary when he stripped down in the medic's tent."

"I was assessing his weight and estimating how much force I would have to apply in a hip throw. I assume it's only a matter of time before I have to fight him again."

"I hope that's not true." Aldari didn't deny that Theli was well trained, but the elves were too good for them to best.

Hawk's gaze shifted to the two mercenaries in the back of the wagon, or maybe the blanket they were stretched out on. His shoulders were slumped with weariness, and she'd caught him wincing more than once that morning.

His hand strayed toward his torso, and he shifted uncomfortably on his reindeer. When he caught her looking, he lowered his hand, nodded to her, and faced forward again.

"How far to your people's outpost, Hawk?" Aldari asked, hoping he could rest and get better treatment there. The gruff mercenary medic hadn't filled her with confidence.

"If we're not attacked along the way and delayed, we should make it by tomorrow afternoon."

"Are we likely to be attacked?"

"Unfortunately, it's rare to travel far in Serth without encountering the Twisted." Once more, Hawk touched his side, but he glanced at her and lowered his hand again. Those wounds were definitely bothering him.

"Is Hawk going to be in your ballad, Theli?" Aldari asked, trying to set aside her worry.

"Yes," Theli said. "He's the villain's sidekick."

"I think it's the other way around." Aldari smiled, though she didn't want Hawk to be a villain in Theli's song or anywhere else.

"I'm not so sure about that."

Aldari almost objected, but could she? Setvik deferred to Hawk, but it always seemed grudging, and the mercenaries were more likely to look to the lieutenant for orders. She remembered her hypothesis that Hawk had beaten Setvik in a fight and taken command of the company from him, but was that likely? Setvik had a lot of experience, but he wasn't old enough that age would slow him down. Would Hawk truly have bested him?

While Aldari was mulling that over, two of the mercenaries

rode off into the woods, pulling their bows off their backs as their reindeer surged between the trees. Setvik watched alertly, his hands on his weapons. It took Hawk a moment to shake his head and focus on the riders.

When Aldari peered between the trees, she didn't see anything except moss carpeting the trunks and running over rocks and roots between them. The reindeer hooves kicked up tufts of it as they raced over the earth. As pervasive as the stuff was here, it was no wonder the elves had turned it into a staple.

If not for the threat of attack and the gloomy sky, Aldari might have called the elven forest beautiful. It was lush and green, and they'd passed numerous streams and waterfalls, but even before the riders had taken off, creepy moans and caws had drifted out of the trees. This wasn't a place that Aldari would want to visit alone.

Once the riders were out of view, Hawk called to Setvik in Elven and received a terse reply. A distant cry sounded from the direction they'd gone, that same eerie keen that the Twisted woman had made.

"If we're going to be attacked," Theli said loudly, "perhaps our captors would see fit to return our weapons."

Aldari nodded in agreement. Someone had brought Hawk's backpack—with their weapons strapped to it—from the ferry, and he was wearing it again. Aldari doubted either dagger or mace would help against the Twisted, but she would prefer having more than the baton to defend herself with. At least the elves hadn't bound their wrists since they'd left Delantria.

Hawk, his gaze toward the forest and his pointed ears cocked, didn't respond to the comment.

After twenty or thirty minutes, the two riders returned and reported in to Setvik. Hawk wiped sweat from his brow and rode forward to join them.

"Does he look sick to you?" Aldari whispered.

Theli shrugged. "I don't spend as much time looking at him as you do."

"How are you going to describe him for your song if you don't study him?"

"You describe villains by their personalities, not their looks." Theli nibbled on the tip of her pen. "What's a word that rhymes with *odious*?"

Aldari shrugged. "Commodious? Acanthopodious?"

"What does *that* mean?"

"Having spiny petioles. I don't think that describes any of the elves though."

"Let's hope not. How do you even know that word? I can't believe it has anything to do with economics."

"Not unless you sell plants, no, but my sister gardens and paints flowers—far more appropriate activities for a princess than economics, or so Father assures us. She knows all about plant anatomy."

"Scintillating stuff."

"*She* thinks so."

While Theli chewed on the pen and muttered more rhyme-friendly alternatives to *odious*, Aldari made herself return to the puzzle of the baton.

There was no way to draw the translations of the tiny numbers and symbols *on* it, so she took some of Theli's paper and painstakingly sketched two-dimensional versions of each segment and its contents. That gave her a dozen rectangles with numbers, letters, and mathematical symbols on them. There was no way to make them rotate on the paper, but she twisted the sections as she mulled, wondering if something would happen if she got what the baton considered the *right* combination. Would it unlock? Revealing something inside?

After a few more twists, a soft *bong* came from the baton, and red light shone out of the end. Aldari almost dropped it. Then she hurried to point it carefully upward, afraid she had turned on a weapon that would shoot out a beam and harm someone.

But the red light only formed a symbol in the air beyond the tip of the baton.

"What's that mean?" Theli's attention had been drawn by the *bong*.

"Ah." Aldari scanned the paper Hawk had given her but didn't see the symbol. "Good question. Hawk?" she called.

The scouts had finished reporting, and Hawk was slumped on his mount with his chin to his chest, but he looked back and slowed his reindeer until the wagon caught up. Right away, he noticed the red symbol floating in the air.

"Do you know what this is?" Aldari asked.

"It's a question mark."

"An elven question mark?" It looked nothing like the one in Aldari's alphabet, but that wasn't surprising.

"Yes."

"Have you seen the baton do this before?"

"No, but I didn't spend a lot of time twisting it around. The king's advisor said it was a tool for academics, not boys who skipped classes in favor of learning how better to fight." Hawk smiled but only briefly, and he lifted a hand to wipe his damp brow again.

"So, it's waiting for something?" Theli asked. "Some kind of input?"

"That could be it." Aldari eyed the symbols that she'd lined up on the baton to cause the effect. There were a lot of blanks and only a couple of letters—variables—and an equals sign. "Can you speak two numbers in your language, Hawk?" she asked, uncertain of her own pronunciation.

"Random numbers?" he asked.

"A larger number and a smaller number." Aldari had a hunch that twisting the segments allowed her to make different equations. Equations for what, she didn't know, but they were what came to mind with the presence of the equals sign. And in the current incarnation, whatever equation the baton was offering was simple, with only two variables and a division sign. Unfortunately, having translations of the elven letters didn't tell her what the variables represented. She would need one of their algebra books, or at least a comprehensive list of formulas.

Hawk spoke in Elven, then offered the translation. "Seventy and ten."

Another number floated into the air.

"That's seven, isn't it?" Aldari double-checked the translation sheet. "Yes," she said at the same time as Hawk nodded.

Assuming the equation had some significance, she dredged up memories of her mathematics studies. After a moment, she snapped her fingers. "Speed."

"Pardon?" Hawk asked.

"That's the formula for calculating speed. Distance over time. Give it some larger, more complicated numbers, please."

"Seven thousand forty and eighty-three."

A number appeared in the air, calculated to ten decimal places.

"Eighty-four-point-eight?" Aldari asked, doing the math in her head.

Hawk nodded, reading the answer out of the air. "Eighty-four-point-eight-one-nine-two and so on."

"So, the baton does calculations. A magical elven version of a slide rule. Though it having all these formulas integrated into it is different. It's not just listing them though. You have to know what you're looking for and spin the segments around until an equation is lined up. I'm... not quite sure what the point is. If you already know the equation, you could do the math yourself." Aldari bent over the baton, trying to think of other equations she knew. Were these all related to engineering and physics? If so, she didn't have many of those memorized. "Oh, hah."

She twisted several segments on the baton, and the question mark appeared again. She said four numbers, but it didn't respond to her language, so she nodded at Hawk to translate.

He dutifully repeated them in Elven, and a new number appeared in the air.

"The answer should be... eighty-thousand four-hundred and six," she said, needing a moment to think through the more complicated equation.

"Yes." Hawk lifted his eyebrows. "What did we just calculate?"

"Compound interest after twenty years." Aldari bent over the baton and found she could make all manner of equations related to finance. "Would anyone like to amortize a loan today?"

"No," Theli said, going back to her ballad.

"I'm puzzled." Hawk scratched his head.

"About how this could get us into a mad scientist's laboratory?" Aldari asked. "Me too. But you just said it belonged to him, right? Not that it opened his secret door."

"That is true. It could be a teaching aid that happened to belong to him and nothing more." Hawk lowered his arm, disappointment flashing in his eyes.

"I'll keep tinkering with it. Maybe there's more. Or maybe, as you said, it offers some insight into how his mind worked." Aldari lowered the baton and waved toward the other mercenaries. Though the riders had returned, they still had their bows out, arrows nocked as they watched the forest as their party continued along the road. "Is there going to be trouble?"

"At some point, likely." Hawk reached out to grip the side of the wagon. "The Twisted might wait until tonight though."

Hawk blinked a few times, as if he were trying to focus.

"Are you all right?" Aldari scooted closer and reached out to rest her hand on his forehead. Heat radiated from his flushed skin. "You have a fever. Your wounds could be infected."

Could be? Or definitely *were*?

Hawk released the wagon and drew back from her. "I'll be fine. The healing potion just needs more time to work."

The reindeer he rode shifted to step over a pothole. It was only a slight movement, but it caused Hawk to lurch sideways. A gasp escaped his lips as he tumbled off the reindeer.

"Hawk!" Aldari blurted.

Though he managed to land on his feet, the startled reindeer running ahead without him, it was only a moment before he crumpled to one knee.

"Medic Mevleth!" Aldari called to the mercenaries. "Your captain needs help."

It was Setvik who looked back, but he spotted Hawk wobbling, the wagon moving past him. Setvik called something in Elven, and the medic, who'd been on foot, jogged back. Unfortunately, Setvik jogged back too.

"Cover your page," Aldari whispered, afraid the elves would see Theli's lines about a heinous death for the mange-afflicted Setvik-villain in her song.

The medic went straight to Hawk's side, but Setvik matched the pace of the wagon and glared up at Aldari.

"What did you do to him?" he demanded.

"Nothing." Aldari left the baton in her lap and lifted her hands. "What could we do? And why would we do it? He's—"

"Your *kidnapper*," Setvik snarled, "and you have been trying to escape since the beginning."

Aldari clamped down on her desire to point out that Hawk was a much better option than Setvik and not whom she would attack if she could. "We didn't do anything," was all she said.

Setvik was tall enough to see into the wagon, and he scowled not at Theli's lyrics but at Aldari's lap. "What is that?"

Before she could reply, he reached in and snatched the baton, his hand too fast for her to stop. He ordered the driver to halt the wagon.

"An elven artifact that Hawk lent me to study," Aldari said as Setvik only glanced at it before returning his glare to her.

"It's magical. What does it do? Is it a *weapon*?"

"Not unless you're trying to very aggressively compound your interest."

His forehead furrowed, and he spoke to the medic in their language. A question. Had Hawk been attacked?

Aldari shook her head, willing Hawk to explain that his wounds were bothering him.

But Hawk crumpled to the ground and passed out in the road.

Aldari exchanged a long look of concern with Theli, worried both about Hawk and about what would happen to them now.

17

ALDARI SAT SHOULDER TO SHOULDER WITH THELI, THEIR BACKS TO the front of the wagon as Medic Mevleth finished examining and applying fresh bandages to Hawk's wounds. The other two injured mercenaries, who'd been deemed healthy enough to walk, had been evicted from the wagon to make room for the new patient.

Setvik stood in the wagon with his forearms crossed, scowling as he watched and snapped at the medic. He wasn't letting Aldari and Theli out of his sight, but he'd stopped accusing them of doing something to Hawk. It was, Aldari hoped, clear that Hawk's wounds were infected, he was fevered, and his injuries were what plagued him, not any plot they could have enacted.

As the two elves spoke, Hawk stirred, mumbling something. Mevleth helped him drink from a canteen and produced the bottle of green liquid again.

Hawk's glazed eyes opened, and he focused on Aldari as he drank.

"Get better, please," she said. "Your lieutenant thinks we poisoned you and used the magic of the baton on you."

Setvik glared at her, maybe thinking he should have gagged her.

"I don't think *poison* is my problem." Hawk waved at his fresh bandages. "Unless the serpent's teeth were dripping with cyanide."

"Tetrodotoxin would be more likely in a sea creature," Theli said.

Mevleth and Setvik frowned suspiciously at her.

"She reads a lot of murder mysteries," Aldari said, hoping Theli hadn't just incriminated them—*further*—with her knowledge of poisons.

"It's true," Theli said.

Hawk only smiled, not looking like he thought they were to blame, but his pale face and the sweat beading on his forehead worried Aldari.

Mevleth pointed a finger at his nose and delivered what sounded like a lecture. Aldari didn't like him. He was too brusque. Someone should have been sponging Hawk and stroking his head, not lecturing him, but she couldn't envision any of the gruff mercenaries volunteering to give sponge baths.

Hawk flicked his fingers as he replied, not fazed by the stern words.

"Will you be all right?" Aldari asked. "What did he say?"

"That the germs on river-serpent teeth are horrendous and that I shouldn't have let it chomp on me. I asked him why I hadn't thought of that. He didn't appreciate my sarcasm." The short speech must have tired Hawk, for he closed his eyes and took several deep breaths.

Mevleth said something to Setvik, pointed at Aldari, then climbed out of the wagon with his bag.

Setvik turned his glare back on Aldari. A bead of sweat trickled from Hawk's temple, and his eyes remained closed.

"Will he be all right?" Aldari asked Setvik, since the medic was walking away and she had nobody else to ask. Hawk hadn't answered her question.

"There are more experienced healers and stronger medicines at the outpost." Setvik nudged a canteen with his boot. "Our mercenary medic thinks I should have you tend Hawk and earn your keep. *I'm* not convinced you weren't somehow responsible."

"I can take care of him and ramble all about my hypotheses on the baton to him. And about economics and what I'd like to see for the future of my kingdom. My lectures often put people into a gentle relaxed sleep."

"No kidding," Theli muttered.

Setvik handed the canteen to Aldari. "We could be attacked at any time. I need to be out there with my weapons ready."

He hopped down from the wagon and swung up onto a reindeer, taking his bow in hand. A few of his mercenaries asked him questions amid a lot of concerned glances toward Hawk.

That relieved Aldari a little. She was glad to know the mercenaries cared what happened to Hawk.

"If he dies," Theli whispered, "his lieutenant is going to try to blame us."

"How could anyone logically think we were responsible?" Aldari crawled to Hawk's side with the canteen and touched his forehead again. She'd hoped Mevleth's treatment might bring down the fever, but he was hotter than ever.

"That idiot isn't logical." Theli glared at Setvik's back.

A screech came from the forest. The same two scouts as before went thundering off to check on it.

Hawk muttered something in Elven. His eyes opened enough for him to focus on Aldari, and he switched to her language. "Need my weapons."

"You're too sick to fight."

"My duty is to defend you and bring you to the outpost. I promised my... I promised the king's advisor."

"If we get attacked right now, we'll have to defend *you*."

"I'm not that weak." Hawk tried to sit up.

Aldari scowled at him, but because he was distressed, she pulled his weapons belt over to him. Mevleth had tossed it in the corner of the wagon when he and Setvik had lifted Hawk inside. Aldari wrapped his hand around the hilt of his sword.

Some of the tension ebbed from Hawk's body, and he let Aldari press him down to his back.

"That's not one of the recommended bodyguard positions," Theli said.

"Ssh." Aldari touched Hawk's flushed cheek. "Do you want some more water?"

His mumbled reply came in his language, but when she tipped the canteen toward his lips and held his head up, he did take a few swallows.

Two mercenaries on foot trotted back to walk beside the wagon and peer in. They spoke rapidly in Elven, hopefully not accusing her of doing anything. Aldari held the canteen up and nodded to them. After a moment's hesitation, they nodded back and jogged off into the woods on the other side of the road.

The constant checking of their surroundings by the mercenaries made Aldari uneasy. Hawk had believed it was only a matter of time until they were attacked, and she suspected they all thought the same.

But mercenaries came and went all morning, sometimes rapidly, as if they were sure there would be trouble, and sometimes, they simply seemed to be checking on things. The birds that chattered from the branches had calls unfamiliar to Aldari, but the fact that they were making noise seemed to imply they didn't feel anything threatening was around.

After lunch—moss bars tossed into the wagon for them— Setvik came back to walk beside them.

"Is he awake?" he asked.

"No," Aldari said.

"Yes," Hawk said without opening his eyes. "I'm guarding the princess."

Setvik eyed the hilt of his sword, still in Hawk's sweaty palm, though Hawk lay completely flat. "Clearly."

"She appreciates my assiduous attention to my duty."

"Uh huh. I came to ask if you want me to *mysandral esvue* if you don't think you're going to make it."

To what? Aldari frowned at Setvik, wondering why he'd switched to his language in the middle of the sentence. Maybe whatever it was had no translation.

Hawk, eyes now open, gazed up at the sky. Since he was still fevered and out of it, Aldari couldn't tell if he was contemplating a response or had drifted off with his eyes open.

"You hear me, kid?" Setvik asked before switching languages again.

"Yes," Hawk rasped. "I'd rather *she* do it." He pointed at Aldari.

That resulted in a chain of curt angry words in Elven, accompanied by clenched fists. "*She* is not one of us," Setvik finished in her tongue.

"Wait," Hawk said. "We aren't far from the outpost. If it comes to that, it is the duty of my father."

"You may not make it that long."

Hawk lifted his chin inasmuch as he could while he was lying down. "I *will* make it. Find my pack, and return their weapons, Setvik."

Setvik's brows rose. "You truly wish her to do it?"

"Uhm." Aldari raised a finger. "Do what?"

"I wish them to be armed so they can protect themselves if we're attacked. She must make it to the outpost. And beyond. She is... hope for our people." Hawk's voice lowered to a whisper. "We need hope. We need a future that's better than the past."

Setvik grunted. "You don't have to tell me that."

He turned to stride away, but Hawk called after him. "Their weapons."

Shaking his head, Setvik snapped something to one of his men. Though the mercenary glanced back in surprise, he hurried to a reindeer that held packs. He untied Theli's mace and Aldari's dagger.

More worried than ever, Aldari rested a hand on Hawk's chest. "What did he say to you? What's *mysandral esvue*?" she asked, enunciating the words carefully.

"It is when the end grows near," Hawk said, "and a family member or ally cuts your throat so you don't die to an enemy blade or illness. I don't think your people have a term for it."

Horrified, Aldari drew back. She could understand wanting a quick death, but the idea of Setvik doing it... The bastard would probably slit Hawk's throat with glee.

"I'll crack him in the head with the baton if he tries to cut your throat," she said.

A clunk sounded as the mercenary threw the mace inside.

"Or shove it somewhere deeper while Theli smacks him with her weapon," Aldari said.

Hawk rested his hand on hers, the fevered heat from his skin noticeable, and turned his head to gaze into her eyes. "You've only known me for three days."

"Is that all? It's been so torturous that it's felt like three years."

"And yet you want to protect me?" He managed a weak smile.

"Well, I told you why."

"So Setvik won't be in charge of your fate?"

"Yes. And because... you're not entirely loathsome. For a kidnapper."

Theli groaned. "I knew it. Give the girl a puzzle, and she falls in love."

"I'm not in love," Aldari snapped.

As much as she liked Theli—they'd been through a lot

together over the years—Aldari didn't appreciate the ongoing comments on that matter. Just because she'd ended up on a detour didn't mean she didn't intend to eventually get to Orath and marry Prince Xerik. And when she did, she didn't need any insinuations reaching his ears that she'd been anything but loyal to him. There was far too much at stake.

Hawk's hand slid to the side, his eyelids drooping.

A screech sounded, and Aldari tensed, expecting an attack at any moment. But one of the elves called out without concern and pointed overhead. A perfectly normal falcon was winging toward them. At least Aldari *thought* it was normal. The fact that it dove from the sky and flew unerringly toward the wagon made her uneasy.

Theli picked up her mace, and Aldari tightened her grip around the baton.

The large brown bird spread its wings and alighted on the front of the wagon, talons biting into the wooden side. The driver glanced back, not appearing surprised.

With a squawk, the falcon lifted its leg, drawing attention to a message tube tied to it.

"Are we supposed to…" Aldari waved uncertainly at the leg.

The falcon's yellow-ringed brown eyes were locked on Hawk, but he was too out of it to know it was there.

The wagon stopped as Setvik trotted back, muttering soothing words—inasmuch as his gruff voice could manage to soothe—as he approached the falcon. It screeched, but it didn't fly away. Instead, it lifted its leg again so Setvik could untie the twine attaching the message tube to it.

Aldari supposed it was silly to hope the falcon would peck him in the head with its beak. Repeatedly.

Setvik opened the tube, pulled out a small rolled-up piece of paper, and read.

"Hawk," he said, "wake up. This is for you."

Though Hawk's eyelashes flickered, he didn't otherwise stir.

Setvik swore. "What am *I* supposed to write in response?"

"If you need help composing a tale," Aldari said, "my body-guard is an aspiring songwriter."

That inspired a glare from Theli. Good. After her love comment, she deserved to be teased.

"Give me your pen." Setvik scowled at Theli's hand and glanced at the box in the back, probably irked that she'd dared open it to take out a writing implement. "*Our* pen."

Judging by Theli's bared teeth, she wanted to stab him with it, but she handed it to him without comment.

Setvik raised the pen to write but paused. An exasperated—or was that *consternated*?—expression spread across his face as he considered the back of the paper. It was blank and presumably where he was supposed to fill in a brief report.

The falcon waited, though it shifted from foot to foot. Did birds get impatient?

"Writer's block," Theli whispered to Aldari.

"Maybe he's trying to think of something to rhyme with *odious*," Aldari whispered back. "Who sent the falcon, Lieutenant?"

"It's the king's falcon, and I think this is his wife's writing. She wants an update on the mission." Setvik glanced at Hawk, then switched languages to complain. A minute ago, he'd been offering to cut his captain's throat. Now, he seemed annoyed that Hawk wasn't well enough to write the message himself.

If the king and queen cared about the mission—and about Hawk's fate—would they send people to help? Maybe a doctor with more skills than the mercenary medic? Or stronger potions?

"Do you want me to write it?" Aldari offered. "I could easily fill in that little paper just letting him know that I'm not pleased he ordered me kidnapped two weeks before my wedding."

"*He* didn't order it," Setvik snapped, anger replacing his exasperation. "This was all *his* idea." He thrust a hand toward Hawk. "Captain Hawk. A mercenary working of his own accord."

"If he's working of his own accord, how come the queen is checking up on him?" Aldari asked.

Setvik snarled like a wolf. "You ask too many questions, Princess."

He dropped the pen and paper and ran up to talk to the medic. Asking for an update on Hawk's condition? Or asking *him* to fill out the note?

Or... what if he was asking if Hawk would die before they reached the outpost and the king and queen? What if Setvik *wanted* that? And didn't plan to mention Hawk's illness at all in the message? After all, he'd been volunteering to slit Hawk's throat. It was early for such drastic action, wasn't it?

Aldari eyed the paper and Setvik. His back was to them. What if she filled out the note before he returned, telling the royals how badly Hawk was injured and that he needed help?

"What are you doing?" Theli whispered as Aldari grabbed the pen and paper.

"Introducing myself to the elven king and queen. And telling them we need help." Unfortunately, there wasn't room for much on the small piece of paper. Did the queen know how to read Hyric? The mercenaries understood and spoke it decently, but that might be because they often worked in the human kingdoms.

"Better hurry," Theli whispered. "One of the scouts is return- ing, and it looks like those two are wrapping up their conversation."

Damn it. There wasn't time or space for introductions.

Aldari wrote that Hawk was dying and needed help immedi- ately, then, inspired by the baton resting next to her, and worried that nobody in the king's court would understand her language, she wrote one of the engineering formulas from the baton. Hawk had said the king's advisor knew about the artifact, right? Even if she didn't speak any human languages, she ought to be able to guess that a critical-load formula hinted at something about to break.

Her gut rumbled as she wrote, the stress of the situation—or maybe the moss bars—not sitting well with her. She missed her quiet days nestled in her room in the castle, reading books and mulling over papers.

Aldari finished writing, rolled up the note, and stuffed it in the tube.

"He's coming back," Theli whispered.

Trying not to alarm the falcon, Aldari scooted closer to it as quickly as she dared. It had been watching Hawk, but its gaze shifted to give her a baleful glare. She might be the one who ended up getting pecked in the head by that sharp beak. But when she raised her hands with the tube, the falcon merely lifted its leg, trained for exactly this duty.

"What are you doing?" Setvik broke into a run.

As soon as Aldari tied the tube, she leaned back and waved her arms. The falcon sprang from its perch, wings almost smacking Setvik in the face.

She worried he would try to snatch it out of the air or even attack it, but when Setvik lunged into the wagon, it was to grab Aldari. With her mace in hand, Theli leaned in to place herself between them. If not for her, Setvik might have wrapped his hand around Aldari's *neck*. As it was, he still got her arm.

"What did you *do*?" he snarled, barely paying attention to Theli, though she raised her mace and was poised to club him.

Aldari's heart hammered against her ribs, but she did her best to stay calm. "I sent the message for you. It was clear you were struggling."

"Because I'm a lowly mercenary, and it's not appropriate for me to write directly to the royal family. It's *definitely* not appropriate for you."

"Certainly it is. I'm a princess. I communicate with royalty all the time." Her father, sister, and brother mostly, but she did have that pen pal in the Razgizar Kingdom.

Setvik's grip tightened painfully. "What did you write to them?"

"Let her go," Theli snarled, then swung her mace at his head.

Without releasing Aldari, Setvik caught her wrist, halting the swing in midair. It hadn't been a slow or inept swing, but it didn't matter. The elf was too fast.

"*What did you write?*" Setvik repeated, his voice a snarl.

"That Hawk is injured and needs help."

Setvik squinted at her. Did he not believe her? Or was it that he *did* believe her, and that wasn't the message he'd wanted to send?

"Let her go," Hawk rasped.

Setvik looked down. His captain still lay on his back, but his bloodshot eyes were open, and he'd lifted his sword. The tip rested against Setvik's thigh. Hawk might have wanted a more deadly spot, but that was all he could reach.

"Did you see what she wrote?" Setvik demanded.

"I did not, but I trust it wasn't anything detrimental to our mission. She cares about us."

"She *cares* about us? You're delusional as well as fevered. She's our *prisoner*. It hasn't even been a full day since the last time she tried to escape. She'd kill us all if she could."

Aldari shook her head as Hawk said, "She would not. Let her go."

"You're a *fool,* Captain. You're letting your penis dictate your actions."

"Trust me," Hawk rasped. "My penis is sublimely uninterested in anything right now. I'm so dehydrated, I haven't even pissed since dawn."

He pushed himself up onto his elbow so he could raise the tip of his sword toward a more menacing target. Setvik's gut. Setvik didn't appear concerned in the least, even when Theli managed to wrest her mace free from him. She shifted her weight—readying for another attack.

Aldari held up a hand toward her.

"Get out of the wagon, Setvik," Hawk said. "I need to rest, and you're interrupting my nap."

"You can nap all you want when you're dead."

Setvik looked at Aldari, his eyes boring into hers. She was the only one without a weapon pointed at him, and yet, she was the only one he was concerned about.

Jaw clenched, she made herself hold his gaze. Though it was taking all of his effort, Hawk kept his sword raised toward Setvik.

"She's your responsibility," Setvik finally said, curling his lip at Hawk.

"Yes," he agreed.

Setvik sprang backward out of the wagon, landing lightly on his feet. Shaking his head in disgust, he strode back into the lead.

The tension drained from Aldari, and she sagged against the side of the wagon. She knew they weren't safe, but at least Setvik hadn't wrung her neck. And maybe her message would make a difference.

"I miss battling foes I'm good enough to defeat." Theli shook her mace. "Next time you want to get kidnapped, please entice common cutthroats."

"Is it delusional for me to hope there won't be a next time?" Aldari was more worried about surviving *this time*.

As soon as Setvik had left the wagon, Hawk had let his sword clunk back down and dropped his head back.

Aldari crawled to his side again and picked up the canteen. "Do you want some more water? It might help with one of your concerns."

"That I haven't urinated all day?" Hawk rasped, his eyes closed again.

"You seemed grumpy about it."

"I'm grumpy that Setvik's main purpose in life is to irritate me."

"I'm not pleased about that either." Aldari lifted the canteen to his lips, holding his head again to help him drink. "I really did ask for help in the note. Is that all right? I wasn't sure... I thought maybe Setvik wanted to see you dead and wouldn't mention how poorly you're doing."

Hawk sighed. "I'm sure he just wants me out of his life."

"Yes, and your death would be one way to accomplish that."

"One that would result in a lot of questions for him."

"What do you mean?" Aldari wiped Hawk's mouth, laid his head back, and capped the canteen.

"Nothing. I didn't want to let anyone see that I was weak, but this isn't so bad. You're a good nurse for a princess."

"Am I? I haven't had a lot of practice."

"It doesn't show." Hawk took her hand, rested it on his chest, then let his arm droop and his eyes close.

"The lieutenant is glaring back at you," Theli said.

"I think it's his new hobby," Aldari said.

"What did you really write in the note?"

"Just what I said."

"I thought you might have been sending our status and location to your father."

"I don't believe that falcons trained by kings to loyally deliver messages can be diverted to other kingdoms."

"Too bad." Theli drew her knees up, wrapped her arms around them, and rested her forehead on them. "I'm ready to go home."

Aldari eyed the baton. What did it say about her that she wasn't?

18

As twilight descended on the forest, Hawk's breathing grew labored. It had been more than an hour since he'd spoken or even opened his eyes. Aldari sat at his side in the wagon, worrying.

A couple of times, the medic had come back to check on him, but his face had been grim. Tears pricked at Aldari's eyes. She didn't know how she'd come to care about Hawk in such a short time, but she had.

Her gut grumbled, and she rested a hand on it, sighing. Already, she'd had to climb out of the wagon several times to visit the trees. Her desire for privacy had wrestled with her fear of being snatched up by enemies if she got too far away from the mercenaries. She hoped that whatever bug was assailing her would pass before full darkness came.

Grunts drifted back to the wagon. The reindeer. They were looking left and right, their dark eyes huge. Their breathing grew heavier, and the ones pulling the wagon tried to pick up the pace. Wheels rattled over cobblestones, and the driver struggled to keep them from breaking into a run. The reindeer sensed something.

All day, the mercenaries had been riding off to check the woods, but a battle had never broken out. Until now?

Uneasy, Aldari patted around and found her dagger and the baton. Next to her, Theli sat cross-legged, her mace in her lap.

One of the reindeer in the lead bucked, trying to throw its rider. The mercenary leaped down of his own accord, landing with his weapons in his hands.

"Aldari." Theli pointed into the deepening gloom between the trees.

In the distance, two yellow dots gleamed. Eyes.

"The Twisted," Aldari breathed, though she couldn't know for sure.

The mercenaries murmured quietly among themselves, pointing into the woods and at the road ahead. They seemed to be debating if they should continue through the night and try to outpace their enemies or stop and make a stand.

One of the inhuman screeches they'd heard off and on all day erupted from the trees, much closer than any of the others had been. More sets of yellow eyes appeared.

Theli rose to her feet and hefted her mace. Also rising, Aldari gripped the dagger and baton tightly. The latter would make a poor weapon, but Hawk had told her not to lose it, and she didn't want to let it out of her sight.

As she moved to stand beside Theli, she bumped something with her boot. Hawk's sword. His grip had loosened as he'd slept—or fallen unconscious—but he'd never put it away.

"His sword would be a better weapon than your dagger," Theli said. "It would give you more reach."

Aldari nodded, remembering Hawk's words about how a bite or a scratch from the Twisted could turn a person into one of them. Still, she hesitated to take his sword from him. Not only would Setvik have a fit, but if Hawk woke up and wanted to help them, he would need it.

More screeches sounded, this time from both sides of the road. Two blue-skinned Twisted darted into view behind the wagon, one baring clawed fingers and the other carrying a huge two-headed axe in its—*his*—hands.

Somehow, Aldari hadn't envisioned them with weapons. They might be in more trouble than the elves had let on.

The rest of the mounted mercenaries sprang off their reindeer, and the driver unhitched the team pulling the wagon—afraid the terrified animals would drag it into the woods otherwise?

The reindeer, eyes wide, sprang away as soon as they were permitted and raced into the forest. The skittish creatures must not have been trained to be ridden into combat.

The Twisted didn't go after them. Their focus remained on the elves—and Aldari and Theli. More appeared from behind the trees and shambled toward the wagon.

Setvik barked orders, and some of the mercenaries charged out to meet the threat. Others circled the wagon to defend it. That was a relief, but Aldari still didn't know if Setvik truly wanted her and Hawk to live—or how far he would risk his mercenaries to protect them.

Aldari reached down, patted Hawk on the chest, and said, "I need to borrow this."

He didn't stir as she loosened his grip further and pulled the sword free.

The big weapon was heavier than others she'd practiced with back home, so she had to set aside dagger and baton and grip the hilt with both hands. More screeches sounded, followed by the clangs of steel.

To the side of the road, the first skirmish had started, two mercenaries battling three Twisted. Three more Twisted charged in from the opposite side of the road, and another pair of mercenaries ran out to intercept them.

In the deepening twilight, Aldari struggled to follow the battle, but she grew aware of more and more shadowy figures gathering between the trees. More and more pairs of yellow eyes. She had a feeling the Twisted had been watching their progress all day, gathering forces. Waiting for an opportunity to strike.

A fight broke out behind the wagon, one of the mercenaries springing to defend against the axeman and his buddy.

Two of the Twisted broke away from the mercenaries fighting to the side of the road and ran toward the wagon. Both blue-skinned creatures were looking right at Aldari.

When Hawk had spoken about them being drawn by magic, had that included magical artifacts? Such as the baton she'd tucked into her belt? Maybe that had been a mistake.

"They're coming for us." Aldari raised the sword, her heartbeat thundering against her eardrums.

"I see them," Theli snarled. "Stand shoulder to shoulder, and don't let them get up here, or we're dead."

"Make sure to keep an eye on Hawk. They could be after *him* and not us."

"They can have him."

"No." Aldari tightened her grip on the sword. "They can't."

An arrow thudded into one of the Twisted running for the wagon, lodging in its shoulder. That didn't stop its advance. The pair of Twisted reached the wagon together and started up the side.

Theli lunged at them, bringing her mace down on one white-haired head. It thudded into the Twisted's skull with what sounded like bone-crushing force, but their foe didn't pause. It hissed at her, gripping the wagon with one hand and slashing at her with the other. She jumped back, barely avoiding its long claws.

Though terrified, Aldari made herself step in and thrust toward the chest of the second Twisted. Her enemy saw her attack coming and jerked a stiff arm up. Not intimidated by the sharp edge, the Twisted knocked the blade from its path. The tip whispered past its cheek, cutting a tuft of wild white hair, but nothing more deadly.

Cursing, Aldari shifted her stance and slashed back toward her opponent's head. She *had* to keep the creature from climbing into the wagon. But it ducked, proving more agile than she would have expected.

Next to her, Theli kicked with her boot, taking her foe in the face. That blow would have sent a man tumbling away from the wagon, but the sturdy Twisted hung on. Its head snapped back, but if that hurt it in any way, it didn't show it. It hissed at her and lifted a leg to climb inside with them.

Fear lent speed to Aldari's arms, and she tried a more complicated attack on her foe, feinting twice for its head and chest. It paused its climb to block the blows, but she hadn't fully committed, and it hit only air. She shifted her grip and lifted the sword high overhead, like a logger's axe. It left her torso exposed, but the Twisted was too wary of the elven sword to ignore it. It looked up, raising an arm to deflect the overhead blow.

Instead of bringing the sword down, Aldari kicked the Twisted in the chest, throwing her entire body behind the blow. Maybe because her enemy was focused on the sword, its grip on the wagon wasn't as firm as the other's had been, and the kick knocked it backward. It hit the cobblestones and rolled to the side of the road.

For a moment, Aldari didn't have an opponent. She spun to help Theli with hers as Theli leaped over another swipe from the Twisted's claws and brought her mace down again. This time, she struck the creature in the face instead of on top of the head, slamming the blunt weapon into its eye.

That stunned it, and it paused in its climb. Aldari swung the sword toward the side of its neck, hoping to behead it and put it out of action—permanently.

The sword cut in, but it was like slicing into a tree, not flesh and blood. The blade sank in only two inches and lodged there. Screeching, the Twisted reached up and gripped it.

Aldari stepped back, trying to tug the sword free, but it was as if she'd caught it in a vise. Theli kicked the Twisted in the face, then planted her heel in its chest.

"Get *out* of our wagon," she snarled, thrusting.

When the Twisted fell back, it almost took the sword with it. Palm sweating, the hilt slipped in Aldari's hand, but she clamped down, refusing to let it have Hawk's weapon.

A horn sounded from somewhere up the road. One of the mercenaries? Or was that the pack of Twisted calling more reinforcements?

The one that Aldari had kicked sprang back onto the side of the wagon. Swearing, she stabbed at it with the sword again.

As it jerked an arm up to knock the attack aside, an arrow whizzed in from behind the wagon. It lodged into the Twisted's ear, and it shrieked, the awful noise rattling Aldari. The creature paused, reaching up to pull out the shaft.

Aldari took advantage and slammed the blade down on the top of its head. It crunched into the Twisted's skull. Theli sprang in, smacking it in the face with the mace.

The trio of blows were enough to knock the Twisted back, and it landed flat on the cobblestone road.

Panting, Aldari dashed sweat from her eyes. For the moment, no more Twisted were trying to climb into the wagon. The mercenaries had downed a few—beheading them seemed to be the main way to stop them permanently—and the reinforcements in the trees had paused instead of rushing in to help.

The horn blared again, closer this time. Aldari wrapped both hands around the sword hilt and stepped back to straddle Hawk protectively.

Hoofbeats thundered on the cobblestone road. Confused,

Aldari squinted into the gloom. The loosed reindeer hadn't been called back by the horn, had they?

No, she realized as she spotted lights. Dozens and dozens of lanterns bobbed in the night as those holding them raced forward on reindeer mounts. Armor and weapons jangled, and the shouts of men—of elves—rang out.

"Reinforcements," Aldari blurted, hoping she was right.

By the lantern lights, she glimpsed pointed elven ears and grim-faced male and female riders. They charged in, surrounding the wagon and the mercenaries, then springing into battle at their sides.

Whatever drove the Twisted wasn't enough to make them suicidal. Once they realized they were outnumbered, they abandoned the fight and drifted back into the trees.

Neither the mercenaries nor approaching elves went after them, and Aldari remembered what the Twisted were—and why the elves weren't eager to mow down every last one.

Once the threat was past, the newcomers recovered the reindeer that had run off while a stern-faced elf with aloof storm-gray eyes and long blond hair headed toward the wagon. Two older warriors flanked him. Bodyguards?

In green and brown clothing, with only his armor appearing of exceptional quality, the elf was dressed little differently than the others, but when he gave orders, people hurried to obey. Perhaps in his mid-twenties, he was younger than most of the other elves, but everyone deferred to him, bowing their heads as he passed. Was this some relative of the king? A son or cousin who'd been sent in response to the falcon's note?

As he approached, he held Aldari's gaze for a long moment, but there was an alienness to his expression that made it hard to read, much different from the affable Hawk or even the scowling Setvik.

As he came alongside the wagon, he stopped his reindeer so

he could peer in at Hawk. His face grew even sterner, and he called Setvik over. The lieutenant dropped to one knee and bowed his head before standing and engaging the newcomer.

Definitely a royal, Aldari decided, having a hard time imagining Setvik dropping to a knee for anyone of less societal importance.

Words sailed back and forth, and the medic was called over for consultation. Once more, Aldari wished she understood their language.

Beside her, Theli still had her mace and appeared ready to protect Aldari from the new elves as well as further threats from the Twisted. Aldari hoped that wouldn't be necessary.

Only after the newcomer waved an older female elf with silver-blue hair into the wagon and looked pointedly at Aldari's hand did she realize she still held Hawk's sword. She shifted uneasily as the cool gray gaze lifted to her face.

"That sword does not belong to you," the elf said in her tongue.

"No." Aldari laid it beside Hawk, resting his hand on the hilt again. "But it was longer and pointier than my dagger and also this baton. Since Hawk wasn't using it, I thought he wouldn't mind. We wanted to keep the Twisted out of the wagon and protect him."

"Protect *him*." Setvik scoffed. "Yes, it was surely *his* welfare that concerned you." He pointed at her and spoke rapidly to the newcomer.

Barely stifling a groan, Aldari exchanged a long look with Theli. If Setvik blathered all of his conspiracies about how she'd somehow caused Hawk's illness, she might get in trouble—*more* trouble.

"I am Princess Aldari ne Yereth," she said, speaking firmly and loudly enough to interrupt Setvik. "And this is my bodyguard, Theli. Who are you, and will you tend Captain Hawk? As you can see, he's badly in need of medical assistance. Assistance superior to that of the mercenaries' medic." Though she couldn't fault Mevleth for what he'd done—even if he was gruff, he'd been attentive—she couldn't help but frown at him.

Her gut grumbled, and she hoped she wouldn't need to run off into the trees again in the middle of this. With the bodies of the Twisted among the leaf litter, this wouldn't be her first choice of outhouses.

"*I* will tend him," the female who'd climbed into the wagon said, shooting Aldari a brief haughty look before delving into a medical kit. She drew out what might have been a magical device and rested it over Hawk's forehead, then also uncorked a small bottle of gray liquid.

Aldari's insides twisted at the reminder of consuming nasty elven potions, but she wouldn't question the female, who was hopefully the very healer she'd hoped for.

"I am Prince Erathian," the newcomer said, confirming her suspicion that he came from the royal court. "What are you doing in our land, Princess Aldari ne Yereth?"

She blinked at him in puzzlement. Surely, if the queen had sent a falcon with a message to Hawk, the royal family knew all about the mercenary captain's mission. The queen must have briefed her son before sending him out.

"You *kidnapped* her," Theli said, giving Erathian an incredulous look.

"I—" Erathian spread a gauntleted hand over his chest, "—have done nothing of the sort."

Again, he shifted to Elven to speak with Setvik. Setvik clenched his jaw, glanced at Hawk, then lowered his chin and dropped to one knee again, giving what was presumably an explanation in a flat tone.

Hawk had implied that this scheme had been his idea, but he'd also spoken of the king's advisor, as if the plan might have been started among his superiors. Aldari wished Hawk were awake so he could talk to the prince—and so these elves would stop acting as if she was in the wrong and had somehow been responsible for his rapid deterioration.

"We will take you to the outpost," Erathian told Aldari after Setvik finished his story. "My father will sort this out."

"And send the princess back to her homeland?" Theli asked. "She has a wedding to get to and an alliance to cement."

The prince gazed coolly at her, and Aldari half expected him to chastise her, a mere bodyguard, for daring to speak to him. But all he did was glance at Hawk again and say, "My father will determine your fate."

Erathian gave what sounded like an order to the healer, then said something to Setvik, releasing him to take charge of his company. As the mercenaries recovered the rest of the reindeer and the wagon driver refastened the team, Aldari wondered if their fate had improved.

Hopefully, the new healer would find out that only the germs from the river serpent were affecting Hawk, and the accusations would drop. And should Aldari also hope that the king would decide to send her home?

Her people needed her, but she couldn't help but glance at the variables on the baton and wonder if she could help the elves with their problem. Other than Hawk, none of them had treated her that well or made her inclined to adore their people, but the challenge of a puzzle that others hadn't been able to solve called to her. Theli would think her a fool, but what if she could talk the elven king into sending word to Prince Xerik that she was only delayed and would come as soon as possible for the wedding?

"What is he doing?" Theli muttered.

Though the wagon and most of the mercenaries had started along the road again, Erathian and his bodyguards were riding among the Twisted, those who had been killed instead of fleeing into the woods. Beside each body, he paused and looked down. If the face wasn't visible, Erathian ordered one of his men to turn the Twisted over.

"Looking for someone he knows?" Aldari guessed, thinking of Hawk's words about the elven princess being taken.

"Someone he *knows?*" Theli hadn't heard the story of the Twisted.

"If what Hawk told me is true," Aldari said quietly, "all of those creatures used to be elves. Apparently, something about the Twisted's touch can cause people to change. Some were turned in past centuries and others in the last year."

Theli's face grew ashen as she looked at a gash on the back of her hand that Aldari hadn't noticed. Cold dread ran through her veins as she stared at it.

"Does their touch *only* affect elves?" Theli held up the wound. "What happens if one of us is clawed by them?"

Aldari risked tapping the healer's shoulder and interrupting her *hms* and *mms* as she surveyed the device she'd put on Hawk's forehead. That earned her another frown but didn't keep Aldari from pointing at Theli's wound.

"One of the Twisted clawed her. Does she need treatment?"

And if she did, would the elves care enough to give it to her?

Still scowling, the healer replied in her own language. Did that mean she didn't understand? Aldari was about to call out to Setvik, hoping he would translate, but the elf reached into her medical kit and pulled out a jar. After waving for Theli to come closer and hold out her hand, she unscrewed the lid, then sprinkled green powder over the wound.

"Please tell me that isn't moss," Theli said.

"Hawk did say they've cultivated numerous strains and found some with a lot of benefits." Aldari smiled, trying to alleviate Theli's concerns, though the same concerns formed a weight in the pit of her stomach.

"It itches."

"That means it's doing something effective, right?"

"Or irritating my skin." Theli scowled.

With the dubious treatment complete, the healer put away the jar and turned her attention back to Hawk.

"Let's just hope that we're not far from this outpost," Aldari said, "and that the king puts value in us and gives us the best treatment possible."

"And a swift ride home." Theli shuddered as she looked out at the dark forest.

Prince Erathian returned to the party and rode beside Setvik. The two elves spoke with their heads bent toward each other, and more than once, Erathian looked back at the wagon—at Aldari.

She couldn't help but wonder if they'd truly been saved.

19

AT DAWN, THEY ARRIVED AT THE ELVEN OUTPOST.

After Hawk's descriptions of what the elves had gone through over the centuries and how they'd lost all of their great cities, Aldari hadn't expected anything grandiose, but the moss-carpeted and vine-draped homes built into, beside, and in the branches of great trees, some as much as twenty feet in diameter, were remarkable. Some of the dwellings were crafted from wood and others had earthen walls, reminding her of the cob buildings that some of her people favored, but they managed an elegance that homes made of such materials shouldn't have had. Full of sinuous curves and even a spire here and there, few were simple squares or rectangles.

With everything covered in plant matter, had a cobblestone road not led to the outpost, one might have missed it completely, for it blended well into the forest. A river ran past one side of the settlement, a *normal* river, not one blanketed in fog or brimming with serpents, or so Aldari assumed. A few young elves on a dock were fishing with nets and poles, with no sign of adults supervising.

The party stopped at an unremarkable spot in the road, and Prince Erathian lifted an arm and called out. A girl with blonde pigtails ran out of a small home in the trunk of a tree, waved vigorously at them, and pressed her palm to a large green stone embedded in the bark. A faint buzz reverberated through the air, and a lick of energy made the hair on Aldari's arms rise. None of the elves appeared concerned, though Hawk stirred, groaning slightly under a blanket the healer had stretched over him.

She'd stayed with him all night, and she rested a hand on his chest now, saying something that sounded soothing. *You're home*, perhaps.

Was this Hawk's home? As mercenaries, his company was likely out on missions for most of the year, but maybe they returned to the outpost from time to time.

Prince Erathian flipped a coin to the girl as the party continued on.

The part of Aldari's brain that wasn't worried about Hawk and worried about her and Theli's fate wondered about the elven monetary system and how the economy of a people who seemed completely cut off from neighboring nations worked. From what Hawk had told her thus far, she would have guessed they simply bartered for goods and services, but perhaps vestiges of the monetary system used in their more prosperous past remained.

After the party traveled forty feet farther along the road, the girl pressed the green stone again. Another faint buzz floated through the air, and then she ran back into her home.

"There must be a magical barrier there that keeps out the Twisted," Aldari said.

"It sounded like a mosquito flying by." Theli didn't look impressed as she eyed the city. She'd been up every time Aldari had woken during the night, and with dawn's light now brightening Theli's face, Aldari didn't miss her frequent glances toward her hand. Every few minutes, she reached for it, as if to scratch an itch, but caught herself and pulled back.

Aldari hoped the wound amounted to nothing, that the green powder had nullified whatever taint the Twisted might have left behind. Theli had been at her side for eight years, and even if they traded barbs as often as heartfelt support, they got along well, and Aldari dreaded the idea of something happening to her. She also didn't want to be left alone among these people.

Though the prince had spoken about taking them to the king and having him straighten everything out, the party stopped at a curving earthen dome tucked between two large trees. A walkway of green moss ran from the cobblestone road to its rounded wooden door, vines and leaves covering most of the planks.

"You will wait there." Erathian pointed, then gestured for Aldari and Theli to climb down. "Someone will come to tend to your needs shortly."

Erathian glanced at the healer and Hawk. She also waved for Aldari and Theli to get out, as if she couldn't wait to get rid of them. Or maybe she simply wanted to get Hawk to better facilities for treatment.

Aldari was tempted to demand to be taken to the king right away, but she didn't want to interfere with Hawk getting the care he needed. She and Theli grabbed their weapons and climbed down. Nobody objected to them taking them, but as they walked toward the dome, Erathian gave an order, and two elven mercenaries jogged down the path behind them. As Aldari and Theli opened the unlocked door and stepped inside, the pair took up guard positions to either side of the entrance.

"I see we're still prisoners." Theli sighed.

Reluctant to let Hawk out of her sight, Aldari stood in the doorway and watched the wagon until it disappeared around a bend. The two mercenaries frowned at her and pointed for her to step inside. As soon as she did, the door thudded shut.

Theli sat on the edge of one of two beds and dropped her face in her hands. "How do I get you home from here?"

She seemed to have given up on Orath. Understandable, since there was no way Aldari could arrive in time for the wedding now. Also, since one could sail from the elven continent to Delantria, that was a more attainable goal. If they made it home, they could regroup, send a message to Orath, and with luck, arrange a new wedding date.

"You don't," Aldari said. "Even if we sneaked out of here past those guards, I doubt that magical barrier will drop if *we* touch the stone. The way home has to be through the king."

"The king who may or may not know we're here locked up in this box?" Theli flung a hand around, though the dome wasn't that bad, as far as prisons went.

A few tall, narrow windows gave glimpses of the outpost, and the beds had pillows and blankets. There were jugs of water or some other liquid on a table, as well as squares of what was presumably food—like almost everything else the elves consumed, the squares were green. Several candles burned, adding to the weak daylight filtering through the branches above the outpost. Whatever the candles were made from, it wasn't beeswax but a dark substance that filled the air with a piney scent.

"I'm sure the king knows," Aldari said. "I did send that note."

"That his falcon might have pecked off his leg and flung into a volcano."

"You're awfully pessimistic. Is that itchy cut making you moody?" Aldari tried another smile, though she'd been struggling to activate her sense of humor lately.

Theli dropped her hands on her thighs. "I'm sorry, Your Highness. I didn't know I needed to remain optimistic in the face of being kidnapped and beaten up by everything from a serpent to pirates to blue-skinned monsters who *used* to be elves. And now, here we are, locked up in a prison. Where we're fed nothing but *moss*." She flung a hand toward the squares on the tray. "No wonder your gut has been troubling you. This place is going to be the death of both of us."

"I don't require optimism, but if you could occasionally chuckle at my wit, I'd appreciate that. I'm fairly certain that was in your list of job requirements when my father hired you."

"I assure you it wasn't. In fact, I'm supposed to remain alert and undistracted at all times. I believe that means I should ignore your wit entirely in favor of peering around for threats."

"Ignore my wit? That can't be right. And besides, you're moping on the bed instead of peering at anything."

"I surveyed everything in this little dome when we entered, and I alerted you to the threat of more moss snacks. I've done my duty."

Though her roiling gut made Aldari reluctant to eat anything, she walked over to investigate the little squares. They had an oily sheen and looked a little different from the cranberry-moss bars. When she bit into one, it was chewy and sweet with a briny undertone. It reminded her of the various seaweed dishes that were often served with meals back home.

"If it helps, I think these might be made from algae, not moss," Aldari said.

"*Clearly* an improvement to be optimistic about."

"I'm actually surprised there's as much vegetation here as there is, given how far north we are. The Nu-nar Tundra on the other side of the world is basically grass-covered permafrost. That's about the same latitude as Serth, don't you think?"

"I can't tell you how much I don't care."

"You're grumpier than the elf lieutenant."

"The elf lieutenant who's telling everyone that you were responsible for his captain's injuries?"

Aldari lowered the algae square. "You caught that too, huh?"

"It was hard to miss."

A gurgle and a sudden cramp made Aldari hunch over and grip her stomach. Though the room wasn't that warm, sweat broke out on her forehead. Maybe she should have told the healer about her problem. But what would the elf have done? Sprinkle green powder over Aldari's abdomen?

Theli pointed to a doorway in the back, wooden beads on lengths of green twine—or maybe those were vines—creating a curtain. "Try that. I'm sure it's a privy rather than the entrance to our own private patio with access to hot springs."

"Yes, I don't think prisoners usually get treated to those." Aldari thought wistfully of the hot springs on the castle grounds back home.

"Cruel."

Since Theli didn't accompany Aldari to investigate the doorway, she must have been certain about her privy assessment. Interestingly, there was another room beyond the bead curtain, a second dome attached to the first. It had far more windows, including a large overhead one set into the curving ceiling. It was translucent, so Aldari couldn't see up to the treetops, but light flowed in for planters and raised garden beds sprouting leafy vegetables. A few vines grew up trellises along the walls, offering bunches of blue or red berries that looked more appealing than those bars.

A large water tank held orange fish that were nibbling at something like lily pads floating on the top. Algae grew along the edge, making Aldari wonder if the bars had been made right back there. If the Twisted were a threat whenever the elves left their outpost, it would make sense that they would try to grow much of their food inside.

When Aldari returned from the privy—a small room attached to the back of the garden dome—she opened her mouth to tell Theli about the berries, but halted as soon as she stepped through the bead curtain. Theli was no longer alone.

A silver-haired elven male stood in front of her, with two warriors poised behind him. He looked like an older version of Prince Erathian, though his weathered face was more weary than haughty, with crow's feet at the corners of eyes that were forest green rather than storm gray. Unlike Erathian's eyes, they were more scrutinizing than condemning or judgmental. He wore the same greens and browns as the rest of his people, but a brown fur cloak with a silver clasp hung from his shoulders, the intricate ornamentation on the chain and clasp suggesting it had more value than most items in the average elven wardrobe. Nothing so banal as a crown rested on his head, nor did he carry any obvious symbols of office, but Aldari had little doubt that this was the king.

His gaze shifted from Theli to Aldari, and she lowered her hand from her troubled gut and lifted her chin, determined to carry herself like an equal rather than a prisoner.

"Captain Hawk is being treated in the palace infirmary," he said without preamble, his voice surprisingly soft and free of an accent.

"I'm glad," Aldari said. "I hope he recovers. Uhm, *are* you the king?"

It occurred to her that this might be a senior healer or someone else in the court, not the ruler she'd suspected. A respected healer might be given bodyguards, especially when being sent to deal with possibly dangerous prisoners. Aldari glanced at Theli, glad she didn't have her mace in hand.

"Yes, yes. Forgive my lack of etiquette." He inclined his head toward her. "I am King Jesireth, twenty-ninth in my line. And you are Princess Aldari ne Yereth, second daughter of King Caylath Yereth. I had not expected to host you or any humans in our homeland. In my lifetime, few have come to visit us." He smiled, though it was tinged with bitterness, and she thought of Hawk's claim that the elves had asked for help many times over the centuries, but no humans had been willing to give it.

"I'll admit it wasn't in my plans for the year." Aldari wanted to ask if he would help her and Theli return home, especially if she'd be willing to look at their puzzle first, but Jesireth had something else on his mind.

"Captain Hawk has been poisoned," he said.

Aldari braced herself against the doorjamb. "It's not...? I assumed it was an infection from his injuries."

An infection that had admittedly come on with amazing rapidness.

"My personal healer is treating him," Jesireth said. "His injuries are grievous, but it is the poison that has afflicted him to such a damaging degree. It's not yet clear if he'll survive."

Aldari opened her mouth, but she didn't know what to say. Emotions jumbled inside of her, everything from sorrow at the thought of Hawk's death to regret for not having gotten to know him better to betrayal that he'd kidnapped her and might now die and leave her alone among his bitter and angry people. Beyond all that, she was stunned. Who would have *poisoned* him? And when? The pirates? There hadn't been time. Someone on that ferry? One of his own mercenaries?

"Lieutenant Setvik believes you did it." Jesireth's face was grave as he studied her. "And he believes you should be killed for the act."

Aldari gripped the doorjamb harder. "I did not. Where would I have kept poison? I don't even have a clean pair of underwear."

The king's face didn't change, and she doubted he appreciated her sarcasm.

Aldari made herself take a breath and form more careful and rational words before speaking further. "When the mercenaries kidnapped us, they didn't let us take our belongings—our carriage had flipped over, rolled down a hill, and crashed—other than our weapons, which they only gave back when we were *all* in danger. Besides, I don't make a habit of carrying poisons along with me on journeys. You can imagine how that would have looked, had someone discovered such a substance when I arrived for my wedding."

As Jesireth watched her and no doubt tried to discern if she was telling the truth, she watched *him* for reactions. Had he known about her wedding? How much did he know about the kidnapping? Had Hawk *truly* acted of his own accord? If so, why had the king and queen known to send a falcon to check in and get a message?

"Talk to Hawk," Aldari urged, the long silence making her uncomfortable. What *did* the king believe? "Please. He'll know who poisoned him, and he'll tell you it wasn't me. I don't want him dead."

"You do not wish ill toward your kidnapper?"

"I'd be all right with Setvik falling off a cliff," Aldari said before she could think better of it, "but not Hawk. He's..." She spread her hand and glanced at Theli, as if she might better explain, but Theli hadn't warmed up to Hawk as much as Aldari had.

"He gave her a puzzle," Theli said.

The king's brow creased. Aldari almost rolled her eyes, but if the king didn't know about that—was it possible that Hawk had a relationship with the king's advisor and had spoken to her about these things but not the king himself?—he should.

"Yes. He gave me this baton—" Aldari pulled it out to show him, "—and told me all about your problem with a laboratory buried under lava rock in an ancient city that you need to get into, in the hope that something inside will help your people put an end to the Twisted. I don't know if I have the knowledge to help, but I'm better than average at puzzles—I guess Hawk found that out, and that's why he came for me. Let me help your people. I'm willing. But it might be useful if you could give me more information on the twin Zedaron and what he was like. Some more of his background and personality. Anything to help me understand how his mind worked. I'm afraid I know very little about your people and your history."

Out of the corner of her eye, Aldari could see Theli frowning at her—probably because she felt Aldari should be negotiating for passage home—or to Orath. But if Aldari helped the elves, surely they would be more inclined to help Aldari. And if Hawk died— she swallowed at the depressing thought—and they were suspects in what ended up being not just his death but his *murder*... they would need someone else among the elves to appreciate them. Or at least not detest and mistrust them.

Long seconds passed as King Jesireth gazed at her. Thoughtfully? Was he contemplating it? Or was he mulling over all the traditional ways to slay murderers of elves?

"Please." Aldari lowered the baton. "Let me do something useful while Hawk is recovering." She refused to admit out loud that he might die, even if she feared the possibility. "And when he wakes up, talk to him. He'll tell you that I wouldn't have poisoned him. I like to solve problems, not cause them."

Thankfully, Theli didn't snort, even though she was still frowning deeply.

"If he wakes up," Jesireth said, "I will most definitely speak with him."

He turned and walked out, the hem of his cloak brushing the variegated green growth of the walkway. The expressionless warriors followed, closing the door behind them.

"I guess that means I'm not getting a tour of the history section of their library." Aldari sank down on one of the beds. Did this place even *have* a library? Or had all the elven libraries been destroyed long ago?

"I don't know why you're so eager to ingratiate yourself to them," Theli said.

"So that if Hawk dies, that man—that elf won't want to kill us in retaliation." Aldari waved at the door to indicate the king; Lieutenant Setvik had already made it clear what *he* wanted. Aldari hoped Setvik didn't have much sway over the monarch. She couldn't imagine why a mercenary would, but for whatever reason, Jesireth seemed to care what happened to Captain Hawk.

"Uh huh. If it's all the same to you, I'm going to go back to contemplating ways to escape."

Aldari lay back on the bed. "Contemplate away."

Despite the words, Aldari didn't know if she would leave if Theli came up with anything. If Aldari could convince the king to give them an escort to a ship and voyage to Orath, that would be one thing, but the thought of sneaking off into the woods and dealing with the Twisted themselves... That would be worse than pirates.

Aldari had a feeling the solution to her problem was to help the elves with *their* problem. But if they wouldn't allow that, what could she do?

20

Hours passed, and after being awake most of the night, Aldari dozed until a knock woke her. When she lurched upright in bed, she caught Theli munching on the green squares while making faces. Hunger must have made her desperate enough to try them.

"Uhm, come in?" Aldari called when whoever had knocked didn't enter.

Since the king had walked in without knocking, she assumed it wasn't he. And if it were Setvik with an assassin's dagger... Well, he wouldn't knock either. They ought to be safe—for now.

One of Setvik's mercenaries poked his head inside, and Aldari immediately questioned her assumption. The lieutenant might have sent one of his men to drag them off for an execution. Or what if he was here to deliver news of his captain's death?

Aldari's stomach twisted. This time, it wasn't from the bug that had been assailing her insides.

"I'm supposed to escort you to the..." The mercenary groped, searching for the term in her language, then peered back at someone holding a lantern. That was odd, since it wasn't dark. The mercenary asked a question in Elven. "Scroll place," he finished after getting a translation.

"Like a library?" Aldari rose to her feet. Had the king decided she wasn't responsible for Hawk's poisoning and that she might be useful? "I'm ready."

When Aldari stepped toward the door, Theli lunged in and caught her arm.

"You're going to take his word and go with him?" she demanded.

"Better than sitting here in bed noshing on algae cakes."

"That's one of Setvik's men, the one who *groped* me. He's probably pissed because we got him in trouble, and he had to swab the deck."

Aldari hesitated. Theli was right. What was the soldier's name? Pheleran.

"Setvik could have ordered him to get us out of here with a ruse," Theli said, "and he's planning to drag us behind a tree outside of the outpost and kill us."

"He could have come and killed us without the ruse," Aldari pointed out.

"You don't think us yelling and screaming and whacking him with my mace would have made noise that brought others? This way, he can lead us off to kill us in privacy."

Even though they were speaking rapidly, Pheleran got the gist. "No, the king said to take you. Setvik is resting with the company."

"Is Hawk still alive?" Aldari asked.

If his captain hadn't yet died, she hoped Setvik wouldn't feel motivated to do something drastic.

"Yes. He is being treated."

"We'll come with you." Aldari gestured for Theli to follow her. "Bring your mace."

"*Obviously.*" Theli grabbed her weapons belt and fastened it. "One doesn't go to a *scroll place* unarmed. Especially if that could translate to pit of vipers."

"My thesaurus suggests library is the more likely translation."

"That's because you're young and naive."

"You're only two years older than I am."

"But vastly more worldly and suspicious of strangers."

"You are more suspicious. As to the rest, you haven't been anywhere I haven't been. You didn't even check out the privy in the back."

"I doubt you gained more worldly wisdom back there. If anything, you've learned not to eat moss bars." Theli grimaced back at the tray of green cakes as they walked out, probably wondering if her gut would start bothering her soon.

It didn't seem fair that her bodyguard wasn't having any trouble with the elven food when Aldari was. Why should her gut be so much more sensitive?

A realization smacked her like a mallet striking a gong, and Aldari almost tripped. She must have blurted out in surprise, for Pheleran and the elf accompanying him looked back.

"That damn potion," Aldari whispered, looking at Theli. "The one *you* refused to sample."

It took Theli a moment to remember what she was talking about. "The stinky green stuff the medic gave you in the tent by the river?"

"Yes. The stinky green stuff that I took a couple of sips of and that Hawk drank a *lot* of."

"I thought it was a healing potion."

"So did I. So did *he.* That's what he told me, but it wasn't until after he drank it that he started getting sick. *Really* sick. And it was also after drinking it that my gut started bothering me." Aldari grimaced and rested her hand on her queasy abdomen.

"Why would his own medic poison him?" Theli glanced at the two elves frowning and shrugging at each other.

"I don't know, but I have to talk to him about it. Just in case that is what happened." Aldari faced Pheleran. "Will you take me to see Captain Hawk first?"

"He is being treated in the palace infirmary." Pheleran pointed upward toward a series of dwellings built in the treetops, vines and moss coating the walls and walkways up there.

The term *glorified treehouse* came more readily to mind than *palace*, but who was Aldari to judge? It wasn't as if her family's castle exuded opulence.

"Mere mercenaries aren't allowed unescorted into the palace, and prisoners definitely aren't," Pheleran added, waving at guards visible on the platforms around the dwellings.

"I'm a princess, not a prisoner. Get someone to escort us, please." In case it helped sway him, Aldari gave him the most heartfelt smile she could manage, though her mind was racing as she dwelled upon the possible repercussions of her hypothesis.

If the mercenary medic *had* poisoned Hawk, what else might he try? Was he against the mission for some reason? Or was it a personal vendetta against Hawk? What if he was a threat to others here? The king and his family? More of the mercenaries?

Pheleran shook his head. "I'm only a *vun*, ma'am. I can't make such requests."

"Will you at least tell someone to pass along the message that I want to see him?" Aldari did her best to tamp down her frustration, keep the smile up, and speak reasonably, though she wanted to find a vine to climb up to the palace and demand entrance.

After a long hesitation, Pheleran said something to the other elf. He also hesitated, but he finally called up to one of the platform guards and spoke. The guard opened a door and gave someone inside a repeat of the message, though a few of the words changed.

"By the time that gets relayed to him," Theli said, shaking her head, "he's going to think you said you never want to see him again and that he can shove his moss bars into his tightest orifice."

"Let's hope that's not true." Aldari wanted to stay there and wait for a response, but Pheleran waved for them to follow him.

"Scroll place," he repeated.

Aldari sighed, but the mercenary didn't radiate menace, and she *did* want to learn more about the centuries-old, puzzle-making wizard, so she followed him onto the cobblestone road that wound through the outpost. They passed numerous mossy pathways meandering off to the sides, leading to dwellings as well as crafting shops where male and female elves were working at looms, banging at carpentry projects, and baking bread. Sweet, pleasant smells wafting from ovens promised they made at least *something* that was more appealing than moss and algae bars.

The elves working outside eyed them curiously as they passed, but nobody spoke to Aldari or tried to stop the group. The clang of metal grew audible as they continued, and the road took them alongside a training arena where shirtless warriors sparred. Their muscular chests gleamed with sweat, and even the repetitive practice exercises displayed their agility and prowess.

A few female elves worked out with them—they wore sleeveless vests—and Theli cast a wistful look toward the practice ground, as if she would rather join in that activity than investigate musty scrolls.

Doubtless, she would. Back home, Theli worked out every day. As far as Aldari was concerned, being attacked by the Twisted the night before and a serpent and pirates the day before *that* were all the workouts she needed. She had no desire to sweat further.

Several of the shirtless males were familiar—the mercenaries. They paused as Aldari and Theli walked past, lowering their weapons and glaring at them. Setvik was among them, and those glares, glares that had been indifference in previous days, promised Aldari that he'd shared his suspicions about her to his mercenaries. Every one of them looked like he wanted to spring onto the road and strangle her personally.

Maybe Theli's suspicion was grounded. If the rest of the mercenary company felt that way, why wouldn't Pheleran?

But what could he do to them in a library? If they walked into a room without any books, Aldari would turn around.

The clangs from the practice arena faded as Pheleran and the other elf led them toward a cliff at the back of the outpost, determined trees growing out of cracks and from tiny ledges in the rock. They'd moved away from the dwellings, though gardens and well-tended berry bushes promised they were still in an oft-visited area, and the gurgling of the river remained audible.

"Weird place for a library," Theli muttered.

Aldari couldn't disagree. She was about to object to this dubious tour and say they wanted to return to their dome when Pheleran descended a ramp and stopped in front of a stout wooden door set into an earthen wall underneath the rock cliff. Great trees rose up to either side of the ramp, and more trees grew atop the cliff some thirty or forty feet up, their roots dangling down the rock face.

Tiny dark globules hung from some of the roots, and as Aldari tried to figure out what they were, a breeze swept through, and a couple of globules tumbled off. She stepped back as they splatted onto the ramp. Numerous dark brown stains implied it happened all the time.

"What is that stuff?" Aldari asked.

While the elf who hadn't introduced himself and didn't seem to speak their language stepped forward to unlock the door, Pheleran waved at the stains and said, "Root pitch. The trees produce it whenever their roots are exposed to air. We have many uses for it, so we encourage some of the trees to grow that way. It's medicinal. Captain Hawk might be getting some smeared on his wounds."

"Do you make candles with it?" Aldari thought of the pine-scented ones burning in their dome.

"Yes. Many uses," Pheleran repeated.

The other elf opened the door, leaned inside, and used his lantern to light two lamps mounted on the earthen walls of what looked more like a root cellar than a library. Or maybe a tunnel to a root cellar.

Kegs were stacked on one side of a dirt wall that stretched back into the darkness, and wooden shelves lined the other. More roots dangled from the ceiling and ran along the walls—sent down through the cliff from the trees all the way at the top? If so, they were tenacious trees and roots.

The lantern elf took several steps inside, squinted at labels on the shelves, and pointed to a particular niche. He said something, shrugged, and waved at a few others before walking back outside and gesturing for Aldari and Theli to enter.

"He says those cubbies hold historical scrolls about the twins and what was going on in our world at the time that they lived," Pheleran explained.

"This is your library?" Aldari hesitantly leaned past him, having no trouble envisioning the mercenary shoving her inside and shutting the door.

"Scroll place. Yes, maybe library is the word. The air from the growing dirt preserves the scrolls. Also alcohol." Pheleran stepped in, waved at the kegs, and placed his palm on the wall above them.

"Growing *dirt*?" Aldari peered at the wall. She *could* see something in the dirt, a fuzzy white growth that reminded her of a spiderweb, but it was embedded in the earth, not lying on top of it. "Mycelia?" she guessed.

Pheleran shrugged. "The growing dirt cleans the air. We also have salt caves. Some things are kept there, but scrolls like it here."

Aldari had leaned in far enough that she could see scroll cases —hundreds and hundreds of scroll cases—in the nooks in the shelves. Symbols in wax on the bottoms of the cases were the only visible labels. Words in the elven language? They reminded her of the maker's mark one might find on a silver plate or bowl.

"Who doesn't like a dark dank cave with roots and fungi growing on the walls?" Theli asked.

"It's actually not dank." Aldari sniffed. Maybe the species of mycelia that grew in Serth *did* clean the air.

"You're right. It's perfectly lovely. Maybe you can recommend a dirt tunnel to Prince Xerik for your wedding locale."

The guide elf said something, waved at a dark lump on the dirt floor at the edge of the lantern light, and pointed at the door.

"He says to make sure to close the door when you're done," Pheleran said. "Sometimes, the *ujari* come into the outpost via the tunnels this connects to, and they will eat livestock if they get out."

"The *ujari*?" Aldari squinted at the lump. Was that... animal scat?

Pheleran shrugged and used his hands to illustrate the dimensions of something in the air. It was about the size of a raccoon.

What livestock could something so small threaten? Did the elves keep chickens? During their walk through the outpost, she hadn't seen or heard any squawking.

"They will not bother you unless you make a lot of noise." Pheleran stepped back onto the ramp and waved for Theli to go inside with Aldari.

"I'll stand guard out here." Theli pointed at the ground outside the doorway.

"Good idea." Aldari stepped up to the first of the cubbies the elf had indicated, frowning at the eleven or twelve scrolls tucked inside. Which one would have what she wanted? And how would she know?

She reached into the cubby, but a buzz sounded, and a tingle ran up her arm. It didn't hurt, but she reflexively jerked her hand back and looked at Pheleran.

"Magic protects them from the animals and moisture in heavy rains," Pheleran said, "but it will not hurt you."

Nonetheless, Aldari examined both sides of her palm carefully before gingerly reaching in again. Another buzz filled the air as the same tingle flowed up her arm, but it didn't seem to do any damage. She pulled out one of the scroll cases, hoping some of them were written in one of the old academic languages that so many modern languages were derived from. So many modern *human* languages. She had no idea if the elven tongue had its roots in any of them.

The first scroll she opened wasn't written in anything she recognized. Nor were any of the others.

"Well, this trip isn't going to be that enlightening, is it?"

Theli grunted an inquiry, though she didn't look inside. The lantern elf had disappeared, but Pheleran remained, leaning against a tree and using a knife to scrape dirt out from under his nails. He already looked bored. Maybe he'd lost a bet and had been stuck with this duty instead of sparring with the others.

"We'll need someone to translate for us. Unless..." Aldari remembered the symbol engraved in the bottom of the baton and pulled it out. She scanned the caps of the scroll cases, hoping to find a match. Would she get that lucky? "Not in any of the cubbies that elf pointed at," she muttered, wondering if he'd been deliberately misleading her.

Maybe not. Finding the same mark on a scroll case as on the baton might imply Zedaron had *written* the text, not that it was something biographical about him and penned by another author.

Aldari grabbed one of the wall lamps and walked deeper into the tunnel so she could examine more scroll cases.

"Don't go far," Theli warned, glancing at her. No, glancing at that pile of scat. Fortunately, it appeared to be several days old. "Unless you've found a possible escape route," she muttered.

"It might be." Aldari thought of the comment that animals could get into the outpost through attached tunnels, but she was more interested in finding what she believed was Zedaron's mark than escaping, at least at the moment. If they left the outpost, the Twisted would be waiting for them outside. "Oh. There it is."

Four entwined leaves. A wax mark on a scroll case matched the one on the bottom of the baton. Even though it might not give her any useful insight into Zedaron—and she would need a translator to read the contents—Aldari couldn't help but feel excitement.

As she withdrew the case, a scurrying sound drifted out of the darkness.

"Uh oh." Aldari lifted the lamp and peered into the shadows.

Another sound followed the first, and her light glinted off two eyes in the dark. A second pair of eyes joined the first. Then a third.

Aldari licked her lips. "Theli, I may need you and your mace."

Did those eyes appear to be higher off the ground than a raccoon's would be? She thought so, but the darkness made it hard to tell.

"And for Pheleran to learn to draw in the air with greater accuracy," she added.

Theli cursed, and a thud followed. "You bastard!"

Aldari turned in time to see Theli hit the ground as the door slammed shut behind her. All daylight disappeared from the tunnel.

Theli recovered quickly, turning the fall—the shove?—into a roll and springing to her feet, but a resounding *click* came from the door. She shoved at it, but it didn't budge. Pheleran had locked it.

Dread curdled in Aldari's gut as more pairs of eyes appeared in the light from her lantern. She backed toward Theli while glancing around for something to throw at the animals to scare them away. Neither the scroll nor baton she clutched were acceptable projectiles. And she wasn't throwing the lamp.

Theli pounded on the door, first with her fist and then the mace. "What are you doing, you idiot? The king doesn't want Princess Aldari dead."

Aldari wanted to nod in agreement, but she didn't know if that was true. What if Hawk had died, and King Jesireth had decided to punish her this way? Or *kill* her this way?

"Setvik said you poisoned Hawk," came Pheleran's muffled accusation through the wood.

"He's an ignorant liar." Theli smashed her mace against the door again. It made a faint dent in one of the stout boards, but whatever species the elves favored for woodworking was hard. Very hard.

A growl floated from the pack of animals. Were they creeping closer?

"Theli." Aldari patted her bodyguard without looking away from those eyes. There were more of them than there had been a few seconds ago. She was sure of it.

After ineffectively smacking the door several more times, Theli turned with an angry hiss. "I'm going to smash his head in."

"You have the opportunity to smash *their* heads in." Using the lamp, Aldari pointed into the gloom.

"They look bigger than raccoons."

"I think so too."

"If Captain Hawk survives," Pheleran said through the door, "I'll come let you out. *He* can decide what to do with you."

"We're about to be eaten by the animals that live in here," Aldari called.

"If you poisoned him, you deserve that." It was hard to tell through the door, but Pheleran's voice genuinely sounded frustrated and full of angst for his injured captain.

Since Aldari hadn't had anything to do with that, she couldn't dredge up any sympathy for the mercenary. All she could do was shake her head and hope the animals wouldn't charge two adults with weapons. But as they crept closer, she doubted she and Theli would be that lucky.

21

"Try to reason with that idiot." Theli grabbed the second lamp from the wall and strode toward the animals with her mace. "I'll keep these things back."

Aldari didn't think she would be able to reason with any of the mercenaries unless Hawk survived, and he told them all that she hadn't been responsible, but maybe Pheleran would listen to her hypothesis.

"I didn't poison Hawk," she called through the door as Theli advanced into the tunnel, waving the lamp and her mace to scare the animals. They shifted and growled at her, but they didn't retreat. "But I may know who did. Your medic gave him a suspicious green liquid. He wasn't sick before that, but after he drank it, he went downhill very quickly. Tell your lieutenant to talk to *Mevleth* about poison. Have someone check his medical kit and take a look at that stuff. Maybe it's not what he says it is."

Growls emanated from what had to be dozens of throats. As more and more animals gathered, they grew braver.

One darted forward, coming into the light as it ran toward Theli. It looked like a giant weasel with a possum's squinty half-blind eyes, and it opened a brown furry snout to reveal pointed fangs. The thing's head was level with Theli's thigh, if not her waist.

"Some raccoon," Theli said as she swung her mace at it.

The slinky-bodied animal darted backward, avoiding the blow, but it didn't retreat all the way into the shadows. More identical creatures were creeping forward. If they charged all at once...

Aldari banged on the door. "Pheleran, do you hear me? How well do you know that medic? How long has he been with the company? Do you trust him?"

She didn't get an answer and had a feeling Pheleran had left. They were on their own.

Another animal rushed Theli, and she kicked it in the jaw. It scurried back but not far.

More of the pack were creeping in, pressuring the others to continue forward, to attack. Two animals darted at Theli. She kicked one and smacked another with her mace. Bone cracked as she connected with its skull. That one dropped to the ground, squealing and rolling, but the other one dodged the kick and lunged in, biting for her leg.

As Theli jumped back, she kicked out again. It shifted aim and snapped down on her boot. Theli yowled and swung the mace at its head, the light level faltering as her lamp wobbled wildly.

"Be careful with the lamps," Aldari warned, giving up on getting help from the outside. They'd *really* be in trouble if they had to fight these animals in the dark.

Theli's only response was a snarl. Aldari ran in to help, swinging the baton at a creature lunging for Theli's side.

The artifact was a meager weapon compared to a mace, but the animal was focused on Theli and didn't see the blow until it struck. The baton slammed into the side of its head. The attack didn't knock it to the ground with a broken skull, but at least it deterred the animal from its target and gave Theli time to deal with another one harrying her.

Once Aldari stood shoulder to shoulder with her, the animals paused their attack. Considering their prey? Or simply waiting for reinforcements? More growls drifted up from the depths of the tunnel.

"This is a hell of a library," Theli panted.

"We need something bigger than a mace to hit them with." Aldari eyed the kegs, thinking of tipping one over to roll at the animals. Most likely, that would only alarm them for a few seconds. "Or to blow up in their faces. How much alcohol do you think is in elven wine or moonshine or whatever they make?"

"I have no idea what the percentage is, but—" Theli lunged in, swinging at an encroaching animal, "—but I'm positive it's fermented from moss."

Aldari snorted. "Probably true. Cover me." She started to set down her lamp to grab one of the kegs and investigate further when her gaze snagged on the roots and the balls of pitch beaded on them.

"I always do." Theli swung at and smacked another animal.

It stumbled against one of the others and struck the shelves, making them rattle. Fortunately, the magical field kept the scroll cases from flying out.

Aldari barely noticed. Her gaze was locked on the pitch. "I've got an idea."

"We could use an idea right now," Theli said, swinging again.

"What we could use is a big explosion." Aldari tipped one of the heavy kegs. It thudded down hard enough that the animals paused. "Lend me your dagger, please."

"Where's yours?" Theli's expression was exasperated when she glanced back, but she paused long enough to pull out her blade and give it to Aldari.

"On the bed in our room."

Aldari used the dagger to scrape pitch from the roots and smear it on the sides of the keg. As sticky as the stuff was, it wasn't an easy task, and she didn't know how much she would need. Nor did she know if it could burn through the wood and ignite the alcohol inside. If all that was in there was wine, flames wouldn't do anything. But if it was something more highly alcoholic, they might.

"That's helpful." Theli jumped as one of the animals lunged for her shin. She kicked it in the head and swung her mace at another one leaping at her.

"I thought we were going to a library." Aldari smeared the pitch as quickly as she could, cutting off more than a few roots in her haste. Hopefully, the trees weren't as vengeful as the elven mercenaries. "Look out," she said when she was done.

"I have been—trust me."

Aldari shoved the keg toward the animals. If it *did* blow up, she didn't want to take out the scrolls—or her and Theli.

"That's not going to work," Theli said, but she cleared the way, keeping the animals from reaching Aldari as she rolled the keg deeper into the tunnel.

As pitch came off on the ground, Aldari grimaced, worried that Theli was right. She stopped rolling the keg, afraid it would lose all the flammable goop if she kept going.

Theli smashed her mace onto the head of an animal trying to slip around the keg. Another one leaped on top of it, snapping its jaws at Aldari. She swung the lamp at it, and it shrieked and backed away.

"These things are awful," Aldari said.

"Awfully hungry," Theli said. "For human flesh, not elven livestock."

"Get back."

Aldari opened the lamp case, poked the pitch-tipped dagger inside, and the gunk caught fire instantly. She pointed the burning blade toward the side of the keg and waved for Theli to retreat. Without a fuse, the keg would catch fire quickly, and the flames might burn through the wood in seconds.

"*You* get back, Aldari." Theli snatched the dagger from her hand and shoved her toward the door.

Though Aldari hated having Theli risk herself on her behalf, that had been drilled into Theli from her earliest days. Aldari had to let her.

She sprinted for the door as Theli used the burning dagger to ignite the pitch on the keg. She whirled and ran toward Aldari as the pitch burned through the wood and started in on the alcohol inside.

They didn't get the thunderous explosion that Aldari had envisioned, but the *thwomp* of fuel igniting terrified the animals. They shrieked as they ran back down the tunnel, and the scent of singed fur mingled with the piney aroma of the burning pitch. As the keg's integrity failed, burning alcohol flowed out in all directions.

"Uh oh." Aldari flattened herself against the door.

Fortunately, the tunnel sloped downward, and most of the flaming liquid flowed in that direction. But some reached the wooden shelves, and they caught fire.

Aldari swore, fearing the magic wouldn't be enough to protect the scrolls, and ran forward, looking for something to use to put out the flame. She hadn't intended to burn valuable historical documents.

A distant gong sounded. An alarm caused by their fire? Or was something else going wrong in the outpost? Like an attack by the Twisted?

"Can you burn down the door too?" Theli asked.

Aldari, busy waving at the flames burning the shelves, only shook her head. Her eyes watered at the growing cloud of smoke filling the tunnel. "I need a wet blanket or something."

Heat scorched her cheeks, and ashes floated in the air. The

flames weren't burning the scrolls yet, but it was only a matter of time. Cursing, Aldari tore off her dress in desperation and used *that* to swat the flames.

A thud came from behind her along with a rush of cool air. The door had opened, and several startled elves peered inside for a shocked moment before someone shouted what had to be an order to bring water. As soon as elves with buckets ran inside, Aldari backed away. Her dress was singed in numerous spots, and swatting at the flames hadn't done much.

As more elves rushed inside, Theli grabbed Aldari and pulled her out. They stumbled up the ramp, smoke flowing out of the tunnel along with them.

With tears streaming down her cheeks and smoke in her eyes, Aldari ran into someone.

"Sorry," she rasped, a series of coughs following. That only brought more tears to her eyes.

"Ah, good afternoon, Your Majesty," Theli said, somehow speaking normally.

Only when Aldari used the dress still gripped in her hand to wipe her eyes did she realize she was naked save for her boots and undergarments. A cool breeze whispered through the trees, rustling leaves and raising gooseflesh on her sweaty skin. The smoke and her vision cleared enough so she could see King Jesireth gazing at her as his people put out the fire in their underground repository.

"Sorry, Your Majesty." Aldari wiped her eyes again before slipping her sooty and singed dress over her head. "I'm just a visitor here, but might I advise that keeping your scrolls and alcohol in a place where flammable pitch drops from the ceiling is perhaps unwise?"

"We haven't had a problem with it before," Jesireth said, "but you have shed light on why such an arrangement could be problematic."

Was it her imagination or was that the faintest hint of humor in his dry voice? Dear God, she hoped so. She would be furious if some stranger lit the library in her family's castle on fire. But she also wouldn't have locked a visitor in the library with giant aggressive rodents.

"Captain Hawk is awake and wishes to see you," Jesireth added.

"Oh, good." Aldari slumped in relief. Even if nobody had shared her hypothesis about the medic with Hawk yet, simply knowing he'd recovered enough to speak filled her with hope.

"Teemohn will take you to see him." Jesireth eyed the dagger in Theli's hand. The pitch had burned off, but the residue remained. "See if you can avoid lighting my home on fire along the way."

"Yes, Your Majesty," they said together.

The bland-faced Teemohn led them away, and Aldari and Theli hurried to follow. Angry and disgruntled shouts were coming from the tunnel. The king's humor might evaporate when he realized how much damage had been done, and Aldari didn't want to be there for that.

22

—————

SOOT DUSTED THE SCROLL CASE ALDARI HAD MANAGED TO RETAIN throughout the chaos, and she kept a tight grip on it as she and Theli trailed their elven guide up a staircase that wound around the trunk of a tree and up to the linked platforms that supported the palace. There weren't any interior hallways, most of the rooms weren't connected, and there was as much outdoor space as indoor space, with roofs supported by posts or trunks creating open-air meeting spaces protected from the elements. Vine-draped doors led into clusters of rooms around such areas.

As their guide led them to a door protected by two guards, it opened, and a silver-haired female elf of perhaps fifty, who was wearing a green dress and carrying an empty tray, stepped out. With her hair swept into an elegant coif, and gold trim edging the hem of her dress, she appeared too regal to be a servant, but all of the elves did the haughty chin tilt well, so it was hard to be sure. The healer with silver-blue hair accompanied her, carrying a medical kit and speaking quietly.

The tray-carrying elf spotted Aldari and Theli approaching and fell silent, her mouth closing and her jaw tightening. Aldari tried to smile instead of grimace, though she feared the rumor that she'd poisoned Hawk hadn't abated.

"He may not speak for long, Princess Aldari," the elf said without introducing herself. "He's been very ill and needs to rest."

"Yes, ma'am," Aldari said, being safe with a generic honorific. "I do have something important to discuss with him."

"Such as why your wardrobe is singed and your skin is inappropriately visible in numerous places?"

Inappropriately visible? It wasn't as if Aldari had *chosen* which parts would burn when she'd been trying to swat out that fire. "Ah, no. I wasn't going to bring that up."

"He may wonder."

The healer tapped her medical kit while saying something in Elven, and the older elf snorted.

"True," she said, responding in Aldari's language while keeping an eye on her. Gauging her responses? "He is woozy. He may not even recognize her."

"I hope you weren't giving him that awful green potion," Aldari muttered, eyeing the medical kit.

The older elf's brow furrowed. Nobody had yet heard Aldari's hypothesis, it seemed. It must have been lost in translation. Or deliberately left out of the translation.

"You may speak with him for twenty minutes. Then he must rest." The older elf nodded curtly as she tucked the tray under her arm.

"That's all I need."

The older elf led the healer across the covered platform and into another building. The guards to either side of Hawk's door hadn't stirred during the conversation, but they eyed Aldari now. Did they understand her language? She hoped the elf hadn't forgotten to let them know she was going in.

"Will you stay out here and keep an eye on things?" Aldari asked Theli, tilting her head toward the guards and glancing in the direction of the practice arena. With numerous trees and dwellings in the way, it wasn't visible from the elevated platform, but the clangs of metal promised that the weapons training continued.

"As long as you promise not to cuddle the patient too intensely," Theli said. "Or let him cuddle *you*."

Aldari gave her the exasperated look the comment deserved. "He almost died. I'm sure *that* isn't going to be on his mind."

Theli poked Aldari through a gap in the side of her dress that showed skin. Aldari rolled her eyes. It wasn't as if she was walking around with her breasts dangling out. Besides, the dirty and torn dress made her look bedraggled, not sexy. She could only imagine what her hair and face looked like after trying to put out a fire by hand.

"Let's hope," Theli said.

The guards didn't stop Aldari when she opened the door and poked her head inside. Hawk lay in a surprisingly plush bed, given the treehouse-style palace, with a soft blanket pulled most of the way up his bare chest. At first, his eyes were closed, and Aldari hesitated, not wanting to disturb him, even if he had requested her presence. But she must have made some noise, for he turned his head and looked over.

Hawk lifted a hand and smiled at her. Once more, relief washed over her, both at seeing him well enough to smile and at having the gesture directed at her. All of the other elves didn't do anything besides glare at her, as if it was *her* fault that she was in their outpost.

"Hi, Hawk." Aldari closed the door behind her. "I need to talk to you."

"Good. I need to be talked to by someone who won't lecture me." He shifted his pillows around and propped himself up against them, wincing as the movements disturbed his injuries. The blanket slipped down around his waist, showing fresh bandages over the serpent-bite wounds and giving her a distracting view of his muscular chest. And here Theli had worried about *Aldari* having skin on display... "You're not going to, are you?"

Blushing, Aldari forced her gaze up to his face. "Going to what?"

"Lecture me."

"I hadn't planned to, but if you'd like, I have a number of talks prepared on free-market capitalism and using differential calculus for representing and explaining economic behavior."

"Those sound more palatable than diatribes on the stupidity of kidnapping a princess and then inserting yourself into a river serpent's maw."

"Palatable isn't an adjective I've heard applied to my lectures before." Aldari looked for somewhere to sit. It was time to bring up the heavier subject of his poisoning.

They appeared to be in a guest room, with few knickknacks or signs of personality around, and furnishings were sparse as well. Besides the bed and a side table with a book, a bowl of soup, and a cup of water resting on it, the only other furniture was a chair, and it was in the far corner from the bed. If Aldari chose it, she would need to speak more loudly than she wanted on a sensitive subject, and with the guards and their keen elven hearing outside the door, she didn't want to do that.

She opted to stand beside the bed and clasp her hands and the scroll case behind her back. For twenty minutes, she could remain on her feet.

"Well, I might fall asleep during it," Hawk said, "but don't take it personally. The healer gave me some strong painkillers and said they'd make me tired and a little loopy." He tilted his head as he looked at her torso. "Does your dress have windows in it now or is the medicine already taking effect and making me see things?"

"Windows? You could call them that, though they weren't

installed to enhance the dress's allure." Aldari had intended to switch to the more important topic, but Hawk frowned and reached out to touch soot on her sleeve.

"What happened?"

Aldari showed him the scroll case and gave him a quick summary of the events in the tunnel—she couldn't bring herself to call an underground keg- and rodent-filled spot a library.

"Pheleran locked you *in*?" Hawk pushed himself up from the pillows, his elbow bumping the book on the side table, and shifted a leg out of bed—a *bare* leg. "I'll wring his neck."

Aldari gaped as she scooted back. Was Hawk naked under that blanket? And about to let her see... everything?

Not sure whether she was horrified or intrigued, she turned her head toward the window. No, she knew exactly how she felt, and it wasn't how she *should* have felt.

Fortunately, or perhaps *unfortunately*, the movement made Hawk dizzy. He blinked slowly as the blanket threatened to fall to the floor, then flattened a hand on it to keep it on the bed—and over himself.

"Oh, sorry." Hawk gripped his abdomen with one hand as he tried to pull his leg back into bed and the blanket more fully over himself, but moving the leg must have hurt, for he grimaced and left it hanging down as he flopped back against the pillows.

"You can wring his neck tomorrow if you wish." Aldari stepped forward, hesitated, then while looking at the book on the table instead of him lifted his leg gently back onto the bed for him. For a moment, she let her fingers rest against his skin to see if his fever had abated. Thankfully, it wasn't as unhealthily warm as it had been the last time she'd touched him. She hoped that boded well and that he was in good hands with the new healer.

"Most nurses look at their patients while they fondle their body parts," Hawk said, his dryness briefly reminding her of the king.

Embarrassed, Aldari jerked her hand away. "Sorry. I'm not— I mean I haven't... seen a lot of naked elves."

"We're mostly the same as your human men, aside from the ears and a tendency toward less fur." Hawk waved at his chest and jaw. Neither were hairless, but they weren't thick with it, and it was likely he didn't have to shave his face often.

"I think you mean hair." Aldari only glanced at his chest and didn't let her gaze linger.

"Oh, I don't know. I've seen some pretty furry humans." He grinned, though his eyes still had that glaze to them, and she was glad he hadn't succeeded in standing. Whether because of the medicine or his injuries, he didn't look like he should be walking.

"There are some, but, uhm, I haven't seen a lot of naked *men* either. My father always discouraged that. Vehemently."

"Ah, right. The virgin bride thing." Judging by his bemused expression, that wasn't an elven custom.

Did he think it strange? Were elven females encouraged to experiment before entering marriages? A part of her was curious, but this wasn't the topic she needed to discuss with him.

"I apologize for teasing you." Hawk scooted over on the bed and patted the edge in invitation.

Instead of accepting it—that seemed far too familiar—Aldari waved at the book, the title in Elven. "What are you reading? Or did that come with the room?"

"No, it's mine. Actually, it was my sister's." Pain flashed in his eyes as he winced, not from his wounds this time. "It's on whales and their declining population in our seas over the last couple of centuries. She studied ocean life and animals and longed to go out into the world to learn more, but with our problems at home... such a lifestyle wasn't encouraged."

"I imagine that for generations, your young people haven't been able to follow their dreams."

"That's the truth."

Aldari blinked, remembering how they'd first met in the library back home. "When you asked for a book on whaling, were you actually interested in the topic?"

"Yes. That's why I originally dragged Setvik into the library. When we learned that we wouldn't be able to report to the king until the next morning, we realized we had some free time to look around. You can imagine how startled I was to find you in the library in a run-down part of your city. Looking back, I should have darted back out before your bodyguard saw us and you had a reason to be suspicious—" Hawk smiled ruefully, "—but it seemed like an opportunity to make sure you really were the person we believed you were. If you weren't *actually* Lyn Dorit, there would have been no point in kidnapping you. As to the whale book...

"Don't take this the wrong way, but I wanted to better understand why your people—why humans from many kingdoms—have been decimating the whale population. When I was growing up, environmental studies weren't exactly a passion of mine—" Hawk's smile was self-deprecating this time, "—but I started reading my sister's books after we lost her, as a way to honor her and remember her. At least at first. But I got interested—and concerned—and wondered if there was anything that could be done to alter what seems an alarming trajectory. Our people also fish and whale, but we only take what nature can replenish, and we use all the parts of that which we kill. In the past, we hunted animals in our land to extinction and learned from our folly, and we'd hate to see it happen again on a global scale."

Aldari grimaced. Hawk's expression wasn't condemning, nor did he seem to blame *her* for the industry, but she was aware how assiduously her people hunted whales for their blubber, so it could be turned into oil and sold. "It's our only natural resource, the only thing we have to export. I've, through my writing under my pen name, encouraged the development of other industries in our kingdom, so we would be less reliant on that, but it's difficult to convince people to change their ways when what they're doing is working and making them money. I think, economically speaking, either the supply would have to dwindle enough that the effort required to find whales would make it no longer profitable—not ideal—or something else would have to be invented to take the place of whale oil in the marketplace, something cheaper and easier to produce. Ideally from a renewable source."

"Such as elven root pitch?" Hawk raised his eyebrows. "It burns better and longer than whale oil."

She almost made a joke about how explosive the stuff was, but she'd heard of tanks of whale oil on the docks blowing up and killing people, so it wasn't as if it was any safer in that regard. "The trees aren't cut down when it's harvested?"

"No, it's like the sap that maples produce. As long as the tree is healthy, it'll create more." Hawk scratched his jaw. "I admit I'm intrigued by the idea that the overhunting of whales might be resolved by inserting a replacement resource into the market. I, being a fighter at heart, was envisioning myself—after I solved our problem with the Twisted of course—leading warships out into the seas to thwart the whalers. With our swords."

Aldari shuddered, realizing that would mean the elves hunting down her own people. "Solving problems with economic solutions is far better than through martial means. I've written papers on that. Would you..." Aldari hesitated, abruptly feeling shy. "Would you be interested in reading them?"

"Yes," he said promptly and gripped her hand, as if he was genuinely excited by the idea. Maybe he was. If she could help him come up with a solution to a problem that concerned him, why wouldn't he be?

"I guess we just have to solve the problem of your Twisted first, so that elves can start cultivating that species of tree and flood the marketplace with a cheap and better alternative to whale oil." She shook her head at the word *just*, acknowledging that finding a way to reverse centuries-old magic wouldn't be easy.

"Indeed." Hawk patted the bed in invitation again, then pointed at the scroll. "Did you find something during your adventure?"

Aldari wrenched her mind away from running calculations on how many trees oozing pitch would be required to put an end to the whaling industry. "Possibly. But I wanted to talk to you about your sickness first. They told you someone poisoned you, right?"

She shifted her weight and looked at the spot he'd cleared on his bed, then over at the chair. Sitting in the chair would be far more proper. Maybe she could drag it over to the bed. It looked heavy, but maybe not *that* heavy.

"They told me." The humor drained from his voice and face, and unease darkened his eyes—he had to wonder who was after him.

The urge to sit down and take his hand came over Aldari, the desire to comfort him. He'd almost *died*.

"I told them you had nothing to do with it," he added.

"Thank you. I... have a suspicion about who did. Did my message get to you?"

"No." Gravely, Hawk gazed up at her face, then patted the bed again and scooted over farther to make more room. "Tell me. It's important. I need to survive long enough to finish this mission and to—I *fervently* hope—change the world for my people."

Trusting he didn't have anything sexual in mind, Aldari sat on the edge of the bed. Right now, worrying about propriety and shoving furniture around would be silly.

"Do you remember when we were both in that tent in your river camp?" she asked.

"Yes. My memory is fine. I didn't hit my head at any point. I don't think." Hawk frowned and reached up to probe his scalp to check. "It's fine." He nodded firmly. "Is yours fine?"

"Ah, yes. I think so." Aldari hadn't seen herself in a mirror yet and hoped half her hair hadn't been burned off.

"Good." Hawk gave her a bleary smile, reminding her that he was medicated.

His eyes had grown even glassier, suggesting it was kicking in. She had better make this quick.

"Your mercenary medic gave me a sip of a green liquid in a bottle."

Hawk nodded. "I had a bunch of it."

"I know. After I had that sip, within a few hours, I started experiencing some—" Her gaze fell upon the bowl of soup on the table, and she halted, gaping at a flotilla of eyeballs floating in it. "What are you *eating*?"

Hawk turned his head. "It's a traditional elven food that's given to the pregnant and injured. It's supposed to be extra nourishing."

"*Eyeball* soup?"

"It's called *sopsathra* soup, and eyeballs are only one ingredient. See, there are some leaves and herbs in there too. My mother could tell you what they are exactly, but eyeballs from *sopsaran* are believed to have great power to heal. They're animals similar to small deer with horns, and they're one of a handful of inherently magical creatures in Serth. Like elves. *Usually* the soup only has a few eyeballs in it, but the more dire your need for magical healing power, the more the chef tends to put in your bowl." Hawk's expression grew wry as he looked over at it. "I suppose I should eat it before it gets cold."

"Er, yes." Aldari resolved to get back to her tale so she could leave him to his meal. She wouldn't object if he ate in front of her, but the idea of listening to someone noshing on eyeballs while she spoke was a little disturbing. "We have fish-head soup for that in my culture. And people don't usually eat the heads. They just kind of float around in there and ooze nutrition into the broth. At least that's my understanding of how it works. I prefer amazale—that's a maple-sugar pastry with frosting drizzled all over it."

"Pastries have healing properties in your culture?" His eyes crinkled with amusement.

"Well, no, but they're good. *Much* tastier than eyeball soup." Admittedly, she hadn't tried the soup, but the eyeballs staring up at her were discomfiting, and she had no urge to pop one in her mouth.

"Perhaps one day, I can try them." His humor faded again. "Though I suppose I'll never be welcome in your land now."

"If you help me get back safely, maybe you will be." And if it wasn't too late for her to marry Prince Xerik and solidify the alliance her people dearly needed...

"I'll do my best." Hawk rested his hand on hers and gazed intently at her. "You have my word."

Aldari swallowed, moved by the intensity of his gaze, of his promise. "Thank you."

Maybe she should have pulled her hand away from the intimate gesture, but she didn't want to. She would simply finish so she could leave him to rest.

"As I was saying, I believe something was wrong with that potion. That it was tainted or poisoned... I sipped from it and have had some discomfort. You drank a lot and have had a *lot* of discomfort. Theli rejected it and has been fine. Maybe you could check in on the other elves who were injured and treated and see if they had any." Aldari hadn't seen them take sips from the potion when she'd been in the tent.

"You think Mevleth poisoned me?"

"I don't know why he would, but is it possible that someone doesn't want to see you succeed at your mission? Could someone have bribed him? Or maybe it was an accident." Aldari shrugged, hesitant to accuse someone Hawk had presumably worked with for years of trying to murder him. Did that even make sense? If

Setvik had given Hawk the potion, she would have no trouble making the accusation, but would a medic who'd dedicated his life to healing do such a thing? "Could it have gone bad or something?"

"That seems unlikely." Hawk held up a finger and called toward the door.

One of the guards stuck his head inside. Theli was still out there, her arms folded over her chest, and she peered in and frowned at Aldari.

As Hawk and the guard exchanged words in Elven, Theli mouthed what looked like, "What are you *doing*?" and pointed at Aldari. Because she was sitting on the side of the bed?

Aldari rolled her eyes and mouthed, "It's fine," before the guard leaned out and closed the door again.

"He'll pass the message to the head of the Royal Guard," Hawk said, "and they'll find Mevleth and bring him up to question."

"Can your people use magic to discern if someone is telling the truth?" Aldari asked before remembering his story of how the elves had to sublimate their magic—she glanced at the bracer on his arm, noting it hadn't been removed with the rest of his clothing.

"It's possible the king has a magical device to help with such things, but I'm not certain. Since we can't unleash our power and make new devices, all we have are the hodgepodge of magical artifacts from the olden days."

"I understand." Aldari stifled a grimace, well aware that it would end up being her word against the medic's, an elf who was trusted among the mercenaries and their people as a whole, whereas she was... definitely not trusted. Not by anyone but Hawk. She didn't even know *why* he trusted her. Given that they should have been enemies, he shouldn't have.

"Are you still feeling ill effects?" Hawk asked gently, his thumb brushing the back of her hand as he looked up at her.

235

"A twinge here and there," she murmured, again thinking that she should pull her hand back, but those little brushes sent pleasant tingles up her arm and throughout the rest of her body. She had to fight the urge to scoot closer and maybe stroke the side of his face and tell him that she was glad he'd survived. "I haven't had to rush to the privy in over an hour, so that's promising."

Maybe that wasn't the most appropriate thing to discuss with a man who was stroking her hand, but he only gave her that bleary smile again. "I think that's good, though our privies are wondrous. Much better than simply squatting in the woods."

"Wondrous? The one in our dome house seems fairly standard."

"Did you activate the plants? Women love them."

"Activate the plants?" She *remembered* plants, a pot next to the privy as well as vines growing up the wall, but with such things so prevalent in the outpost, she hadn't thought anything of them.

"Ask a guard to show you. They fill the room with pleasant fragrances. Even males can appreciate such things, especially if they've been poisoned and are having discomfort in their lower regions." His mouth twisted.

Aldari shook her head, not sure if he was serious or woozy from the medication, but the last thing she planned to do was ask one of the dour guards how to *activate* the privy.

"I appreciate you," Hawk said softly, squeezing her hand.

"Uhm? I mean, thanks, but why?" Aldari didn't usually fumble her words around men, but they also weren't usually stroking her hand when they spoke to her.

"You've been helping me almost since we kidnapped you. Since *I* kidnapped you. You protected me in the wagon when I was too weak to raise my own sword to fight. I saw you. And you could have struck against me when I was locked in battle with the serpent, and you didn't. You helped me drink and cared for me in the wagon. I don't think I deserve any of that from you." He brought her hand to his mouth and kissed her knuckles.

It wasn't an erotic kiss, nothing like that, but it sent another tingle through her and made her want to lie down beside him and wrap her arms around him, maybe even to *kiss* him. Not on the knuckles but on the cheek. Or... the lips?

Aldari swallowed, knowing she should move, should put some distance between them, but her body refused to get off the bed. If anything, she caught herself leaning closer to him.

"I know you have your duty that calls you," Hawk said, lowering her hand so that it rested on his chest—his *bare* chest, "and that when you help me it's in conflict with what you need to do for your people. You're willing to give up your happiness and maybe your freedom and everything you know to help your kingdom. I... understand that."

Not trusting her voice, Aldari only nodded. She knew he did. He might be a simple mercenary, but he'd taken on this duty for the sake of his people, whether they'd approved of his unorthodox approach to problem-solving or not. He was risking his life—he'd already almost *died*—because he wanted to help them.

"I understand," he repeated, "but I admit... I wish you weren't engaged to marry another man. I find myself... appreciating you more than I should."

A warm shiver went through her, and she didn't know what to say. It was the first time he'd admitted he found her appealing in any way. None of the elves had suggested that, but when his eyelids drooped, and his gaze lowered from her face to one of the *windows* in her dress, she realized he might be attracted to her.

"I hope he'll be good to you," Hawk whispered. She was on the verge of being touched by his concern, but then he added, "I'd be tempted to kill him if he wasn't," and that jolted her as much as the eyeball soup had.

"Uh," she managed to say. "That might be bad for our alliance. I mean, the alliance between his people and mine."

"Maybe, but you deserve..." He lifted his gaze, but a yawn broke his words, and he blinked slowly. "You deserve someone fun and nice. Is he nice?"

"I haven't met him."

"Tell him to be nice." Hawk smiled, his eyelids threatening to close, and released her hand.

Even though she liked talking to him, liked *being* with him, Aldari was relieved that he was falling asleep. Sitting there with him, with him holding her hand, was too tempting. She *was* sworn to do what she had to do for the good of her people. She didn't need temptations, especially when that temptation could lead her to do something foolish—and permanent. As Theli kept pointing out, Aldari couldn't forget that her marriage was contingent on Xerik getting a virgin. She might think that was stupid and shouldn't matter, but it was what her father had agreed to. And she'd agreed to it too. At the time, she'd been largely indifferent to men and sex and hadn't thought anything of waiting until marriage. That had been before—

"Tell him," Hawk repeated, "that if he's not nice, I'll come to his kingdom and kill him." His eyes were closed, but he smiled and shifted his arm to pat her on the thigh. "Don't let him not be nice, Aldari. You're too good for someone who doesn't treat you well."

Even though he was half-asleep, the words seemed sincere, and they touched her. She had a hard time coming up with a response, because she was so aware that he was touching her, his hand lingering on her thigh. Her dress—thankfully window-free in that spot—was between them, but the thin fabric wasn't much of a barrier. She had no trouble feeling the warmth of his hand through it.

She cleared her throat diffidently, intending to tell him to move his hand, but his head tilted to the side, chin to his chest, as sleep seemed to claim him. But not fully. His hand lingered, and he massaged her thigh gently. When he'd kissed her knuckles, that might not have been erotic, but this... This sent heated pleasure through her body, every part of her tightening in anticipation. She couldn't help but wonder what else he might touch if she encouraged it.

But she couldn't encourage it. She took a deep breath and picked up his hand and moved it aside. He didn't stir, and she had a feeling he wasn't aware that he'd been touching her. Strange that her body could be so affected by such absent fondling.

His breathing was even, his eyelids closed, and she told herself to rise. Whatever happened with the medic, Hawk would update her, but it wouldn't likely be until the next day. It was time for her to return to her dome with Theli.

Or maybe she would lean forward and kiss Hawk on the cheek. He was asleep. He wouldn't even know, and there was nothing overly intimate about a kiss on the cheek. She felt grateful to him for saying that he appreciated her, even if she was more disturbed than grateful about his promise that he would kill her future husband if he wasn't *nice*. She hoped he wouldn't remember having spoken such words when he woke.

"Rest well, Hawk," she said gently, patting him on the chest.

Then she leaned forward, assuring herself once more that a kiss on the cheek wouldn't be inappropriate. As she touched her lips to his skin, her mouth not far from his, she wondered what she would do if he woke up and turned his face toward her.

But he wasn't the one to stir. Without warning, the door opened.

Aldari lurched back and lunged to her feet as King Jesireth walked in with the healer coming after him. Guilt and embarrassment swarmed her as she wondered if they'd seen her with her lips on Hawk. The king frowned at her, but he didn't say anything, and she couldn't tell. He stepped forward and shook Hawk's shoulder to wake him.

Aldari opened her mouth, feeling protective and that Hawk's sleep shouldn't be disrupted, but she couldn't stop the elven king. Besides, this might be about the medic.

Hawk woke with a smile that turned to a frown when he spotted Jesireth scowling down at him. He looked blearily around the room until he saw Aldari, then managed a smile for her. That only made the king's scowl darker.

Theli was in the doorway, her hand resting uncertainly on the hilt of her mace, and a guard stood next to her, watching her, with his hand on the hilt of *his* weapon.

Aldari shook her head at Theli. She didn't think she was in trouble at the moment. Jesireth spoke tersely, drawing Hawk's focus to him.

Hawk rubbed his eyes and blinked as he nodded. He looked like he was trying to shove aside the grogginess. Again, Aldari wished they would all leave him alone so he could rest.

When Jesireth finished, Hawk looked at her again. "They can't find Mevleth. He was seen leaving the outpost and hasn't been back. Did you tell anyone else your hypothesis?"

"I told Pheleran when I asked to see you an hour or two ago."

Hawk sighed. "That's about when Mevleth was seen leaving. *I* didn't get that message, but someone must have warned him."

"Aren't the mercenaries loyal to you?"

"They should be," Hawk said darkly. "Someone is getting Setvik from the practice arena now. The king will have him questioned."

Aldari winced, afraid this would turn Setvik even more against Hawk. If he'd colluded with Mevleth, or even given the order for the medic to poison Hawk, then maybe he would be arrested and wouldn't be a further problem, but if he'd had nothing to do with it, Setvik might be indignant at the accusation and have more reason to dislike Hawk.

Jesireth said something, and Hawk sighed and nodded again.

"Someone will take you and Theli back to your rooms." Hawk squinted over at Theli, who had thankfully lowered her hand from her mace. "The healer will come see you later and give you something to help your stomach."

"Thank you."

Jesireth glanced at Aldari, then launched into what sounded like another lecture to Hawk. No wonder he would have considered one from her on economics more palatable.

Aldari allowed the guards to usher her out, though for the tenth time, she wished she understood the elven language.

23

THE NEXT MORNING, ALDARI WOKE WHEN SOMEONE KNOCKED. THELI rolled out of her bed with her mace in hand.

Without waiting for an answer, two elven females walked in, one carrying a stack of clothing and the other a tray with pitchers, a tureen, bowls, and spoons. Not speaking or reacting to Theli's defensive posture, they set the items down on the table next to the scroll case. The day before, Aldari had placed it there, chagrined when she'd realized she'd been too distracted to ask Hawk to translate the contents—though he might have been too weary to manage the task even if she'd asked.

After the elves bowed and walked out, Aldari flopped back onto her pillow and rubbed her face. The vestiges of a dream lingered in her mind. A *lurid* dream. That was the only word that came to mind to describe it. She'd been back in Hawk's room, doing things with him that she'd only read about in books. Warmth flushed her cheeks and made her glad that her body-guard couldn't read her mind. What lecture would Theli deliver if she could?

This wasn't the first sexual dream Aldari had ever had, but it was the first time she'd dreamed about a real person. In the past, her dreams had usually involved some fictional hero from a ballad or a novel. Were she a dutiful fiancée, she supposed she would keep a portrait of her future husband in her room and try to dream about him. But she doubted it worked that way, that simply looking at a portrait before bed could instill proper dreams. Maybe she shouldn't even be *having* such dreams. It wasn't a sign of subconscious disloyalty, was it?

"This soup has eyeballs in it." Theli had put away her mace and lifted the lid on the tureen, but she clanked it back down.

"How many?" Aldari forced a smile.

The evening before, the healer had come by to examine them, sprinkling a fresh dusting of powder on Theli's cut, and giving Aldari a red potion that she'd sipped on but not finished. After her *last* potion, she'd been hesitant to put her full trust in another elven concoction. But it had soothed the vestiges of her affliction and even invigorated her. Maybe she could blame the potion for her *active* dream.

"I saw at least three floating on some leaves," Theli said. "Some might be hunkering underneath them."

"The healer must not have thought we were very ill then. Hawk had at least thirty floating in his bowl."

"Is that what you were discussing with him?" Theli sniffed one of the pitchers, then poured purple juice into a cup. "You were in there a long time just to tell him about the poison."

"I know." Maybe she should have left it at that, but Aldari felt conflicted and wished she had someone to confide in—or at least talk things through with. Could Theli listen attentively without judging her? Probably not, but at the same time, Aldari didn't think Theli would blab any secrets she shared with Aldari's future husband or anyone back home. "I like his company. A lot more than that of any of the other elves."

"I know you do." Theli poured another cup and brought it

over. "That's why I'm worried. My father is a military man, and so are my brothers. If the kingdom ends up at war with the Taldar Empire, my entire family will be sent to the front lines."

She didn't say *we need this alliance*, but she didn't have to. Aldari knew, and she also knew how badly things would go for her people if they had to fight the empire.

"You don't have to worry, Theli. Nothing's going to happen between Hawk and me. I won't let it." As if to mock Aldari, the memory of her dream flooded back into her mind, of her mouth locked to Hawk's, of his hands continuing the exploration they'd started the day before.

"I believe that you believe that, but come on, Aldari. I see the way he looks at you, and the way you get all dreamy when he smiles. I know you intend to go through with your marriage and don't *want* to do anything to hurt our people's chances at retaining their independence, but it's easy to make bad decisions when you're attracted to someone."

"I'm not going to make a bad decision."

"You looked like you were about to make one when the king walked in yesterday."

"Hawk was sleeping. I was just going to kiss him on the cheek."

"While your hand was caressing his chest?"

"It wasn't *doing* that." Or had it been? Damn, maybe she *had* still had her hand on his chest. Not *caressing* it but touching it. If Theli had seen that, the king, who'd walked in first, certainly had.

Aldari rubbed her face again, mortified and longing to go home. Not to Xerik's home but to her own, where she could stay in her room, researching and writing papers, and not worry about men of any kind, human or elven.

"I trust it wasn't Xerik that you were dreaming about while you were over here moaning in your sleep," Theli said. "I've seen his portrait. He's not as drool-inspiring as Hawk and the other mercenaries."

"I wasn't *moaning*."

Theli arched her eyebrows.

Aldari slumped and buried her face in her hands, tempted to bury her entire body under the covers. Why hadn't their captors been polite enough to give them separate bedrooms?

"Look, Your Highness—Aldari." Theli sat on the edge of her bed. "I understand, and I really don't want to be your chaperone—Hell, I've had dreams about them too. Who doesn't love a tautly muscled warrior with the athleticism of a gazelle? And if you weren't supposed to be walking to the ceremonial platform for your wedding in a week, I wouldn't stand in the way in the least, but... I think you'll regret it if you do anything. I know you care about this alliance too."

"I *do*. That's why nothing is going to happen. Dreams aren't... It's not cheating if it's a dream, right?" Aldari looked a little uncertainly at Theli, afraid she would have a different opinion.

"No. As long as it doesn't go beyond dreams."

"It won't." It wasn't a lie; Aldari meant it.

"Good."

As they finished their dubious breakfast—the salty broth was delicious, but the leaves were bitter, and Aldari avoided the eyeballs—another knock came at the door. This time, the person waited for Theli to open it before entering.

"At the king's behest, you are commanded to attend an inquiry," a male elf said, looking past Theli to Aldari.

Theli scowled. "Are we being accused of something? Something *else*?"

"Please dress promptly. I will wait and escort you to the audience platform." The elf closed the door without acknowledging Theli's questions.

"I guess a dress with windows isn't appropriate for an audience with the king." Even before the fire, Aldari had been tired of living and sleeping in the travel-stained garment, so she pulled it over her head and flung it aside with relish before examining the stack of clothing.

"*Windows*? Is that what you're calling those rips?"

"It's what... someone called them."

Theli snorted. "I told you he would be intrigued. The one on your side shows the curve of your breast."

"Thanks so much for letting me know." Aldari kept herself from saying it had been her *thigh* that Hawk had touched. She would keep that to herself, but as she selected a green dress with silver trim, she couldn't help but hope Hawk would be at this audience. It would be nice to have one elf present who didn't glare at her. But given how dizzy and tired he'd been the day before, he would likely still be in bed.

Her gut twisted as she paused in dressing. What if something had happened to him since she'd last seen him? What if he'd gotten worse? Would she be accused of harming him *again*?

The thought distressed her so much that she lunged for the door and flung it open while Theli was in the middle of putting on a tan dress she'd selected.

"Is the captain all right?" Aldari blurted as soon as the elf turned toward her.

He tilted his head. "Who?"

"Captain Hawk. Nothing's happened, has it?"

"Ah, yes. Captain Hawk. The last I heard, his condition had improved and he was speaking."

That had been yesterday, and she almost said so, but if he'd gotten worse, news would have leaked out about it. That probably meant he was fine, or at least not any worse.

The elf looked past her shoulder to where Theli was pulling her dress up over her shoulders. He must have been a fan of muscular women, for he smiled and nodded appreciatively, crossing two fingers in a gesture Aldari hadn't seen before. He turned around even before Aldari shut the door, but she apologized to Theli for having facilitated the gawking.

"No need." Theli grabbed her boots. "That's the first elf who's acknowledged how sexy I am. I was tempted to give him a little wiggle."

"*Theli.*" Normally, Aldari wouldn't have judged her, but Theli had been giving *her* such a hard time that it seemed fair.

"What? Most of them seem to think humans are no better than dogs. But you know what? I've seen their females. They're not that great. Half of them are sticks. A man likes a little something to grab on to." Theli patted her butt, then thrust her breasts out. "Remember that when you're going to your prince's bed."

"What, to wiggle my breasts?"

"Among other things."

When they walked out together, the elf was still smiling and gave Theli another nod, though he didn't touch her or do anything inappropriate. Aldari didn't know if she should read anything into that. If the elven people still believed Aldari and Theli were heinous criminals, would the guard sent to escort them have flirted with Theli?

Who knew? The guard might not know anything.

The audience platform was a covered area with numerous groups of seats and a fire crackling in a circular stone pit. King Jesireth and the silver-haired female who'd been coming out of Hawk's room the day before stood on a dais in front of a railing that looked over the river. Lieutenant Setvik faced them, his back to Theli and Aldari as they approached.

Setvik was without his weapons, but his hands were clenched as he faced the pair. He gazed toward the river instead of challenging them with direct stares. A few other elves sat in the nearest group of seats, two of them scribbling in notepads. Numerous guards were positioned around the area, including two with nocked bows pointed at Setvik.

"Did they find out he's responsible?" Aldari whispered before she could think better of it.

Setvik, his hearing as sharp as Hawk's, looked back at her. He glared, as he usually did, but not for long before Jesireth spoke and drew his attention back to him.

Their escort directed Theli to a seating area. Aldari started to follow, assuming their turn would come later, but he held up a hand and pointed for her to join the group at the railing.

"Oh, good," she muttered, not wanting to get anywhere near Setvik, even with archers keeping an eye on him.

Aldari didn't see Hawk. Too bad. She would have preferred to get an update from him, rather than joining this... whatever it was. Hawk had mentioned Setvik would be questioned. Had that already happened?

King Jesireth looked at Aldari as she reluctantly approached, and she remembered that he'd caught her about to kiss Hawk, with her hand on his chest—*fondling* it, if Theli hadn't been exaggerating. Aldari hoped she had been.

"We have a few questions for you, Princess Aldari," Jesireth said.

"Yes, Your Majesty." Aldari glanced at the silver-haired female and realized abruptly that this had to be his wife, the elven queen. Even though she hadn't thought the woman she'd seen the day before had looked like a servant, it surprised her that the queen would have personally brought soup to an injured mercenary.

"Has *Veth* Setvik done anything suspicious in your eyes since you've been with the mercenary company?" Jesireth asked, watching Setvik more than Aldari.

She hesitated. This wasn't the line of questioning she'd expected.

Setvik's jaw tightened, and he didn't so much as glance at her. He shifted his hands behind his back to clasp them, his fingers tight, and continued to stare out at the river.

"Suspicious... other than kidnapping us?" Theli muttered from her seat several feet away.

Aldari almost missed hearing it, but the elves doubtless had no trouble catching the comment, for the king frowned at Theli.

And then at Aldari. "Perhaps, Princess Aldari, you could ask your servant to mind her tongue during this audience. We do not mind her witnessing it, as we may call upon her to testify, but we would prefer she show respect in this sacred hall." He waved to four statues mounted in the rafters above the dais—elven gods?

Aldari looked at Theli and put a finger to her lips, hoping the elven royals didn't require stronger punishment for wayward *servants*—Aldari was sure the proud Theli was roiling inside at being called that. Theli rolled her eyes and folded her arms over her chest, but she didn't open her mouth again.

"I didn't witness the lieutenant giving the medic any orders," Aldari said, "if that's what this is about."

"Yes," the queen said, speaking for the first time. "The Moon Sword medic fled before our people could capture him, but he left his medical kit behind. Our healer found the dreadful potion that he gave to Hawsy—to *Hawk* and analyzed it. There was indeed a poisonous substance in it. You are fortunate that you did not drink more of it."

"The fact that this *mercenary* encouraged Hawk to..." Jesireth flexed his fingers in the air, as if he were imagining wringing the medic's neck.

Aldari was glad the king and queen appeared to care for Hawk, though it was a little surprising, especially since the Moon Sword Company worked, as far as she'd heard, outside of Serth and had for years. How close could the captain be with the royal family here?

It crossed her mind that Hawk might be from a noble family— or the elven equivalent. If he'd grown up around the royals, maybe that was why the king and queen cared for him. He was about the same age as the prince. Maybe they'd been playmates during their schooldays.

Setvik spoke stiffly in his own language.

"We'll see," Jesireth said in Aldari's, then looked at her again. "You never saw them conspiring together?"

"I saw them speaking after Hawk took ill, but I can't understand your language, so..." Aldari spread a hand. "Before we reached this side of the river, I didn't interact with the medic and wasn't paying much attention to him. I was busy working with my bodyguard to try to escape." She raised her brows, not too proud to remind the king that his people had taken her prisoner against her wishes.

Jesireth sighed softly and looked at his wife for a long moment before facing Aldari again. "I do apologize that you were brought here against your will, Princess Aldari, for what many consider... a far-fetched scheme."

Aldari let her eyebrows climb higher. "Hawk said your scientists had uncovered some puzzles that need to be solved if your people are to gain access to an ancient laboratory that could hold the secret to changing the Twisted back or at least ending their threat. Is that not true?"

Thus far, she'd taken Hawk's words at face value, but maybe she'd been naive to do so.

"That is our belief, yes, but the notion that a young human woman who knows nothing of our people could assist in some way..." Jesireth smiled gently—and condescendingly—at her.

It made Aldari want to gnash her teeth.

"I never would have authorized such a mission," he said. "Had *Captain* Hawk asked for permission, I never would have granted it. Even if I believed you *could* help, *kidnapping* you wouldn't have been the way to go about requesting that help."

Theli made a strangled noise. At least she didn't mutter her thoughts this time, though Aldari had no trouble guessing them. *That's what* we've *been saying.*

The queen stirred, as if she might speak, but she didn't say anything.

"Now that it's clear you had nothing to do with Hawk's poisoning," Jesireth continued, "I will, of course, arrange an escort to take you safely back to your homeland."

Aldari rocked back in surprise. It was what she wanted—what *Theli* kept reminding her she wanted—but she hadn't expected them to let her go so easily. As strange as it was, she felt no relief. If anything, she was insulted that this arrogant king didn't think she could help. If she offered to stay, would he even allow it?

"I thank you for that, Your Majesty, but... since Hawk explained the peril that your people have been suffering for so long, I feel I should try to help, if at all possible. I may be young, but I'm not bad at puzzles." Bragging was frowned upon in her culture, but she realized the description *not bad* might not sway him, so she changed it. "By that, I mean I'm good at them. I have a knack for solving them, and if it's possible that I could help, I would like to."

Jesireth tilted his head in puzzlement.

The queen gazed thoughtfully at Aldari. "The puzzle that currently bars entrance to what we believe was Zedaron's laboratory is in a dangerous place. Even if you could be of assistance, we could not in good faith allow you to go and endanger yourself."

"Hawk said he would protect me."

"*Hawk* nearly got himself killed," Jesireth snapped before taking a breath and smoothing the emotion from his face. "He is a capable warrior, but even he cannot stand against a horde of the Twisted."

"Or a betrayal from within his own company," the queen murmured, frowning at Setvik.

Setvik flinched. He hadn't reacted like that when the Twisted had been barreling down upon him, but maybe he was genuinely distressed at what had happened to Hawk. Or, more likely, he was distressed to have been dragged in front of the king and queen. Aldari recalled how Setvik hadn't felt he had the authority to reply to the message the queen had sent via the falcon.

"Do you not have a marriage that you were en route to?" Jesireth asked Aldari.

From her seat, Theli nodded vigorously. She had to be having a hard time refraining from speaking out.

Aldari blushed again under the king's gaze, though he hadn't brought up the kiss he'd seen her giving Hawk.

"Yes, Your Highness. An arranged marriage." Aldari realized that made it sound like she was making an excuse for her behavior and implying she didn't approve. She took a deep breath and corrected herself. "An arranged marriage that I agreed to in order to cement an alliance between Orath and Delantria. You may be aware that my kingdom has been encroached upon by the Taldar Empire. My people are struggling even as we speak to retain Delantria's independence, and we're counting on Orath to ally with us and keep the empire at bay."

Jesireth nodded. "We are unfortunately embroiled in our own problems, so our people aren't able to participate in the politics of the human kingdoms, but I do my best to keep abreast of what goes on in the world. Because of the tenuous situation, you must be eager to return."

"I am, yes, but I also... sympathize with your people and your plight. Admittedly, I was aware of very little of it before, but now that I know, it would be difficult for me to leave without offering to help."

"*Aldari,*" Theli blurted. "Take his offer."

Aldari lifted her palm toward her as she held the king's gaze. "Your Majesty, is it possible you could send a message to Prince

Xerik with one of your falcons and let him know I'll be coming and just be a little delayed? Then I could go with Hawk and—"

"No," Jesireth said, cutting her off. "If you were injured or killed, what then? Our people would be blamed. Rightfully so." He shook his head. "It is too dangerous. I will arrange an escort to take you home. You'll leave in the morning."

Theli slumped in her seat in naked relief.

Aldari couldn't feel anything but distress, distress at having come all this way and not being allowed to help, at never seeing the puzzle that nobody had managed to solve, and at never seeing Hawk again. The latter shouldn't have bothered her more than everything else, but it did.

"Let us first finish the matter at hand." Jesireth gestured again at the silent Setvik. "Princess Aldari, who locked you in the scroll repository yesterday?"

"Ah."

Setvik shot her a dark look. She had a feeling he already knew —and that he didn't want her to say anything to the king.

"Princess?" Jesireth prompted.

"One of the mercenaries. Pheleran." Aldari lifted her chin. If Setvik had wanted her loyalty, he should have been less of an ass to her and Hawk.

"So," Jesireth said, "not only did Setvik's *medic* poison Hawk, but one of his troops tried to end your life."

"And mine," Theli muttered.

This time, nobody paid attention to her comment.

Jesireth scowled at Setvik and said, "As the leader of those men, you are responsible for their actions," before switching to Elven.

Setvik spoke in protest, pressing a hand to his chest and shaking his head. What punishment was the king threatening? Aldari wished she knew. Alarm and then distress entered Setvik's eyes, eyes that had been fearless in the face of battle and death.

A voice spoke up from the back of the platform. Hawk.

He walked slowly, the healer at his side and a staff in his hand for support, but he came forward with firm determination.

Jesireth asked a question. Hawk repeated whatever he'd said, pointing at Setvik, then at himself. That prompted an argument, with Hawk and the king going back and forth. Aldari was surprised Hawk kept coming, kept speaking back, and wouldn't back down to his monarch. She worried he would get himself in trouble.

"What's he saying?" she whispered, though she doubted the nearby guards would translate for her.

"That *he's* the leader of the company," Setvik surprised her by translating, "and therefore responsible for the actions of the men, and that he will take any punishment meant for them."

Aldari couldn't tell if Setvik was relieved, but for the first time when he looked at Hawk, it wasn't with irritation or frustration.

As the argument between Jesireth and Hawk grew louder and more agitated, the queen walked to Aldari's side. "Come, Princess Aldari. We've no more questions for you. I'll take you back to your quarters and arrange that escort. Tomorrow, you'll go home."

"But what about Hawk? It's not his fault that his men misbehaved. The medic was targeting *him*, and Pheleran only locked us in because he believed I'd been responsible for the poisoning. None of that was Hawk's fault. Why are they arguing?"

The king's raised voice turned to a roar, and he pointed at the floor in front of him. Hawk fell silent, though he clenched his jaw as he lowered his head and dropped to one knee. The pose of supplication didn't keep him from continuing his argument, though he spoke more quietly now. Quietly but stubbornly.

"He's made some poor decisions aside from that." The queen took her arm.

Aldari wanted to stay, to argue further on Hawk's behalf, but Jesireth was red in the face now and not looking at her. Neither was Hawk. How could she help him when she didn't even understand the language?

"Come." This time, the queen applied force, her grip surprisingly strong.

Aldari slumped, having no choice but to allow herself to be guided away. She couldn't help but look back, afraid for what would happen to Hawk and wondering if she would ever see him again.

24

As the sun set, Aldari sat on her bed and stared glumly at a fresh tray of food the servants had delivered. Theli hummed as she puttered around, packing the clothing, combs, and toiletries that had been brought for them, gifts for the return trip. She hadn't been in such a bright mood since before they'd been kidnapped.

Aldari should have been pleased as well, but she couldn't stop worrying about Hawk. All day, she'd listened with hope every time an elf walked past their window or when a sound outside might have meant someone coming to the door. But Hawk hadn't visited.

Would he find a way to do so before she left? Or was he in an elven dungeon cell, awaiting punishment for crimes he didn't deserve to be blamed for? Why hadn't he let Setvik accept the onus for everything? The king had seemed willing to hold the lieutenant accountable. Aldari certainly would have been.

Still, she couldn't be surprised that Hawk had stepped forward. Even though he'd kidnapped her, she believed he was honorable, that only desperation and a need to help his people had led him to take that action. She understood that need perfectly well.

A soft knock sounded, and Aldari sprang to her feet.

"I'll get it," she blurted as Theli grabbed her mace and tried to reach the door first.

"*Aldari*, you're *impossible* to protect," Theli said as Aldari flung the door open, hoping to find Hawk on the threshold.

Surprisingly, the queen stood there. After she'd escorted them back to their dome that morning, Aldari hadn't expected to see her again.

Theli backed away and lowered her mace, looking sheepishly at the queen's regally raised eyebrows. She held a small silver chest but nothing resembling a weapon. Two guards had accompanied her, but they stood well back.

"Come in, please, Queen... I'm sorry. I don't think anyone has told me your name." Aldari stepped back. "I'm ashamed to admit I don't know it. My father would, I'm sure, but..." Aldari bit her lip, wishing she hadn't confessed to that ignorance. She knew the names of most of the rulers in the world, but the elves were so reclusive that she hadn't known either the king or queen before all this started.

"Tsaritha." The queen stepped inside. "Our people keep to ourselves. I would be more surprised if you *did* know the names of those in the royal court. I'm sorry we won't have time to better get to know you. You seem to be... more than I expected."

Aldari glanced at Theli. What did *that* mean?

"I felt I knew you somewhat," Tsaritha said, "in an academic sense through your papers, but I wouldn't have expected you to want to help our people, not when it would involve danger to you. And when I believed you had something to do with Hawk's poisoning, I thought the worst. I apologize for that."

"It's all right... Uhm, you've read my papers?"

"Professor Lyn Dorit's papers." Tsaritha's eyes crinkled.

Aldari's jaw sagged open. Why would the elven queen have been researching her pen name? Unless... was this the *king's advisor* that Hawk had spoken of? If so, why not mention that she was also the queen?

"We can't allow you to risk yourself, of course," Tsaritha continued, "but it means a great deal to me that you offered. I brought you a small wedding gift. It is nothing significant, as we don't have great riches to share, but perhaps you will value it. I hope that if we ever find a way to end the threat of the Twisted and venture out into the world again, your kingdom will not consider us to be enemies for having allowed your kidnapping."

"I don't blame you for that, Your Majesty."

"I'm not without blame, unfortunately. Oh, I wasn't responsible for it and didn't know *that* was what Hawk intended when he said he would go find you, else I never would have sent the mercenaries along with him."

"Is Hawk all right?" Aldari bit her lip, afraid both the king and queen were condemning him and that he was being punished with more than the lectures he loathed.

Instead of answering, Tsaritha gazed at her with her head tilted, as if studying her. "I sense that you do not blame him either," she finally said.

"For kidnapping us? Well, I understand why he did it."

"That is unexpected."

"That I can understand things? I hope elves don't think too poorly of human intellectual capabilities."

Tsaritha surprised her by laughing. "That you *forgive* him."

"Oh, well, he's kind of... charming."

Tsaritha chuckled again. "I suppose he can be." She handed the small chest to her. "Please accept this gift from our family. It's a necklace that is believed to repel the Twisted. I wouldn't rush out into the wilds to put it to the test, but my grandmother did swear that it worked when they tried to get to her many decades ago."

Surprised, Aldari opened the chest to reveal a beautiful golden chain with a vibrant emerald-green leaf medallion. It gleamed, almost as if it had an inner light. If it was magical, maybe it did.

"I... this is far too valuable, Your Majesty." Aldari tried to return it, hardly able to believe the queen wanted to give it to her. "I can't accept this."

"I wish you to have it." Tsaritha clasped her hands behind her back, refusing to let Aldari foist it on her.

"But we don't have the Twisted in Delantria. It belongs here, protecting your people."

"You must cross through our land to reach the ship that will sail you to your future husband," Tsaritha said. "It is possible your party will be attacked along the way. I want you to have it."

"I..." Aldari swallowed.

Tsaritha had a good point, but once Aldari set sail, she wouldn't see the Twisted again. After she reached the port, maybe she could give it to a trustworthy member of her escort to return to the queen. Would that be rude? To refuse the gift? Aldari would decide when she reached the port.

"Thank you, Your Majesty," she said.

"You are welcome. Best wishes on your journey." Tsaritha nodded to Theli as well as Aldari, though as she stepped back into the doorway, she held Aldari's gaze, smiling faintly. "I'm touched that you find Hawk charming."

"Will you tell him..." Aldari trailed off, not sure what she wanted her message to be. Was it foolish to hope that she might see him again? That he would show up in the morning before she left?

Tsaritha raised her eyebrows. "That you find him charming? Goodness, no. He would be smug and full of himself."

"I'm sure that's not true, but if you could please tell him I forgive him and am glad to have met him..." Aldari's throat swelled with emotion, and she struggled to get out the rest of her words. "I would appreciate it."

"I will." Tsaritha inclined her head before stepping out.

Aldari sank onto the bed with the chest and amulet, contemplating the gift and mulling over Tsaritha. At first, Aldari had been inclined to dislike the queen *and* the king, but this changed her opinion, at least of her. They were probably both fine leaders though, just trying to lead their people in harrowing times.

"She should have given that to *me*." Theli waved her hand to draw attention to the gash she'd received from the Twisted, though it appeared to be healing nicely. "I'm more likely to get clobbered by them than you."

"Only because you insert yourself between them and me. You might recall that they're drawn by magic, which I believe that baton is." Aldari wondered if she should have given that to the queen. She couldn't take it with her when she left Serth.

"*Inserting myself* between you and a threat is my job."

"True. Do you want to wear it?" Aldari offered her the chest.

Theli's eyes grew wistful as she gazed upon the beautiful amulet. "Yes, but I won't. She gave it to you."

"Do you want to wear it after we leave the outpost and she won't see us again?"

"Maybe."

Aldari smiled.

A soft knock sounded, not at the front door but at the wall beside the beaded curtain that led to the garden dome and the privy. Theli sprang into an aggressive crouch, her mace in hand once again.

Aldari reached for her own dagger. She hadn't noticed an exterior door leading out of the back of their quarters and wouldn't have guessed anyone could enter that way. Unless someone had been skulking among the garden beds and berry bushes all day.

The knock came again. Whoever their intruder was, he or she was polite.

"Come in?" Aldari asked more than called.

Theli gave her an incredulous look and tightened her grip on her mace. "It could be one of those mercenaries, or Setvik himself, out for revenge."

"Revenge for what? They kidnapped *us*."

Before Theli could answer, the beads parted. "Are you sure?"

Aldari nearly fell off the bed. That was Hawk's voice.

"I don't know," Aldari said. "Did you hobble out of bed and over here against the wishes of your healer?"

The curtain opened wider, beads clattering, and Hawk stepped in. His face was pinched, and he used a staff for support, so she had a feeling she was right.

"Against *everybody's* wishes," he admitted. "But I didn't hobble. I strode over here in a virile and masculine fashion."

Aldari eyed the staff.

"This is an unstrung bow." Hawk lifted it and turned to show a quiver of arrows on his back. "A masculine weapon I'm simply carrying along in case there's an attack."

He didn't hold the bow staff up for long before setting the tip back down and leaning on it while trying to hide that he was leaning on it.

"If you'd sent an invitation, I would have come up to your room to visit," Aldari said. "I actually wanted to give you some work, but you fell asleep before I could yesterday, so I didn't get a chance."

"You like to deliver lectures *and* give work? Are you sure you're not a professor instead of a princess?"

"I wouldn't mind being a real professor and being able to publish my papers openly."

"They're great papers—at least my, uhm, the king's advisor says so."

"You mean the queen?"

"Ah? You figured that out, did you?" Hawk smiled at her, more in approval than consternation that she'd seen through his omission. "When she shared the paper mentioning the puzzle with me, it was a little over my head, but I look forward to reading anything you've got that could help solve the whale problem."

"I'll send over everything that's relevant as soon as I'm able." Aldari didn't know if Hawk would find her other papers more accessible, especially given that Hyric wasn't his native language, but maybe she could make some notes in the margin. The thought of sending him personalized annotations warmed her heart, and she hoped her future husband wouldn't object to her having correspondence with an elf mercenary. Though she feared he might, and that thought made her glum. Forcing a smile, she added to Hawk, "Some light reading helps one fall asleep after a rough day of battle."

Theli sighed dramatically, dropped her mace onto her pack, and flopped down on the bed with her arm over her eyes.

"Is your bodyguard all right?" Hawk asked.

"She's aggrieved that there's a boy in my room."

"Well, I *did* come to kidnap you again, so if she's vexed with me, that's understandable."

Aldari raised her eyebrows. "Truly?"

Theli lowered her arm, scowled at Hawk, and glanced at her mace, probably wondering if she'd set it down too early.

Hawk wavered his hand in the air. "This time, I'm asking your permission to do so first." He took a deep breath and looked at the wall instead of her. "The king and queen believe that you should be returned to your homeland in order to avoid an international incident and possibly your death."

"Extremely *valid* things to want to avoid," Theli said.

Aldari waved for her to stay out of it—or possibly explore the gardens in the other room. "I told them I'd be willing to risk those things and help. I mean, I don't want to start an international incident, but if your king was to send a note to Prince Xerik, explaining that I'll be along shortly... I'd still be game to help. The king did, however, give me the impression that he didn't think I could be useful."

"*I* think you can." Hawk flattened his hand to his chest. "And she may not have admitted it, but the queen thinks you can too."

"Oh?"

"The queen is an academic and a historian and truly does advise the king on such matters. I didn't want to implicate her in my plot, so that's why I was evasive, but as I said, she's the one who found your papers and believed you could help. If you'll come with me—" Hawk rested his palm on his chest, "—I want to continue to the north, to our fallen capital and the camp we established there this spring. A number of scientists are still there, working on the puzzle and digging more of the ruins out from under the lava rock. By now, they might have unearthed more clues to help with the puzzle. We can't give up, not when we're this close." Hawk held thumb and forefinger out, almost touching. "I don't know for sure that there's a solution to the Twisted in Zedaron's old laboratory, but if there's even a *chance* there is, I have to go. And I'd like you to come."

"I'm willing, but..." Aldari glanced toward the window, wondering if the guards were still stationed out there. She hadn't checked since they'd returned that morning. "It sounds like this would be against the wishes of your monarchs."

"Yes. We'll need to sneak out."

"Just us?" Aldari remembered Hawk's touch on her leg and how tempted she'd been to kiss him. If they were alone out in the woods, would she be even *more* tempted?

No, Theli would be there. Besides, how much kissing and groping could they do when the Twisted might be skulking in the bushes?

"Us and the mercenaries," Hawk said.

Aldari grimaced. "Setvik? The medic?"

"Mevleth disappeared. And Setvik has agreed to this. Technically, he agreed to it weeks ago. Not much has changed."

"Other than your king forbidding it?"

"He hasn't *technically* forbidden it." Hawk was using that word a lot. "We didn't ask for permission, so there was nothing for him to forbid. We're just... going to go. In the dark of night. Actually, the dark of pre-dawn. Because the Twisted favor the night and are much more likely to be about then, we'll wait as long as we can, but we would need to slip out of the outpost before people get up." He hesitated. "If we don't get enough of a head start, it's possible the king will send troops after us."

"Are you *sure* he hasn't forbidden this?"

Hawk's gaze shifted back to the wall. "Even if he had, it would be worth defying him and suffering punishment for the chance to end this centuries-long darkness that threatens to destroy what little is left of our people."

"I understand." Aldari picked up the sooty scroll case and dumped out its contents. "I believe Zedaron might have written this." She showed him the mark on the case and the matching mark on the baton. "Can you translate it for me? I thought it might give me some insight into his mind."

Hawk studied the scroll. "I'd *like* to translate it for you, but it's in the old academic language. I'd be hard pressed to pick out more than a few words."

Aldari sagged against the table. "Would one of the scientists at that camp you mentioned be able to?"

"Possibly, but the queen could too, if I can figure out how to ask in a way that doesn't suggest we're going to sneak off with you in the morning." Hawk rolled up the scroll, tucked it back in the case, and stuck it through his belt. "If I can't, I'll find someone else in the outpost who can. Tonight." He smiled. "I was wondering what I'd do while waiting until we can leave on our excursion."

"Some people sleep at night."

"I slept all day. I'm well rested." Hawk waved a nonchalant hand.

The pain creases at the corners of his eyes and the bags underneath them suggested his healing body could use a lot more rest, but Aldari didn't argue with him. She wanted to know what the scroll said.

"Will you meet me outside an hour before dawn? At the road where we came into the outpost. I'll have reindeer for you." Hawk glanced at Theli. "For both of you."

"I guess we have to if I want to find out what the scroll says," Aldari said, though she'd known she would go with him as soon as he'd hobbled—as soon as he strode in a virile and masculine way —into the room.

"Yes. *Clearly*." Hawk patted the case. "Consider it a bribe."

"I hope it's not something insignificant. Like Zedaron's shopping list."

Hawk snorted. "*Those* aren't usually kept in our scroll repository of ancient knowledge." He clasped Aldari's hands and bowed over them. "I look forward to once more adventuring with you."

Theli groaned and threw her arm over her eyes again.

"I look forward to solving your puzzle," Aldari said, hoping it didn't sound too cocky to imply that she could. She also hoped she wasn't overestimating her abilities.

"Excellent." Hawk released her and did his best to stride out without leaning on the bow staff.

"I don't know why I got my hopes up that we'd be leaving," Theli mumbled. "I should have known. As soon as he gave you a puzzle, we were doomed."

"Do you think Prince Xerik will give me puzzles?" Aldari felt guilty for postponing the wedding even if she believed it was for a good cause. She hoped the delay wouldn't inconvenience her people—or Xerik's people—overmuch. And that nothing happened to her on this mission. Would Xerik agree to marry her sister if Aldari died and wasn't available to cement the alliance?

"If he's a normal man, he'll give you flowers and candies."

Aldari made a face.

"Quit wrinkling your nose. There's nothing wrong with such gifts. *Here*, we get moss cakes and eyeball soup."

"The eyeballs weren't that bad." Fortunately, the tureen had contained mostly broth.

"They pop in your mouth. It was the most disgusting thing I've ever eaten."

"That *can't* be true. What about Chef Beltzi's tripe stew?" Aldari wrinkled her nose again.

"Tripe doesn't pop. It's just... chewy."

"For a long time."

"Promise me if you run away from your marriage to an elf lover, you won't live in this kingdom."

"That won't happen." Alas. "But why would it matter to you?"

"I'm your bodyguard."

"You wouldn't be if I ran away. I'm sure Father would take you off the payroll."

"I'd stick with you."

"Truly?" Aldari was touched, even if she couldn't allow it.

"I'd have to. If you lived here, you'd need a bodyguard more than ever."

"To protect me from the food?" Aldari smiled.

"Among other things." Theli gave a pointed look to the singed dress dangling over the back of a chair.

Aldari's smile turned bleak at the reminder that one of the mercenaries had tried to arrange their deaths—and that they were about to go off into the wilderness again with those mercenaries.

25

AN HOUR BEFORE DAWN, ALDARI AND THELI GATHERED THEIR weapons and the packs they'd been given and stepped out of their dome. Either because Hawk had arranged it, or they were no longer considered prisoners, there weren't any guards standing by the door. This early, few elves were walking around in the outpost, but someone was singing in a nearby kitchen, and the smell of baking bread wafted to their noses, a hint of rosemary accompanying it. Or maybe that was moss or algae.

Aldari snorted as she and Theli headed for the cobblestone road. If she *were* to run away to live with an elven lover, she might insist they reside in a kingdom with more scintillating dietary staples.

The mercenaries waited on the cobblestone road near the invisible barrier that protected the city, its faint buzz tingling over Aldari's skin as they approached. This time, there wasn't a wagon, but the group had acquired more reindeer, enough for everyone to ride.

The medic wasn't among them. Aldari was relieved, but it was short-lived. Setvik glowered over at her, as if his need to get up early and travel into danger again was all her fault, and she remembered Pheleran's attempt on her life. He was among the mercenaries, sitting atop a shaggy gray-and-white reindeer. He looked at her and Theli, bit his lip, then looked away.

Feeling guilty? Aldari hoped so.

Hawk strode up the road and into view, his armor back on and his sword hanging from his belt. Instead of using the bow as a crutch, he'd strapped it to his pack along with his quiver of arrows. Aldari hoped that meant he was feeling better, but he yawned as he reached them, and she remembered he might have been up most of the night, trying to get her scroll translated. Had he succeeded?

As if he could read the question in her mind, Hawk nodded to her when he joined them. "I'll tell you as we ride." He waved her to a reindeer and offered her a boost up. "We need to get out of the outpost before we're noticed."

As people mounted, the reindeer grunted and shifted, their hooves clattered on the cobblestones, and Hawk winced and glanced in the direction of the aerial palace.

"How much trouble will you get in if we're caught?" Aldari asked him quietly.

"I don't know, but it's worth the risk." He gave her a smile, but it appeared forced.

Worried for Hawk and his future, Aldari couldn't return his smile with anything but bleakness. But she still wanted to go along with him and help solve his people's problem. Maybe, if they succeeded, all would be forgiven.

After everyone was mounted, Hawk drew Aldari and Theli into the lead alongside his reindeer. As the group headed for the barrier, the same girl that had lowered it before came out of the nearby tree home. Apparently not one to question her elders, she pressed a hand to the stone in the trunk, and the buzz disappeared from the air.

"Is she special?" Aldari asked. "Or could any of you do that?"

"Any of us who know the activation and deactivation words," Hawk said, "but someone has to remain inside to raise it again after the group has gone out."

"Ah."

Hawk thanked the girl and tossed her a coin.

"You haven't told me about your monetary system," Aldari said as they rode out, the mercenaries tense as they eyed the forest around them and the outpost behind.

"Most people curious about elves are more interested in hearing about our history or our fighting and training techniques." Hawk glanced at her. "I suppose an economist would naturally find coins more interesting."

"Naturally."

"They're all centuries old. We lost the mints when we lost the great cities. When our civilization—I hate to say *fell*—grew simpler, we had less need for complicated monetary systems. Our accounting and taxes are very basic these days. Some people still use the coins for exchange, but many have been lost or hoarded over the years."

"So, you have a deflationary money supply? That can come with some challenges."

A few of the mercenaries grew noticeably more relaxed as the road curved, and they rode out of view of the outpost.

"The coins are very slightly magical—as the mints were—and they're considered lucky. Hence the hoarding. Most people barter for what they need, those with services they can perform or goods they can make and trade. Soldiers—and mercenaries—are paid by the crown in coin, salt, or moss."

Aldari blinked. "*Moss*?"

Was he joking? Dawn hadn't yet come, but it was growing lighter, enough to see that he wasn't smirking.

"Anyone can grow the basic mosses, if they have a home and

room for a garden, but some kinds are more difficult to cultivate and have great nutritive or medicinal properties. Those are usually grown by master gardeners on the sides of specially treated tree trunks or in particular soils. There are blends that can alleviate headaches, cure digestive ailments, and are even believed to stave off greater diseases."

"But it's what you use for trade and commerce?"

"It's an important part of our lives." Hawk looked at her. "I suppose you think our people are primitive because we've defaulted to such a basic financial system."

"No." Aldari shook her head. "As an economist, I'm intrigued. Just as you said. You've got me wanting to do research and write a paper on your people. Coin is typical, and salt isn't that unusual, but I've never heard of a culture that trades in *moss*. It's fascinating."

"As we strive to be." Hawk gave her a lopsided grin.

Her insides fluttered. She glanced at Theli, hoping she hadn't caught her reaction—and wondering if she should have kept her dreams to herself. But her bodyguard was yawning as she alternately gazed at the road ahead and into the woods alongside it. Talk of economics never interested her, so maybe she wasn't watching them for hints of... flirtation.

Not that Aldari was doing that. She was asking perfectly reasonable and professional questions—and not joking about writing a paper. So what if a smile or a grin made her insides squirm?

Hawk nudged his reindeer closer to hers and lowered his voice. "I'd like to apologize for something."

"Oh?"

"The day before yesterday. My memory is a little fuzzy. Helyna gave me some potent painkillers, and they made me a little woozy."

"I remember." Aldari resisted the urge to say something dumb, such as that he was cute when he was woozy. Maybe she should have pretended it hadn't happened at all, since he appeared uncomfortable by whatever he remembered.

"I think I may have gotten a little... handsy." Hawk winced and wriggled his fingers while eyeing her warily. "I apologize. I know you're engaged to another man, and I wouldn't— It wouldn't be honorable of me to try to entice you away from him." Was that the briefest wistful flash that passed through his green eyes? "I was just moved because you wanted to help us. And like I said, woozy." He shrugged. "It won't happen again."

She told herself that was a relief, not a disappointment. "It's all right. I, uhm, didn't mind it as much as I should have."

"That's reassuring. I *have* been told by women that my touch isn't entirely loathsome, but given the circumstances..."

"Not entirely?" Aldari decided humor would be better than letting this make them uncomfortable going forward. "Women only find it *partially* loathsome?"

"Indeed. I'm hoping to improve my skills to be exceedingly inoffensive, but I've only had male mercenaries around to practice on lately."

"Such as Setvik?" Aldari looked toward the grumpy lieutenant, but he'd drifted farther away to give them their privacy—or because he had no interest whatsoever in their discussion. "Does he enjoy being touched?"

"Not that I've noticed."

Setvik didn't look in their direction. Several of the mercenaries had paused their mounts on the road and were peering back. Two elves in the rear drew swords, one calling softly to Hawk and Setvik.

"They say someone is coming," Hawk translated.

"Elves sent by the king to drag us back?" Aldari looked at Theli, not surprised to catch a hopeful expression on her face.

"We'll find out soon enough," Hawk said.

Setvik rode toward the rear of the formation, and Hawk turned his mount, looking like he wanted to join them, but he glanced at Aldari and Theli and stayed close and drew his sword. Aldari suspected she'd acquired a second bodyguard.

A single cloaked figure rode into view, also on a reindeer, the shaggy creature slowing from a gallop to a walk as it neared the formation.

Setvik called out a warning. A wary response came from the rider, a male voice that sounded familiar.

Hawk swore, but it took Aldari a moment to place it. She groaned as the newcomer pushed back his hood to reveal his face. Mevleth.

"What is *he* doing here?" she whispered harshly, her hand jerking to her dagger as fresh rage and indignation poured through her. The medic had *poisoned* and almost killed Hawk. Why would he have *dared* return to the company?

Angry mutters came from the other mercenaries. Aldari hoped that meant they'd heard the truth, that she hadn't been responsible for Hawk's illness—and that the medic had.

Mevleth stopped behind the company, and Setvik asked a few terse questions. *He* didn't sound that angry. But all along, he'd demonstrated no love for Hawk and might not have cared if he'd died. After all, he'd offered to slit Hawk's throat himself.

The medic launched into what sounded like a story, or at least a lengthy explanation.

"What's he saying?" Aldari whispered.

"He heard that his potion contained poison," Hawk translated quietly, "but he says it was new information to him. He had no idea. He'd purchased it while in the Taldar Empire some weeks earlier and hadn't yet used it on any other patients. Since none of the mercenaries were badly injured during the kidnapping, he hadn't needed to. Not until he gave it to us."

"Do you *believe* him?" Aldari didn't.

Hawk sighed and released his sword hilt. "I don't know, but he's been with the company for years. He's served with Setvik for a long time, and he doesn't know what else he can do if he doesn't return to the mercenaries."

"Wait, is he asking to come *along*?" Aldari shook her head, not wanting someone along who'd tried to kill Hawk. Mevleth would have happily taken her down too, if she'd drunk more of that concoction. "If he's so innocent, why did he hide from the king's elves who went to question him?"

Setvik was asking a few more questions, but again, he didn't sound disgruntled—or skeptical.

"*Hawk*." Aldari might not be in charge, but she wouldn't stand silently by while the mercenaries made a mistake—one that could endanger her and Hawk again.

"You make a good point." Hawk switched to Elven and raised his voice.

Mevleth looked past the mercenaries to meet Hawk's eyes for the first time and winced. From atop his reindeer, Mevleth bowed deeply several times toward Hawk and issued what sounded like numerous apologies.

Aldari couldn't resist rolling her eyes. Hawk's face was harder to read. Did he buy this? Like special moss from a master elf gardener?

"He says he was afraid the king wouldn't believe him," Hawk said, "and that he would be put to death. That is the punishment for killing another elf outside of the heat of battle. It's not the punishment for *attempting* to kill another and failing, but he might have been locked away or—as is our more typical custom—ostracized to the wild lands. There, he would have been forced to fight for his life day in and day out against the Twisted."

"Why would that be so bad for him? He's a mercenary. Doesn't your company fight for their lives every week for coin?"

Wait, *was* it his company? The queen's words echoed in her mind: *I never would have sent the mercenaries along with him.*

"The company works *outside* of Serth." Hawk's mouth twisted with distaste. "They find battling the Twisted unpleasant—as we all do. They would rather fight in human wars for coin." There was that twist of distaste again.

As Aldari watched Hawk's face, the queen's words lingering in her mind, she realized how apart from the company he seemed. They called him captain and deferred to him, but...

Setvik turned and spoke to Hawk. It sounded more like a statement than a question.

Frowning, Hawk replied.

"I need to learn this language," Aldari whispered to Theli, wondering if she could press Hawk into tutoring her along the way.

"If you're going to run away with an elven lover, that seems wise," Theli replied.

Hawk had been in the middle of speaking with—or maybe arguing with—Setvik, but he looked over at them, grabbing his reindeer for support.

"She's joking," Aldari hurried to say. Then, because Theli deserved a dig for that comment, added, "*She's* the one who's been fantasizing about elven lovers." She pointed at Setvik as Theli glared at her.

Hawk turned back to his argument with Setvik, who, if he'd heard their asides, didn't indicate he cared about them. They continued to argue about the medic. Even though Hawk shook his head and spat in disgust, Setvik turned back around and waved for Mevleth to join them.

Aldari's stomach sank. "He's being invited back in?"

"As Setvik pointed out," Hawk said, "he never kicked Mevleth out."

"It's never too late to give someone the boot," Theli said, flexing her own boot.

Hawk sighed. "As Setvik also pointed out, he's the company's only medic, and we're going into a dangerous situation."

"I don't want him tending any of *my* wounds." Aldari shuddered.

Hawk rested his hand on the hilt of his sword as he nudged his mount forward again. "I'll do my best to make sure you don't receive any wounds."

"See to it that you don't either." When Aldari looked back, she found Mevleth looking past the other mercenaries and straight at them. Her stomach dropped with the certainty that this was a bad idea and that the poisoning hadn't been accidental.

But how did she prove it to the mercenaries?

26

EVEN THOUGH ALDARI HAD FOUGHT HARD TO GET THE ZEDARON scroll, she struggled to concentrate as Hawk shared the contents with her, awkwardly holding both the original and the translation open across his thighs as they rode. It had rained all morning and half the afternoon, and they hadn't wanted to risk damage to the ancient scroll—or the fresh ink on the new translation—so he was only now, twenty miles into their journey, sharing the information.

But Aldari kept glancing over at the medic, her mind picking at the inconsistencies in his story, as well as the one Hawk maintained about being the captain of the mercenaries. All along, there had been clues to the contrary, or at least that he wasn't telling her the whole truth, but she liked him and had been reluctant to believe he was lying to her.

Mevleth now rode beside Setvik, chatting easily with him. It didn't seem the lieutenant was holding a grudge. Hawk hadn't said anything to Mevleth since their initial discussion that morning, and Aldari hoped that meant he hadn't been fooled and would keep a sharp eye on the mercenary medic.

"...and numerous mathematical patterns have been observed in nature," Hawk read, translating as he went.

Aldari made herself focus. This could be important when it came to solving the puzzle.

"Fractals can be found in flowers, river networks, snowflakes, and even our blood vessels," Hawk continued. "There are also many instances of what our ancient philosophers called the Golden Ratio, which can be observed in flowers, seed heads, pinecones, and seashells, as well as on a much grander scheme in the flows of a hurricane or the formation of a spiral galaxy." He looked over at her. "Is this enlightening to you?"

"It sounds like it's a basic paper on mathematics in nature. I don't know if anything in there will help specifically with your puzzle, but what do you know about Zedaron? Was the natural world a field of study for him? Did he enjoy applying science and mathematics to it?"

Hawk shrugged. "He's most well-known for his inventions, the various contraptions he made, especially. Ambulatory constructs that trundled about the city, giving rides and carrying goods without need for a cart and horse—or reindeer. It's also rumored that he made some flying contraptions, though the stories say they often crashed. His inventions were believed to use a mixture of engineering and magic, though since our people have all but forgotten how magic works—" he glanced at his bracer, "—been *forced* to all but forget how magic works, few know what is, or was, possible in that regard."

"If he was trying to make mechanical constructs to move around, he might have spent a lot of time studying nature, especially animals and birds and insects. Maybe he attempted to replicate how animals move and insects fly." Aldari drew the baton and ran a finger over the ridges between the segments. Earlier, she'd thought of finger bones with knuckles, but she'd also been reminded of a branch with knots. Maybe a tree had been the inspiration for it.

As she recalled from her tutoring days, the Golden Ratio could be expressed as the Serrithon Sequence, named after the elven mathematician who'd discovered more than a thousand years earlier that each term was the sum of the two preceding terms, with the numbers starting at zero. Zero, one, one, two, three, five, eight, thirteen, twenty-one, and so on, continuing to follow the pattern infinitely.

Excitement thrummed through Aldari. If Zedaron had loved and been inspired by nature, that might be the clue she needed. Maybe Zedaron had even used the Serrithon Sequence in his puzzles. She wished she'd had time to hunt more thoroughly through the scrolls in the outpost to see if there had been more written by him in that collection.

"Are there any formulas on that scroll?" she asked, but Hawk wasn't paying attention.

Two of the mercenaries had ridden off to one side of the road, charging into trees that had changed over the journey from evergreens to alders, their green leaves hiding whatever was out there. Aldari couldn't help but remember similar behavior from the mercenaries on the way to the outpost, the scouts riding out to check on threats throughout the day until the company had eventually been attacked at dusk.

Though clouds obscured the sun, she glanced toward it, guessing at how many hours they had left before nightfall. Not many.

"Will they attack tonight?" she asked when Hawk turned his attention back to the road.

"According to the scouts, there aren't many out there right now," Hawk said, not having to ask who *they* referred to.

The Twisted seemed to be the main threat for the elves. Now

and then, she'd heard a mountain lion or similar large cat roar in the distance, but the forest was otherwise peaceful, full of birdsong and softly rustling leaves. She wished she could relax and enjoy the journey.

"It's possible we won't be disturbed when we camp," Hawk said. "Setvik is also talking about the merits of continuing through the night. We could reach the canyon lands tomorrow if we did that."

"Does the road continue on in as good of a condition?" Aldari couldn't imagine traveling through the night unless a bright moon came out, but the elves seemed to have better vision after dark than humans. Maybe nocturnal travels were normal for them.

Hawk rocked his hand back and forth. "It's not bad. Our people have attempted to maintain the highway to the ports and ancient cities, to facilitate travel and keep Serth from falling entirely back to nature, but when road crews are constantly at risk of being attacked and killed..." He shook his head. "It's difficult to get people to leave the outpost and venture out, no matter how much you offer to pay them."

"No matter how much moss?"

He smiled faintly. "Moss, salt, coin, eyeball soup... Few things are worth risking one's life for."

"Not even the eyeball soup entices them? I'm appalled."

"I assumed that news would shock you." Hawk started to read from the scroll again, but Setvik barked something at him and rode off to join the scouts.

Hawk waved an indifferent hand.

There was nothing extraordinary about the exchange, but in that moment, the truth clicked home like a puzzle piece, a truth Aldari had sensed all along but hadn't wanted to accept, not when it would have confirmed that Hawk had been lying to her.

"He's the captain, isn't he?" she asked quietly.

Hawk looked up from the scroll. His expression wasn't confused or surprised but carefully blank as he gazed over at her.

"They defer to him more than you, he gives orders as if he's been commanding them for years, and he resents having to follow you... because he's not used to it, I assume."

Hawk's face didn't change, not so much as an eyebrow twitching. He didn't look away, as if guilty that he'd been caught in a lie; he simply waited. Or was he trying to figure out what to say?

"Further, you mentioned that Setvik had worked with the medic for years and trusted him, not that you had." Aldari raised her eyebrows. "So, if he's the captain, who are you?"

Hawk finally sighed. "I have a plausible lie that I've rehearsed for when you inevitably saw through our ruse, but after all we've been through, I'm reluctant to keep lying to you."

"I would appreciate the truth." Aldari hoped that was true. Already, it was starting to sting that he'd been lying to her all along, but if he offered a reasonable explanation, maybe it wouldn't feel like a betrayal.

"Setvik is the captain of the Moon Sword Company, yes. And he's far more capable of leading his mercenaries on this mission than I am." Hawk offered a self-deprecating shrug. "I'm not an inept warrior—I hope I've demonstrated my ability in that area—but I grew up in the outpost, in the king's court, not commanding people in battle."

"As a noble? Do your people have nobility as such? I assumed from your treatment in the tree palace that you weren't just some scruffy mercenary, at least not to the king and queen."

"We don't have nobility in the sense of people owning estates and helping to govern—our nation has grown so small that there's little need for that much hierarchy—but there are those with blood ties to the monarchs, yes, and they're often called upon to carry out duties for our people and our nation. Once, the nobles were diplomats and military leaders. I am related to the king, yes. I was sent on a mission to the buried city, to lead the scientists who were digging out Zedaron's laboratory. I relayed what they'd found to the queen, and when she learned about you and your paper that mentioned a formula for solving one of our ancient puzzles, I... volunteered for this mission." Hawk's lips flattened. "I came up with the idea to, uhm, convince you to come help us."

"But you didn't mention kidnapping to her?"

"No. I believe she thought I would use my charm." There was that self-deprecating shrug again. "I hoped that might work, but when we arrived in your land and realized you were about to head off for your wedding in another kingdom, I realized... more desperate measures would be required." He raised his eyebrows, as if to ask if he'd been correct. Or, if he'd openly asked for help, would she have given it?

No. Aldari couldn't have delayed her wedding to help a stranger. Even now, she feared there would be repercussions for her choice to continue on with him.

Even though she didn't speak her thoughts out loud, Hawk nodded, certain he was right. "The queen thought it would be dangerous for me to go into your kingdom alone, so she contacted the Moon Swords, calling them back to our land to ask them to help. I never wanted to use them. They're..." Hawk glanced around to make sure the nearby mercenaries weren't listening, but they were focused on the woods and whatever their scouts had found. "They're fine warriors, but I worried they wouldn't be loyal to the queen, to me, or the mission. As I mentioned before, they left Serth long ago." His tone turned hard. "They abandoned our people, leaving us to deal with the Twisted while they went out and earned coin for fighting *lesser* opponents." He paused, glancing at her. "I'm sorry. I don't mean to insult humans, but you're not—your *people* generally aren't as capable in battle as ours."

"I'm not insulted."

"I might be," Theli muttered. She'd stuck close enough to hear the conversation.

"You've admitted that the elves are annoying opponents because you can't hold your own against them," Aldari told her. "I distinctly remember a request that I next time arrange to be kidnapped by common cutthroats."

Theli grunted. "I wouldn't mind if there wasn't a *next time*. I'm not that delighted by *this time*."

Aldari waved away the aside, far more interested in what Hawk was revealing.

"Setvik agreed to the queen's request. Before he was a mercenary, he was a soldier in the king's service, and even those who have abandoned their homeland may feel some loyalty and obligation to the monarchs they once swore fealty to." Hawk shrugged. "Even so, he and his company... I doubt they care about our success the way I do. I doubt they're as committed to it—as willing to die if it'll make the world better for the rest of our people. That's not what mercenaries are known for." Hawk pushed a hand through his blond hair. "I am relieved he hasn't turned his back on us yet."

That *yet* bothered Aldari, and it worried her that it seemed to bother Hawk too. But despite his reservations, he'd gathered the mercenaries for the second half of this excursion.

Because he'd had no other option. Because the king and queen had forbidden him from taking Aldari off into danger.

"I still don't understand why you lied to me," she said. "Why the elaborate ruse?"

"In case you got away, or even if we succeeded in kidnapping you, getting you to help, and everything worked out like I hoped. I worried that your people—and your future husband's people —" Hawk grimaced, "—would retaliate. Serth can't afford a war with outsiders when we're embroiled in our own eternal war right here. I thought that if mercenaries who'd had nothing to do with the crown for the last twenty years were the ones to kidnap you, and it all fell apart, the *company* would be held accountable, and blame wouldn't go toward the king and queen and the elven people in general. Setvik even knew of a monarch who'd failed to pay his company in the past, and he was prepared to say that man was responsible, that he'd hired the company to kidnap you." Hawk paused to huff out a breath. "I didn't want to go that far, to be *that* dishonorable with our lies, as the need to perpetuate a ruse already went against what I believe is right, but I also agreed that we dared not make enemies abroad."

"I guess I can understand that." Aldari looked at the road behind them, though the outpost had been out of view for a long time. "What happens if the king sends troops after you?"

"It's a possibility, but I think... I think he won't. He may not agree with my methodology, but he's prayed all of his life for a solution to the Twisted. Now that he's made the obligatory protests, I believe he'll wait and see what happens."

"Do you think, if we succeed, your transgressions will be forgiven?"

Hawk's eyes grew wistful. "I hope so, but even if they're not... if we succeed, it will have been worth it." His eyes sharpened and focused on her. "I do know that he sent a note to let your father know that you're alive and well. I'm sure they're worried, and I apologize for that. My grand scheme seemed a lot more brilliant before I got to know you and... care. Based on what I'd read and heard about humans..."

They'd refused to help his people in the past, they were responsible for overhunting the whales in the seas that their lands shared, and they'd apparently cheated Setvik and his mercenaries out of payment at least once. She could understand if Hawk had been predisposed to think poorly of her people.

"Well, it wasn't right of me to judge you before I knew you. I'm

glad you turned out to be a good person. The queen likes you too."
Hawk smiled at her.

"She likes me? We barely spoke." Aldari lifted a hand to the
necklace the queen had given her. Before leaving that morning,
she'd put it on, tucking the leaf medallion under her dress.

"She liked that you wanted to help us and weren't the spoiled
brat she assumed all human princesses are."

"Really."

"She's interacted with a few monarchs and their children over
the years, so I don't think she believes her opinions are
groundless."

"I've heard Princess Zebia in Darvy has her servants whipped
if her food isn't warm enough when it's brought on fuzzy soft
ervatha leaves to her private dining chamber," Theli said.

"You read that in a book." Aldari squinted at her. Neither of
them had ever traveled to Darvy. "Probably a mystery novel."

"I heard it from another bodyguard."

"Gossip. An even more legitimate source."

"Regardless, whatever you tell your people when this is over,
I'm prepared to accept the consequences." Hawk gazed sadly at
Aldari. "I don't want to lie to you anymore."

"I appreciate that."

He almost looked like he would say something else, but Setvik
and the scouts galloped back to the road and rejoined the
company. Aldari hoped that meant they'd scared off—or dealt
with—whatever threat they'd found out there, and that another
big attack wasn't imminent. Especially since no falcons had
arrived recently with messages. If the mercenaries ended up
needing help, there would be no way to call for it.

"For what it's worth," Aldari told Hawk, "I wouldn't ask my
father to retaliate. Even if I were so aggrieved by my experience
being force-fed moss and eyeball soup and *wanted* retaliation, my
people lack the resources to start a war with anyone."

She'd hoped to lighten his grave mood with the food comment, but he only looked somberly over at her and asked, "And is that also true of your fiancé's people?"

She hesitated but could only say, "No."

For good or ill, the Orath Kingdom had resources aplenty. That was the reason her father so badly wanted an alliance with them.

Hawk smiled sadly.

27

ASTRIDE THE PLODDING REINDEER, ALDARI DOZED WITH HER CHIN TO her chest, but she jolted awake frequently, grabbing at the animal's shaggy fur for support. The elven reindeer were placid enough mounts, and had uncanny stamina that she couldn't imagine from horses, but the mercenaries didn't use saddles, and she didn't feel that secure even when she was awake.

A hand touched her shoulder, ready to grip her more firmly if needed. Hawk. As he had throughout the night, he rode beside her, watching out for her. Their gazes met, she nodded that she was fine, and he withdrew his hand. He yawned as frequently as she did, but if he'd dozed off at any point, she hadn't caught it.

Now that it was daylight again, her butt long since having gone too numb to register the discomfort of riding a reindeer, it should have been easier to stay awake, but the monotonous scenery didn't inspire alertness. They'd left behind the forest and entered a bleak landscape dominated by boulders, with only stunted shrubs, tufts of grass, and the occasional stalwart flower growing between them.

The scouts hadn't ridden off since before dawn, and Aldari

hoped the lack of trees meant it would be harder for hordes of Twisted to sneak up on them, but those boulders were large enough to hide enemies. *Many* enemies.

Theli rode on Aldari's other side, singing softly, trying out the lyrics she'd been working on and choosing a tune to go with them. More than once, Setvik looked back at her, no doubt catching her depictions of his villainous ways within her ballad. Theli only lifted her chin and gazed defiantly back at him. If anything, she sang louder when she thought he was listening.

Aldari expected ongoing glowers from the surly lieutenant, but his expression was more one of bemusement. Or even *amusement*? Maybe he was tickled to be featured in a ballad.

A scout in the lead called back to Setvik and Hawk, and Aldari straightened, willing alertness into her limbs. Setvik held up a finger to Hawk, then rode ahead.

"There's something lying on the road up there," Hawk said. "Probably a dead animal."

The croak of a crow came from the sky ahead. In addition, vultures circled, and several flew up from the road as the mounted elves approached. Theli stopped singing, and Aldari exchanged a long look with her. Would a scout have bothered mentioning a dead animal?

As the party rounded a bend, a dark lump in the road came into view. Hawk sat taller to peer at it.

"It's not an animal," he said, his voice grim. He started to nudge his mount to run ahead so he could join the others, but he glanced at Aldari and hesitated. Because he felt compelled to stick close?

"We'll go with you." Aldari didn't know if she wanted to see what—or who—was dead up there, but she forced a smile for him and waved to Theli.

Hawk nodded and led the way.

As they rode closer, Aldari picked out a swath of blond hair on the dark form, and she shifted uneasily on her mount. It was a person. One of the Twisted? No, all the ones she'd seen had white hair. This looked more like one of the elves lying face down in the road.

A scout swung down from his reindeer to check. A bow staff lay clenched in the elf's pale hand, and arrows had spilled out of a quiver onto the cobblestones. After checking for a pulse, the scout looked up at Setvik and shook his head.

When Aldari, Hawk, and Theli reached the gathering, Setvik had a hand up as he peered not at the body but toward the fields of boulders stretching to either side of the road. His reindeer's nostrils were twitching. *All* of the reindeer were reacting to something they smelled, Aldari's mount grunting and shifting about.

Setvik started to give an order to the scouts, but two male Twisted sprang out from behind the boulders, yellow eyes squinted shut against the sunlight. That didn't keep them from screeching and running toward the group.

Setvik raised a bow and fired as Hawk drew his sword. Theli hissed and pulled out her mace.

Not wanting to fight from her reindeer's back, Aldari slid to the ground. As soon as she landed, stumbling on the uneven cobblestones, the creature darted away before she could catch its reins. She swore, tempted to run after it, but she didn't want to leave Hawk and Theli's protection and make it easier for the Twisted to catch her.

Hawk stayed on his own mount, his sword ready as he watched the mercenaries fire at the Twisted. Arrow after arrow thudded into their chests, but they kept coming.

How they could see with their eyes shut, Aldari didn't know. More arrows came from the rest of the mercenary party, plunging into necks and what should have been vital targets. But the nearly immortal Twisted kept coming.

With a chill, Aldari realized they were heading toward *her* again. The damn baton had to be drawing them. She touched the amulet the queen had given her. It might keep the Twisted from turning her into one of them, but it wasn't discouraging them from coming at her.

Maybe the draw of the baton's magic was too great. But she couldn't cast it aside, lest they get it.

Theli jumped down to stand protectively beside her as Setvik and the scouts exchanged bows for swords and axes and charged at the Twisted. An ululating cry that Aldari hadn't heard before tore from the creatures' throats, and every hair on the back of her neck rose. The Twisted were like nightmares out of a children's tale.

Though they remained focused on Aldari, they clawed and bit at the elves who drew close to them. Setvik swung an axe like an executioner and lopped off his target's head. That finally killed the Twisted—or at least stopped it. The body pitched sideways as the head flew off, striking a boulder and thudding to the ground ten feet away. Aldari winced and looked away from the grisly sight.

Another mercenary swept his sword toward the head of the second Twisted, but it ducked with surprising speed. It sprang sideways and clawed one of the reindeer. The animal squealed and bucked so hard that it threw even the agile scout. Twisting in the air, the elf would have come down on his feet, but he clipped a boulder, and that threw him off. Their blue-skinned enemy lunged for him, deadly claws raised on those eerily human—*elven* —fingers.

Before the Twisted could strike, Setvik rode in again. Once more, he cleaved off the creature's head.

Beside her, Theli gasped with approval.

There was no blood on Setvik's axe, only a dark ichor. He hurried to pull out a cloth and clean off the blade, as if the substance were an acid that would eat through steel if he let it. Maybe it was.

Several mercenaries dismounted to climb onto some of the higher boulders and peer in all directions, searching for more enemies.

Hawk lowered his sword and frowned thoughtfully at Aldari. "They seem determined to reach you."

"I noticed. I'm glad the mercenaries stopped them."

"More might come. That ululating noise can travel for miles. It was a call for reinforcements, a promise that prey has been found."

"Do they have a language that your people can understand?"

"They don't, but I've heard that call and seen the results enough times to know what it means. We can't linger for a funeral pyre, but..." Hawk held up a finger, dismounted, and jogged to the body of the slain elf.

He rolled it over, revealing a face frozen in a rictus of fear and pain, blue eyes unseeing, blond hair a tangle. The bow had been clutched in one hand, but the other gripped something else. A scroll case?

"I recognize him. He's one of the scientists from the camp. It looks like he was bringing us a message. Maybe a warning." Hawk gently pried open the elf's fingers to take the scroll case, but something on the bow caught his eye. The string was broken.

"Bad luck," Aldari whispered, though the arrows the mercenaries had fired had been so ineffective that she wondered why the elves carried the weapons.

"Maybe more than that." Hawk held up one of the broken ends of the bow string. "This was cut. A partial cut, but you can tell. It's clean on one side and frayed on the other."

"He had a reindeer." One of the scouts had returned to check the ground around the body, and he pointed at prints to the side of the weathered cobblestones. "It ran off in that direction."

"Give me a second opinion, Rauloth, because this doesn't make sense." Hawk showed the bowstring to the scout.

"It was cut, sir."

"Who would have done that, and why?" Hawk frowned down the road in the direction the party was heading—in the direction the slain elf had come from.

"Someone didn't want his message to get back to your people?" Aldari guessed.

Perhaps realizing he might be holding the answer, Hawk pulled his gaze back to the scroll case and opened it.

"Read that along the way," Setvik said, riding closer. "There are more of them out there. We need to get going. We're still at least two hours' ride from the camp."

"Will we be safe there?" Aldari wondered.

"There are two *phyzera* placed there to guard the scientists and their supplies," Hawk said. "At least there were when I helped set up the camp. There's no reason why they shouldn't still be there, and they'll repel the Twisted."

"We have to reach them first," Setvik said.

"I know. Mount everyone up." Despite the words, Hawk didn't move. His gaze was riveted to the message. "It's a warning not to send more people. Not now. It's too dangerous. For some reason, even more Twisted have come to the canyons, as if they've collectively decided to guard the ancient city. The scientists haven't been able to get in close enough to dig out any more of the structures, and they've made no progress with the puzzle. They are recommending waiting for a few months until the Twisted in the area return to more manageable numbers."

The rest of the mercenaries, most back on their mounts, gathered around Hawk and Setvik.

"Mevleth." The scout that had been thrown from his reindeer lifted a hand, showing a bloody gash. "One of them clipped me. I need your powder."

"Right." The medic opened his kit.

Aldari looked at Hawk, wondering if they should allow

Mevleth to treat more people, but he was still frowning down at the message.

After sprinkling what appeared to be the same powder that the palace healer had used on Theli onto the man's hand, the medic gave him a potion. Aldari winced. It was a different bottle from the one Mevleth had given to her and Hawk, but what looked like the same green substance sloshed inside. The trusting mercenary took a long swig.

As if he sensed her gaze, Mevleth looked over at Aldari, then said something to Setvik.

"It's a new batch," Setvik told her. "He acquired it from a trusted herbalist and potion maker at the outpost. He won't be foolish enough to trust humans to make the *vevithar* again." Setvik cocked his head as another ululating call floated out of the distance. "Hawk, get your women on their mounts, and let's go. They're gathering out there."

"Understood." Hawk stuck the message back into the scroll case.

Aldari looked around for her reindeer, hoping it hadn't gone far, but with the mercenaries crowding close, she didn't spot it. Hawk grabbed her wrist and pulled her up behind him. As she gripped his waist, he and the other mercenaries nudged their reindeer into runs.

"Theli?" Aldari peered back.

"Right behind you." Theli had kept her reindeer and was back astride it.

"Hawk?" Aldari asked, thinking of the mercenary swigging the potion.

"Yes?"

"Back at the tent by the river, did the medic give that potion to the injured elves who were in there before we arrived?" Aldari closed her eyes, trying to remember everything that had happened. The two mercenaries had been on their backs on cots, so it was possible they'd received the potion before she'd arrived, but...

"I'll check." Hawk guided his mount between others and drew even with one of the two mercenaries who'd been there. He asked a quiet question.

The elf shook his head as he replied.

Aldari waited impatiently for Hawk to translate, but his gaze was locked on the road ahead. There weren't any Twisted waiting for them, not yet, but even from behind, Aldari could tell he was troubled. Probably more by the contents of the message—and the death of an elf he'd known—than anything about the medic, but Aldari couldn't help but think that if Mevleth had given the potion to her and Hawk, and deliberately *not* given it to his mercenaries, it would prove that he'd known it was tainted.

Another ululating cry floated through the boulder field. Aldari glimpsed something white in the distance. The hair of one of the Twisted?

The mercenaries rode with their hands on their weapons and exchanged uneasy glances with each other.

"Hawk?" Aldari prompted softly.

"Sorry. I'm just thinking about things. About far too many things." He glanced back and forced a smile for her, though there was nothing here to smile about. "You're right to be suspicious of the medic. He didn't give the other two mercenaries his draught. Erithor even requested it, and Mevleth said he was fine and didn't need it."

"His injuries were worse than mine."

Hawk nodded. "They were, and I agree with what you're thinking, that it's highly likely Mevleth knew about the poison in advance. He probably put it there himself."

"Why aren't you furious?"

Hawk still looked like he was half lost in thought.

"I'm not pleased, but I'm afraid it's the least of our problems right now." Hawk waved toward the road ahead, the cobblestones winding through the boulders toward the canyon lands he'd spoken about. "If we're not able to get to the ancient city because there are too many Twisted, then all of this—kidnapping you and making this journey—will have been for naught." His eyes were bleak as he met her gaze. "We'll have stolen you from your wedding and threatened the alliance your people need, and have gained nothing. Nothing for our people—nothing for the world."

"I'm sorry."

Setvik barked an order to his mercenaries, then repeated it in Hyric. "They're after us. Full speed."

The beleaguered reindeer, weary from traveling through the night, must have been afraid, for they obeyed the nudges from the mercenaries without balking. As Hawk's mount sped up, Aldari wrapped her arms more tightly around him, fearing she would fly off if she didn't.

It was too hard to speak as they thundered along like that, and all she could do was press her cheek to Hawk's back while hoping the Twisted couldn't catch reindeer. She also wondered if there was any relation between the medic trying to kill Hawk and someone in what should have been a camp of allies cutting the bowstring of a messenger.

As Theli would be quick to point out the next time they spoke, Aldari might have made a mistake in not allowing the queen to send them home. A big mistake.

28

THE REINDEER RAN, THEIR EYES WIDE AND THEIR NOSTRILS FLARING. They had to be exhausted, as their deep huffs and shuddering legs attested, but the Twisted followed on the road behind them, dozens of them. Maybe hundreds.

With her eyes closed and her cheek pressed to Hawk's back, Aldari tried not to look. Every time she did, there were more of them, with reinforcements running in from the boulders and adding to the size of the pack. Worse, they were gaining ground.

The magic-cursed creatures were seemingly unaffected by a need for air, by muscles burning, by the weariness of a long run. One of the reindeer went down without warning. Its rider yelled a startled oath and managed to leap free. He landed on his feet and ran, his legs fresher than those of the reindeer. He was able to keep up with the four-legged animals, at least for the moment, but would his stamina last?

Aldari glanced back and wished she hadn't. Already the Twisted had caught up with the fallen reindeer. Several of them sprang upon the creature, tearing it apart to dine on its flesh. But far, far more of the Twisted kept going. They screeched, the noises inhuman and chilling.

In the lead, Setvik barked orders. He'd pulled quite far ahead. No, Aldari realized. That wasn't it. It was Hawk's mount that had fallen behind, only a few other stragglers as far back in the party as it was. Riding beside them, Theli kept glancing over with concern.

"Your mount is struggling," she called over the noise of the hooves pounding on the cobblestones. "Because it's carrying two."

Hawk glanced at Theli but didn't reply. He had to know she was right, but Aldari's reindeer, along with the handful of others that had been brought to carry supplies, had disappeared. With nobody holding their reins, they'd run off into the boulder fields to save themselves.

"There's nothing else for me to ride," Aldari told her.

Even if there had been, she never could have jumped down to swap mounts while they were all running. She would have ended up trampled.

"Mine isn't as tired. Here, join me." Theli offered her hand.

Aldari shook her head. She had a good view of Theli's mount, and it appeared as exhausted as the others. If she doubled up with Theli, they would have the exact same problem.

"No." Hawk held up a hand. "Let go of me, Aldari. I'll get off and run."

"That's suicidal," Aldari said, though the other mercenary on foot was keeping up.

She glanced back to check on him and gasped. He *wasn't* keeping up. Though he hadn't fallen far behind yet, he was at the back of the pack now, his legs strong but not as powerful as the reindeer's, not over distance.

"We're almost to the camp." Hawk gently tugged at Aldari's hands to extricate himself from her grip. "You'll have a better shot of making it this way."

"We *both* need to make it." Aldari was tempted to fight him, to squeeze tight and keep him astride, but she couldn't keep him from going if he was determined. Besides, they'd fallen back to the rear and were only ahead of the mercenary on foot. And the Twisted had grown even closer.

A few of them had bows that they were waving in the air as they ran. If they paused and opened fire, they would be close enough to hit their targets.

"We will," Hawk said. "I've got plenty of wind left in me."

"Yesterday, you were using a cane to walk."

"That was two days ago, and it was a bow staff. Hang on tight and keep going. We're almost to the camp, and you'll be safe there." Hawk looked over his shoulder, holding her gaze. "I'm not giving up. I promise."

"Hawk..."

He twisted, touched her cheek, then launched himself off the reindeer, barely even brushing her. Instinctively, she grabbed for him, but he was too fast. He landed lightly, already facing in the right direction and already running. He smiled up at her and nodded, keeping up with the reindeer.

A fresh round of screeches came from the Twisted, as if they were excited that another elf was on foot. As if they knew they would eventually be victorious.

Setvik glanced back, saw that Hawk wasn't mounted anymore, and yelled what might have been a curse—or to tell Hawk he was an idiot. Hawk's reply was terse. He kept smiling up at Aldari, but already, he breathed heavily.

"There's something up ahead." Theli pointed up the road.

Aldari made herself look, though all she cared about was Hawk surviving.

Several tents and canopies were perched at the edge of a cliff amid stacks of crates, trunks, and a broken wagon. There was nothing impressive about the camp—Aldari had been imagining, or at least hoping for, a great fortified structure with walls the Twisted couldn't climb—but she did spot a glowing purple orb mounted to one side of it. And, yes, there was a second one on the other side of the camp.

Unfortunately, it was still a mile away if not more. And Hawk was falling behind. Maybe deliberately, for he was running alongside the other mercenary now. Both elves had drawn weapons and kept glancing back.

Seeing their prey ahead and vulnerable spurred on the Twisted. They were only twenty feet behind Hawk and the scout.

"We have to do something," Aldari told Theli.

"What can *we* do?"

Setvik was the one to bark an order and lead several of the mounted mercenaries to turn around. Others fired at the Twisted, arrows arching over the running elves' heads to thud into the chests of the lead enemies. As before, the projectiles barely did anything. A few of the Twisted jerked, their steps faltering, but only for a few seconds.

Setvik and five other mercenaries with axes rode past Hawk and curved their paths to angle past the lead Twisted. Clawed fingers swiped at their mounts as the elves leaned in, swinging the sharp blades.

Focused on Hawk, Aldari didn't see if any heads rolled. She couldn't imagine it would matter if they did. There were too many Twisted. *Hundreds* by now.

Shrieks of pain came from the reindeer that had been forced close to the Twisted. One bucked, almost throwing its rider.

Setvik cursed and issued another order. He and the others rode away from the Twisted, urging their mounts back toward the pack—and toward the camp.

It was only a half a mile away now. Aldari prayed they would be safe once they reached it. And that the scientists there wouldn't all be as dead as the messenger they'd sent.

As Setvik rode closer to the mercenaries, he drew abreast of Hawk and swept him up onto the back of his reindeer. Another of his mercenaries tried to do the same with the other elf on foot, but his mount stumbled, and the rider slid off. He landed on his feet, weapons in hand, and he and the other mercenary spun toward the horde.

Setvik and Hawk yelled the same word in Elven at them. *Run!*

It couldn't have been anything else, but the two elves exchanged looks and sprang toward the horde, weapons slashing and stabbing. Bile rose in Aldari's throat as she realized they were sacrificing themselves, trying to buy time for the rest of the company to escape.

Tears ran from her eyes, and she wished she could do something. Hawk's face was stricken as he rode behind Setvik, his sword raised, but thanks to the two mercenaries, the Twisted weren't close enough for him to attack. Setvik's face was a hard mask. If losing his people meant anything to him, he didn't show it.

Aldari's reindeer stumbled, a hoof catching on an uneven spot in the ancient road, and she flung her arms around its thick neck. If she tumbled off, she doubted there would be time for anyone to reach her and pull her onto another mount. Already the two mercenaries had fallen, the horde too massive for even skilled warriors to stop. They disappeared under the Twisted, trampled as surely as if a stampede of bison had crushed them.

A tingle encompassed Aldari's body, similar to what she'd felt near the barrier at the outpost. They'd passed into the protection of the orbs, the magic somehow knowing who to let in and who —*what*—to keep out.

Theli, Setvik, and Hawk also made it across, their reindeers' sides heaving. All of the mercenaries except the two who'd sacrificed themselves reached the camp.

For the first time, the Twisted slowed down. They sensed the barrier. Several glanced toward the two orbs at opposite sides of the camp. The magical barrier they created was invisible, but it was there.

As her mount slowed, Aldari straightened and wiped sweat from her brow. She exhaled a long relieved breath, but as she looked at the hundreds of blue-skinned Twisted spreading out around the camp, with even more running out of the boulder-strewn landscape to join them, she realized that what she'd been thinking of as a sanctuary was also a trap.

If the Twisted didn't leave, there would be no way to escape.

29

ALDARI TRIED TO KEEP HER BACK TO THE TWISTED AS SHE STOOD beside Hawk, listening as he discussed the situation with a white-haired female elf named Siadra. She'd been introduced to Aldari as a scientist and the camp leader, but then she and Hawk had switched to speaking in their language.

Beyond the barrier—which, judging by how the Twisted had spread out, was a dome about a hundred feet in diameter—the elven enemies numbered in the hundreds if not thousands. For whatever reason, the arrival of the mercenaries had brought them in droves. They were lucky there hadn't been Twisted guarding the camp and blocking the entrance when they'd arrived, but it was hard to feel fortunate with so many sets of hollow yellow eyes staring at them with an ancient magic-infused hatred, a palpable desire to kill.

Something told Aldari that the Twisted didn't need to leave to sleep or eat, that they could stay out there indefinitely. She hoped that wasn't true, but the grave faces of the scientists and merce-naries made her believe her hunch was right.

From what she'd seen, there were only four scientists, two

males and two females, most older than the mercenaries. Though they carried bows and could no doubt defend themselves with the swords at their waists, it was hard to miss how few arrows remained in their quivers. The camp had been attacked before. Aldari didn't need a translation to be certain of that.

"We could have been on a ship home by now," Theli said softly.

Her voice was wistful rather than full of condemnation, but as she gazed over the back edge of the camp and into the first of a maze of canyons that stretched as far as the eye could see, defeat lurked in her eyes. Aldari knew Theli believed they'd made a mistake. Maybe they had, but could Aldari truly regret having delayed her wedding to aid a beleaguered people in need of help?

If they weren't able to reach that puzzle, she might. After all these days, she itched to see it. To *solve* it.

Setvik's angry voice rose over those of the others as he pointed his bow toward the Twisted-filled road—or maybe the spot where his mercenaries had died. Hawk pushed a hand through his hair, and it sounded like he was trying to remain calm and reasonable, but doubt plagued his green eyes. Maybe he also wondered if they'd made a mistake.

When he looked at Aldari, he winced. Yes, he wouldn't have brought her here if he'd known it would be like this.

Since she couldn't understand the discussion, Aldari walked to the back of the camp. A telescope set up on a raised platform drew her curiosity, and she also wanted to know if more Twisted were in the canyon below. If not, and if the elves had ropes, that could be a possible escape route.

A glance was all it took to confirm that there were enemies down there. Not as many, but a hundred feet down, six Twisted wandered over black lava rock, remains of the ancient flows. There might be dozens more Twisted beyond the bends that hid much of the canyon from view. And who knew how many more in the attached canyons? Looking out at the landscape from above reminded Aldari of a diagram she'd once seen of the bronchial trees in lungs.

After climbing up the raised wooden platform, she approached the telescope, careful not to bump it. It was positioned toward a precise location in the distance, a spot in one of the canyons.

Her breath caught at what it showed her, not only the hardened lava flows but partially excavated buildings made from an intriguing iridescent glass. No, crystal, Hawk had said. Magical crystal.

The walls had survived being buried under molten lava. Tools and scaffolding were scattered about the area, evidence that someone had been chiseling the structures out of the rock.

It was as Hawk had described it, and doubtless he'd been expecting to be able to return to the excavation site. Zedaron's laboratory had to be among those buildings, as well as the puzzle she'd been brought all this way to solve. But how could they reach it?

Even as she observed, a Twisted shambled into view. It ignored the abandoned archaeological work, though it stepped on a wooden toolbox and broke it, seemingly without noticing. The Twisted turned toward her, eyes boring into hers through the distance and the telescope. Aldari jerked back, her heart pounding.

Why did she get the feeling that they sensed she was a threat and wanted her dead?

Maybe that was her imagination, but she couldn't shake the idea. Even though she told herself it was just because she had the baton, she couldn't help but wonder if that was true. Surely, she wasn't the only one around with a magical item.

"Are you all right?" Hawk asked, making her jump again.

Aldari hadn't heard his soundless feet on the steps. He rested a hand on her shoulder, concern in his eyes.

"I'm fine." *She'd* made it. She shivered as she glanced back toward the road. Beyond the horde, she could see the dead elves—the smashed remains of their bodies. "Thank you for asking," she made herself add. She didn't want to be short with Hawk, her only ally among the elves. "What happened? This isn't what you expected, is it?"

"No." Hawk lowered his hand. "Over the past week, the scientists sent out their three falcons with messages." He nodded toward a tree of empty perches under one of the pavilions. "But they must not have made it to the outpost, or the king would have warned us. The Twisted rarely use weapons like bows, but they are capable of it. It's possible they shot them down. If so, that shows... a surprising awareness that the Twisted haven't demonstrated in the past. They *are* intelligent—since they were once elves, it would be hard to imagine anything else—but they're usually single-minded, wanting to kill us or subsume us, but they haven't shown a propensity for coming up with elaborate schemes to infiltrate our outposts or destroy our homes. *This* is more typical for them." He waved toward the shifting horde, their hollow eyes pointing toward the camp. "Though even this is unusual in that they don't typically gather in such numbers to try to kill us. And they don't usually concern themselves with our machinations, at least not as far as we've observed."

Aldari shivered at the idea of the Twisted developing some new determination to work together to stop... What was it they wanted to stop? Did they understand what the elven scientists had uncovered? And was it possible they wanted to make sure Hawk and his team weren't successful at changing them? At *ending* them?

"Why did they kill that messenger?" she asked. "Instead of turning him into one of them?"

"I think I mentioned that the Twisted don't always turn people.

Sometimes, they simply kill them. There don't seem to be any rules they follow faithfully, but we know they prefer to turn those with stronger magic, or at least the potential to have strong magic." Hawk touched his bracer.

Did *he* have the potential to wield strong magic?

"When Siadra didn't get a message back," Hawk said, "she suspected the falcons were being intercepted. She sent Yoresh—the dead messenger we saw—on a reindeer. She deliberately picked a time when there weren't any Twisted in view and none had been seen for a while, but it didn't matter. You saw the result."

Aldari nodded numbly. "Did all the messages say the same thing?"

"Mostly. Siadra wanted to let the king and queen know that the numbers of Twisted in the area had grown and that they had to abandon the dig at the main and ancillary sites and retreat to this camp." Hawk waved in the direction the telescope pointed. "They were lucky the king had given them two of the *phyzera* to create the barrier. The ancient orbs are exceedingly rare and usually placed where they're most important, either to protect population centers or to keep our remaining highways and ports open."

"Is it possible the Twisted *know* what you uncovered out there?" Aldari glanced toward the distant dig site. "And what you're trying to accomplish?"

"It's possible."

"Maybe you should find all this resistance encouraging then." Aldari forced a smile, though with death lingering in the air, there was little to smile about.

"How so?"

She shrugged. "If you weren't on to something, they wouldn't care about stopping you."

His gaze sharpened as it locked on to hers. "That's an interesting hypothesis. As I said, they haven't demonstrated excessive interest in our goings on before, but..."

"If they're as smart as you are..." She turned her palm toward the sky.

He squinted toward the dig site. "That makes me want to take you out there more than ever, but it's far more dangerous than I thought it would be. I won't risk losing you."

"I appreciate that and prefer not to be lost. But I also want to help." She *wanted* a chance to solve that puzzle, to pit herself against the ancient elven mastermind and win. Her fingers twitched at the thought of rising to the challenge and defeating it. But she made herself temper that desire with the rational thought that she might *not* be able to solve the puzzle. And what then?

"I'm glad, but—"

The camp leader—Siadra—called up to Hawk in Elven and pointed at a table.

"Ah?" For the first time that day, Hawk's face brightened. "She says they made a replica of the puzzle and have been practicing trying to solve it here."

Siadra pointed at Aldari and waved an invitation.

"Does she think I can help?" Aldari asked.

Thus far, only Hawk—and maybe the queen—had shown any belief in her.

"I told her you're a brilliant puzzle solver," Hawk said, though the only puzzle-like thing he'd seen her figure out was the baton.

Aldari appreciated his faith and hoped she could live up to the expectations.

"I'll try to be." Nerves mingled with anticipation as she descended the steps to join Siadra.

The scientist's weathered face wasn't brimming with belief, but she also didn't emanate skepticism. If anything, weariness was the prevalent emotion that she exuded—that everyone in the camp exuded.

"What are their specialties?" Aldari waved at the scientists as she and Hawk followed Siadra toward the table where a mound of discs rose up in a stack ten high, jagged triangular indentions removed from several of the discs. They were made from clay, with plaster molds resting on the ground next to the table.

Aldari assumed someone had made the molds from the original puzzle before being driven away from the dig site. The elven numbers zero through nine and a dot—a decimal point?—were engraved in order around the edge of the bottommost disc. On the subsequent tiers, some of the numbers were missing, thanks to the triangular indentions where they should have been.

"They're archaeologists," Hawk said. "They all think they ought to be able to solve it, and a couple of times they believed they were close, but when they tried to plug in the solution to the real puzzle, they were almost incinerated."

"Incinerated?"

"By the booby traps that survived being buried by lava centuries ago," Hawk said.

Siadra said something in Elven and lifted a cloak draped over a crate, half of it burned away, the rest blackened.

"You need to be prepared to roll away, or have someone pull you away, if you fail to enter the correct solution," Hawk said. "Now, they can't even get close enough to the site to try."

"Ah."

A hiss came from the barrier. Several of the Twisted were watching them, shifting and reaching out clawed fingers, testing the magic. Nerves jittered in Aldari's belly again, as she imagined trying to work with that audience observing. A flash of purple light came from one of the orbs, and Hawk and Siadra exchanged concerned words.

"Is it supposed to do that?" Aldari stepped up to the table to study the puzzle more closely. Books and notes stacked under rock paperweights taken from the landscape filled the surface around it.

"No," Hawk said. "They don't know what's wrong. There's

some concern that the *phyzera* may be failing, but even the archaeologists have no personal knowledge of magic and how the ancient artifacts work. They only know what they've read about, since none of us dares channel the power dormant within us."

Hawk prodded at his bracer again, his expression wistful as he looked toward the *phyzera* and the Twisted. Envisioning himself heroically channeling his sublimated power to lay their enemies low and save everyone? Aldari couldn't blame him for the fantasy.

"May I write my people's version of the numbers on there?" She picked up a pen and pointed it at the replica puzzle, thinking her brain would be more likely to see solutions if she didn't have to translate as she fiddled with it.

"Yes." Hawk drew his sword, leaned his hip against the table, and whether by accident or design stood so that he blocked her view of the Twisted—and their view of her, or at least of what she was doing.

Aldari opened a notebook amid the tomes and looked at the pages, though she couldn't read them. Presumably, they were the scientists' thoughts on the puzzle and what they'd tried thus far.

"Will you translate this for me while I start trying to solve this?" Aldari asked.

"Yes. As long as there aren't too many big words." Hawk smiled as he took the notebook.

"Somehow, I doubt you have much trouble with those."

"If you're calling me smart, I'll ooze my appreciation onto you. My father, who has never let me forget how often I sneaked away from my studies as a boy to hunt and practice swords with friends, usually implies the opposite."

"Maybe he's a jerk."

Hawk snorted. "I'll be sure to mention that possibility to him."

"You haven't spoken much about your family." Aldari finished writing the translations of the numbers on the various tiers and studied them as she started rotating the discs. "Except for the sister you lost."

Hawk hadn't spoken much about her either, but when he had, his eyes had grown so haunted that Aldari hadn't wanted to pry.

"There have been a lot of distractions on our journey," Hawk said. "I don't think I've told you my favorite color or place to take women on dates either."

"Is it not to barren, remote camps surrounded by deadly enemies?"

"Not in the least. There's a bridge over the river at the outpost, and at night, phosphorescent algae in the water glow silver. Sometimes, when the moon is out and it hits the water just right, it creates a silver beam arcing between it and the algae, like a nighttime version of a rainbow. It's a romantic place to have, ah, tender moments."

Aldari imagined him wrapped in an embrace with a beautiful elf maiden, and she blushed for some reason. Though she tried to concentrate on the puzzle, she couldn't help but ask, "Have you taken many women there?"

"Not... that many. Not lately, especially. When I was still a boy, concerned more about having fun and avoiding my studies, I was a little more likely to try to woo a girl off for romance, but since my sister's death... I guess that sobered me and made me grow up. Dedicate myself to being the kind of person my people need, someone driven, someone willing to risk his life to make theirs better." He swallowed and looked toward the canyons. "To try to create a world where others don't have to worry about losing their family members."

"You were close to her," Aldari guessed.

"Yes. We are—we *were*—twins. Not that similar in looks or personality—*she* never climbed out a window to evade a tutor coming with a book—but close, yes. We teamed up often to torment our older brother. He deserved it, mind you. He always lorded over us and thought that because he was older, he was akin to a god. That's how he acted when he was younger, anyway. He's grown *slightly* less pompous as an adult." Hawk held up thumb and forefinger with a minuscule amount of space between them. "*Slightly.*"

"I see." Aldari found a blank page in the notebook and, hoping nobody would mind, penned the numbers on the discs in tidy rows so she could look at them all at once and see if anything struck her about the ordering or the missing digits.

The presence of the decimal points made her believe the solution was a non-integer or a sequence of them. Maybe one simply spun the discs to line up digits in the correct order. But one had to know the answer ahead of time to do that, possibly to nine decimal places. The missing triangles were clues, since they eliminated certain numbers, but that still left a lot of options.

"What about your family? Do you think..." Hawk shifted his gaze from the canyons to her. "Do you get along with them well? Do you miss them? As I said before, I didn't think about all of those who might be upset by your disappearance. I guess the Twisted aren't the only ones with a singular focus." He grimaced, and she genuinely believed he regretted his choice to kidnap her —or at least that he'd been driven to feel that it was his *only* choice.

"I do miss them, and I'm sure they're worried." Aldari couldn't bring herself to brush off that concern. If anything, his words roused guilt in her, making her realize she'd been so caught up in her own adventure that she hadn't thought often about her father and siblings and how worried they had to be. "You met my sister before we left, I think. She's a little more worldly and less bookish than I am, and we insult each other frequently, but we do care for each other. And my brother... You sound like you have a lot in common with him. Since our people only allow male rulers—" even though Aldari had never longed for her father's throne, she couldn't help but roll her eyes at that, "—he's the heir, and he spends a lot of time evading his tutors as well."

"Oh? How old is he?"

"He's the kid Setvik pulled out from under the carriage."

Hawk snorted. "So, eleven or twelve?"

"Ten."

"And I'm a lot like him?" Hawk scratched his jaw. "That's distressing. I may need to work harder at maturing into a respectable elf."

"I think you've matured fine." Aldari looked him up and down, not realizing until afterward that he might interpret it as her checking him out, as if she were some elf maiden interested in a make-out session with him on that bridge. "I mean, from what I've seen of you this past week, I wouldn't call you immature. You probably don't spit out your broccoli, sneak it into a napkin, and try to feed it to the castle dogs under the table. Though maybe that's not a correct assumption. You didn't mention your favorite food."

"It's *tafferzel*, a sugar-coated candy from the Taldar Empire. Every now and then, a trader risks the Forever Fog River and brings some home. I can stomach broccoli, and the hounds in the outpost don't show much interest in anything green."

"Good to know your moss reserves are safe from canine interest."

"Indeed."

"It's not the Golden Ratio," Aldari said, crossing out numbers on the page. "That would have been one-point-six-one-eight-zero and so on, but the eight is missing if you start from the bottom and go up, and the one is missing if you try to input it in the other direction.

"Is that... disappointing?"

"Well, it would have been convenient if it had been that easy."

Aldari couldn't give up the niggling idea that a nature-related answer might have appealed to the old inventor elf.

Aldari flipped through the pages of notes in Elven. Though she couldn't read the language, she could pick out spots where others had written down the digits available on the puzzle and tried various combinations. When she spotted the Golden Ratio, she wasn't surprised that someone else had guessed that.

She glanced at the singed cloak. "Maybe it's some other number that's significant in nature. Pi?"

Though she was certain the scientists would have tried that already, she attempted to write it in, using the numbers on the puzzle. Once more, a missing digit thwarted her.

"That's not it either," she said.

"Hm." Hawk stepped closer, his shoulder brushing hers, so he could look down at her notes with her.

The image of him on that bridge in the moonlight came to mind again, and she had to squelch an urge to ask him what kind of girls he'd invited there in the past. The shifting and sighing of the Twisted reminded her to focus on the present. Even if they hadn't had pressing problems, it wasn't as if she could have asked him on a date.

"Do you think—" Hawk broke off when Setvik called to him.

The lieutenant stood at the edge of the camp, pointing toward the sky.

"Messenger falcon." Hawk jogged over to join him.

Setvik drew an arrow and nocked it. Not to shoot the falcon, Aldari hoped. That wouldn't make any sense.

Setvik pointed the arrow not toward the sky but toward the horde of Twisted. In the back, a blue-skinned male standing on a boulder had raised a crude bow and was targeting the approaching falcon.

Swearing, Hawk pulled his own bow off his back. He was so fast that he fired at the same second as Setvik. Their arrows zipped over the heads of the Twisted toward the one in the back. One sliced through their enemy's bowstring, and the other pierced his eardrum. Before he could fire, the Twisted pitched off the boulder, disappearing from view.

The falcon pulled its wings in and dove for the pavilion. A few more Twisted grasped at the air as it passed, more than one waving an axe, but they couldn't reach the raptor, and it landed on an empty perch.

The barrier either allowed in animals and birds, or it knew the falcon had been sent by an ally. Angry buzzes filled the air as the Twisted hammered at the invisible shield, but it must have shocked them, for they stumbled back.

For now, the barrier remained firmly in place, but another flash came from one of the two orbs, the same one that had flashed earlier. A signal that its power was waning? Aldari hoped not. As talented as the mercenaries were, so many Twisted would be too much for even them to handle.

Siadra untied a message attached to the falcon's leg. Doubting it had anything to do with her, Aldari made herself turn back to the puzzle.

But only a minute later, Hawk called her over. Once again, his face was grave.

"King Jesireth sent a message personally." Hawk waved at a small scroll and the falcon waiting on its perch. "The Taldar Empire has sent a legion of troops out of the Shark Tooth Mountains and into your homeland. Because the king sent word to your father that you're here and safe—or were the last he knew—" Hawk grimaced as he glanced at the horde, "—your father knows where you are and is imploring Jesireth to return you immediately. Apparently, the imperial army is attacking your villages. Your father has sent troops to intercept them, but he fears they'll be overwhelmed. According to him, Prince Xerik and his father are *considering* sending forces to help, but they're reluctant to take hostile action against the Taldarians when they and your nation aren't officially aligned yet."

Aldari closed her eyes and sank into a crouch, bracing her elbows on her knees and gripping the back of her neck as she stared bleakly at the ground. "Because the wedding hasn't happened yet."

Guilt and distress washed through Aldari. She could have said *no* to Hawk and this quest to solve a puzzle. The queen had offered to send her home; she could have accepted. By now, she might be nearing her castle or even Orath for her wedding. Instead, she'd been intrigued by the challenge of the puzzle. She had wanted to help the elves, and now, people who'd been tormented a scant week earlier by the vorgs might be slain by invaders with swords and bows and who knew what else.

When Aldari lifted her head, she found Theli gazing at her. A few steps away, she must have heard Hawk's words. Her father and brothers might even now be among the soldiers marching toward the Taldarian army.

Theli's troubled eyes didn't seem to blame Aldari, but it didn't matter. Aldari blamed herself.

"I have to get out of here." She pushed herself to her feet. "I have to go home."

Hawk looked at the Twisted again. "Unfortunately, none of us can go home right now. I'm sorry, Aldari. Had I realized you would be trapped here, I wouldn't have brought you."

"Worse than trapped," Setvik grumbled, stepping up to Hawk's side. "The *phyzera* are being worn down by the constant strikes at their magic, and they're on the verge of failing. The scientists don't have many arrows left, and we'll run out before long too if we can't retrieve them. Worse, while there's food for a couple of weeks, we'll run low on water soon."

"We'll have to make a run for it," Hawk said.

"How?" Setvik scowled at him. "The Twisted don't sleep, and

for whatever reason, they're fascinated by this camp and us and won't leave. They're gathering in greater numbers in the canyon below as well, so climbing down isn't an option."

"Is there a way to cross to the far side?" Aldari pointed to the boulder-dotted ground opposite their camp. Unfortunately, the canyon was hundreds of yards across.

"Did you bring *wings*, Princess?" Setvik asked.

"No, but do any of your people have an engineering background? With the right supplies, maybe we could build gliders." Admittedly, flying across the canyon to the far side would be far more feasible if it were lower than their current perch. Unless a very stiff wind came up to help them in just the right way, a glider would lose altitude too quickly. "Unless there was a ledge halfway up that we could angle onto," she mused, though it was hard not to envision crashing into the canyon wall and breaking bones. "And then climb up to the top."

"We do have ropes and grappling hooks. As to the rest, I can ask." Hawk glanced at the pavilion above them. Possible material for a glider?

"Don't be ridiculous, Hawk," Setvik said. "Even if you could get over there, to what end? The Twisted will simply follow. Don't risk your life—or ours—just because the princess wants to go home. If her future husband's people cared a whit about her and that marriage, they would have sent troops to help already. More likely, they found out how many soldiers the empire has, pissed themselves, and are making excuses because they don't want to risk losing thousands of men over somebody else's peninsula."

Aldari frowned at him, but she'd had doubts of her own. With the wedding and the alliance imminent, why wouldn't Orath send help?

"We would be taking the risk," Hawk said coolly, holding Setvik's gaze, "because we're trapped—we're *dead*—if we do nothing."

"Send the bird back and ask the king to send troops." Setvik flung a hand toward the falcon. "We can hold out until they arrive."

"According to Siadra, the *previous* falcons haven't made it to the outpost. The Twisted are picking them off."

"Tell that one to fly higher."

"Yes, I'll use my magical telepathic powers to communicate with it."

Setvik glanced at Hawk's bracer. "Your ancestors could do that."

"*Many* of our ancestors could do that, but even if I took off the bracer and tried to call upon my power, it's not like I know how to use it. Nobody does anymore."

Setvik spat.

"We'll figure something out." Hawk rested a hand on Aldari's shoulder and drew her away. "Will you work on the puzzle? I know you're worried and want to go home, and that it's my fault that you're here and not at your wedding right now, but..." He gazed into her eyes. "My people need to get into that laboratory and find a solution. Find *something*."

"I know," Aldari said, though she couldn't help but gaze across the boulder-strewn landscape to the southwest, toward where her homeland lay.

Hawk squeezed her shoulder. "If we're successful, and we find something to stop the Twisted forever—or even to drive them away for a time—I'll bring troops to your homeland, and we'll help your people drive back the empire."

"The mercenary company?" Aldari appreciated the offer but couldn't keep from glancing at the twenty-odd elves and comparing them to the thousands of soldiers that were invading her homeland. Elven warriors would be powerful allies, but twenty were far too few to turn the tide. They needed armies, not a few squads of warriors.

"I can get more troops than this," Hawk said. "You have my word."

"I'll try." It wasn't as if there was anything else Aldari could do until they found a way past the Twisted. "But I'll only be able to make guesses with that replica puzzle. I need access to the real one."

"I'll get you that access," Hawk said with determination.

As he strode toward Setvik and the scientists to speak with them in Elven, thrusting a finger toward the pavilion fabric, Theli came up to Aldari's side.

"I know, I know. We need to escape, but we can't until *they* can. Our fate is tied inextricably with theirs." Aldari eyed her friend and bodyguard warily, anticipating a barrage of I-told-you-sos.

Theli took a deep breath. "I was just going to ask if there's anything I can do to help."

"I have a feeling you're going to be needed to cut fabric and saw wood to construct gliders in a minute."

"Given how little engineering experience I have, that might not go well."

"Maybe you can sing heartening ballads to those working," Aldari said. "Setvik seemed to like it when you villainized him."

"Pleasing him is of paramount importance to me."

"Maybe he'll take his shirt off again so you can admire him while he works."

"Your wit continues to awe me." Theli looked toward the far canyon wall. "You truly think we can get across without crashing and dying?"

Aldari sighed. "I don't know."

30

THE STEPS OF THE WOODEN PLATFORM CREAKED AS THE ELVEN scientist Siadra climbed down from the telescope. Night had fallen, but a few root-pitch lanterns burned around the camp. Outside, the Twisted shifted and pointed, some tapping at the barrier. Testing it.

Aldari straightened, her back aching from leaning over the table with the puzzle and the scientists' notes. With Hawk's help, she'd translated a lot of them, skimming through numerous ideas. A few possible combinations were underlined with hypotheses explaining them while hundreds of others had been crossed out.

When Aldari had read the hypotheses, none of them had quite gelled for her. If the price of guessing wrong was having a gout of fire spewed into one's face—she glanced at the charred remains of the cloak—she would hate to step forward to fiddle with the puzzle with anything less than confidence in her solution.

"This is the line of thinking I believe is most likely." Siadra joined her and pointed at a book under several others.

"Oh?" It was one of a handful on the table that were written in Hyric, and Aldari had skimmed it, though she'd only been able to guess at the notes written in Elven stuffed between the pages. It was a botany text, *Compendium of Plants*. "Do you also believe Zedaron might have leaned on his interest in nature for inspiration for his puzzles?"

"I do, yes. I was the one who kept trying numbers based on the Golden Ratio. Fayrooth keeps reminding me that Zedaron was known for his *engineering* abilities, but I'm not certain." Siadra shrugged and pointed to another tome. "His notes are all in that book. *Advances in Construction and Building Design in the Old Elven Cities.*"

"Hm."

Siadra frowned over her shoulder as the noise coming from what had turned into a glider production station increased, with tearing, hammering, and cursing filling the camp. Earlier, Aldari had gone to look at a sketch one of the archaeologists had come up with and offered a few criticisms and a suggestion for one large triangular sail—for greater surface area to catch the wind—instead of wings. She'd been shooed away with pompous-sounding Elven words. Nonetheless, when Aldari had checked back later, they'd shifted to using her design. Largely, she suspected, because Hawk was in charge, not the archaeologists.

Even though she'd scoffed at the idea earlier, Theli was over there helping—helping and singing. It was a work chantey used by sailors to coordinate the hoisting of the sails, but the elves seemed willing to cut wood and stretch fabric to the rhythm. Even Setvik, who'd joined the group, was working in time to the tune.

"I'm aware that Zedaron had an affinity for nature," Siadra continued when the noise died down. "Early on, on the original puzzle, I ignored the decimal point, thinking it might be there to throw us off, and tried lining up as many numbers from the Serrithon Sequence as possible. That was the *first* time I triggered flames and lost a piece of clothing. And my eyebrows."

"Ah." Aldari wouldn't have tried to force a solution that didn't seem to fit, but she couldn't blame the scientists for attempting it. She was encouraged that someone else believed the answer might be related to the natural world. These people had to know a lot more about their own historical figures than Aldari did.

"After that, I thought some other ratio might work, perhaps representing the distance between petals on flowers or scales on cones that are native to this area." Siadra opened *Compendium of Plants* to a section in the back. "These are the flora of this particular part of Serth."

She turned pages, showing paintings of various plants and trees that included close-up and to-scale diagrams of leaves, flowers, seeds, and the like. Pausing on a picture of an evergreen, Siadra pointed to a twisted juniper rising from a split boulder within the camp.

"That's a thought," Aldari mused. "The Golden Ratio is everywhere in nature, but there are exceptions. For example, not *every* flower has a number of petals that shows up in the Serrithon Sequence. It might make sense that Zedaron chose one of the exceptions rather than the rule." One might use math to figure out a ratio for such an exception. Could something like that be the answer?

As they were gazing at the juniper, the *phyzera* flashed. It wasn't the one that had been flashing earlier, and Siadra grimaced.

"They won't last much longer." Siadra glanced at the empty perch.

Before starting the glider project, Hawk had sent the falcon off with a message for the king, one that begged for legions of soldiers, Aldari hoped, but there was no way to tell if the bird would make it all the way to the outpost. As it had flown off, several Twisted had fired arrows at it. The mercenaries had fired arrows at *them* and succeeded in distracting them, but if the falcon flew past more Twisted along the way, there would be nobody nearby to protect it.

Even if the message made it to the king, it would take nearly two days for troops to arrive. Did they have two days?

"Do you have any ideas for these exceptions?" Siadra asked.

Aldari hesitated. "I'm not familiar with your flora, and I'm not sure you haven't already tried what I'm thinking. And until we can actually test it on the real puzzle..."

"You need to figure it out here. If you can make it to the real puzzle at all, you'll have Twisted on your heels."

"I know, but I doubt your people were able to replicate the inner workings so that we'd know if we successfully solved it."

"No. It's set into the wall, and the walls are made from crystal and rock and infused with ancient magic. They're durable against even lava flows. Also durable against elves with tools and swords trying to chip away the puzzle or carve an alternate doorway into the laboratory."

Aldari paged through the botany book, seeking inspiration. "I'll do my best to come up with a few numbers to try."

Siadra eyed her, the elf's face unreadable. "I'm skeptical that a human female from a country who knows nothing of our people and our ways can come up with anything *we* can't."

"I am too." Aldari smiled faintly. "But I'll do my best."

Siadra squinted at her. "You're not as pompous as I expected from a princess."

"Are elven princesses pompous?" Aldari asked before remembering that the queen had lost her daughter.

"There's not much for our people to be pompous about anymore. Hundreds of years of dealing with—of *dying* to—them —" Siadra waved at the Twisted, "—has stolen our arrogance. Some believe it's the punishment for the hubris we once had."

Aldari followed her gaze, but it snagged not on the Twisted but on Mevleth. He and one of the scientists were conferring near one of the gliders, their heads bowed together as they spoke in hushed tones. Maybe it was her imagination, but there was something secretive about their postures.

"Who's that?" Aldari pointed casually at the elf she didn't know.

Siadra frowned. "Waylith. You'd do best to avoid him. He's turned out to be a *vadir*."

"A what?"

"Someone who believes our people deserve this fate." Siadra waved again toward the Twisted. "That we were once too proud and arrogant, and that this is our comeuppance. We didn't know before the mission, or we wouldn't have brought him. We don't give him many duties related to the puzzle and our goal of getting inside. He's been studying the weather patterns since we got here."

"Would he... believe that so much that he would sabotage someone getting back to your king with a message?" Aldari thought of the dead elf on the road and the bowstring the mercenaries believed had been severed.

Siadra looked sharply at her but only briefly before shaking her head. "Not that message. Even if Waylith disagrees with what we're attempting to do, it would have been suicidal to have done something to stop that message from getting through. We're trapped here, and we need help." She glanced at the faltering *phyzera* and lowered her voice to whisper, "Before it's too late."

Even if Aldari was young and insulated by her position, she'd read numerous historical accountings of people being such zealots that they would give up their lives for their beliefs. But she didn't have a relationship with Siadra and doubted the elf would believe her over her own teammate if she pushed the matter. Later, Aldari would give the information to Hawk, if he didn't already know about it. He could keep an eye on the elf.

Aldari looked at the juniper tree, then out at the canyons. Nearly full, the moon shone silvery light over everything.

The raised land between the canyons was dotted with juniper

trees and other stunted vegetation, but there wasn't much besides rocks and boulders in this desolate area. Daylight and a more thorough exploration might reveal some of the smaller plants and flowers in Siadra's book, but this was a surprising place for a capital city, especially for what had once been the jewel of the elven kingdom. It lacked the verdant beauty of the forests and rivers to the south. Perhaps it hadn't always been like that.

That sparked a thought, and Aldari turned back to Siadra. The elven scientist was watching her with a mixture of skepticism and hope.

"What was this land like before the eruption?" Aldari asked. "Obviously, the lava flows buried the city, but what else did the volcano change? I've read about great eruptions of the past filling the air with smoke and ash and blocking sunlight for a time."

Siadra nodded. "Ours was cataclysmic, at least to this part of our continent. Some believe Zalazar used his magic to confine the environmental effects to our kingdom—to only punish *us*." She grimaced with distaste. "I don't know if that's true, but if you go on an archaeological dig, most of the lava rock is within a twenty-five-mile radius of the city, and while you'll find great amounts of ash below the current soil level, it's also confined to roughly fifty miles around the eruption site. The Wrathwild Forest marks that boundary to the south."

"Did the event alter what could grow here?" After all, not *every* tree had the tenacity and biological ability to grow up through a cracked boulder.

Siadra squinted thoughtfully at her. "I believe a number of species *did* go extinct." She bit her lip, a hint of excitement quickening her movements as she patted around the books and notes on the table. "I hadn't thought of that. Maybe none of us did, that the puzzle might represent a cone or petal pattern from an extinct species, or at least one that doesn't grow in this area anymore. Let me see if any of our books cover the flora from that time."

Aldari nodded and made herself step back, though she experienced the same excitement. Had she been able to read the Elven texts, she would have joined Siadra in scouring the books.

"Your Highness?" Theli walked up, two coils of rope over her shoulders.

"Are we going somewhere?" Aldari looked from her, then around the camp until she spotted Hawk.

A few mercenaries had rolled out their blankets to try to sleep, but most remained up, either on guard or engaged with Setvik and Hawk in what looked like planning. At the least, they were pointing at the Twisted often, as well as the canyon below and a distant ridge off to the east. The gliders appeared to have been completed. Eight of them were lined up along the edge of the canyon, each one capable of carrying one person. That would leave a lot of people up here, though maybe the rest of the mercenaries planned to climb down if the Twisted below were drawn away by the gliders sailing over their heads.

"I want to be prepared," Theli said. "Nobody will tell me anything, but the elves keep looking uneasily at those orbs, and the way they're flashing makes me think they might be failing."

"They are."

"I thought so." Metal clanked as Theli lifted the ends of her coils to reveal grappling hooks. "There are Twisted down there, but far fewer than up here, so if we're going to try to escape..."

Since Aldari had peered down to the canyon floor several times, she had a good idea about how far the drop was, and she didn't think the ropes Theli had selected would be long enough to reach the bottom. *Maybe* if she tied them together, they could, but a misstep in the descent would send them to their deaths.

"The plan is to take the gliders," Aldari said, though she was well aware that those might send them to their deaths too.

"There aren't enough for everyone, even if people share."

"I know. The elves were limited by the wood and fabric they

had in the camp." Aldari pointed upward. The pavilion canopy had been taken down, and only stars were over their heads now.

"I'm going to assume bodyguards are deemed expendable," Theli said.

"You're *not* expendable."

"The elves may see it another way, and they're in charge."

"If they won't give you a glider, you'll ride with me."

"What if they don't give *you* a glider?"

Aldari started to protest that idea, but what if Siadra had the clue she needed now to solve the puzzle, and the scientists no longer believed they needed a princess from a foreign kingdom?

"The gliders were my idea," Aldari said, though it sounded like a weak argument. It wasn't as if she'd assisted in building them. "Besides, Hawk said he would help us with our problem at home."

"A promise he won't have to keep if you are dead."

"You're full of cheer tonight, aren't you?"

One of the orbs flashed, and several Twisted groaned and tapped the barrier. Their yellow eyes glinted wickedly with the reflection of the lanterns burning in camp. Or maybe they glowed in the dark on their own.

"I can't imagine what would move me toward gloom." Theli hefted the ropes. "I'll be ready if we have to make a decision fast."

"Thank you." Aldari patted her on the shoulder, then returned to Siadra's side.

Another scientist had brought over an old book, and their heads were bent over it as they flipped through the pages, looking at faded drawings of flowers. Determined to help them, whether she could read the language or not, Aldari turned up the lantern light so she could see better.

"The *dayartha* plant has fifteen petals," Siadra murmured. "That's not one of the numbers in the Serrithon Sequence."

The other scientist said something in their language.

"I know," Siadra murmured, turning more pages. "There are a

lot of exceptions. And the Sequence may have nothing to do with the puzzle."

Aldari tapped her chin as they continued through the book. There were a *lot* of drawings of flowers. Hundreds of species. Which ones were extinct in this part of the world now that hadn't been before the eruption? And did that truly have something to do with the solution to the puzzle?

"The baton," Aldari blurted, a thought coming to her. "I've wondered a few times if it's meant to resemble a branch. If it is, is it from a distinct species of tree? Perhaps one with flowers or cones that grow in a way that represents a different and less familiar ratio found in nature?"

If the baton *was* meant to emulate a specific species, would it be possible to tell which one by looking at it? Without a background in botany, Aldari wouldn't have the faintest idea. But maybe the elven scientists could look at a branch and know what kind of tree it came from. Admittedly, the baton was made from metal, so it was a replica at best.

"The baton?" Siadra asked.

"Hawk lent it to me." Aldari pulled it out and laid it across her palms. "He said it was a teaching tool that belonged to Zedaron. We found that you could turn it this way and that to line up numbers and variables to create formulas and solve problems, but I'm wondering if the design of the baton itself could be a clue."

Siadra accepted it and examined it in the light. "It's a stretch to think a random artifact, one among hundreds of items he made over the years, would have anything to do with the puzzle at his door."

"Maybe, but can you tell what species this represents? If it's local, it might be worth trying."

Judging by Siadra's grimace, it *wasn't* easy to guess the species of a tree from a foot-long "branch" made of metal. She leaned over and consulted with the other elf, who raised his eyebrows and offered what sounded like a couple of guesses.

"It could be a *yulaylar* tree," Siadra said. "They're deciduous and grow along the rivers out here."

Aldari sagged. "Meaning they're not extinct and you've already checked their flowers?"

"They don't actually flower anymore, at least not around here. We believe that after the eruption, the trees stopped producing seeds and pollen because they sensed the ground was no longer hospitable to their species. The ones out there are very old and largely in a dormant state. Their branches are skeletal and a little haunting when the leaves fall. They're very symmetrical, so they have a distinctive look."

"Symmetrical?" Aldari could envision a math-loving nature appreciator being drawn to a symmetrical tree.

"This book covers many extinct and ancient species, so diagrams of their flowers should be in here." Siadra returned the baton and flipped to a page with a tree, flower, and a close-up diagram of a branch.

Her fellow scientist pointed excitedly at the branch and at the baton. They *did* look similar.

"The flower has nineteen petals," Aldari whispered, her fingers twitching toward the drawing. "Another exception to the Sequence."

Did the elves have rulers? She wanted to measure the distance between petals, as well as their length and width. And might analyzing those symmetrical branches reveal some interesting angles?

"We'll trace the flower and take measurements," Siadra said, fishing out drawing tools, "but if the author of this book eyeballed it, and the measurements aren't precise..."

"I understand." Aldari frowned at the thought of having to physically hunt down one of the trees. Even that wouldn't be enough if they were all dormant. They would need a fossil of the flower.

While Siadra took measurements of the length and width of the petals and the distance between them, Aldari grabbed a protractor to get the angles between the branches. One of her sister's factoids came to mind, that orchard growers liked to see forty-five-degree branch angles to maximize growth and fruit production. The branches of the *yulaylar*, at least the one in the book, tended to be thirty, forty-five, or sixty degrees. Every angle she checked was one of those. The preciseness was uncanny, and she wished she had an actual tree that she could measure. It was possible the artist had used tools to draw the *yulaylar* rather than exactly rendering what had been in nature.

Siadra lowered her pen after writing a single digit, a decimal point, and eight digits following the point. She'd written several other numbers above that and crossed them all out, but she underlined this one. "I tried a number of ratios based on the measurements, which the author was kind enough to include in the text. This one is what I got when I divided the number of petals by the distance between the petals."

"And it fits?" Aldari had no idea if that was a common ratio that people checked in botany—it looked like Siadra had simply been conjuring up ratios based on every measurement she'd been able to take from the diagrams.

Siadra spun the discs and lined everything up using the number she hadn't crossed out. The triangles with the missing numbers didn't affect her ratio. Aldari watched intently, memorizing the number, in case this was indeed their solution.

When Siadra finished, she rested her hands on the table to either side of the puzzle. "Everything fits that way. That doesn't necessarily mean this is the solution, as we've had other possible solutions, but since this was inspired by the species Zedaron modeled his baton after..."

"It could be the solution to his puzzle?" Aldari asked.

"Yes. It even makes sense that he would have put a clue out into the world somewhere. One doesn't create puzzles unless one wants someone to solve them." Siadra picked up the book and replica and slid them carefully into a backpack. "I'll tell the others. We need to find a way to the real puzzle so we can try it."

Aldari nodded as Siadra ran over to Hawk and the others. Her pace and the fact that she'd swept everything right into her pack gave Aldari hope. Siadra believed they had something.

But could they get past the Twisted to try it?

31

WHILE HAWK, SETVIK, AND THE SCIENTISTS CONFERRED, ALDARI SAT shoulder to shoulder with Theli, their backs to one of the few crates that hadn't been broken down for glider parts. They slumped against it, a blanket draped over them, and tried not to shiver as the night deepened and it grew colder.

Somehow, Theli was managing to sleep, but that eluded Aldari. An icy wind blew across the boulder-dotted lands, reminding her that autumn wasn't far off. Back home, the first frosts would come soon—they were always early in their northern kingdom.

An awareness of time passing made her worry about her father and brother and sister, as well as everyone else she cared about back home. How far had the imperial army advanced? Were they harrying the villages near the border, or had they marched straight to the capital city? What if her family was in trouble at that very second?

She rubbed at moisture in her eyes and might have let tears fall, but a cloaked figure stepped away from the meeting that had been going on for more than an hour—since Siadra had gathered the elves to report on a possible solution for the puzzle. She hadn't pointed at Aldari as she'd explained, and Aldari wondered if the scientist would give her any credit if the solution turned out to work. While she didn't *need* credit, she couldn't help but hope Hawk would learn that she'd helped, if only in a small way. She wanted him to think well of her, and she also didn't want him to feel that he'd made a mistake in risking everything to get her.

Maybe she shouldn't have believed that, given the position her people were now in, but even if things had gone according to plan, she wouldn't yet have married Xerik. The wedding had been set for the week after she would have arrived in his homeland. Maybe the empire had known that and had deliberately invaded before the ceremony. It wasn't as if invasions were carried out on a whim. Taldar had to have been planning to take Delantria for some time. It was possible the men who'd attacked her caravan had done so to ensure she was killed and the wedding couldn't take place. For the first time, it occurred to her that she might have died that day if the elves hadn't been with her.

The cloaked figure turned out to be Hawk, and he sat beside her, his shoulder brushing hers. She offered him a corner of the blanket she and Theli were sharing in case the wind bothered him through his leather armor.

Hawk barely noticed; his eyes were focused outward, toward the threats and his plans for the future. "We'll leave in the morning. I'm tempted to try now, but the mercenaries need rest, and jumping off a cliff in the dark while dangling from a glider seems unwise, especially with enemies below." He glanced toward the night sky, a few clouds dimming the moon's brightness.

"You need rest too." Aldari hoped he hadn't forgotten it had only been a couple of days since he'd been lying near death. Mounted on reindeer, none of them had slept much the night before either.

"Yes." Hawk gave her a quick smile. "Though it's hard to sleep with them milling and growling out there."

"I know." The single time Aldari had dozed off, she'd woken with a start, dreaming of the barrier failing and the Twisted lunging through to tear her head off with those deadly claws. "Have you found out who sabotaged the messenger's bowstring?" she asked, keeping her voice low.

"No," Hawk said. "I asked Siadra if there was anyone she didn't trust, but she said everyone here was loyal."

"Even the *vadir*?"

Hawk frowned at her. "Who told you about them?"

"Siadra. One of her younger scientists is one."

Hawk turned his frown on the camp. "They don't usually do much. It's just a religious sect that branched off from the fundamentalists at the time of the eruption. They believe that they'll be rewarded in the afterlife, not for pursuit of excellence—as our people have traditionally believed—but by being humble and living in sync with nature while accepting that the Twisted are a trial we must endure in this life to thrive in the next."

"Are there a lot of *vadir*?" Aldari asked.

"No. It's not a popular idea. Most people want to find a way to end the Twisted and return our kingdom to what it once was. I'm keeping an eye on him and will check the gliders before we leave. Just in case any of the scientists have ideas about sabotage."

"Would it make sense to confront that one and tie him up if it's believed he's guilty of sabotaging your messenger's bowstring?"

Hawk blew out a slow breath. "In these times, without the telepathic powers that our magic once gave us—" he brushed his bracer with his fingers as he continued on with longing in his voice, "—it's hard to know when someone is lying or telling the truth."

"Is it the convenience that you'd gain with your magic that makes you long for your power, or does not using what's inherent in your blood cause physical distress?" Aldari waved toward his bracer, having caught him touching it wistfully more than once.

Hawk lowered his hand. "I'm not physically distressed, no, though I have heard of people going crazy and blaming the magic they have but can't access. It's just that I believe—I *know*—that winning battles would be easier if I could use my power." He glared at the Twisted.

"Didn't you say that it takes years to master it?" She hoped he wouldn't cast off the bracer and try something foolish, like running out into the Twisted, hoping magic could somehow save him from being clawed and trampled.

"It does." Hawk tilted his head closer to hers and lowered his voice. "I've never told anyone this—my parents would be aghast—but when we were younger, my sister and I used to take off our bracers in secret and try to use our magic. We played games, as elven children long ago did, to develop our power, and she was good at them. Very good. I wasn't bad either." He tightened his hand into a fist. "If I dared take off the bracer now, maybe I could force that horde away from us."

Worried that he might try—and that using his magic would make them all target *him* when the orbs inevitably failed—Aldari leaned against his shoulder and rested her hand on his sleeve. Even through his tunic, she could feel the corded muscles of his arm, the tension in his body.

"I know little about magic, but forcing a thousand enemies away would take far more power than something used in a game, wouldn't it?" she asked. "And you'd be putting yourself in great danger."

"Yes, but it would be worth it if it worked. Though that may be what my sister was thinking when she was taken." Hawk slumped against the crate—and Aldari.

The heat of his body warmed her better than the blanket, but she resisted the urge to snuggle closer. Even if Theli hadn't been leaning against her on the other side, and apt to wake up at any time, that wouldn't have been wise.

"Well, don't get yourself killed or taken, please." Aldari forced a smile. "You're the only one here who doesn't think we're expendable, and Theli is worried we won't get a glider."

"Did someone say that? That you're expendable?" Hawk met her gaze, his fist still tight, as if he would punch someone on her behalf if she pointed out an offender.

"Not directly, at least not to me, but you're the only one who thinks we have a use."

"That's not true. Siadra said you led her down the path to what she believes might be a solution to the puzzle." Hawk loosened his fist and lifted a hand to her face, tucking a stray lock of hair behind her ear.

A shiver of pleasure ran through her, and she had to stifle the urge to lift her own hand to his face, to trace the strong line of his jaw. "Oh, good. I wasn't sure... Well, it doesn't matter if I get credit. I just hoped to be able to be useful to your people." Her gaze drifted from his eyes to his lips.

They were parted slightly, as if he were thinking of kissing her. Was he?

His fingers ran from her ear to her chin, and he brushed his thumb across her lips. "You *are* useful. Even though you have every reason to fight us."

"I'm more of an academic than a combatant," she murmured, leaning her head into his hand, not wanting his touch to leave.

It was warm in contrast to the cold air. *He* was warm. Would his lips be as well?

She should have drawn back, but she wanted him to kiss her. If he didn't, maybe she would. Would that be so bad? Just a kiss, so she knew what it was like, before she had to marry another man. It wouldn't be a betrayal, would it? Prince Xerik might be kissing some concubine at that very moment. They'd never met. What loyalties did they truly owe to each other at this point?

But as she leaned her mouth closer to his, voices pulled Hawk's attention away. It was Mevleth talking to one of the scientists—the one Siadra had identified as the *vadir*.

"Is there any reason why they should be buddies?" she whispered.

Hawk squinted at the pair. "No. It may be time for me to confront Mevleth."

He started to rise, but Aldari tightened her grip on his arm. "Wait. He's your only medic, isn't he? If you confront him, what if that makes him more dangerous? If you're injured again..."

If *any* of them were, would the medic take the opportunity to kill them by less subtle means than a tainted potion?

"He won't be able to do anything if I kill him," Hawk said.

"Will Setvik allow that?" Aldari glanced toward where the mercenary lieutenant also leaned against a crate, trying to get some rest. Given his keen elven hearing, he might have heard them whispering.

"I'm in charge," Hawk said but didn't push himself to his feet. Hopefully, he was debating the wisdom of killing one of their own people when an enemy horde loomed only thirty feet away.

Not that Aldari would cry over the loss of the elf who'd been responsible for poisoning Hawk.

"Is Mevleth one of those *vadir*?"

"It's possible," Hawk said. "I'll ask Setvik."

Aldari grimaced, suspecting Setvik was an unreliable source. He might be one of those people himself. That could explain why he was so quick to argue with Hawk. What if he didn't want this mission to succeed?

"Are you *sure* he's on your side?" she whispered, remembering

Setvik's willingness to slit Hawk's throat when he'd been ill. "What if neither of them wants—"

Setvik rose, shedding his blanket, and looked right at them.

Certain he'd heard everything, Aldari shrank back. They should have gone somewhere more private to speak, but it wasn't as if the camp was that large or offered privacy nooks.

Hawk stood up as Setvik approached. Next to Aldari, Theli stirred. She shifted under the blanket, gripping the hilt of her mace.

"I do not care if your human female *likes* me," Setvik said, challenging Hawk with his eyes, "but I will not be accused of being a *vadir* or have it said that I do not care about the fate of our people. If you do not make the truth clear to her, *I* will." Setvik launched a scathing look at Aldari but only briefly before locking his gaze back on Hawk.

"It's your medic that we were doubting," Hawk said, meeting his lieutenant's cold eyes, "but you haven't given me much reason to believe that you care either."

"I went back for you." Setvik flung a hand toward the road, though the ancient cobblestones weren't visible under the Twisted, the blue-skinned creatures never growing weary and sitting or lying down.

"And I appreciate that, but you haven't been behind this mission from the start. You've argued with me at every opportunity."

"Just because I argue with *you*—" Setvik pointed a finger at Hawk's chest, "—doesn't mean I don't care about our people. Of course I want the Twisted to stop plaguing them."

"If you cared, you wouldn't have taken your mercenaries— elves who were in the king's guard then—and left all those years ago. We *needed* people like you, and you abandoned the kingdom."

"How would you know what was needed? You were a toddler at your father's knee when I left."

Hawk lifted his chin. "I knew."

"You barely cared about any of this until your sister died."

"That's not true. I've done everything my father ever asked of me. And I stayed. Even when it was hard to stay. Even after I watched them take her. I was helpless as my brother grabbed my arms and held me back and shouted that it was already too late. That she was already gone and that all I'd accomplish if I went after her was to give myself to them as well. That was the hardest —" Hawk broke off, his voice thick with emotion. "That was the hardest thing I ever experienced," he whispered, "but I stayed. I stayed to support my family and our people. I didn't walk away from them and our kingdom. Like a coward."

This time, Setvik lifted *his* chin, his eyes blazing. "I'm no coward. I've fought in countless battles and faced death a thousand times."

"This is worse than death, and you'd know it if you ever watched them take someone close to you. If you'd watched them turn someone you loved into a monster, into one of them, condemning them to lose themselves and roam the wilderness forever, no rest for their soul as magic compels them to prey on their own people. If you'd watched that—" Hawk's voice broke again as he pointed a finger at Setvik's face. He swallowed and finished with, "That was the one thing you couldn't stomach, and *that* makes you a coward. You didn't want to follow my lead, because I'm young, and I can understand that, but you need to understand why I question your loyalty when you turned your back on your people and disappeared for twenty years."

Setvik snarled in disgust. "You're a child and impossible to reason with."

He walked back to his blanket, grabbed it, and strode to the far side of the camp. Dozens of sets of eyes watched him. All of the mercenaries and scientists had witnessed the argument, and Aldari rubbed her face, afraid that it would have ramifications.

Long seconds passed before Hawk sat back down next to her, not as close as he had been before. She had little doubt that she wouldn't receive the kiss she'd been hoping for. Theli would tell her it was for the best, but if it had meant that argument wouldn't have taken place, Aldari wouldn't have been quick to agree. She hadn't trusted Setvik not to act against them before, and she trusted him even less now.

"Human female," Setvik called across the camp.

Aldari touched her chest uncertainly.

Setvik looked not at her but at Theli. "Human female who sings."

"My name is Theli." She shook her head and muttered, "You'd think he could have mastered that by now."

"Sing us a song, Theli," Setvik said, holding her gaze. "To help us sleep."

"Is he kidding me?" Theli whispered. "I'm not his servant at his beck and call."

"Maybe if it makes him less crabby, you should do it," Aldari said.

"That's asking a lot of a song."

"Sing us a song, Theli," Setvik repeated, the words an order, not a request. What an ass. "For we all may die tomorrow."

"Hell." Theli surprised Aldari by shrugging off the blanket. She didn't walk over to Setvik but climbed the platform to stand next to the telescope. From the elevated position, she started singing a ballad that Aldari didn't recognize but that had a haunting melody that spoke to their situation and the danger all around them.

Aldari might have preferred something perkier and more optimistic, but Setvik and several of the other elves made contented grunts and settled back to listen.

"Do you think goading him was... wise?" Aldari whispered to

Hawk, wondering if she might talk him into apologizing to Setvik and if it would make a difference.

She'd wanted Mevleth outed and ideally left behind or sent off in another direction. Not the lieutenant—the captain—who was the rightful leader of the mercenaries and whom the men might follow even against Hawk's wishes.

"No." Hawk pushed his hair behind his shoulders and sighed. "My father often says he hopes he lives long enough to see me develop wisdom. I shouldn't have snapped. But he... Before this all started, when he first learned of the mission and that I would lead it, he called me a childish brat and refused to follow me. There was arm-twisting, and he eventually agreed, but I've been struggling to rise above that insult and command him well. To command *all* of them. It's not easy being in charge of your seniors. Or in charge at all. I'm trying to do better, but I'm... fallible."

You're young, Aldari thought but didn't say. He wasn't much older than she, and she wouldn't have deemed herself capable of commanding men either. It was bad enough that she felt the weight of her nation on her shoulders—and that she wasn't at home to bear it for her people.

"What if someone sabotages the gliders tonight?" she asked.

"I'm keeping an eye on them." Hawk nodded toward the gliders—they were all visible from this spot. Maybe he'd sat where he had because of that rather than a desire to cozy up next to her. "Do you trust me, Aldari?" He looked at her.

"More than I should," she admitted.

Hawk lifted a hand toward her face again but dropped it, as if acknowledging that the kiss they'd almost had would have been a mistake. "I meant what I said before. If your... fiancé won't help you, *we* will. Even if he does send troops, we will too. After all this, we owe you that. I'll make sure it happens, no matter what the outcome here."

"Thank you," she said softly.

Touched, Aldari leaned her head against his shoulder. Too bad it wouldn't be enough. Hawk only had a couple dozen men, and they were more loyal to Setvik than to him. All she could do was hope to get back in time and hope it would matter. The thought of returning home only to find that her family was dead and the Taldarian emperor had declared Delantria part of his empire terrified her as much as the threat of the Twisted.

32

ON THE HARD GROUND, WITH A CRATE AT HER BACK, ALDARI SAT awake most of the night, long after Theli had finished singing, receiving a few compliments from the elves, and returned to their corner of the camp. Aldari didn't think she dozed off at all, but when someone touched her shoulder, she woke with a start.

"We need to go." Hawk crouched before her. "The barrier is about to fail."

Next to Aldari, Theli rolled to her feet and grabbed her pack and mace. Hawk pointed to one of the *phyzera*. It was not only flashing repeatedly now, but it had grown much dimmer. The barrier itself must have shrunk, for the Twisted had been able to move in, the closest only twenty feet away now.

It was still dark out—still dangerous to take off in the gliders— but they didn't have a choice.

"I'm ready," Aldari made herself say, wincing at the quaver in her voice.

"You, me, three of the scientists, and three mercenaries will go. We'll leave the young scientist with Mevleth and the rest of the mercenaries." Hawk lowered his voice. "I've kept an eye on the gliders and just checked them to make sure there are no cuts or loose connections."

Aldari wondered how well he could have watched and checked them in the dark but made herself nod. It didn't sound like they had much time. "What about Theli?"

He'd named eight people for the eight gliders, and she hadn't been among them. Aldari wouldn't leave her.

"Yes." Theli grabbed the coils of rope she'd had the day before. "What about Theli?"

"Do you think the gliders are strong enough for you two to share one? You're lighter than the mercenaries, so I'm hoping that will work." Hawk's wince promised he might *hope* that, but he wasn't sure of it.

Aldari wasn't either. Even though she'd known enough to make suggestions on their construction, she fully admitted she was an economist, not an engineer. And they hadn't been building the gliders from the most ideal materials.

"We may land a little more quickly." Aldari tried to quash the quaver lingering in her voice and sound brave. "It's fine."

It wasn't as if the gliders would have carried them across to the other side under any circumstances. Their goal was to sail over the heads of the Twisted and land a couple of miles up the canyon.

"I'll let go of mine and jump if your glider goes down faster than mine. Especially if the Twisted are there. I'm *hoping* this will catch them by surprise, and we'll get the few minutes we need to get out ahead of them. You and the scientists will run to the ruins —they know the way—and we'll buy the time you need to solve the puzzle and get in." Hawk touched his sword scabbard.

"What happens if there are more puzzles—more traps inside the laboratory?" Aldari allowed Hawk to guide her toward one of the gliders as she spoke.

She touched her belt to make sure she still had her knife and the baton, though perhaps it would be better to leave the artifact, especially if it drew the Twisted. But even as she had the thought, she couldn't imagine abandoning something so valuable and instead secured it better so it wouldn't fall out when they leaped off the cliff.

"There may be," Hawk said grimly, pointing her and Theli to a glider that one of the mercenaries was holding up for them. "You'll have to do your best. I'm hoping that once you're in, the puzzle-lock will reset, and the Twisted won't be able to follow. We'll try to catch up with you, but if we're not able to, you'll have to... be careful. Please." He held her gaze earnestly. "Stay safe, and find whatever it takes to put an end to the Twisted. Siadra will be your guide."

"I understand."

The urge to kiss him returned, not for romantic reasons but for luck. She worried he would sacrifice himself for the mission—for her and the others to get in—if necessary. What if she never saw him again?

Maybe it was unwise, but Aldari gripped his arm and leaned in close, intending to kiss him on the cheek. But Hawk turned his face toward hers, and their lips met.

At first, he froze in surprise, and so did she, marveling at the warmth and appeal of his lips—of him. She expected him to pull away and say there wasn't time for this. Instead, he lifted a hand to the back of her head and threaded his fingers through her hair as he pressed his lips to hers. It wasn't the chaste good-luck kiss she'd been thinking about but a passionate I-want-to-remember-this kiss that left her knees wobbly. She returned it with equal passion, knowing it had to end soon but wanting nothing more than to sling her arms around him and keep him tight against her forever.

Hooves clopped on the hard ground, Setvik riding up on a reindeer. Aldari and Hawk pulled apart, and he drew his hand back but he caught hers for a squeeze before turning to face the mercenary.

For once, Setvik didn't scowl or say anything sarcastic. The rest of his mercenaries—those who hadn't been selected for the gliders?—were also mounted or on foot, all with their weapons in hand. All ready to go.

"What are you doing?" Hawk asked. "You're supposed to climb down after us once the ones on the ground see us and give chase."

"And what happens when *they* all climb down after you as well?" Setvik thrust his hand toward the horde, the Twisted watching their every movement.

"We'll fight," Hawk said. "It's all there is left to do."

Setvik snorted. "The scientists will need time to figure out how to get in and find whatever you've been praying is in there to end all this."

"Yes. We'll buy that time."

"Against thousands? Without the *phyzera* for protection?"

Hawk opened his mouth, but Setvik cut him off.

"Just let us lead them away. It'll be for the best."

"It may not work," Hawk said.

"Take this." Aldari held the baton up toward Setvik. She hated to give it away, especially when it might provide more clues, but... "I think they're drawn to it. They've been trying to get to me ever since Hawk gave it to me."

Setvik squinted at her. "Maybe they just don't like you."

"Impossible. I'm witty and a delight. Just ask Theli."

Theli made a noise akin to a cat hawking up a hairball. It was amazing that such a talented singer could manage such an awful sound.

Setvik snorted, took the baton, and pointed toward a distant ridge. "We'll ride that way."

"Setvik," Hawk said, "that's a suicide mission. There'll be more out there, and they'll cut you off. You know they're smart and you know how they hunt."

"Yes, but contrary to what *you* believe, I am not a coward and do not fear death. And even though I haven't spent much time here these past twenty years—" Setvik glowered at Hawk, "—I know the ways of the Twisted well. I was fighting them before you were born. We'll do the best we can. If nothing else, if we succeed, you'll only have the ones below to worry about. If we can break away somehow and lose them, we'll try to find a way down to help you. Hold out as long as you can. If we don't make it..." Setvik twitched a shoulder. "If that falcon got through, the prince should arrive in a couple of days with troops."

"We should have brought everyone we had from the beginning," Hawk said.

"Yes. But we had to sneak away because of political foolishness." After another lip curl, Setvik pointed to the ridge again and gave his mercenaries an order.

Break through the barrier and the Twisted and run as fast as they could? Aldari hoped that would be possible.

"Aldari." Theli poked her on the shoulder.

Aldari wrenched her attention from the mercenaries. Theli had the glider off the ground, the great triangular sail over her head, her weapons belted, and her hands wrapped around a handlebar attached to the frame. There was another bar to hook their feet over to keep their bodies horizontal as they took to the air. As long as they didn't slip.

The canyon stretched out before them, dark and ominous. The moon had set, so no silvery light illuminated the ground far below. This might be as suicidal as Setvik's mission. If Aldari died, would her father ever be able to arrange the alliance her people needed?

Setvik bellowed a final order, and the mercenaries charged through the barrier and into the Twisted. The orbs that had been failing went dark together. There was no choice but to go forward. No, to go *down*.

Swallowing, Aldari brushed shoulders with Theli as she

gripped the handlebar. At the mercenaries' behest, the scientists launched themselves first, helping each other over the edge.

"Go," Hawk barked, springing for the glider next to Aldari's. "They're coming."

As they eased toward the edge, the wind already tugging at the glider, Aldari risked glancing back. Hundreds of the Twisted were charging the mercenaries—one managed to tear an elf from his mount even as the company swung their swords with lightning speed, dull meaty thuds echoing across the boulder-strewn land.

Despite the distraction of the mercenaries, more Twisted ran for Aldari and the others. Hawk raised his sword, yelling again for her to go, making it clear he would wait to go himself, defending her even if it meant his death.

Aldari couldn't allow that. She turned, tightened her grip on the bar, and she and Theli sprang.

Utter terror gripped Aldari, and she gasped as they left the ground, struggling awkwardly to hook their feet and level themselves. A breeze she hadn't felt before whistled through the canyon, caught the glider, and they lurched sideways. Her gasp turned into a scream as the handle almost slipped from her grip, and the framework creaked. She tried to clamp down on the cry, but her terror needed an outlet.

Several other voices cursed and yelled, and another woman screamed. Siadra?

Theli panted and swore as she struggled to keep her arms straight and maintain a hold on both bars. When Aldari had worked out the mathematics of this, she'd envisioned a smooth flight, their glider guided down by a gentle breeze, but the wind battered them alarmingly. The framework and sail shuddered as gusts struck them from the side instead of nudging them from behind.

"Try to turn it sideways," Aldari said, certain the glider would work better with the wind behind them—they'd designed the front with a point in an attempt to gain an aerodynamic flight. As the dark canyon wall on the far side loomed ahead of them, she realized they had another reason to turn. "*Hard.*"

She twisted her body as much as she could, attempting to turn the tip. Theli released one foot from the bar and kicked her leg, as if they were in water instead of air. Though Aldari doubted that would work, she didn't stop Theli, for they were turning. Some of the other gliders were too.

Aldari wanted to look back, to see if Hawk had made it, but the large sail blocked their view of anything above them. The only things she could see were the dark wall of the canyon and the dark ground below, and those were only vague outlines lost in shadows. Wind tugged at her hair, batted at the side of her face, and brought tears to her eyes that further impeded her vision.

"Aldari and Theli," Hawk called from somewhere behind and above them—the gliders with single riders were descending more slowly. "Are you all right?"

"Jolly," Theli snarled.

"Yes." Aldari wanted to complain about the wind, the terror in her belly, and how badly her hands shook as she gripped the bar, but she didn't. "We're fine."

"*Fine* may be an overstatement," Theli said.

"We're alive."

"For now, maybe. I can't see what's down there. Can you?"

Aldari shook her head, her full concentration on keeping the glider pointed into the canyon instead of veering toward one of the walls. They were gradually sinking, but she didn't think they could do anything to stop that.

She wished she knew how fast they were going—and if they were outpacing the Twisted. Their enemies in the canyon must have seen them take off and had to be following. They had a single-minded purpose. Unfortunately.

Distant screams and the squeals of reindeer dying—of elven

mercenaries dying?—reached their ears. Aldari winced, wishing Setvik and the others had tried something else. She didn't know what else they could have done, but being clawed and torn to pieces had to be a horrible death.

She couldn't bring herself to feel glad that Mevleth had ridden off with them. All she knew was that she was glad he wouldn't be the one to treat her if she broke her leg landing. She would rather have Theli with her limited medical skills do it.

Or maybe Hawk would simply carry her to safety. If there was safety to be found. She doubted it.

"Aldari!" came his call. He sounded even higher above her now.

Fresh fear darted through her body as Aldari realized she and Theli would land well before the solo riders, and they would have only Theli's mace and her dagger with which to defend themselves.

"You're close to the ground now," Hawk yelled. "Can you see it? Do you know how to land?"

"Not well." Aldari peered into the dark gloom, but with the moon down, the stars behind clouds, and the canyon walls cutting off most of the sky, they might as well have been descending into a bottomless abyss.

"Be ready to free your legs. You're almost there, and the ground is rocky and hard. Only ten or twelve feet!" Hawk's *ears* weren't the only thing better than the human equivalent.

The tearing of fabric sounded in their ears, as ominous as a gunshot.

"What—" Theli started, but the glider jerked, fabric tearing even further, and her words devolved into curses.

Aldari unhooked her boots as the frame shuddered and they lost what little control they'd had, careening toward one of the canyon walls. They tried vainly to tilt the glider away from it.

Aldari's arms quivered from the effort of holding on, and she couldn't do enough.

The left side of their sail clipped the rock wall. The glider jerked again as wood crunched, the makeshift frame not able to take the impact. Aldari's sweaty palms slipped, and she cursed and tightened her grip. But as they bounced away from the canyon wall, tilting wildly, she realized it might be better to let go.

Assuming Hawk was right and the ground was close below them. Was it?

Do you trust me? he'd asked.

More than I should.

"I'm letting go," Aldari told Theli and did.

She tried to push away from the bar so she wouldn't be tangled in the frame or bump into Theli, but she had no leverage. The sail whooshed by as the glider continued on. Aldari twisted in the air, trying to get her feet under her. Even though she was ready, the ground came fast, with a jarring impact that sent her flying.

Stabbing pain came from her ankle as one foot hit before the other, and she tumbled to her side, momentum throwing her legs over her head. The ground was as hard as Hawk had promised and battered her on all sides as she rolled.

Theli's pained grunt and more curses came from farther up the canyon. Had she held on until the end?

Aldari's momentum slowed, her head hitting a rock as she finally rolled to a stop on her back. The blow dazed her, and she struggled to move—to even remember what was going on.

A thud sounded beside her, and a shadow stirred. One of the Twisted? Aldari cried out, trying to roll away, but she bumped into a boulder.

"It's me." Hawk knelt and swept her into his arms. "I've got you."

Aldari groaned, relieved but distressed. He was supposed to

guard the scientists from the Twisted, not have to carry her. The plan hadn't been for her to collapse and be a burden.

"Sorry," she rasped. Her ankle throbbed, and she prayed it wasn't broken.

"No, *I'm* sorry. I heard that rip. One of them might have sabotaged your glider, and I missed catching it."

"It might have just been the hasty construction. Or the weight of carrying two."

"And it might not have been," Hawk said grimly, squeezing her —no, *hugging* her. "I'm sorry you crashed."

More shouts sounded, the mercenaries and scientists landing farther up the canyon. Grunts and screeches came from the opposite direction. The Twisted.

Carrying her in his arms, Hawk ran toward the rest of the group. The hilt of his sheathed longsword jabbed Aldari in the back, but she didn't care. She wrapped her arms around his shoulders and kissed him on the neck, remembering the last time she'd done that, back on the pirate ship. He kept saving her. The thought of leaving him forever filled her with anguish, but she had to focus on the present, on surviving this night.

"Theli?" Aldari craned her neck. "Are you with us?"

"I'm here," Theli said from beside them. "But lacking a porter."

"I hurt my ankle," Aldari said, embarrassed to be carried and feeling the urge to justify it.

"I hurt everything."

"We should have invited Setvik along to carry you," Aldari said before remembering that Setvik and all the other mercenaries might be dead by now. She shut her mouth on her humor.

Hawk called to the others in Elven and got several responses. Once he was sure they had everyone, he then sped up. "The Twisted are coming."

"Of course they are." Theli sighed, grunting and cursing again as she attempted to maneuver over the rocky ground in the dark.

Aldari wished she'd grabbed a lantern from the camp, but she never could have held it while gripping the glider with both hands.

Hawk managed to keep up with the others, even though he carried her, but Aldari continued to feel like a burden. Siadra had the possible solution to the puzzle. Could Aldari even be of use in this elven laboratory?

Grunts and hisses and screeches echoed from the Twisted behind them. Aldari couldn't see them, but her ears told her they'd already closed the gap.

"You can let me down," she whispered, though her ankle throbbed, as if to deny the statement. "I'll try to run."

"I can carry you to the camp." Hawk didn't yet sound breathless, but this had to be much harder for him than the others. And Theli was no better able to see where she was going than Aldari—as her grunts attested.

"I don't want to slow you down," Aldari said.

"You won't. I'm strong."

"And cocky."

"As nobles usually are." He squeezed her again and surprised her by kissing her on the forehead.

It was a ridiculous time for it, but emotions welled up, the fear that she would lose him, and that what she would one day have with Xerik wouldn't be nearly as appealing as what she felt for Hawk. Tears moistened her eyes, and this time, she couldn't blame the wind.

"I don't suppose you can carry Theli too?" she asked when Theli grunted again.

She'd fallen behind, and fear returned, overriding Aldari's other emotions. How far was it to the ruins she'd seen in the telescope? A mile? Five miles?

Hawk glanced back, then barked an order in Elven. In the dark, Aldari didn't notice that a mercenary ran in and swept Theli over his shoulder until she squawked in surprise, and they caught up with Hawk. The elves' powerful legs carried them up the canyon, hopefully as fast as the Twisted were giving chase.

"*Vythra*, Pheleran," Hawk said to the other elf.

"Pheleran?" Theli groaned, the sound muffled since she was draped over the mercenary's shoulder, her face pressed against his back. "Why'd *he* get chosen to come? He's the one who likes to grope prisoners."

"He won't do that." Hawk was starting to sound a little breathless now. Could he truly keep up the necessary pace while carrying Aldari?

A screech tore through the canyon, the battle cry—or cry of the hunt—coming from the throat of one of the Twisted. Maybe the creature had been watching Theli and hoped to catch her, and the sound was evidence of its frustration.

"Maybe I wouldn't mind so much now," Theli admitted. "Tell him if we get out of this, I'll give him a kiss."

Hawk looked over at her. At first, Aldari thought he wouldn't say anything, being too focused on running and saving his breath, but he managed to sound amused as he translated the offer to Pheleran.

"*Syray?*" Pheleran asked in wonder.

Hawk confirmed.

Pheleran said something else, a much longer sentence.

"He apologizes for touching you without permission before," Hawk said, pausing and breathing heavily every few words. "He says he was overwhelmed by your beauty and getting to hold you."

Aldari didn't think Theli would buy that, but maybe the possibility of death had her feeling magnanimous.

"Tell him I forgive him," she said.

Hawk translated.

Theli snorted.

"Did Pheleran do something?" Aldari asked.

"Patted my ass." Theli sounded more amused than annoyed. "The elves are somewhat amazing at what all they can do while running full out and carrying someone."

Hawk said something else in their language.

Whatever Pheleran said in response sounded smug.

"I think they agree," Aldari said.

"I have no doubt."

Heavy breathing came from beside them, and rocks shifted and clattered as someone slipped. Siadra cursed. The puzzle and book-filled pack had to be almost as much of a burden as a passenger.

Hawk asked her if she was all right. The response sounded like an affirmative but a frustrated and breathless affirmative. He juggled Aldari, so he could reach out a hand and steady Siadra as he called for someone else to come back and help.

He'd only brought three other mercenaries. They would run out of porters soon, and—

Another screech echoed off the walls of the canyon. The Twisted had gotten closer. Aldari still couldn't see much in the gloom behind them, but she could tell there was movement back there.

One of the elves in the lead called out and pointed. A hint of light came from up ahead.

Night was still deep, and Aldari couldn't imagine what natural source of light would be out here. A faint yellow glow—a *magical* glow—came from around a bend, brightening the reddish-brown walls and highlighting the blackened ground, the lumpy lava rock the elves were maneuvering over.

Unfortunately, it also provided enough light that Aldari could pick out the Twisted running after them. She'd preferred it when she *couldn't* see them. At least ten were visible, not hindered by the terrain as they ran, and moving shadows farther back promised more of them.

Hawk ran faster, his legs propelling them around the bend, through the confluence of two canyons, and into a much wider one. It had to be more than a mile across, and the ruins Aldari had seen from the telescope came into view. The half-buried crystal walls of numerous ancient structures, only a few of which had been partially excavated from the black rock.

The group raced toward ruins nestled against one side of the canyon—or maybe even built *into* one side of the canyon. But mounds of rock—debris from the excavations—piled everywhere made it hard for them to navigate, and the elves had to slow down.

Ahead of them, two Twisted sprang out from behind a rock pile, startling Aldari as they ran straight at her and Hawk.

In one swift motion, he set her down, drew his sword and dagger, and lunged at them. They slashed at him with their claws even as they tried to get around him to reach her.

Confusion swarmed Aldari—she wasn't carrying the baton anymore, so why were they determined to get *her*?—but pain distracted her, her ankle protesting as soon as she put weight on it. Her leg almost gave out.

As Hawk fought their enemies, Aldari stumbled to the side and braced herself on a pile of rubble. A rock shifted and came away in her hand.

The mercenaries rushed forward to help Hawk, but two more Twisted leaped out, and they had to detour to fight them. Before they closed to melee range, Aldari threw her rock. She had the satisfaction of watching it pound one of the Twisted in the head, but the blow didn't stun it in the least. It whirled and ran toward her. Fortunately, one of the mercenaries leaped onto its back to stop it.

It—she—was a woman, breasts jiggling under her torn tunic, and Aldari wrenched her gaze away as the mercenary pulled a knife across her throat. Even that blow didn't kill the Twisted. She grabbed over her shoulders for him. He snarled and dug the blade in deeper, sawing off her head.

"I hate this place," Theli snarled, stumbling as she left Pheleran and hurried to Aldari's side.

"Get to the puzzle," Hawk called, then gave the same order in Elven. He'd downed his two opponents, but the ones that had been chasing them had almost caught up, and more followed after them. "We'll hold them off for you."

With Theli's help, Aldari hobbled after Siadra and the other scientists, trusting they knew the way. With each step, the pain in her ankle brought tears to her eyes, but she did her best to ignore it. If they couldn't find a way in—and a way to keep the Twisted out—they would all die before sunrise.

33

THE MAGICAL GLOW INCREASED AS ALDARI, THELI, AND THE scientists drew closer to the ruins. Thanks to the light, Aldari had no trouble spotting the puzzle mounted vertically on the rocky wall of the canyon. The tiers of discs with numbers embedded around the edges were made from the same crystal as the buildings and appeared to be fused to the rock.

A crystal arch embedded in the rock next to it rose up twenty feet and spread ten. It had to be a doorway, but Aldari couldn't tell how it opened. It didn't even look like there was anything behind it, nothing but the rock of the canyon wall. But maybe that was an illusion or some other form of ancient elven magic, and there was a cave—or laboratory—back there.

Behind them, shouts mingled with the screeches of metal striking claws. Siadra sprinted for the puzzle, and Aldari hobbled after her as quickly as she could manage, her ankle still throbbing. She was afraid to look back, afraid she would witness Hawk or one of the other mercenaries falling under the onslaught of enemies.

Siadra slung her pack off and dug for her notebook.

"I remember the number you came up with to solve it," Aldari said and jumped for the puzzle.

"Solve it then, but be careful." Siadra pointed at barely noticeable circles marking the outer edge of the arch and both sides of the puzzle. "Those spout fire if you arrange the numbers incorrectly, or if you pause too long once you've started."

Remembering the charred remains of the cloak at the camp, Aldari swallowed and nodded.

Theli put her back to the rock wall, raised her mace, faced the battle, and nodded toward Aldari. "I'll watch your back."

The other scientists also drew weapons and crouched in ready stances, though Siadra pulled out her notebook, probably intending to try herself if Aldari screwed up and got herself killed.

Taking a deep breath, Aldari gripped the bottom of the topmost disc, hoping they would turn smoothly. She couldn't reach the top or even the sides so she would have to massage everything into place from below.

They glided almost without effort, as if the puzzle had been created the day before, not eight centuries earlier, but doubt assailed Aldari as she clicked the first number into its slot. Had she truly memorized the ratio to all ten decimal places? Maybe she shouldn't have been cocky and should have double-checked. But the grunts and yells coming from the battle reminded her how short they were on time. And now it was too late. She'd already started. All she could do was spin the subsequent discs and line up the numbers.

Next to her, Siadra lay the replica on the ground. Aldari glanced at it for confirmation as she slid the next digit into place. Yes, it was as she'd remembered. As long as they had indeed come up with the correct answer, this would work.

"I hope," she whispered.

A screech erupted, echoing from the canyon walls. It came not from the battle but from the ruins. Two new Twisted appeared atop the lava rock, running around half-buried structures toward them.

Theli swore.

"Keep going," Siadra urged, waving for her scientists to fire at the Twisted. "Don't pause." She raised her voice to call back to Hawk and the others, a warning that they were being flanked.

Theli stepped between Aldari and the new threat, and Aldari made herself keep spinning the discs. Once they got inside, Hawk and the others would have an easier time with defense. They could hold the doorway, assuming the Twisted didn't have explosives or anything else that could bring down the canyon wall to bury them.

That distracting thought caused Aldari to over-spin a disc and move a digit too far. A faint click emanated from the rock wall—the booby traps arming?

Cursing, she hurried to rotate the disc back and get the number in the right spot. Sweat dripped from her hairline and ran down the side of her face. As she turned the next disc, she glanced at the circles in case any nozzles appeared, ready to spray flames. For the moment, they remained dormant.

"Next digit," she whispered, focusing with great difficulty.

As Theli sprang into battle alongside the scientists, more Twisted appeared in the ruins. They raced toward Aldari, as if they knew exactly what she was doing and wanted to stop her. Maybe they did. All along, they'd seemed to be targeting her.

She still wore the queen's amulet, but unfortunately, it seemed to be little more than a luck charm. Maybe it would have swayed the Twisted if they'd randomly encountered her on a road and had no real interest in her. But here and now... they were *very* interested.

"Last digit," Aldari said to warn the others, though they were all fighting by now.

Theli swung her mace and kicked, anything to keep the

Twisted from getting close enough to claw her or squeeze past to Aldari. But as the enemy numbers grew, Aldari feared her allies would be overwhelmed. If they had to flee, where would they go? There were Twisted in both directions and probably up the other canyon too.

After the final digit clicked into place, Aldari stepped back. In case she had to fight, she drew her knife, but her gaze locked onto the arch as she prayed she'd solved the puzzle.

Clicks and clanks sounded, and she held her breath. *Something* was happening.

But a doorway didn't appear. Instead, the top disc on the puzzle split into six sections and popped open, revealing a flat surface with glowing numbers inside. Once again, zero through nine in Elven. The glow of the numbers seemed to invite her to press them, to solve another puzzle.

"Siadra, you know anything about this?" Aldari called, wanting to drive her dagger into the numbers. She had no idea what it wanted now.

Siadra only grunted as she swung her bow, using it like a staff to keep the Twisted at bay. The blue-skinned creatures fought Theli, Siadra, and the other scientists, but their eyes were toward Aldari.

Not only could Siadra not spare a moment to glance over and offer an opinion, but she was being forced back. Her heel came down on the replica, crunching the topmost disc. One of the Twisted lifted a clawed hand and lunged for her cheek. As she whipped her head back, Theli managed to dart in and deter the assault with her mace. The Twisted's head jerked back as she connected, but another enemy merely pulled the creature aside and took its place.

"Hawk!" Aldari called. "We need help!"

At a loss, with no time to mull over what the puzzle might want now, Aldari tried tapping in the same number that she'd just entered. When she was done, the glowing digits flashed three times at her. What did *that* mean?

She glanced at the arch as the circles sank back into the rock. Crystalline tubes extended, not nozzles, but that only made it worse. They turned as one to point toward her.

By now, Siadra and Theli and another scientist were right behind her, driven back by the Twisted. Hemmed in, there was nowhere for Aldari to go to avoid the flames the tubes would spew at her. All she could do was duck low, but she doubted that would be enough.

They didn't, however, fire. Not yet. Had she been close enough with her guess that the mechanism hadn't immediately judged her effort a failure?

Maybe it wanted the ratio calculated to more decimal places? Or maybe—

Her breath caught. Could it be some other number inspired by that same tree? Such as the angles for those symmetrical branches?

"Thirty, forty-five, and sixty. But in what order?"

Aldari straightened, dashed sweat from her eyes, and tapped the numbers, hoping the order wouldn't matter.

Hawk bellowed as he, Pheleran, and the other two mercenaries charged into the Twisted attacking their little group. They slashed and cleaved, beheading enemies, but they'd had to leave their own battle to join this one. The Twisted they'd been keeping back had the opportunity to run closer.

Aldari finished entering the digits as she eyed the tubes. If she was wrong, they might all be fried by flames before the Twisted's claws could take them down.

"Hurry, Aldari!" Theli gasped, staggering back and bumping Aldari in the shoulder. "We can't hold them any longer."

"I know, I know!" But Aldari had already finished, and nothing was happening. "What more do you want?" she demanded. "The angles in another order? The length of the branches? Something else entirely?"

The six sections flipped back closed over the numbers. She stared. Did that mean she'd entered the right thing? Or lost her opportunity at a second chance?

Shouts and the thud of hoofbeats sounded in the distance, not in the direction of the ruins or from where they'd crashed their gliders. The noises were coming from the other canyon that converged with this one. Someone yelled something.

"It's Setvik!" Hawk cried.

More clinks and clanks emanated from behind the puzzle, and Aldari dared not look away, except to glance at the tubes. If smoke started wafting from them, she would have to warn the others.

"He's only got five soldiers with him," Hawk added, his tone grimmer, punctuated with grunts as he used his sword to deflect attacks. "Aldari?"

"I—" she started, but the entire puzzle sank into the rock wall.

A pulse of energy buzzed against her skin, and what had appeared to be solid rock between the arches disappeared, revealing a dark chamber beyond it.

"We got in!" she blurted.

Setvik and the others arrived, and a few more of his mercenaries appeared around the bend. They'd lost their reindeer mounts and were running on foot. Blood streamed from their faces, and more than one limped, but they ran into the battle to help Hawk and the others.

"Be careful of more booby traps," Hawk warned without looking back, his focus on his enemies and the barrage of claws swiping toward him.

"Siadra, can you break away?" Aldari eased into the doorway and squinted into the gloom. Whatever lay inside, she would likely need a translator.

Setvik yelled something in Elven. Hawk yelled back. Setvik

swung his sword, his eyes blazing with fury, and lopped off the head of the Twisted that had been attacking Hawk. He thrust his sword toward the doorway and must have ordered him to get inside.

Hawk nodded once and relinquished his position. He pulled Siadra and Theli through the doorway after him, and cool darkness embraced them.

"He says he'll buy us the time we need to find something to stop them," Hawk said. "They'll guard the doorway."

Some of the glowing light from the canyon filtered inside, and Aldari's eyes adjusted to the gloom, only to realize they had another problem. The rectangular chamber they'd entered wasn't large, there was no apparent other way out, and there was another puzzle mounted on the far wall. Or *embedded* in the far wall.

This one was a square with marble blocks of different sizes and shapes fitted together, some jutting out and some flush with the wall. And was that the outline of another door beside it?

Aldari couldn't keep from groaning as she envisioned ten or twenty chambers in the place, with a puzzle to solve to gain entrance into each. The mercenaries would never be able to hold the Twisted off for that long, and she had no idea what extinct elven flower would give them the secret to the next puzzle.

"Aldari, Siadra," Hawk said, also spotting it. "I need you to figure that out." He met each of their eyes, then turned to help the mercenaries. "You can do it. I know you can."

Though daunted, Aldari didn't want to disappoint him. She stepped forward to examine the puzzle as Hawk returned to the battle. Setvik and the others were backing through the doorway as they fought, clearly wanting to use it to limit how many enemies could come at them at once.

"I don't know what to suggest." Siadra looked as daunted as Aldari felt. "There aren't any numbers."

"Maybe we arrange them in a pattern? Or find a way to make

them all flush with the wall?" Aldari stepped forward to see if she could slide the blocks around or pull them out.

The first one she grabbed came away easily in her hand. Siadra sucked in a worried breath and peered around for booby traps. Theli lifted her mace to bash any threat that came from the puzzle or the wall.

Aldari didn't see any sign of a trap, but that didn't mean much. Still, she couldn't hesitate. She pulled out more blocks, lined them up on the floor, and moved them around, trying to guess what shape they could be arranged in that wouldn't leave anything sticking out.

Siadra flipped through her notebook at a frantic pace, but if the answer was in there, she wasn't able to find it.

Setvik roared in frustration as he swung at an opponent pushing through the doorway. Something thudded down beside Aldari, startling her. A blue-skinned hand that had been cleaved from its owner's arm. The fingers twitched, claws clacking on the floor, as if it lived independent of the rest of the body.

Horrified, Aldari kept moving the blocks around, but she couldn't keep from asking, "Could someone do something about that?"

Theli smashed the severed hand with her mace. The fingers went limp and stopped twitching.

"Thank you," Aldari said, her voice squeaking and belying the calmness in her polite words. "I can't wait to hear what ballad you compose about our adventures here."

"This verse will be great," Theli said. "Lots of words rhyme with *severed hand*."

"A pyramid?" Aldari mused, finding a pattern in the blocks.

Siadra looked up from her book. "I don't see it."

Trusting her instincts, Aldari worked to assemble the collection of shapes into a pyramid. "It makes a perfect one. Let's see if the puzzle thinks so."

She waved for Siadra to help her lift the pyramid without the pieces tumbling free. As they tilted it to insert the bottom into the waiting square frame, Aldari worried everything would fall apart. But a strange sucking sensation came from the wall, and some magical force drew their pyramid into place. The frame around the blocks flashed once, and another doorway appeared.

"We're heading deeper," Aldari called back to Hawk, who was fighting side by side with Setvik.

He said something to Setvik, then ran to join them. "I'll stick with you. I don't trust this place not to have traps."

"I think the traps only go off if we fail at the puzzles," Siadra said.

"That could happen," Aldari admitted.

"You're doing fine." Hawk nodded at her and smiled, though it was an odd expression on a face painted with blood, sweat, and grime. "More than fine. You can do this, Aldari."

She nodded, hoping he was right.

With Hawk and Theli leading, they entered another dark chamber, this one with wide stairs leading up to a balcony and what appeared to be an empty wall but had to hold another hidden doorway. On their level, other doorways were open, almost in invitation, and offered other options. Aldari found them suspicious, and her instincts told her the stairs led to what they needed. At least they'd come into what seemed more like a home—or laboratory?—than a booby-trapped dungeon.

"There's another puzzle." Siadra pointed at a collection of red rectangles mingling with pale blue triangles and white cylinders that were set into a large rectangular frame in the floor at the base of the stairs.

The geometric pieces might have passed as an artist's mosaic, but Aldari knew better. "It looks like it could be the skyline of a city," she said, envisioning the white cylinders as towers made from the same crystal that comprised the walls here. "Maybe what was once *this* city?" The red rectangles might represent the reddish rock of the canyon walls and the pale blue the sky above.

"Try it," Siadra said.

When Aldari crouched down and reached for the triangles, the air buzzed with what felt like a warning. "Uhm."

A cry of pain followed by vehement curses came from the entrance, a reminder that the battle was still going, that the Twisted could overcome the mercenaries and flood inside at any moment. Hawk stepped in that direction, his sword out.

Ignoring the warning buzz, Aldari touched one of the triangles. A shock of electricity charged up her arm. She reeled back, gasping in pain.

Hawk lunged back to her side, kneeling and wrapping an arm around her shoulder. "What happened?"

Theli also sprang up, her mace in hand, but there was no opponent she could attack, only the puzzle. She eyed it menacingly.

Aldari held up a hand, afraid she would lose her temper and bash it—and that something worse than a zap would occur.

"I don't think the puzzle is going to let me solve it." Aldari shook her hand and pulled out her dagger, wondering if she could move the pieces around with it, and it would insulate her.

"Look." Theli pointed to the left of the staircase, then jerked her finger toward the right.

Thick fog gathered to both sides, with sparks of electricity forming inside. It was as if they were storm clouds.

While keeping an eye on them, Hawk leaned forward and touched the same triangle that had zapped Aldari. He didn't react.

"Did it shock you?" Aldari knew the elven warriors had plenty of experience enduring pain, and it was possible the jolt simply hadn't bothered him that much.

But Hawk shook his head and touched another triangle. "No.

Maybe Zedaron designed it so that only elves can unlock the door
to his inner sanctum."

Siadra touched one of the triangles but jerked her hand back.
"*Some* elves, perhaps."

"Tell me what to do, Aldari." Hawk pushed on the triangle, and
it depressed into the floor. Another one slid atop the first, and the
one he'd touched appeared on the far side of the frame, popping
up as if from underwater.

"Rearrange them into a view of the city outside—what it
looked like before the volcano erupted."

"I don't know what it looked like."

"Just... push that one there. And that there. Then that there."
Aldari pointed, guiding him. She had no idea what the city had
looked like either, but if she was right with her guess, there were
only so many logical ways the shapes could be arranged.

"Better hurry." Theli shifted her weight. "That fog is coming."

Aldari could hear as well as see the electrical charges in the
clouds, buzzes that licked at the air. And they were creeping closer,
threatening to converge on the puzzle—on *them*.

"Put that one there." Aldari made herself continue to guide
Hawk, even moving his hands for him.

If those clouds covered the puzzle, and they couldn't get back
to it, they would be stuck here, with more Twisted arriving at every
moment. As Aldari helped Hawk slide shapes around, she tried
not to think about what would happen if the solution to the
Twisted *wasn't* in this laboratory. What if they got in only to learn
that whatever the elven wizard had left behind had been cleared
out by puzzle-solving scavengers centuries ago?

"I see it." Hawk started to move the pieces without help.
"Almost there."

The clouds crackled closer, the air sharp with the scent of
lightning and the buzzing growing painful against their skin.
Siadra backed away. Theli gritted her teeth and swung her mace at

one of the clouds, but there was nothing to connect with. She only ended up yelping in pain and springing away.

"Get back, Aldari." Theli grabbed her by the shoulder. "It'll shock you."

"No." Aldari tried to brace herself to stay, to keep helping, but Theli was too strong.

"It's all right." Hawk's hands moved more quickly. "I've almost got it."

The clouds converged, flowing across the puzzle as he manipulated the last few pieces. At first, Aldari thought the electricity didn't hurt him, that the magic was allowing him to keep working, but he clenched his jaw, cheek muscles twitching as sweat dripped down the side of his face, and she realized he was enduring the pain.

A desperate yell came from the entrance amid another clash of weapons. Setvik ordering them to hurry up.

The last puzzle piece snapped into place. Aldari held her breath. They'd both seen the cityscape, but what if they'd both been wrong?

The clouds disappeared, and the completed puzzle sank two inches into the floor. Hawk stumbled back, sucking in a deep breath. Aldari ran forward to give him support, but a doorway appeared at the top of the stairs, and he charged up them.

Stepping more gingerly, Aldari skirted the puzzle and followed him up, Theli and Siadra behind her.

"This is it," Hawk called down from the threshold. "The workshop!"

Aldari broke into a run, hoping the solution he needed was there—and that they could get to it.

34

ALDARI WANTED TO CHARGE THROUGH WHAT SHE HOPED WAS THE last doorway, but Hawk held up a hand and drew his sword, easing warily over the threshold.

"I think this is it," he whispered, peering around inside.

"It's beautiful," Siadra breathed, creeping in behind Hawk.

"Looks like a bunch of junk," Theli muttered, lingering on the landing.

Aldari didn't agree. Inside the chamber, magical yellow light gleamed off walls and a ceiling all carved from the same ancient crystal as the city, but unlike the walls of the ruins outside, these weren't plain. Colorful artwork was embedded into the surfaces, everything from landscapes to animals to blueprints and schematics, each piece as vibrant as if it had been crafted the day before.

The floor space was filled with metal and wood contraptions, many with giant gears, cogs, and wheels. Tables and workbenches held crates overflowing with tools, and dozens and dozens of containers lined shelves. Somehow, everything gleamed with no hint of dust or cobwebs dulling the surfaces.

Hawk glanced at the items as he prowled the chamber,

probing the floor with his sword while waving his bow ahead of him. Looking for tripwires or the magical equivalent? Siadra gripped her chin as she peered at the various items. Would she recognize the thing that could put an end to the Twisted if it was here?

Just inside the doorway, Aldari shifted from foot to foot, aware of the clangs, shouts, and battle cries still drifting up from the entrance. How long could the injured Setvik and his remaining mercenaries hold off the Twisted?

A scream of pain made her lurch into motion. There wasn't time to wait for Hawk to check every inch of the chamber for traps.

They needed to find... Wait, what was that?

Aldari crept toward the far wall. The crystal was thinner there, the translucent material letting in light from somewhere behind it. The canyon outside?

In addition to being thinner, the wall held a puzzle with thirty-five square tiles within a larger square and an empty spot in the middle. A jumbled-up picture was painted on the squares.

"Slide puzzle?" she mused.

If so, it would be the simplest—or at least most familiar—thing she'd seen in here.

"Aldari," Hawk warned and jogged over.

He caught up with her as she reached for the tiles, stopping her before she could lift a hand and start rearranging them. "Let me..."

Again using his bow, Hawk tapped the wall next to the puzzle. It shimmered, and he pulled Aldari back, shifting to protect her.

But nothing shot out at them. Aside from the puzzle, the entire wall shifted from translucent to transparent, turning into a genuine window that looked out over the centuries-old lava flows and ruins. Dawn had arrived, and when Aldari stepped close and peered down, she could see the white-haired heads of dozens of Twisted converging on the entrance to the laboratory.

"We have to figure out a way to stop them soon," Hawk said, "or the mercenaries will be overrun. There's a never-ending flow of them."

"This puzzle." Aldari pointed. "Let me solve it. It must do something."

"They've all *done* something, but nothing beyond opening doors. For all we know, this opens the way to the privy."

"I don't think so," Siadra said, joining them. "We've reached his workshop."

"You don't think he had a privy here?" Hawk grumbled, but this time, he didn't stop Aldari when she reached for the tiles.

Another scream of pain came from below. That had sounded like Pheleran.

"Theli, will you go help them?" Aldari was tempted to send Hawk too, but his hands had been needed for the earlier puzzle and might be again.

Theli scowled. "It's my duty to protect *you*."

"If those Twisted get through down there, we'll *all* die."

Theli's scowl deepened, and she looked like she would stubbornly remain where she was, but the next cry of pain came from Setvik's throat.

"Fine." Theli backed away. "Don't do anything stupid."

Focused on the puzzle, Aldari didn't reply. As she'd suspected, the tiles slid easily within the confines of the square, the empty slot giving her the space to move them around. She glanced back, wondering if Siadra wanted to work the puzzle—she might have more of an idea of what the picture was supposed to be.

"Go ahead." Siadra nodded encouragement. "You've been better at this than I so far."

Though nervous, with sweat dampening her palms, Aldari set

to the task. She'd solved numerous slide puzzles. This one had a lot of pieces, but she knew she could do it.

The tiles clunked softly as she moved them around, attempting to manipulate them into a complete picture. She could make out faces—elven faces with pointed ears—but they glowed, as if lit with magical light. Or divine light? It shined down, as if from the heavens.

"I think that's our little pantheon," Siadra said. "The Hunter, the Crafter, the Mother, and the Forager."

"No warrior god?" Aldari had heard Hawk mention the Hunter, but she would have expected a deity related to battle for the fighter elves. Though her people followed the One God, warrior gods were familiar figures in many cultures around the world. And the elves were some of the strongest warriors Aldari had ever seen.

"We don't have one," Hawk said as she continued to move the tiles around, forming the four glowing bodies Siadra had suggested. "Up until the Twisted were created, and our entire continent was thrown into upheaval, we weren't fighters. We used our bows for hunting, and few young elves took up swords. When necessary, we used magic to defend our shores from invaders." He frowned down at his blade. "As a people, we just wanted peace, to pursue the arts and academics and magic. We never wanted war."

"I'm sorry it was thrust upon you." Aldari kept working, not taking her eyes from the puzzle as she spoke.

"I've wondered what I might have studied, what I might have been, if I hadn't had to train to defend our people from the ever-present threat," Hawk said.

"A cetologist?"

"I don't know what that is," Hawk said.

"Someone who studies whales and dolphins."

"Ah. What's someone who *protects* whales and dolphins?"

"An elf with a mission."

"Sounds right for me." Hawk smiled fleetingly, but as more clangs and shouts rose up from below, Theli's war cries among them now, he shook his head and took a step in that direction. "I better go help Setvik and the others."

"She's almost got it," Siadra said, watching the puzzle. "There, there. Move that one there. That's the tip of the Hunter's bow."

Hawk paused to watch Aldari slide the last tile into place, revealing the four gods standing at the edge of a forest pool, divine light bathing them as they contemplated who knew what. The wall hummed.

Though the illustration had come together, Aldari lifted her hands defensively and stepped back. Just because she'd solved it didn't mean the workshop would reveal its secrets to her.

A rumble sounded to the left. A doorway appeared between two workbenches, but a crystal door blocked it, with no hint of a knob or latch to turn.

When Siadra stepped up to it and pushed, it didn't budge. Red letters—words in the Elven language—appeared on the wall above the closed door.

"Only an heir with the power of the royal line will have the strength to step within and activate the nullification device." Siadra clasped a hand to her chest. "This could be it. An artifact to nullify what his brother created." She spun toward Hawk.

"Uh, did we bring along an heir?" Aldari thought of Prince Erathian and King Jesireth.

"Yes," Hawk said, though his brow furrowed, and he stepped warily past Siadra to the door.

Aldari blinked. Hawk had admitted to being a noble, but would that be good enough?

"Wait." Aldari rushed forward and gripped his arm. "What if there's a booby trap that goes off if you try to get in and you're *not* a direct heir?"

"Just in case, you better stay back." Hawk extricated his arm from Aldari's grip and glanced at Siadra. "Both of you."

He took a breath, determination replacing his wariness, and planted his palm on the door. It ground open at his touch, revealing a small room, also with a clear window wall looking out over the canyon. A single crystal chair sat upon a dais in the center, the only piece of furniture inside.

When Hawk stepped in, light glowed from the ceiling and the floor, highlighting the throne. Did that mean it accepted him?

He leaned his bow against a wall and turned to sit in the throne, his face toward the doorway—toward Aldari and Siadra. Warm light from the throne bathed his features. Yes, it accepted him.

"He's the king's son?" Aldari asked as the ramifications came to her.

Siadra nodded, as if she'd known all along. Of course she had. *All* of the elves had. That was why Setvik had deferred to him, however grudgingly.

A part of Aldari felt betrayed that he hadn't confided that to her, but she told herself it didn't matter right now. Besides, if Hawk had withheld that information, it had been for a reason. Probably the same reason he'd already shared. If things had gone wrong, he hadn't wanted the royal family or the elven people to be blamed for Aldari's kidnapping.

The throne brightened further, silver light enveloping Hawk. He closed his eyes, then grabbed the bracer on his forearm and pressed his thumb to the *ryshar* embedded in it. Long seconds passed before it flashed three times. The bracer loosened, clunking to the floor.

A grating noise came from the crystal ceiling above the throne —maybe the lava rock above it. Hawk's eyes remained closed.

Envisioning the ceiling collapsing and burying him, Aldari

almost lunged inside. Maybe Siadra knew what she was thinking, for she reached out and gripped her shoulder.

"Let him do this," she said. "He can handle it. Besides, the throne may object to such lowly beings as us walking in."

"I *am* a princess," Aldari couldn't help but say stiffly, but she doubted an elf who'd lived almost a millennium ago had cared about her people. Her kingdom hadn't even been formed back then, and her nomadic ancestors had lived in huts made from whale bones and reindeer hides.

The grating continued, and a hole in the ceiling appeared. A hole that went all the way up into the rock and to the top of the canyon. A hint of daylight filtered down.

Hawk gasped, his back going rigid.

"What's it doing?" Again, Aldari wanted to lunge in and pull him out of danger.

"I'm not sure," Siadra said. "Mingling its magic with his?"

Down below, the screeches escalated, the Twisted growing more agitated. Did they sense that Hawk had taken off his bracer and want his magic? Want *him*?

Setvik shouted something. The equivalent of *hold the line*?

"We may have to get ready to fight if they get past them," Siadra whispered, glancing toward the exit from the workshop.

Aldari couldn't tear her gaze from Hawk. The light brightened around the throne until she couldn't see him anymore. A hum came from within it, and that light created a beam that shot upward into the hole.

Outside, the light in the canyon brightened as well. Not the glow of the ruins that had been there all along but the silver light coming from the throne. It had shifted from a beam into something more, something that bathed the entire canyon.

More screams and screeches sounded, torn from hundreds of mouths. The Twisted within view of the window jerked in spasms, some even pitching to the ground, as the light enveloped them. The *magic*.

The Twisted writhed in pain, and Aldari felt sorry for them. They might have been trying to kill her and the others—and they'd already killed some of Setvik's mercenaries—but they hadn't asked for their fate. They'd been torn away from their people against their wishes and turned into these monsters.

The light in the canyon grew so bright that Aldari had to look away. She turned her back on the window and the throne and squinted her eyes shut. If only she could shut out the screams as well as the sight of the writhing Twisted.

Setvik shouted up to them.

"He says they're dropping," Siadra translated. "Something's happening to all of the Twisted."

On the throne, Hawk gasped, but he turned it into a determined growl. Maybe he'd also been thinking that the Twisted didn't deserve death but also knew that it was the only answer, the only way to free his people from their eternal war.

Long moments passed, and the screams outside dwindled. Hawk panted, the ragged sounds filling the room. Whatever his role was, it was clearly more than pressing a lever and letting the artifact do the work.

The sounds of fighting stopped, and the last scream finally died away. After a few more seconds, the silver light disappeared, though its effects lingered even after Aldari opened her eyes.

A thump came from the center of the room. Aldari turned back to the throne, no longer caring if a booby trap lashed out at her. With tears streaming from her eyes, she struggled to pick out Hawk. He'd fallen from the throne to the floor beside it and wasn't moving.

Terrified, Aldari dropped to her knees and reached out to him. He didn't stir, and his skin was surprisingly cold.

What if he was dead? What if he'd had to pay for the freedom of his people with his life?

She had no doubt that he would have happily made that trade, but the thought horrified her.

"Hawk," she whispered, touching his face as tears ran down her cheeks. "Please don't be dead. I care for you, damn it, and your people need you."

Siadra came in and knelt on his other side, resting a hand on his chest. "Hawsylereth?"

That was his real name. Prince Hawsylereth.

Back at the outpost, the queen had almost used it, but she'd cut herself off. So Aldari wouldn't know who he truly was.

She tried to tamp down that feeling of betrayal again, or at least of hurt. That Siadra had known his real name and Aldari hadn't. That he'd never told her.

Aldari reached out and touched his throat, afraid she wouldn't find a pulse there, but she had to know.

"I prefer Hawk," he rasped, turning his head not toward Siadra but toward Aldari.

"Since when?" Siadra asked.

"Since I met a princess who likes hawks," he said, reaching up to brush a lock of Aldari's hair behind her ear. His fingers were still cool, but they were alive. *He* was alive.

Aldari slumped across his chest, and Siadra drew back. Hawk wrapped his arms around Aldari, and her feelings of betrayal and disgruntlement faded. What did it matter if he hadn't told her his real name, his real position in the royal family? If she was right, he'd succeeded with his mission, and that was what counted.

Hawk stroked the back of her head. "I'm sorry I couldn't tell you."

"It's all right." Aldari shifted her weight, assuming he would like to get up, but he kept his arms around her, and she ended up gazing down at him, her lips inches from his.

"Is it?" he asked uncertainly. Maybe the lie had weighed upon him.

"Yes."

Nothing had changed for her, and she still had to go off to marry Prince Xerik, but she couldn't keep herself from lifting her lips toward his. She wanted to kiss him again as she had in the camp but for longer this time, without interruptions.

Hawk's lips parted, agreement in his eyes, but footsteps in the workshop made them pause and glance toward the doorway. Hawk released one of his arms around Aldari and pushed himself to his elbow, glancing toward where he'd leaned his sword against the wall. But a friendly face appeared in the doorway, Pheleran.

He blurted something to Hawk, then ran back out of view.

"He says we have to see this," Hawk translated.

"This?"

Aldari wished that whatever it was, it could have waited until they'd kissed, but duty reigned supreme for Hawk. He patted her on the back and rolled to his feet. He helped her up, but his eyes were toward the doorway, and he paused only long enough to grab his weapon before hurrying out after the mercenary.

He'd left his bracer on the floor. Did that mean he didn't think he would need it again?

Not sure, Aldari picked it up for him. Just because that throne had helped him deal with the Twisted in the canyon didn't mean its power had extended across the whole continent.

When she caught up with Siadra and Hawk, her injured ankle making her slower than they, they were walking out the main entrance. The mercenaries must have succeeded in keeping the Twisted out, for no bodies littered the floor. Certain there would be hundreds of them outside, Aldari braced herself as she stepped through the doorway, squinting at the daylight.

Hawk, Siadra, Theli, and the remaining mercenaries and scientists formed a semi-circle around the doorway. Beyond them, hundreds of sets of grimy and torn clothing and boots lay on the lava rock among the ruins. Mounds of blue-gray ashes were among them, though a breeze was already whisking them away. Was that all that remained of the Twisted? Ashes?

Movement near one of the ruins drew Aldari's eye, and Setvik was pointing in that direction. A gaunt woman—a female elf with puzzled green eyes—in her forties or fifties shambled uncertainly toward them. She wore the ragged clothes of the Twisted, but her hair was blonde instead of white, and her skin was pale peach instead of blue.

The mercenaries muttered uncertainly among each other, their swords half-raised. They didn't seem to know if they should drive the female back or draw her close for a hug.

Hawk stepped forward and asked her a question. *Do you understand me?* That was Aldari's guess.

The female focused on him for a long minute, her lips moving but no sound coming out. It was as if she'd forgotten how to speak. Maybe she had. How long had she been among the Twisted? How long had she been *one* of the Twisted?

She finally got out something that might have meant *yes.* Then, brow creasing, she whispered, "*Hylar* Hawsylereth?"

Hawk nodded and walked forward and rested a hand on her shoulder. She inhaled a shuddering breath, then collapsed against him, weeping.

Siadra whispered something and, when Aldari gave her a questioning look, said, "They remember who they are, but they also remember what they've been." Horror filled her eyes.

Hawk called out toward the city in ruins. A few more people had reverted to their elven forms and were approaching with the same lost uncertainty that cloaked the woman.

A breeze stirred some of the clothing, more blue-gray ashes scattering.

"Why did most of them die?" Aldari asked.

"I would guess," Siadra said slowly, "that most of the Twisted were taken long ago and had outlived the years their mortal bodies would have given them. It must have been the magic of the spell that kept them alive, in a sense, beyond that time, and once it was gone..."

Aldari gazed bleakly at the clothes and ashes. What a horrible way to live out one's final years. *More* than one's final years. Hawk had once said that the Twisted didn't die unless a blade took them down, so some of them might have been walking the world for centuries. At least now, they might have some peace, an end to what must have been a miserable existence.

"Since she recognized Hawsylereth," Siadra added, "she must have been turned in the last decade or two. And those as well." She waved toward the tentative elves, some peering at them from the ruins and some creeping closer, then went forward to help Hawk explain to them what had happened.

Aldari wondered if Hawk would find his sister eventually, or if she'd died. What if she'd been one of the ones who'd attacked them or other elves and had been killed?

"Are you all right?" Theli asked, speaking not to Aldari but to Setvik.

Blood ran from his wounds, and he was leaning heavily against the wall next to the door. *Most* of the mercenaries were bleeding. Pheleran might have been sent up to get them because he was one of the few who could still walk.

"I am alive." Setvik shrugged, as if indifferent to the rest. "I did not expect to live, but I had to show someone that I wasn't a coward."

Hawk glanced back, said something to Siadra, then came to stand in front of Setvik. He lifted his chin. "I apologize for calling you that. I was wrong."

"Yes. You were. I will follow you anyway." Setvik raised his sword in a salute, though he winced from the effort of lifting it.

"Stop that," Theli told Setvik crossly. "Sit down and rest. We've got to get your bleeding stopped. Do you have a medical kit around?"

Setvik looked at her with amusement, but he tugged a pack off his back and pushed it toward her as he slumped to the ground, apparently ready to let Theli treat him.

Aldari didn't ask what had happened to Mevleth, but she didn't see him among the survivors. If he'd been the one to sabotage her glider, after he'd already poisoned Hawk, she wouldn't feel bad about his passing.

Medical kit in hand, Theli started to kneel beside Setvik, but Pheleran trotted up and blurted a cheerful, "I'm ready," to her.

"For what?" Theli frowned at him.

He took her hands and kissed her soundly on the lips. Theli's eyebrows flew up, and her fingers curled into a fist.

"You did promise him a kiss if we survived this," Aldari pointed out.

"Oh, hell," Theli muttered as Pheleran kept mashing his lips to hers.

Hawk opened his mouth, but he didn't seem certain if he should put a stop to the kiss or not. Setvik was the one to snap at his soldier and shoo him away. The chagrined Pheleran backed off, but he blew a kiss to Theli and gazed enraptured at her before bouncing away to join the remaining mercenaries.

Judging by the twist to Theli's lips, the kiss hadn't pleased her quite as much.

Setvik reached up, gripped her arm, and rasped, "Treat me, bodyguard."

"Haven't you learned my name yet?" Theli snapped, though she let him guide her down to his side.

"Treat me, Theli," Setvik said, lifting a hand to her face. "I have seen you watch me. I know you will enjoy touching me."

Aldari was about to tell Hawk that his mercenary commander

might not be a coward but that he *was* an ass, but Theli smirked at the pompous statement.

"You think so, eh?" she asked.

"I know it." Setvik slid his hand through her hair to grip the back of her head and pulled her down for a kiss.

Theli planted a hand against his chest, and Aldari expected her to pull back and slap him, but she gripped his breastplate and leaned in, returning the kiss. With great enthusiasm.

"That's unexpected." Aldari looked away to give them their privacy.

Hawk's lips parted in surprise. He must have agreed. But he recovered, glanced at Siadra and the growing number of converted —*reverted*—elves, and drew Aldari aside.

She handed him his bracer, and he accepted it but put it in his pack instead of back on his arm.

"I wasn't sure what would happen in there," Hawk said. "When I realized what the magic was doing, I hoped it might give us all of the Twisted back, all alive, but... this makes sense. I wanted more, but it's better than if we'd lost everyone."

"Do you think it affected the Twisted everywhere or just the ones nearby?" Aldari asked.

"I'm not sure." His eyes grew distant as he continued. "But if there are more out there—if my *sister* is still alive out there—we'll find them and force them back to this canyon to treat. Every last one of them. I swear it."

Instead of being finished, his mission might have only begun. That would mean he would be too busy to help her and her people, but Aldari couldn't blame him for that. She'd known all along that the elves wouldn't be the answer to Delantria's problem.

"I thank you for your help in this." Hawk shifted his attention to her, pulling her into a hug. "We couldn't have done this without you," he whispered, his lips brushing her earlobe, and a zing of pleasure ran through her, that desire to kiss him returning.

She gripped his strong shoulders and leaned into him. If Theli could kiss Setvik, couldn't she kiss Hawk? It wasn't as if Xerik would ever find out.

Except that she wanted to do more than kiss Hawk. That was the problem.

"I'll escort you to our port and get you on a ship home to your people," Hawk said as he stroked the back of her head. "I wish you could stay for a time, but I know you need to go."

"I do," Aldari made herself say, but her body had other ideas. She pressed her face into the side of his neck, tears threatening again, and nuzzled his warm skin as she trailed her fingers up his jaw to trace his pointed ear.

"Aldari," he whispered, almost a groan, his arms tightening around her.

Damn it, she wanted one kiss. One kiss when they weren't rushed. One kiss that she could remember for the rest of her life.

Maybe Hawk wanted the same, for he touched her jaw, tilting her face toward his, and kissed her. She molded her body to his, enjoying the warmth of his embrace, enjoying his lips pressing against hers. The air tingled all around them, as if the inherent power he'd finally let free were crackling about them, making the kiss magical. Making her want to be with him even more.

But it couldn't be, and when the call of a hunter's horn floated down from the top of the canyon, they both sighed and broke the kiss. Hawk rested his forehead against hers and held her until a second call came, closer than the first. The sound of hooves on rocky ground also floated down. *Hundreds* of hooves.

Hawk released Aldari and turned to face the top of the canyon wall. Dozens of elven riders came into view, Prince Erathian among them. He gazed down at them and lifted a hand toward Hawk. Hawk returned the wave and called up. The prince —Hawk's brother—replied with a nod, then bowed deeply on his mount. The bow wasn't for Hawk but for Aldari. The other elves also bowed toward her. Thanking her for her help, it seemed.

She appreciated the sentiment but would have preferred it if they hadn't shown up so soon. She wished she could have spent more time with Hawk, maybe finding a private place where she could let him know that she was glad things had worked out for him and his people. And that she cared for him.

A lump formed in her throat. Maybe she *more* than cared for him. But there was no point in saying that, not when she was betrothed to another man. More than ever, her people needed her to return home and complete the alliance with Orath.

"We need to search the area and find all the elves who've been turned back," Hawk said, "but my brother is sending a squad down to get you and escort you and Theli to the port. They'll get you on a fast ship home, and hopefully, it won't be too late for your people."

"Thank you."

He kissed her on the cheek, his lips lingering, as if he wanted to do more, but he only smiled sadly and stepped back. One of the scientists called a question to him, and he stepped away from Aldari.

With that lump still in her throat, Aldari walked back to Theli, where she was still locked in a kiss with Setvik, his hand on her butt, holding her against him. They were either indifferent to the prince's arrival or so distracted they hadn't noticed it.

"We're going home, Theli," Aldari said. "Our people need us."

35

ALDARI CLIMBED TO THE CASTLE WALL WITH HER SISTER SHYDENA AS Theli trailed behind them.

Theli had spent the night with her family—her brothers and father hadn't been sent off to fight yet and were stationed here to protect the city—but she'd refused to take time off from her body-guard duty. Unfortunately, a new threat to Aldari loomed on the horizon. *Closer* than the horizon. And she was by no means the only one in danger.

Over the years, Aldari and Shydena had often stood on the castle wall and looked out over the town and the harbor, watching ships sail in. They'd always been curious about those rare foreigners who came to visit. Now, a fleet of imperial vessels floated in the harbor, and Aldari felt little curiosity toward them. Fear was her primary emotion.

The armed and uniformed men striding along the decks were far different in appearance from the mountain brutes who'd attacked her caravan weeks earlier, but Aldari now believed they'd been sent by the same emperor, a part of the same plot.

When she and Theli had sailed into the harbor the afternoon

before, it had been just in time to see a massive army march up the highway to the capital and brazenly set up camp outside of the city wall. At dawn, the matter had grown even more desperate when the imperial fleet sailed unopposed into the harbor.

Delantria didn't have a navy, fielding only fishing and whaling ships and the occasional merchant vessel. The paltry cannons mounted on the towers overlooking the docks wouldn't be enough to keep the imperial fleet at bay. The cannons on the castle and city walls would do even less against the masses of soldiers that had marched in. Their tents and supply trains stretched almost as far as the eye could see. Why couldn't roving packs of vorgs come down and nosh on *them*?

Aldari looked farther out to sea, hoping to see sign of Orath's ships. Over dinner the night before, after a glum reunion with her family, her father had briefed her on everything, including the latest message Prince Xerik had sent, repeating that his people wouldn't send aid until after the wedding joined their two nations together. As Aldari had feared while in Serth, Orath seemed to have gotten cold feet and decided it wasn't willing to take on the empire, not for her. And not for her kingdom.

"If you hadn't come back so bruised and battered—" Shydena pointed at the cane Aldari was using for support, her wrapped ankle still sore, "I'd say you should have stayed where you were."

"I couldn't be safe there while you and Rothi and Father were enduring this."

"We wouldn't have begrudged you. The other day, Father was trying to get me to sneak off in a whaling ship headed to a neutral country. He's afraid the Taldarian emperor will take me as one of his wives, to cement the annexation of our kingdom into his. He already has *three* wives, and I've heard he doesn't treat them well."

"Hawk—the elves—promised they would send help, but I don't know if it'll be soon enough."

Aldari's heart ached as she thought of Hawk, but would he even remember her now that he was back with his family and had his sister to find? With so many corpses all over his kingdom, and all those Twisted who'd been changed back but been so lost and vacant-eyed, Hawk would be busy dealing with his own problems for a long time. Even if he remembered his promise... what could the remnants of the Moon Sword Company do against all this? If Xerik was afraid to oppose the empire, the elves would be too. Their king hadn't even wanted to risk ruffling feathers with Delantria or Orath.

"The elves that kidnapped you promised to send help?" Shydena raised skeptical eyebrows.

"One of them did. Hawk and I... got to know each other."

"*Hawk* doesn't sound like the name of an elf with a lot of sway."

"He's the younger prince, actually." Aldari had almost forgotten about that, the secret he'd kept until he'd torn off his bracer and sat in that throne, the magic in his blood singing to it, allowing him to command it. Now that he was infused with power, would he think at all of a human woman who didn't know a magical orb from a children's ball?

Aldari shook her head, knowing she'd been foolish to let herself develop feelings for him. All along, she'd sensed that he'd been more than he seemed, that he'd been withholding something from her. But she, she who usually loved puzzles and solving mysteries, hadn't wanted to pull on that thread to unravel the truth. She hadn't wanted him to be anything other than Hawk. The mercenary with the charming smile and quick wit. And magical kisses that made her tingle all over.

Two imperial officers flanked by numerous soldiers strode up the road toward the city gate and called up to the guards in the towers. From the castle wall, Aldari couldn't hear what was said, but they convinced the guards to let them in. Was this a party being sent to demand their surrender? To offer them a chance to give up the city—and the kingdom—without a fight?

Maybe that would be for the best. As much as Aldari hated the idea of rolling over and presenting Delantria's belly, she also didn't want to see their people needlessly killed.

As the officers approached the castle gate, one looked up at Aldari and Shydena and scowled. His black hair stuck up in tufts, he had bags under his eyes, and he looked frazzled. Maybe he'd slept poorly in his invasion tent. Such a shame.

Aldari lifted her chin, determined not to appear intimidated. It wasn't that hard. After being harried by the Twisted, dealing with mere men wasn't as daunting.

Her father, flanked by his own bodyguards, stepped out onto the castle wall to speak with the officers. It seemed he wouldn't invite them into the castle for a chat. Aldari wasn't that surprised, especially since they appeared to be middle-ranking officers, not the commander or any of the other higher-ups.

"Your new allies are ruthless, King Caylath," one officer called up. "Do you approve of their methods?"

Aldari blinked in surprise. Did her father know what they were talking about?

He gazed down at them without giving anything away. "One can't be choosy when one is in our situation."

"We will, of course, report this egregious behavior directly to our emperor."

"As is your right as a loyal subject."

"Do you know what they're talking about?" Aldari whispered to her sister.

"No idea, but... who are *they*?" Shydena pointed out past the harbor.

A moment ago, nothing had been out there, but now, dozens and dozens of green-hulled ships were sailing toward the capital.

For the first time, Aldari allowed hope to rise up in her chest. Could it be...

Did the elves have that many ships?

"Skulking about in the night and assassinating an army's high-ranking officers is a crime against humanity," the imperial man continued, "but their kind are known to be ruthless. You may find that allying with them is far worse for your people than becoming a vassal-state of the empire."

"I doubt that." Father looked over at Aldari and raised his eyebrows.

He wanted a cue, but Aldari didn't know if she could give it. *Their kind.* The officer had to be talking about the elves—he wouldn't have spoken of humans using such words, would he? But how—

A horn blew from out among the field of tents, and more started up. The officers frowned at each other.

Warriors in black leather armor were riding on horseback— no, on the backs of *reindeer*—up the road. Dozens of them. Maybe more than a hundred. The sunlight glinted off the pale blond hair of the warrior in the lead.

The hope in Aldari's chest grew even stronger, and she gripped the stone wall, peering out. It was Hawk, but she couldn't believe he dared ride through legions of enemy soldiers, *especially* if he or his troops had been assassinating those enemies during the night.

The ever-scowling Setvik rode at Hawk's side, and she had little trouble envisioning him cutting the throats of sleeping men. Another time, she would have objected to such tactics, but if they kept her people free...

More horns blew, and riflemen and bowmen fired upon the elves.

"No!" Aldari blurted, tightening her grip in terror.

A shimmering bubble appeared in the air around the elven party, deflecting the projectiles. Relieved, she slumped against the low wall. She didn't see the orbs that could create such barriers—nor had she gotten the impression that they were mobile—but Hawk wasn't wearing his bracer. Did that mean he or another of the elves had used magic to create the protection? If so, he was learning to use his power quickly. Though he had admitted to the games he'd played with his sister in their youth.

The imperial soldiers backed away from the elves while exchanging uneasy looks with each other.

Grim-faced, dressed all in black, and with deadly weapons on display, the elves would have appeared dangerous even if they hadn't had any magic, but witnessing the power of their barrier had to make the thought of doing battle with them even more daunting.

Hawk's face was as stern as the others as he rode at the head of the procession, and Aldari remembered when she'd first seen him and Setvik in the library. During her time with the elves, she'd forgotten how fierce they appeared—to their enemies. But their allies shouldn't have to worry.

"I didn't expect to see him again," Theli whispered.

Aldari glanced at her.

"I mean *them*." Theli blushed.

Aldari smiled. "Will you kiss him again?"

"Of course not. He's a pompous jerk who can barely remember my name."

"Which is why you crawled into his lap and let him grab your butt."

Theli's cheeks grew even pinker.

"I was just relieved we survived," she muttered, looking at the elves—at *Setvik*—instead of meeting Aldari's eyes.

"Your butt was especially relieved."

"I'd punch you if it were allowed."

Aldari only smiled again, feeling Theli deserved teasing after all the comments she'd made about *Aldari* needing to remain chaste around the elves.

When Hawk lifted his head to gaze along the castle ramparts, looking first at her father and then spotting Aldari, her smile broadened, and she waved to him. His grim face brightened, and he lifted a hand.

As the elven party drew near the city gate, the guards looked to Father, as if asking if they should deny access. Aldari snorted. They'd let the imperial invaders send a party in unopposed.

Father looked over at Aldari, as if to defer to her. She nodded firmly and walked along the wall toward him.

"Those the elves who kidnapped you?" Shydena asked, following her. "They look quite ferocious."

"They are when they fight."

"Some of them are quite handsome too." Shydena waved toward the front of the party, or was she picking out Hawk? She *couldn't* be picking out Setvik. He was far too dour and dark to be considered handsome. "I didn't realize that when they were here before."

Since they'd joined Father, Aldari didn't comment on the elves' looks. She doubted he would approve of his daughters' speculation.

The imperial officers puffed out their chests and rested their hands on their weapons as the elves drew near. Both groups were in front of the closed castle gate, with Father's defenders in the towers pointing bows in their direction, but their focus was on each other.

"Who are you who dares walk through our army and interrupt this meeting?" the senior imperial officer demanded, looking at Setvik instead of Hawk. Dismissing the younger elf as less of a threat?

Though he'd revealed his true name and heritage to her, Hawk still wasn't wearing anything to hint of his royal lineage. In his armor and travel clothing, he blended in with the other mercenaries. Had there even been time for him to go back home before getting passage over here? She didn't see how he could have. How had he even arranged for all those ships to come so quickly?

"Oh, is this a meeting?" Hawk asked casually from astride his reindeer. "If you're here surrendering to King Caylath, we can wait."

"*Surrendering!*"

"Yes, it's what one does when outmatched. As you're no doubt aware, an elven fleet is approaching the harbor, the ships full of warriors like us." Hawk tilted his head toward Setvik instead of pointing at himself, though he was as much of a talented warrior as the mercenary. "They wield magic, not only swords and bows, and if your troops are here when they arrive..." Hawk lost his humor, and his tone turned cold. "Our people will *destroy* yours. Your invasion force isn't welcome in Delantria, as I'm certain King Caylath will inform you."

Father nodded, though he couldn't have expected any of this.

The officer only glanced at him, instead focusing his glower on Hawk. "Who in the Nine Celestial Heavens are you?"

"I'm Prince Hawsylereth, second son of King Jesireth of Serth, sent here to offer an alliance with King Caylath and destroy any who seek to usurp the sovereignty of our neighbors across the Forever Fog River. Now that we've dealt with our problems at home, we'll be turning our eyes outward to be sure no hostile and ambitious nations are operating near our borders. If they do... we'll deal with them."

Setvik caressed the hilt of his sword.

"You assassinated our leaders," the officer blurted. "There will be reprisal."

"I'll task you with trotting home to your emperor and delivering the message that there had better not be." Hawk hopped off his mount, landing to face the officer. The other imperials raised their weapons toward him, but his magical barrier remained intact and bumped against them, forcing them to stumble back.

The senior officer tried to back away, but Hawk sprang at him, pouncing with the speed of a cougar. He reached through his own barrier, his hand blurring as it caught the officer's wrist before he could lift his sword. Hawk's other hand whipped in too quickly to avoid, and he caught the officer around the throat, his fingers tightening.

Again, his men tried to attack and stop the threat to their officer, but the elven magic protected Hawk. Setvik and his mercenaries watched blandly, certain their prince wasn't in danger.

"Our people have spent centuries honing their skills in battle," Hawk said softly, the words barely audible to Aldari on the wall above.

In that moment, Hawk appeared as deadly—as apt to kill—as Setvik, and she couldn't help but wonder which one of them had been responsible for the assassinations. She wouldn't have thought Hawk would use such tactics, but could she object? If it drove fear into the hearts of the imperial soldiers and convinced them to leave...

"Thanks to Princess Aldari," Hawk continued, "that which we fought all that time is no longer a threat. We're going to have a lot of free time going forward. Pray we do not have a reason to turn our attention to your empire, which I believe has no magic to protect it."

"Humans don't have any magic." The officer gripped Hawk's forearm, trying to wrench his hand away from his throat, but Hawk didn't budge.

"That would put you at a grievous disadvantage in battle then. Don't you agree?"

"I..." Once more, the officer tried to break Hawk's grip.

Maybe Hawk was using his magic to strengthen himself, or

maybe the hardened elves were simply that much stronger than the imperials, but again, he didn't budge.

The officer glanced up at Aldari in bewilderment, no doubt wondering how she could have possibly done anything to help the elves.

Aldari kept her face neutral and offered nothing to enlighten him on that, but she did say, "I've seen them in battle. The elves are very formidable. We welcome them as allies."

"Take a message to your people," Hawk told the officer. "From this day forward, Delantria is under *our* protection."

He released the officer, who staggered back and lifted his sword, but he didn't try to attack. He eyed Hawk and the elves and must have decided their magic was too much to overcome.

"Also take your army and march home," Hawk said, "without doing any damage or so much as stepping off the road onto someone's field along the way."

"I will take your message, but don't think the emperor will be cowed."

"He's welcome to cross the Forever Fog River if he wants to have a chat with us. Just tell him to watch out for the serpents. They can be nettlesome."

The officers departed, casting glowers at the elves over their shoulders. None of them spoke a word to Father, who stood with a stunned expression on his face and a finger to his lips.

He lowered his hand and whispered to Aldari, "Can we trust them? Are we sure we *want* this alliance, if that's what they're offering?"

"Yes," she said firmly. "And yes."

"What will they demand in exchange?"

With the imperial threat departing, Hawk turned to look up at Aldari.

My hand in marriage, she wanted to blurt but didn't. "I think nothing. They're returning a favor."

"That's some favor," her father whispered.

"My apologies for acting as a bully, Your Majesty, Princess Aldari, and princess I don't know." Hawk bowed toward their trio. "But Captain Setvik informed me that the best way to defeat a bully is to use their own tactics against them. And we were a little desperate to make an impression. This is…" Hawk glanced around, including toward the harbor, and lowered his voice to finish. "A bit of a bluff."

"Oh?" Father looked toward the imperial armada in the harbor and the rows and rows of tents in front of the city walls. The soldiers were breaking camp, but with so many troops to organize, it would take them a long time to depart.

"May I come in and speak to you about it?" Hawk asked.

"Certainly."

Hawk bowed to him.

"Aldari," Father said, drawing her toward the steps that led into the courtyard. "Since you seem to know *much* more about this than I do, please stay with me for this meeting." He looked at Shydena.

"I'll stay too," she said. "If you need a daughter to marry off to an elf, I'm available."

Father's eyebrows flew up. "They're stained with the blood of our enemies."

"I like a man who isn't afraid to get his hands dirty."

Father rocked back.

Aldari elbowed her sister before trotting down the steps ahead of Father. The guards were opening the gate, and she wanted to greet Hawk before Father dragged him off into his meeting.

While the other elves rode their reindeer into the courtyard, Hawk walked in on foot, and he smiled broadly when he spotted Aldari. Her heart soared, and she almost tripped over her dress as she ran to greet him. No, to throw her arms around him. It hadn't been that long since they'd been together, but she hadn't known if she would see him again, and she squeezed him tightly as she buried her face in his shoulder.

He wrapped his arms around her and stroked the back of her head. "I would kiss you," he murmured, "but your father is frowning at us, possibly while considering flogging me."

"It's inappropriate to flog one's allies," Aldari said into Hawk's shoulder, doubting her father would object to a hug for the person who'd driven off the empire. A kiss... she was less certain about.

"A status we haven't solidified yet. The last time he saw me, I was plotting—successfully—to kidnap you."

"Yes, but you just scared away the imperials. You're an ally."

"I'm glad you feel that way after all you endured at our people's hands. You might wish to know that Mevleth didn't survive the battle against the Twisted but that we questioned the young scientist Waylith. He and Mevleth had met in the past and recognized their shared religious beliefs... of wanting the Twisted to continue to exist, of believing they were something our people needed to endure to be rewarded in the afterlife." Hawk shook his head. "Waylith, not wanting our mission to succeed, was the one to cut the messenger's bowstring. That night before we left, he and Mevleth conspired, Mevleth distracting Setvik and me while Waylith sabotaged the gliders. He attempted to damage several but didn't have any engineering expertise or know what he was doing. It was just bad luck that he effectively sabotaged yours, and it fell apart when nobody else's did."

Aldari's ankle twinged at the memory of her hard landing, but none of that had been Hawk's fault. "It's all right. We survived."

"I'm glad."

"What about your sister?" Aldari knew he hadn't had time to search—he must have realized he could hand things over to his brother and left shortly after she and Theli had—but she raised her eyebrows, hoping on his behalf.

"I actually received a message from my mother as I was about to get on the ship." Hawk waved his hand to indicate a falcon's flapping wings. "Hysithea has been found. She's... not herself, but I hope that, in time, she'll recover. That they all will."

Not having to ask who *they* were, Aldari hugged Hawk again, relieved for him.

Father cleared his throat.

Aldari made herself draw back but didn't release Hawk completely, instead clasping his hand as she faced her father. "Father, this is Prince Hawk—Hawsylereth. Hawk, my father, King Caylath."

"Wasn't it *Captain* Hawk the last time we met? When I hired you to look after my daughter?" Father's gaze shifted to Aldari's grip on Hawk's hand.

She refused to release that grip.

"Yes, Your Majesty. I deemed you would be more likely to hire a mercenary to guard her caravan than a prince. Everybody knows how fluffy and useless royalty is." Hawk slanted a look toward Setvik, and Aldari suspected he was echoing something the grumpy mercenary had said.

"Is that so?" Father said. "What's the bluff you spoke of?"

"We *did* bring a fleet, but it's on the smallish side." Hawk gestured toward the harbor. "A lot of those ships are illusions— mirror images of the real ships. A navy wasn't useful in fighting the Twisted, so we don't have a lot of warships."

"How many ships are in a smallish elven fleet?" Aldari asked.

"Two."

Father blinked and looked toward the harbor, though they couldn't see the vessels from down in the courtyard. "It looked like a hundred ships out there."

"A hundred ships that are staying out beyond the breakwater in the hope that the imperial fleet doesn't get a good look at them," Hawk said. "We have a substantial number of warriors, and my father is preparing to send more if needed, but this is what I could get together on short notice." He nodded toward Setvik and the mercenaries.

"Are you saying, Prince Hawk," Father said slowly, "that you scared off thousands of imperial invaders with a few dozen mercenaries and two ships?"

"There was also magic." Hawk wiggled his fingers in the air. "As I said, we can bring in more forces if necessary, but I knew time was of the essence and wanted to get some people here immediately."

"We appreciate that." Aldari was tempted to hug him again.

"Good. I hope we were timely enough." Hawk met her gaze, an apology in his eyes. "I know it would have been better if we hadn't interrupted your journey in the first place, but... I was hoping to make up for that."

"You have, and *I* don't know if it would have been better," Aldari said. "Prince Xerik doesn't seem to care much about time and essence."

"Under Setvik's advisement, we took out some of the Taldarian military leaders in the night to discombobulate them," Hawk admitted, not commenting on Xerik. "It's not the tactic I would have preferred, but when we saw how many people they'd sent and that they were already at your gate, desperate measures were required."

"Yes," she said softly. "They were."

Had the elves not shown up, her nation might have fallen before noon.

Hawk squeezed her hand, then extricated his so that he could withdraw a scroll case. "My father sent this, Your Majesty. Our protection, if you need it, has already been paid for, so it's not a request for anything, nor do we require an alliance, but he wants you to know that we will open our borders to your diplomats if you wish to pursue official relations."

"Already paid for?" Father wondered softly as he accepted the case. He opened the scroll to read it.

"Didn't you tell him about your journey?" Hawk asked Aldari.

"Some, but I only returned home yesterday afternoon, and with the imperial army poised to lay siege to our city, Father was distracted. We all were."

"I suppose your failure to bring up our adventure was understandable then. Though I would have thought *I* warranted at least a passing mention."

"I wasn't sure you'd come, or that I'd see you again."

"No?" Hawk rested a hand on his chest. "I said I would, and you said you trusted me."

"I did—I do, but you had so much to deal with at home, and I..."

Hawk arched his eyebrows.

"I didn't know if, now that you're... magical..." Aldari waved to the spot on his forearm where he'd worn that bracer. "Now that you're *powerful*, will you have any interest in cavorting with humans?"

"Oh yes. I particularly enjoy cavorting with economists who want to write papers on our moss trade."

Aldari smiled. "Not just papers. A whole book, I should think. *The Elven Moss Trade: the Untold Story.*"

"That sounds like a scintillating tome. And I hope we'll also be able to work together to bring elven root pitch to the market as a whale-oil alternative."

"I would like that." Aldari looked at her father as he lowered the scroll, realizing he might be wondering why his daughter would have anything to do with economics and writing papers.

"Can *Lyn Dorit* write about something as pedestrian as moss?" Father arched his brows. "She tends toward the idealistic and esoteric."

"Uhm." Aldari didn't know if her father had known about her

pen name all along or if he'd been poking around in her absence, but it appeared he knew now. Was he angry? She couldn't tell. "She could write about moss. And definitely about elven root pitch. She has, ah, first-hand experience with the latter."

"Hm," was all Father said. Well, even if he wasn't enthusiastic about her pen name, at least he wasn't chastising her about it or forbidding her from writing more. He turned toward Hawk and held up the scroll. "I will write a formal response for you to take back to your father. It may take some time for our people to learn to trust each other fully, but I thank you for bringing your men and convincing the imperials to leave. You've lifted a great weight from my shoulders."

"I'm glad, Your Majesty." Hawk bowed to him.

"I hope you can assure me that you won't kidnap any of my children again." The squint he gave Hawk suggested that transgression might not be quickly forgotten.

Aldari was glad she hadn't blurted out that joke about Hawk requiring her hand in marriage. It might take her a while to warm Father up to that idea. Was there any possibility she would get the chance?

"No kidnappings at all?" Shydena asked, her voice tinged with disappointment.

She'd drifted over to the mercenaries and was talking to— Aldari groaned. Pheleran. Maybe he'd realized he wouldn't succeed at wooing Theli, for he smiled shyly at Shydena.

"*No.*" Father frowned at her.

Theli was speaking with the mercenaries too, Setvik of all people. Aldari caught her saying something about how she'd decided he wasn't a true villain and that she wouldn't need to kill the character based on him in her ballad. He said he *liked* being a villain and asked her—or maybe that was a cocky command—to sing for him later.

"Kidnapping tactics won't be necessary again, Your Majesty," Hawk said, "and I apologize for employing them."

"We accept your apology," Aldari hurried to say before Father uttered something less forgiving. "And Father?" Maybe this wasn't the best time to bring up her delayed wedding, but... "Now that we have new and powerful allies, allies who aren't afraid to show up to help us when there's an invasion, is it still necessary for me to marry Xerik?"

Father rocked back, but he didn't immediately blurt a *no*. He drew his fingers to his chin and combed them through his beard. "I suppose it wouldn't be necessary. In truth, I would prefer you remain here in Delantria, not in a far-off land where we'd rarely see you again."

"But a diplomatic visit to Serth now and then might be all right?" Aldari asked.

"You want to go *back*?"

"Only for visits. The food is dreadful, so I'd hate to stay there permanently."

"Perhaps, we'll be able to arrange more imports in the future," Hawk murmured. "The magic that made the Forever Fog River so daunting is fading."

"That's good news. You *need* imports."

"That maple-sugar pastry you once spoke of?"

"At the least."

"I suppose an occasional visit to an ally nation would be permissible," Father said. "Once you've recovered from your injuries."

"Good. Thank you." Aldari gave him a heartfelt smile and hug before spinning away to clasp Hawk's hand. Her ankle twinged a protest, but she barely felt it. She was too delighted with how the day had turned out. "Would you like a tour of our castle?"

"I would." He squeezed her hand and allowed her to guide him away from the others. "Is there a private romantic spot we might visit?" he murmured, gazing at her in appreciation.

"We don't have anything quite like your bridge over the river, but I find our library terribly romantic."

"Your library that's filled with dust motes and the must of ancient tomes?"

He had, she recalled, been in one of the city's more run-down libraries.

The castle one was better kept, but to tease him, she said, "I consider those aphrodisiacal scents."

"And you think our tastes in moss are eccentric."

"I do indeed, but I'm growing to appreciate elven eccentricities." Aldari led him into the castle for a thorough tour of its more private and romantic spots.

THE END

Printed in Great Britain
by Amazon

13241581R00236